Dangerous Liaisons:
Propositions

BRENDA JACKSON

ANDREA LAURENCE

BARBARA DUNLOP

MILLS & BOON

First Published in Great Britain 2020
By Mills & Boon, an imprint of HarperCollins*Publishers*
1 London Bridge Street, London, SE1 9GF

DANGEROUS LIAISONS: PROPOSITIONS
© 2021 Harlequin Books S.A.

Private Arrangements © 2012 Brenda Streater Jackson
The Boyfriend Arrangement © 2018 Andrea Laurence
An Intimate Bargain © 2012 Barbara Dunlop

ISBN: 978-0-263-29889-5

MIX
Paper from
responsible sources
FSC® C007454

This book is produced from independently certified FSC™ paper to ensure responsible forest management.

For more information visit: www.harpercollins.co.uk/green

Printed and bound in Spain
by CPI, Barcelona

Dangerous Liaisons

About the Authors

Brenda Jackson is a *New York Times* bestselling author of more than one hundred romance titles. Brenda lives in Jacksonville, Florida, and divides her time between family, writing and travelling. Email Brenda at authorbrendajackson@gmail.com or visit her on her website at brendajackson.net

Andrea Laurence is an award-winning contemporary author who has been a lover of books and writing stories since she learned to read. A dedicated West Coast girl transplanted into the Deep South, she's constantly trying to develop a taste for sweet tea and grits while caring for her boyfriend and her old bulldog. You can contact Andrea at her website: http://www.andrealaurence.com

New York Times and *USA Today* bestselling author **Barbara Dunlop** has written more than fifty novels for Mills & Boon, including the acclaimed Whiskey Bay Brides series for Mills & Boon Desire. Her sexy, light-hearted stories regularly hit bestsellers lists. Barbara is a four-time finalist for the Romance Writers of America's RITA® award.

PRIVATE ARRANGEMENTS

BRENDA JACKSON

To the man who is my first, my last,
my everything, Gerald Jackson, Sr.

To my fellow author, Adrienne Byrd, the
Queen of Plots. Thanks for letting me borrow
Quentin Hinton and his Doll House for a spell.

You do not have because you do not ask.
—James 4:2 NRSV

Prologue

"So, Jonas, what do you think?" Nicole Cartwright asked as she handed the man standing in front of her desk another photograph she'd taken a few days before.

She watched as Jonas Steele studied the photograph and then his green eyes found hers. The smile that touched his lips made her heart pound like crazy in her chest. His company, Ideas of Steele, was on the upward move, getting a lot of attention, and she felt fortunate to be a freelance photographer working with him on this particular project.

"These are great, Nikki, and just the shots I wanted," he said, handing the stack of photographs back to her. "I'm glad you agreed to help me out on such short notice. Three weeks wasn't a lot of time," he added.

"Thanks, and like I told you, I work better under pressure."

He opened his mouth to say something, but at that moment his cell phone rang.

She inhaled deeply as he shifted his gaze from her to focus on his telephone call. She wondered why on earth she was drawn to him so much. She certainly wasn't his type. Just last Sunday his face was plastered across the gossip pages; his name was linked to some former fashion model. And the week before, the papers had connected him to some senator's daughter. It was obvious he much preferred the Barbie-doll type—sleek and sophisticated, without a strand of hair out of place.

She pushed an errant curl back from her face and thought that certainly wasn't her. And there definitely wasn't anything sleek and sophisticated about her. Jeesh. She couldn't recall the last time she'd worn a dress.

She tried not to listen but couldn't help overhearing his conversation. He was confirming a date for tonight. She tried to not let it bother her that the man she'd had a secret crush on for close to a year was making plans to spend his evening with someone else. Story of her life.

For the past twenty-seven years she had been living in a dreamworld and it was time for her to wake up and realize she'd been living a friggin' fantasy. As much as she wanted to believe otherwise, she didn't have a soul mate out there after all. There was no knight in shining armor who would come charging in and whisk her away to a place where the two of them would live happily ever after. It was time for her to accept that marriages like her parents' and grandparents' happened just once—maybe twice—in a lifetime. They weren't the norm.

And, she thought as she glanced over at Jonas, a leopard couldn't change his spots. So why had she fallen for a man who didn't know the meaning of an exclusive affair with a woman? She looked down at her computer keyboard, trying to ignore the pain that sliced through her chest.

"Oh yeah, now where were we, Nikki?"

She glanced up, tempted to say, *Nowhere.* Instead she said, "I believe you needed me to print out more photos."

"Yes, that's right," he said, smiling.

She wondered if his smile was for the photos or the phone call he'd just ended. Deciding it wasn't any of her business, she stood and crossed the room to the printer. Her office was small but efficient. The one huge window had a beautiful view of Camelback Mountain.

At that moment he took another call and she figured it was probably another woman. But when he let out a loud whoop, she glanced over at him and saw the huge smile on his face.

When he hung up the phone, he was smiling from ear to ear. "That was my secretary. Gilbert Young's assistant called. We got the Thompson account! They were impressed with those brochures we gave them last week and don't need to see any more!"

She clapped her hands while grinning, not able to contain her own excitement. "That's wonderful, Jonas."

"Wonderful? That's fantastic. Simply amazing. Do you know how many other marketing outfits wanted that account?" he asked, crossing the room to her.

Before she knew what he was about to do, he reached out and pulled her into his arms for a hug. "And I owe it all to you, Nikki."

It was meant to be just a hug. She didn't know what happened, but the next thing she knew Jonas Steele was lowering his head and slanting his mouth over hers in one hell of a kiss.

Chapter 1

Eighteen months later

Jonas Steele felt an argument coming on.

"I hear you, Mom, but I just don't feel what you're saying," he spoke into his iPhone.

His lips tightened to a frown as he alighted from the shiny black BMW two-seater Roadster and glanced around while sliding his aviator-style sunglasses into the pocket of his jacket. *Whoa! But I'd love to feel all over on those,* he quickly thought when his gaze landed on the legs of a woman who was getting out of her car. And they were definitely a gorgeous pair. Long, smooth and shapely.

"You and I need to do lunch to discuss this further, Jonas."

His attention was immediately pulled back to the

conversation with his mother. He rolled his eyes heavenward. "I'd love to, Mom. Anytime. Any place. You are my number-one girl. But certain topics are off-limits."

He glanced back to where he'd seen the pair of sexy legs just seconds earlier only to find the owner gone. *Crap!* Frustration seeped into his pores. He would have loved seeing the rest of her; certainly he would not have been disappointed.

His frown deepened when his mother said, "That's utter nonsense, Jonas. You can't restrict me from certain topics. I'm your mother."

He shook his head as he made his way across the parking lot. He loved his mother to death, but lately, talking to the beautiful Eden Steele, former international fashion model and the woman who had captured his father's heart close to forty years ago, was draining on his senses. "True. However, you leave me no choice. With Galen and Eli married off, now you want to give your remaining four single sons grief, but we won't let you."

"You won't?"

"No. Although I can't speak for the others, I can speak for myself, and like I've told you numerous times before, I intend to be a bachelor for life."

Her soft chuckle flitted across the phone. "You sound so confident about that. Do I need to remind you that Galen and Eli used to tell me the same thing? And quite often, I might add. Now look what happened to them. Both got married in the last year."

Jonas didn't want to look. In fact, he didn't want to spend a single moment analyzing what could have possibly made two intelligent, fun-loving, die-hard womanizers like his brothers Galen and Eli fall in love. Galen had gotten married ten months ago, and Eli had tied the knot on Christmas Day. Granted, Jonas would be the first to admit they had married gorgeous women, but still, look how many women they'd given up to be committed for the rest of their lives to just one. It made no sense. Bottom line, Galen and Eli were whipped and the sad thing about it was it didn't seem to bother them.

And he was sure his mother had heard by now that another bachelor friend of theirs by the name of York Ellis, who lived in New York, was taking the plunge this weekend in time for Valentine's Day. Again, Jonas was convinced that like Galen and Eli, York needed to have his head examined for giving up his bachelor status.

"You will be here for dinner Thursday night, right?"

Her words intruded on his thoughts. "Do I have a choice?"

"There are always choices, Jonas."

Just like there are always consequences, he thought, remembering what had happened to his brother Mercury when he'd decided to skip one of their mother's weekly Thursday-night dinners. Before Mercury could get out of bed the next morning, Eden Steele had arrived on his doorstep. She had informed her AWOL son that since he had missed such an important family function, she was duty-bound to spend the entire day with him. And then she had the nerve to invite the woman Mercury had spent the night with to tag along. Their mother had deliberately overlooked Mercury's bed-them-but-never-wed-them policy when it came to women.

Since then, none of Eden's sons had been brave

enough to miss a Thursday night chow-down. The last thing any of them needed was an unexpected drop-in from Mommy Dearest.

"I'll be there, Mom," he said, deciding he needed to get her off the phone.

"I'll hold you to that, and you're welcome to bring a lady friend."

He caught himself. He was about to tell her he didn't have lady friends, just bed partners. "Thanks, but no thanks. As usual I'll come alone."

Then an idea popped into his head. "Since Galen and Brittany will mark their one-year anniversary in a couple of months, you might consider convincing them that you need a grandbaby or two. Heck, they might hit the jackpot and luck out with triplets like Cheyenne," he said of his cousin living in Charlotte.

"Hmm, triplets. You might have something there," his mother said thoughtfully.

He hoped so. Then maybe she could turn her attention away from him, Tyson, Mercury and Gannon. His brothers would owe him big-time if he could get her to do that. He smiled, deciding to go for the gusto and said, "You might not want to scare them with the multiple-births idea though. Just push for the single birth for now. Come to think of it, I'd love to have a little niece or nephew, and I know you and Dad would make the best grandparents any child could possibly have."

He inwardly chuckled as he moved toward the revolving doors. He'd just laid it on rather thick and if word got back to Galen of the seed he'd planted inside their mother's head, his oldest brother just might kill him. But then drastic times called for drastic measures.

"Personally, I would prefer a niece," he added. "I can see her now, cute as a button dressed in lacey pink." In all actuality, he couldn't see a damn thing, but his mother didn't have to know that.

"Yes, I can see her as well," Eden replied in a voice filled with excitement. Apparently the idea was growing on her and fast.

Jonas breathed out a deep sigh of relief. "Good."

"But I'm envisioning her dressed in lacey lavender instead of pink."

Whatever. He glanced around hoping that he would run into the owner of the legs he'd spotted a while ago. Although he didn't have a clue how the woman looked, with legs like hers she shouldn't be hard to spot.

"Well, I'm at the hotel for my business meeting and—"

"Hotel? Business meeting? Really, Jonas, I think you can do better than that. I wasn't born yesterday."

He fought back a smile. It was pretty damn sad when your own mother didn't trust your motives. "What I should have said is that I'm meeting someone for dinner at Timothy's." He was well aware that Timothy's, the restaurant inside the five-star Royal Blue Hotel, was one of his parents' favorite places in Phoenix.

"Oh. Nice choice. Are you still celebrating?"

He smiled. "Kind of."

Had it been a week ago already since he'd gotten word that his company had been chosen to spearhead a marketing campaign of a lifetime? Over the years, his marketing group, Ideas of Steele, had made pretty decent profits, but with this new project there was no doubt in his mind that he was about to pull in the big bucks. Eighteen months ago the Thompson account had helped to get his company's name out there, and now the Fulton account would blast it off the charts.

"Well, don't celebrate too much tonight. I don't want you to get sick. You know you can't hold liquor well."

He breathed out a deep sigh. "Thanks for reminding me. Now, I really have to go."

"I'll see you Thursday night."

"Okay. Goodbye, Mom." He clicked off the phone, both amused and curious, wondering which one of his brothers she would be calling to harass next.

He felt confident that whoever her next victim was, his single brothers would be able to keep Eden out of their business. Like him, when it came to the women they were involved with, they didn't think any further ahead than the present.

He glanced around the luxurious, immense lobby of the Royal Blue Hotel, taking in the polished marble floors, high ceiling and rich mahogany crown moldings. He could remember the first time he'd come here as a boy of ten. It was to attend a fashion show raising money for charity, and his mother had been one of the models. On that day he'd realized Eden Steele might be just "Mom" at home, but to the rest of the world, she was Eden, a renowned international fashion model whose face graced the covers of such magazines as *Vogue*, *Cosmo* and *Elle*.

Jonas's gaze shifted to the massive windows on one side of the lobby to take in the panoramic view of crimson-hued mountaintops. It had reached a high of seventy today, a beautiful day in February, which accounted for the picturesque sunset he was now seeing.

He checked his watch and saw that he was a good ten minutes early. He could use that extra time to get a drink at the bar, but he knew his mother was right. His system had very low tolerance for alcohol, and too much of the stuff made him sick. So to play it safe he kept within his limits and would usually end up being the designated driver.

Deciding against the drink, he slid his hands into his pockets and crossed the lobby to the restaurant. There was another reason he wished he could take that drink. Nikki Cartwright. The thought of meeting with her had him feeling tense. For any woman to have a Steele feeling that way was unheard of. But he knew the reason.

The kiss they had shared a year and a half ago.

He'd kissed plenty of women, but none had ever left any lingering effects like the one he'd shared with Nikki. And none had managed to haunt him like a drug even after all this time. It had been an innocent kiss, one neither of them had meant to happen, one that had caught her off guard as much as it had him.

He could clearly recall that day in her office. He had been so excited when he'd heard he'd gotten the Thompson account that he had pulled her into his arms to hug her, and the next thing he knew they were locking mouths. And it had been a kiss that had nearly knocked him off his feet. It had made him feel emotions he hadn't known he was capable of feeling. And it had scared the shit out of him.

Jonas would be honest enough to admit he'd been attracted to her from the start and could vividly recall the day they'd met.

It had been raining all week and that particular day was the worst. She had burst into his office soaked to the skin with her blouse and jeans plastered to her in a way that should have been outlawed. He doubted he would ever forget how her jeans had hugged that tight and round bottom of hers.

He had rushed to get her a towel, but not before taking in everything about her, even the way her short curly hair had gotten plastered to her head. And he hadn't missed how her nipples had shown through her wet blouse, or what a curvy body she had.

She had looked a total mess, but at the same time he thought she'd also looked simply gorgeous. He'd also fallen over backward when he'd gazed into her eyes. They were so dark they almost appeared navy blue. And her lips...with their seductive curve had tempted him to taste them on more than one occasion.

His attraction had been stronger than anything he'd ever encountered, and during the three weeks they had worked together it hadn't diminished one iota. And the thought that any woman could have that kind of hold on him unsettled him immensely.

He hadn't understood why the attraction was so intense. And at the time he definitely hadn't wanted it and had done a good job of fighting it until that day. He doubted that she knew what he'd gone through those three weeks. Nikki Cartwright was a looker, no doubt about that. But then all the women he dated were. However, none had provoked the kind of strong reaction from him that she had with that kiss.

In all his thirty-three years, no woman had dared to invade his dreams or made him envision sexual positions he'd like trying out just with her. His taste in women often varied, but he usually was drawn to the slim and sleek. But it was just the opposite with Nikki. She had curves. The jeans she always wore showed off a perfectly proportioned body. A body that had been plastered against his while he'd drowned in the sweetness of her mouth.

The kiss had nearly knocked him to his knees, which was the reason, when he'd finally released her mouth, he had quickly left her office and intentionally put distance between them for eighteen months.

Then why was he now seeking out the very woman he had tried staying away from? The one whose single kiss had him longing for more.

Shivers ran down his spine, and for an instant, he thought about turning around and canceling the meeting. But there was no way he could do that. For this new marketing campaign he needed the best photographer in the business and as far as he was concerned, Nikki was it.

He would just have to steel his senses and hold his own against her. He had hoped with the passing of time his desire for her would lessen, but he found that wasn't the case. When he'd seen her on Christmas day at his brother's wedding, he had been drawn to her even more, which was why he'd left the reception early.

When Jonas reached the top step that led to the restaurant, he could feel lust beginning to stir his insides and anticipation invading his senses. It was happening again and it seemed he couldn't do anything about it. No woman was supposed to have this sort of effect on him. Not Jonas Steele. The master of one-night stands. The man who had a revolving door in his bedroom and who was enjoying the single life and didn't mind the reputation he and his brothers had acquired over the years.

He loved the opposite sex—all shapes, sizes and

styles. Race, creed or color didn't mean a damn thing to him, nor did religious affiliation.

He was the fourth-oldest of Drew Steele's sons. Drew had been run out of Charlotte while in his twenties when his reputation as a womanizer had gotten the best of him. Fathers were threatening him with shotguns, and mothers were keeping their daughters locked behind closed doors. Jonas had heard the stories from family members many times over.

Luckily, Drew had finally met the woman he'd wanted, fallen in love, gotten married and had kept his wife pregnant for seven straight years, which accounted for he and his brothers being born within a year of one another.

Jonas didn't know of a better-suited couple than his parents. Or a more loving one. But then, happily married or not, unfortunately, his father had passed his testosterone-driven genes on to his six sons.

He quickened his steps, thinking testosterone be damned, he was determined to stay in control. He was the womanizer the society tabloids pegged him to be and was making no apologies. He had a reputation and was proud of it and felt he was living a good life. And to top things off, last week he had been awarded the marketing deal of a lifetime and he didn't intend to screw things up.

When he entered the restaurant he glanced around and saw Nikki sitting at a table across the room. She smiled when she saw him and he felt his stomach do a somersault. And as if on cue, his pulse began hammering away and air felt as if it were slowly being sucked out of his lungs. *Holy hell.*

He drew in a deep breath and tried purging the deep,

unwanted attraction for her out of his system. He moved across the room toward her, thinking that no matter what, he was in full control. And this time he would make sure things stayed that way.

Nikki Cartwright watched the man approaching her table with a stroll that was so sexy it bordered on sinful. She tightened her grip on the glass of water while trying to downplay the sensations rolling around in her belly.

Her instinctive response to Jonas Steele was something she should have gotten out of her system by now. There was no reason why a warm rush of desire was invading her insides, almost making it difficult for her to breathe.

Then she quickly decided that yes, there was a reason. Walking toward her had to be one of the most gorgeous men she'd ever seen. Tall, powerfully built, with dark wavy hair flowing around his shoulders, he was pure masculine sex on two legs.

A quick glance around the room indicated she wasn't the only female who thought so. There was nothing quite like a group of women taking the time to appreciate a good-looking man, and Jonas was definitely a looker. Eye candy of the most scrumptious kind.

She'd known working with him on that brochure wouldn't be easy. After all, he and his brothers were the hottest bachelors in Phoenix. They weren't known as the "Bad News" Steeles for nothing, and their reputations for being die-hard players were legendary. There was a joke around town that a woman hadn't been bedded unless she'd been bedded by a Steele. From what Nikki had heard, their skills in the bedroom were off the charts.

The air seemed to shiver the closer he got with a stride that emitted the masculine power that all Steele men seemed to possess. Like his brothers, he had inherited his mother's green eyes. Smokey Robinson eyes, she called them, as they were the same color of those of the legendary R & B soul singer. And then there were the rest of his prominent features—medium brown skin, strong chiseled jaw and one luscious looking pair of lips.

She'd heard that of all the Steele brothers, Jonas was the one everyone considered a rebel. He wore his hair longer than the others and owned a Harley. She understood he had several colorful tattoos on certain parts of his body. She definitely knew about the ones on both shoulders since she'd seen him a couple of times wearing muscle shirts.

Nikki wished she could look right past all six feet three inches of him, see beyond the well-toned muscles beneath the designer business suit that symbolized the growing success of his marketing company.

And more than anything, she wished she could look at his lips and not remember the kiss they'd shared that day.

Had it been a year and half ago when they had last worked together? When she'd constantly fought to control her attraction to him? An attraction that definitely had been one-sided.

Still, he had kissed her that day—she hadn't imagined it. They'd both been caught off guard; however, when he should have ended it, he'd kept right on kissing her, even deepening the kiss. And of course, she'd let him. When he'd finally come to his senses and let her go, he had mumbled something about being late for an appointment and had hightailed it out the door without once looking back.

The memory of that day sent a warm rush of sensations flowing through her, and she sighed. The man was not husband material. He didn't even believe in having a steady girl. She'd heard about his one-and-done policy. It had come as a surprise, a real shocker, when two of those "Bad News" Steeles had fallen in love and gotten married. In fact, Jonas's older brother Galen had married her best friend Brittany.

That left four brothers still single and swearing up and down Bell Road that they'd never fall in love. And she had no reason not to believe them. And as if to make that point solid, she'd heard the four had stepped up their game and were chasing skirts more so than ever these days, especially Jonas.

To break eye contact she glanced around the room again and saw every single female eye was still on him. And then, as if of its own accord, her gaze returned to slide over him. She appreciated what she was seeing. *Oh, mercy.*

With the eye of a photographer, she thought Jonas's features were picture perfect. She tried not to be one of those women who judged a man on looks, but his looks were so sharp, so compelling, so pinch-a-sister-in-the-butt gorgeous, it took everything she had not to start drooling.

"Hello, Nikki. Thanks for agreeing to meet with me."

She jumped at the deep baritone of his voice, which sounded like Barry White reincarnated. She had been so deep into her "Jonas" thoughts that she hadn't been aware he'd gotten close.

"Sorry if I scared you just now," he said.

"You didn't," she replied simply, forcing a smile to her lips. "I'd gotten lost in a few thoughts, that's all."

"I see."

Pulling herself together, Nikki watched as his body slid easily in the chair across from her. Sensations stirred in her tummy again. Unknowingly, he was playing havoc with her senses. Deciding there was no reason for her senses to suffer any more abuse, she spoke up. "When you called you said that you wanted to discuss something with me. A business proposition." Like there could be any other reason for him calling and asking to meet with her. In a way she was surprised that he wanted to use her services again, considering how they'd parted eighteen months ago.

Nikki crossed her legs, hoping the action would tamp down the tingling vibrations she felt between them. The man emitted testosterone that was attacking her big-time.

"We'll talk business later," he said, smiling.

Later? She lifted her brow, a little surprised by his comment. If they didn't talk business then what else were they supposed to talk about? Surely, he didn't intend to bring up that kiss.

"We haven't worked together in months. How have you been?" he asked her.

She stared at him. Evidently he had forgotten they had just seen each other at his brother's wedding on Christmas day. If he'd really wanted to catch up on her life he could have inquired about her well-being then. Instead he'd been too busy checking out the single ladies, friends of the bride from Memphis. He had done the courteous thing and spoken to her, but that was about all. It was as if he'd been careful to avoid any lengthy contact with her.

"I've been doing well."

He nodded. "That's good. I saw Eli and Stacey's wedding photos. As usual you did a great job."

"Thank you."

He was about to say something, but paused when the waiter approached with menus. Seriously, why all the small talk? she wondered. Why did he feel the need to lay on that lethal Steele charm in such a high dosage? Sharing a table with him had her nerves on edge. There was that usual degree of desire she always felt whenever she was near him, making a rush of heat flow through her body. She shifted in her chair.

"And what about you, Jonas? What are you up to these days?" she asked, like she didn't know. Like she didn't read those society tabloids.

"I've been staying busy. Just got back from a business trip to South Africa a few weeks ago. Enjoyed the trip."

"That's good," she said, deciding to study the menu that had been handed to her. He did the same, and she couldn't help taking a peek over the top of hers to do a close-up study of him.

Why was he smiling so much?

As if he read the inquiry in her gaze, he looked up and said, "Last week I received a very important call from Wesley Fulton."

She nodded, very much aware of who Wesley Fulton was. Who wasn't? The man was a self-made billionaire who was building a global financial empire.

"And I have reason to celebrate."

His words cut through her thoughts. She could hear the excitement in his voice. "Do you?"

"Yes. You might have read in the papers that Fulton Enterprises expanded into the airline industry by introducing what they're calling a luxury airship."

She nodded. "Yes, I did hear something about that."

There was no way she couldn't have since it had dominated the media lately. Fulton had hired the best technological minds and engineers to build what everyone was saying was the largest airliner in the world. In fact she'd heard it was so large it made the Airbus A380 look small in comparison. She had seen photographs and it appeared to be an airplane and zeppelin rolled into one, with such amenities as individual sleeping quarters, a nightclub, a movie theater, a casino and a restaurant.

"Ideas of Steele was selected to head up marketing for this venture."

Now Nikki understood why he was in such a cheerful mood. That was certainly good news for his firm. To be selected by Fulton was a feather in any business owner's cap. "That's wonderful, Jonas. Congratulations."

"Thank you." He features turned serious when he met her gaze. "And the reason I wanted to meet with you, Nikki, is because I'll need a good photographer and I want you as part of my team."

Her chest tightened. To know he wanted to include her as part of his high-profile marketing project was almost overwhelming. Especially considering how their relationship had somehow crossed the line the last time they'd worked together. Being a part of something as significant as the project he was talking about could make her career. And it definitely needed a boost right now, especially financially. The economy had taken a toll on just about everybody and freelance photography assignments weren't coming in as steadily as before. Lately she'd had to resort to doing weddings, anniversary parties and private photo shoots.

"I don't know what to say, Jonas."

He chuckled. "Say you'll hear me out over dinner while I tell you about the project. Hopefully, I'll be able to convince you to come on board."

She drew in a deep breath. "Of course I want to hear about it," she said. But then a voice out of nowhere whispered, *Go ahead and hear him out, but you might also want to consider turning him down. Think about it. Will you be able to endure being around him constantly? How will you handle that intense and mind-boggling attraction that eradicated your common sense the last time? Do you honestly want to go through that sort of torture again?*

Nikki inwardly sighed, thinking that no, she really didn't. But she would be crazy to turn down his offer. She had bills to pay, a roof to keep over her head and a body that needed to be fed on occasion. But then, it was that body she wasn't sure about when certain parts of it were so attuned to him. He could charm the panties off a woman without blinking, and that's what bothered her more than anything. When it came to Jonas Steele she needed to keep her panties on. She had a weakness for him and it was quite obvious the kiss they'd shared that day in her office had meant more to her than it had to him.

His voice broke into her thoughts. "I hope my timing

isn't bad and you're not involved in a project that I can't pull you away from."

She thought about the job offer she had received a few days ago. It was election year, and one of the candidates wanted her as part of his team. Following around a politician as his personal photographer for six months was something she'd prefer not doing. But she didn't want to hang around Jonas and constantly drool, either.

She drew in a deep breath and said, "I do have a job offer that came in a few days ago, but I haven't accepted it yet."

"Oh, with whom?"

"Senator Waylon Joseph's election campaign."

He stared at her. "Whatever amount they've offered you as a salary, I'll double it."

She blinked, not believing what he'd just said. "You will?"

"Yes. My business has been doing well, but what Fulton is offering is a chance of a lifetime. It'll take us to a whole other level and I want the best people on board to work with. And I consider you as one of the best. Your photography speaks for itself."

She was definitely flattered. The Joseph campaign had offered her a decent salary and to think Jonas was willing to double it had thrown her in shock. She forced herself to regroup. She needed to weigh her options and think things through with a level head.

"I'll cover the strategy plan I've come up with over dinner. I think you'll like it."

There was no doubt in her mind that she would like it. When it came to marketing strategies, Jonas was brilliant. His company was successful because he was picky about those he did business with. In the world of marketing, a stellar reputation was everything. And unlike some CEOs, who liked to delegate duties and play golf whenever they could, Jonas was very much hands-on.

She knew what coming on board as his photographer meant in the early stages of any project. They would work closely together again, just like that time before— sometimes way into the wee hours of the nights and on weekends. He would come in Monday through Friday dressed in his designer business suits, and then on the weekends, he would wear his T-shirts and jeans and ride around on his Harley. It was as if he were two different men, yet both were sexy as sin.

She would drool during the day and have salacious dreams of him at night. It had gotten harder and harder not to react to him when he was around. Hard to keep her nipples from pressing against her blouse and to keep her panties from getting wet each and every time he opened his mouth to release that deep, sexy baritone voice of his.

He kept looking at her now and she knew he was waiting for her response, so she said, "All right, Jonas, I'm curious to hear your plan."

He smiled, winked and went back to studying his menu. Nikki drew in a deep breath as she turned her attention to her own. But she couldn't ignore the play of emotions that spread through her. As usual, he was having that sort of effect on her and there was nothing she could do about it but sit there and suffer through it.

She wished there was a way after hearing him out that she could just thank him for considering her for the project and then graciously turn him down. But whether she wanted to admit it or not, she wanted the job.

She needed the job.

But what she needed even more was the use of her common sense when it came to Jonas. And she wasn't sure that was possible.

Chapter 2

Being around Nikki was doing a number on him, Jonas thought, taking another sip of his wine. Wasn't it just a short while ago he'd given himself a pep talk, confident that he would be the one in control during this meeting? But that was before he'd had to sit across from her for the past half hour or so. More than once he had to bite down on his tongue to keep from telling her how good she looked or how sweet she smelled. And her hair, that riotous mass of curls that she tossed about, made her features even more attractive.

Crap. When would this intense attraction for her end? And why was he feeling as if he was about to come out of his skin? And to make matters worse, he had a hard-on that was about to burst his zipper. Why was the thought of doing intimate things to Nikki so much in the forefront of his mind? Why hadn't time away from her eradicated her from his thoughts? And why did he remember that kiss as if it were just yesterday?

He shifted in his seat again, feeling edgy. Horny. Lusty. Those were physical states he usually never found himself in. Never had a reason to. As a rule, he got laid whenever he wanted, which was usually all the time. But at the moment, he felt sexually deprived. Overheated.

Where was a Tootsie Pop when he needed one? Sucking on one of those usually took his mind off his problems. Eight years ago when he'd quit smoking, his brothers had given him a huge bag of the lollipops as a joke. They had told him to lick one every time he got the urge to smoke, and pretend he was licking a woman's breast instead. It worked.

Now if he wouldn't feel so friggin' hot…

If there was any way he could remove his shirt and just sit there bare-chested, he would. His attraction to Nikki was overpowering his senses and he didn't like it at all. No woman was supposed to have this sort of effect on him. But he knew no way to stop it. He took another drink and felt a bit queasy. Why was he drinking the stuff? He knew why, and the main reason was sitting across from him.

He glanced at Nikki again. She wasn't what he would consider drop-dead gorgeous, but her beauty seemed to emit some sort of hypnotic appeal. Her eyes were dark, her nose the perfect size and shape for her face, and her lips were sensually full…and tasty, he remembered. Combined, the features on her medium-brown face were arresting, striking and expressive. For him a total turn-on.

He just didn't know what there was about her that tempted him to clear the table and spread her out on it and take her for the entrée as well as for dessert. Then he would proceed to lick and lap a body he had yet to see or touch underneath those jeans and shirt she normally wore. But he had a feeling she was hiding a body that was ultra sexy. Her curves hinted as much. What color bra was she wearing? What color panties? Bikini cut, hip huggers or thong? He had a thing for sexy underwear on a woman.

He shifted in his chair, thinking he needed a Tootsie Pop and bad.

He put down his wineglass to cut into his steak. But each and every time he would glance up and stare at her lips, he would remember that kiss. And the memories were filling his head with more foolish thoughts... as well as questions he didn't have any answers to.

One question that stood out in the forefront was that if he'd been so attracted to her when they'd first met, why hadn't he hit on her long before that kiss? It wouldn't have been the first time he'd broken his strictly business rule by making a professional relationship personal. Hell, he was one who believed in taking advantage of any opportunity, business or personal. Then why hadn't he placed her on his "to-do" list long before their kiss that day?

He knew the answer without thinking hard about it. From the first, there had been something about his desire for Nikki Cartwright that wasn't normal. He'd sensed it. Felt it. And it had scared him. He had never reacted so viscerally to a woman before. She had a seductive air about her that had come across as effortless as breathing, and he was sure it was something she wasn't even aware she possessed.

Thoughts of her had begun taking up too much of his time, and he couldn't shake them off like he did with other women. It was as if they occupied the deep recesses of his mind and intended to stay forever. And Jonas Steele didn't do forever with any woman.

And there was also the fact that around her his active imagination was worse than ever. Some were so downright erotic they had startled even him. That much desire made him feel vulnerable, and it was a vulnerability he could and would not tolerate.

Things had gotten worse after the kiss. He had started comparing every single kiss after that with hers, and so far none could compare. And then at night, he would wake up in a sweat, alone in his bed, after dreaming of making love to her in positions that were probably outlawed in the United States and their territories.

At one time he'd thought the best thing to do was just to work her out of his system by sleeping with her. He figured that one good night of sex ought to do the trick. But then there was this inner fear that an all-nighter might not do anything but make him want some more. Then he would start begging.

And the thought of a Steele begging was unheard of. Totally out of the question. A damn mortal sin. Definitely something that wouldn't be happening anytime soon. Never.

Then why was he freaking out about a kiss that happened eighteen months ago?

He figured one of the main reasons was that he had tasted something in that kiss he'd never tasted before—

the type of passion that could ultimately be his down-fall, his final hold on the world that he wanted for himself. The only world he could live in. A world filled with women, women and more women. He refused to let his body's reaction to one particular woman end what he considered the good life.

He needed a Tootsie Pop.

"So what's your marketing strategy for this project, Jonas?"

Her voice was low and seductive. He knew it wasn't intentional. That's the way it was. He glanced over at her. Was she wearing makeup? He couldn't tell. She had what most women would call natural beauty. And this wasn't the first time he'd noticed just how long her eyelashes were. Most women wore the fake ones to get that length, but he knew hers were the real deal.

His fingers tightened around the glass, and he took another sip before saying, "Fulton wants me to capital-ize on the fact there hasn't been an airship of this kind since the Hindenburg…while at the same time mini-mizing the similarities." He breathed in her scent again, liking it even more, and getting more and more aroused by it.

Nikki nodded. She understood the reason Mr. Fulton would want that. It had been decades since the luxury airship exploded while attempting to dock. Of the ninety-seven passengers and crew on board, thirty-five people had lost their lives. If Fulton had built a similar airship, the last thing he would want people to remem-ber was the fate of the original one.

"That tragedy was seventy-five years ago," she said. "I'm surprised no one has attempted to build another luxury airship of that kind before now."

"People have long memories," he said, pushing his plate aside and leaning back in his chair since he'd finished his meal. "Fortunately, the ones who do remember are no longer around to tell the story of that fateful day in May 1937."

He paused a moment and then added, "I remember reading about it in school. I had a history teacher who ranked the Hindenburg explosion right up there with the sinking of the Titanic."

Nikki could believe that. Both had been major catastrophes. She had studied the Hindenburg in school as well, and was well aware that the disaster had effectively destroyed the public's confidence in any type of giant, passenger-carrying air transportation of its kind, abruptly ending the era of the airship. But at the time they didn't have the technological advances of today. She'd heard the airship that Fulton had built was in a class all by itself, definitely a breakthrough in the world of air travel.

"My ultimate plan is to rebuild people's confidence in this type of air travel." Jonas interrupted her thoughts. "After the Titanic, people were leery of cruise ships, but now they don't give a thought to what happened with the Titanic years ago. I want the same mindset in getting the public back interested in luxury air travel. Especially on the airship *Velocity*."

She arched her brows. *"Velocity?"*

"Yes, that's the name of Fulton's airship, and when you think of the meaning I believe it will fit."

He leaned back in his chair. *"Velocity* is being billed as the wave of the future in air travel, and is capable of moving at four times the speed of sound and uses biofuel made from seaweed with minimum emissions."

"Seaweed?"

He chuckled. "Yes. Amazing, isn't it? Fulton will bring a hypersonic zeppelin-design aircraft into the present age. It guarantees a smooth flight and will trim the time getting from one place to another by fifty percent. Ideas of Steele's job is to tie everything together and present a package the public would want to buy into. When the *Velocity* is ready for its first series of air voyages in April, we want a sold-out airship. Fulton's designers have created a beauty that will be unveiled at a red-carpeted launch party in a few weeks."

Jonas paused a moment when the waiter returned to clear their table and give them a dessert menu. Jonas looked over at her and said, "Fulton is well aware the only people who will be passengers on his supersonic airship are the well-to-do, since a ticket won't be cheap. My job is to pique everyone's interest, restore their confidence in the safety of hypersonic travel and make sure those who can afford a ticket buy one. I will emphasize all the *Velocity* has to offer as a fun and exciting party airship."

He paused a moment, then continued, "I'll need photographs for the brochures, website, all the social networks I'll be using, as well as the mass media. The launch party will be held in Las Vegas. Then the next day the *Velocity* will take a trial flight, leaving Los Angeles, traveling to China, Australia, Dubai and Paris on a fourteen-day excursion. That's four continents. Fulton has invited certain members of the media, and a few celebrities. You will need to be on board for that too, to take as many marketing photos as you can."

Jonas met her gaze. "As my photographer I'd like you to attend all events as well as travel with me. We'll want to highlight the airship to its full advantage, to give it the best exposure."

Nikki breathed in deeply in an attempt to downplay the racing of her heart at the thought of all the time they would spend together. Here he was, sitting across from her, all business. She drew in a deep breath. Evidently he had put the kiss they'd shared out of his mind and was not still dwelling on it like she was. Had she really thought he would?

Get real, girl. Do you honestly think that kiss had any sort of lasting effect on him like it had on you? You're talking about a man who's kissed countless women. In his book, one is probably just as good as another. No big deal. So why are you letting it be a big deal for you? If he can feel total indifference then why can't you?

She knew the answer to that without much thought. As much as she boasted about no longer believing in fairy tales of love and forever-after, and as much as she told herself that she could play with the big boys, she knew she could not compete with the likes of Jonas Steele. Nor did she want to.

She had deep apprehensions when it came to him and they were apprehensions she couldn't shake off. What if her attraction to him intensified? What if it moved to another level, one that could cause her heartbreak in the end? Could she handle being a Jonas Steele castoff?

"Um, this dessert menu looks delicious. What would you like?" he asked.

What would I like? Having him wasn't such a bad idea. Deep, dark chocolate. The kind of delectable sweetness that you could wrap around your tongue, feast on for hours and still hunger for more. She wondered about those tattoos she'd heard he had. Where were they? How did they look? How would they taste under her tongue?

Suddenly she felt breathless and her heart was thumping like crazy in her chest. She should feel outright ashamed at the path her thoughts were taking. She needed to get a grip.

She took another sip of wine thinking any time spent around Jonas would drive her over the edge. Already she was imagining things she shouldn't. Like how his lower lip would taste being sucked into her mouth. She shifted in her seat and forced the thoughts away. And he thought they could work closely together again. Boy, he was wrong.

At that moment, considering everything, she knew what her answer regarding his job offer would be. She would be giving up a golden opportunity, one any photographer would love to have. But she had to think about her sanity.

"Nikki?"

She met his gaze. "Yes?"

"Dessert?"

It was hard to keep her mind on anything but Jonas, and that wasn't good. "Yes, the apple pie sounds delicious, but the slice is huge. That's more than I can eat."

He closed his menu. "No problem. We can share it."

She swallowed deeply. He wanted to share a slice of pie with her? To him that might be no big deal, but to her that was the beginning of trouble. It was so sad that he didn't see anything wrong with it.

"Nikki?"

If she kept skipping out on their conversations he

would begin questioning her attention span. "Okay, we can share it," she said and regretted the words the moment they left her lips. Sharing a slice of pie seemed too personal, and this was a business meeting. Wasn't doing something like that considered unprofessional? Evidently he didn't think so.

The waiter returned to take their dessert order. After he left, Jonas said, "I need to be up front with you. If you do take the job it will require long workdays, but I don't see it as being as exhausting as the last project we worked on together."

In a way Nikki wished that it would be. Then she would be too tired to do anything but collapse in bed each night. Too tired to replay over in her mind every nuance of feelings she'd encountered around him. And too tired to remember that one darn kiss that he'd already forgotten.

Jonas made it through dinner—barely. His gut had tightened each and every time he'd glanced up to see her mouth work while chewing her food. He imagined that same mouth working on him.

And sharing that slice of apple pie with her hadn't helped matters. They'd had their own utensils, but more than once he had been tempted to feed her from his fork, hoping that she licked it so he could cop her taste again.

He'd meant what he said about doubling whatever salary Joseph's campaign was offering her. One thing she didn't know was that Jonas had kept up with her over the past few months. He knew no big accounts had been knocking on her door.

Like he'd told her more than once, she was the best

and could handle a camera like nobody's business. And from the way she was acting she probably didn't even remember that kiss. She hadn't even brought it up. In fact she was acting like it had never happened. He didn't know whether he should be relieved or insulted. He wasn't conceited, but to think one of his kisses hadn't left a lasting effect on any woman was pretty damn annoying.

His thoughts drifted to what he'd told her about the job and the time they would spend together. She'd nodded and asked a few questions. Otherwise, she'd mainly listened while he had explained the marketing strategy to her. It was something he knew she could handle.

He only hoped and prayed he could handle it as well. That he would be able to keep his libido in check and his hands to himself. He had a voracious sexual appetite, and considering the fact he was already strongly attracted to Nikki, that meant he had to do whatever was necessary to stay in control at all times.

Control suddenly took a backseat when he looked at her chest. He really liked the shape of her breasts, which were pressing against her blouse. The tips of her nipples seemed like little hardened buds, as if she was aroused. That couldn't be the case when she was sitting over there eating the last of her pie and not paying him any attention.

His stomach tightened when she finished it off by licking the fork. He again imagined all the things he'd like her to do with that tongue. And since he already knew how it tasted, he could feel sensations stirring in his gut.

Knowing he had to stop thinking such racy thoughts,

he cleared his throat. "So, now that you know what the project will entail, do you have an answer for me now or do you need to sleep on it?" *And how about sleeping with me in the process?* He had to tighten his lips to keep from adding such a suggestion.

Before she could respond, the waiter came again to remove the last of their dishes and to leave him with the check.

It was then that she said, "Thanks for your consideration of me for the job, and I appreciate the offer. But I won't be able to take it, Jonas."

He blinked. Had he heard her right? Had she just turned him down? Shocked, he fought to keep the frown off his face. No woman had ever turned him down for anything. Business or pleasure.

There was a long pause and he knew she was waiting for him to say something, so he did. "Uh, all right. Would you like to order another cup of coffee?"

Hell, what else was he going to say? Tell her that it wasn't all right?

"No, I'll pass on the coffee. One cup was plenty for me. And thanks for being understanding about me not taking the job," she said.

Was he being understanding? He doubted it but decided to let her think whatever she wanted. Shouldn't he at least ask her why she had refused his offer? He quickly figured it wouldn't matter. There was nothing left for him to do but to move to the number-two person on the list, George Keller. George was a good photographer but could get on his last nerve at times. The thought of spending two weeks with the man had his teeth grinding.

"Well, thanks for dinner. I need to leave now."

And now on top of everything else, she was running out on him. Automatically, he stood as well. "You're welcome. If not this time, then maybe we can work together again on another project in the future."

She shrugged. "Possibly."

Possibly? Was she for real? Just what was with this *possibly* crap? His lips curved into a forced smile. "I'm glad you're willing to keep your options open," he said, trying to keep the sarcasm from his voice.

At that moment she moved around the table getting ready to leave, and he felt a sucker punch deep in his gut. Nikki Cartwright was wearing something other than jeans. She had on a very short dress that showed all of her curves and legs he was seeing for the very first time. Long, gorgeous legs.

His gaze ran up and down her body and his breath caught in his throat when he realized that she was the same woman whose legs he'd seen in the parking lot earlier. Damn. Holy, hot damn.

Before he could stop himself, he looked up, met her gaze and said in an incredulous voice, "You're wearing a dress."

There was something about the look in Jonas's eyes that gave Nikki pause. Was that heated lust in the dark depths staring at her like she was a slice of strawberry cheesecake with a scoop of French vanilla ice cream on top? He had never looked at her like this before. Not even after the time they'd kissed. She was more than certain that she would have remembered if he had.

She was definitely confused. Did seeing her in a dress finally make him aware that she was a woman in a way that kiss hadn't? She would have worn a dress around him a long time ago if she'd known it would grab this much attention.

She drew in a deep breath, feeling sexy and seductive for the first time in years. "Yes, I usually wear jeans or slacks because they're more comfortable for the work I do. But I decided to wear a dress tonight since I'm going to spend some time upstairs."

He lifted his brow. "Upstairs?"

"Yes, at Mavericks. Tonight is jazz night."

Jonas nodded. Mavericks was an upscale nightclub on the thirty-fifth floor that had a rooftop bar and a wraparound terrace that provided a panoramic view of the mountains and Phoenix's skyline.

He stared at her and her outfit for a moment, wondering if perhaps she had a date. Of course if she did it was none of his business. But still, for some reason, he wanted to know.

"Sorry, I hope I didn't detain you unnecessarily. I wouldn't want you to be late for your date," he heard himself saying.

She smiled. "I don't have a date. I like jazz and thought I'd spend my evening doing something other than watching television."

He lifted a brow. "You aren't meeting anyone?"

She frowned. "No. I don't need someone to take me out if I want to enjoy good music."

He was well aware of that. However, a woman who was alone and looked like her would be inviting male attention whether she wanted it or not. There was no way he wouldn't hit on her if he saw her sitting alone. Men made plays for attractive women with only one thing in mind. It was the way of life. He of all people should know.

Imagining her sitting alone in a club while listening to jazz didn't sit well with him. He met her gaze. "I don't have anything else to do tonight and I love jazz as well. Mind if I join you?"

Chapter 3

Nikki struggled to retain an expressionless face as she walked into Mavericks with Jonas by her side. She was determined that nothing would make her come unglued, even the feel of his hand in the center of her back as he led her toward an empty table.

"I think this is a good spot," he said, pulling out her chair.

She had to hand it to him and his brothers when it came to manners. They were on top of their game, and she knew their mother could be thanked for that. Eden Steele had raised her sons to be gentlemen. Becoming notorious playboys was their own doing.

"There's a nice crowd here tonight."

She had noticed that as well. She had found out about the lounge's jazz night from a woman in her aerobics class this morning. Like she'd told Jonas, she enjoyed jazz, mainly because her parents were huge fans and she and her brother had grown up listening to it.

"Would you like anything to drink?" he asked when a waiter materialized at their table.

Remembering what he'd told her over dessert about having to limit his drinks, she smiled and said, "Just a glass of water with lemon."

Jonas gave her order to the waiter. "And I'll have the same."

He glanced toward the stage. The musicians were still setting things up. "Looks like we made it before the start of the show."

"Yes, it looks that way."

She had turned her head to look around the lounge, but Jonas got the distinct impression she'd done so to avoid eye contact with him. Did he make her uncomfortable? Nervous?

Then again, she could be avoiding his eyes because she was upset that he had invited himself to join her. The waiter returned with their waters and he watched as she took her lemon and gently squeezed it into the water before lifting the glass up to her lips and taking a sip. He sat there, transfixed and aroused, as he watched her part her lips.

She caught him staring, tilted her head and asked, "Is anything wrong?"

If only you knew, he thought when he shifted his gaze from her lips to her eyes. Her short, curly dark brown hair crowned her face like a cap and emphasized the darkness of her eyes and her high cheekbones.

Her question didn't give him pause. His brothers claimed he could BS his way out of any question so he said, "No, nothing is wrong. I was thinking about your lemon."

She lifted a brow. "My lemon?"

"Yes. Did you know there aren't any in India? They use lime instead. I was disappointed when I visited there a few years ago and couldn't get any lemonade."

She smiled grimly and he figured she was probably thinking, *Whatever.*

"So what's your favorite jazz group?" he asked her as he squeezed his own lemon into his water, still picking up on her nervousness.

She shrugged. "I basically love all of them, but I grew up on music by the Diz. My parents were huge Dizzy Gillespie fans. I also like Branford Marsalis."

He nodded and smiled. "Same here. My parents enjoy listening to jazz as well, and my brothers and I grew up on the music. But nothing dominated our house like the Motown Sound."

He chuckled and then added, "My parents are actually members of Motown Is Forever Association, which is a group of die-hard Motown fans who meet once a year to get their old-school, back-in-the-day groove on."

Selecting another lemon off the tray he squeezed it into his drink. She had gotten quiet on him again. The conversations at the tables around them were low and steady, which made the quietness at their table all the more noticeable. He took a sip of his water and wondered what the heck he was doing here. Why was he determined not to let their time together end at Mavericks just yet?

He knew the answer. It was simple. He needed to know why the kiss they'd shared had done him in.

* * *

By the time the first artist hit the stage, Nikki's brain cells were almost fried. She was certain Jonas was generating just that much heat. She could actually feel it all over her body, in some places more so than others, which was why she tightened her legs together.

What was his secret when it came to women? Not only did he have the looks but he also had the gift of gab. Although she had very little to say, it seemed he was determined to keep the conversation going. She had discovered there were no lemons in India, that Walt Disney's body had not been put in cryonic storage and he was convinced a bar of soap between the bedsheets prevented your legs from cramping. She figured if anyone would know about the latter it would be him, considering the amount of time he probably spent in bed with women.

She tried shifting her focus off Jonas and onto the performer. He was killing his saxophone, emitting sensuous sound waves that floated in the room. She recognized the piece and always thought she liked it better with the words, but the sax player was giving her thought. Without the words of undying love, the music still had a message of its own. And the message was stroking her senses, stirring across her skin and caressing certain parts of her body.

"I don't understand why you'd come here alone, Nikki."

She glanced over at Jonas and saw he had tilted his head while studying her as if she was a complex object of some sort. Was she that hard to figure out? Evidently he was a man who thought a woman wasn't complete without a man. She would be the first to admit she assumed a man and woman complemented each other, but only when they were on the same accord. When they wanted the same things in life and when there were no misunderstandings about their relationship.

"Why wouldn't I come here alone?" she asked.

"Why would you feel the need to?" he countered.

At that moment she felt that she could respond to his questions several different ways since he evidently didn't understand that some women preferred peace to drama, solitude to unnecessary commotion. But more importantly, a loving relationship to a purely sexual one.

She left his question hanging for a few moments before finally saying, "I don't date much by choice. At the moment I don't have time for the games men like to play."

He met her gaze, held it while he took a sip of his water. "So you're one of *those* women."

He'd said it like "those" women were a dying breed. Probably were if he had anything to do with it. Since she knew exactly what he meant, she said proudly, "Not really. I stopped believing in forever-after a while ago. I don't mind having a good time myself. But on my own time."

Nikki was convinced when he curved his lips into a challenging smile that her already wet panties got even more soaked. "Your own time? An interesting concept. One you'd toss to the wind with the right man," he said, as if he knew that for certain.

She knew his words were both a challenge and an invitation. He was one of those Steeles, those "Bad News" Steeles, so he would think that way. He was of the mind-set that everything would begin and end in the bedroom. And the end result would be hot, sweaty, sexually satisfied bodies.

Nikki noticed the sudden darkening of his eyes and flaring of his nostrils. If she didn't know better she would think that the pure animal male in him had picked up an arousing element in her scent. She'd heard some men had the ability to do that. Men who were acutely in tune with a woman.

And she wished Jonas wouldn't look at her the way he was doing now, like he could see more than normal people could with those green eyes of his. It was as if he could see right through her blouse, past her bra, directly to her nipples, which were responding to everything male about him. Certain things a woman couldn't evade, and her response to a gorgeous man was one of them, no matter how wickedly sinful the man was. And he was wickedly sinful. From the crown of his wavy hair to the soles of the Salvatore Ferragamo shoes he was wearing.

Thinking too much quiet time had passed between them, she decided to address what he'd said. "By the 'right man,' you're talking about a man like you, I presume."

That sinfully sexy smile widened. "And what kind of man am I, Nikki?"

Why did he have to say her name with such passion, such sensuality? And why was he intent on engaging in what she considered wasteful conversation? He knew the kind of man he was; he certainly didn't need her to spell it out for him. But if he wanted to hear it directly from her lips then…

"You're a man who loves women. Not just one or two, but plenty. You'll never settle down with just one, nor do you want to. Life is about women and sex, but mostly sex and more sex. You play safe. You play fair. But you play. And you will always play."

Jonas shrugged. Yes, that pretty much sized him up and he had no shame. There would never be a single woman to capture his heart like they'd done to Galen and Eli. There would never be a woman to make him feel anything other than a tightening in his groin. And that's what was so hard for his mother to understand and accept. But eventually she would. She had no choice.

Instead of responding to what Nikki had said, since her words really needed no response, he settled back in his chair to continue listening to the music. And to think some more about the woman sitting across from him. She might not want the hot sheets, sex and more sex, but something about being here with him was getting to her. He was a hunter and could pick up the scent of an aroused woman a mile off. And some part of his presence, and their conversation, had turned her on. He was certain of it.

He had no doubt she wanted to believe everything she'd said. Although she hadn't admitted such, he had a feeling that deep down she did believe in that nonsense about forever-after. He'd bet at one time she'd been wrapped up in the notion of a house with the white picket fence, babies and the words of undying love from a man's lips.

Who was the real Nikki Cartwright? his mind demanded to know. She'd peeled off a layer tonight by wearing a dress instead of jeans, and he liked what he saw. Who would have thought she had legs that looked like that? Legs that could probably wrap around a man real tight, grip him pretty damn good while they had nitty-gritty, between-the-sheets sex.

He took a sip of his water and appreciated how the cold liquid flowed down his throat to cool his insides. He knew the score with her and conceded he needed to leave her alone. Her turning down his job offer was probably a smart move. And to be quite honest, he really didn't have any reason to be sitting here with her, sharing her table, and listening to jazz.

He had tried not to notice her at Eli's wedding when she'd moved around the room snapping photographs. She had looked cute then...and busy. To keep his attention off her he had pretended interest in a couple of single women who'd flown in to attend. He'd eventually left the wedding reception with one of them.

And talk about leaving...Jonas knew he should go, tell her it was nice seeing her again and that he regretted they wouldn't be working together again and that he understood. His jaw tightened knowing that was one lie he could not tell because he did not understand it. Why was she walking away from an opportunity that could ultimately boost her career?

"That was beautiful," she said when the saxophonist ended the song. Like others, she stood to applaud, and Jonas's gaze automatically lowered to her legs. What a pretty-damn-stunning pair of legs they were. He had never considered himself the leg man in the family—everyone knew that was Eli. His favorite part of a woman's body usually was the middle. Specifically, what lay at the juncture of her legs. All the others parts—the legs, the breasts, the thighs, hips and backside—just whet his appetite. And as he continued to stare at Nikki's legs he could feel not only his appetite being whet but also himself becoming fully aroused in one hell of a way.

"Wasn't that just great?" she asked him, sitting back down.

"Totally tantalizing," was his response. He knew she was talking about the jazz instrumental that had just been played. He was talking about her legs and her curves in that short dress.

When the waiter came and refilled their water glasses and brought more lemons, he settled farther into his seat. He would stay, enjoy the rest of the show and at the same time enjoy the woman…at least enjoy the company of the woman. He'd learned his lesson with women who thought they could change their thinking that a wedding came before the bedding. Nikki might think she had it down pat, but deep down she would still look for wedding bells. There were really no sure converts when it came to that sort of thing. Just the pretenders.

He'd run into several of those in his lifetime. And the last thing he wanted to do was get mixed up with another. He glanced at his watch, thinking it was time to bring this evening to an end. But for some reason, he couldn't. At least, not yet.

Nikki ran her fingers through her hair as she walked beside Jonas to her car. It was close to midnight and he had hung with her longer than she'd thought he would. She had figured he would leave at some point during the evening but surprisingly, he hadn't. In fact he genuinely seemed to have enjoyed the music as much as she had.

But she wasn't fooled into thinking that he hadn't

been trying to size her up, figure her out. More than once during the course of the evening, she had glanced across the table in the semi-darkened room to find those green eyes leveled on her. It had been during those times, when her heart would beat like crazy in her chest, that she wished she had something stronger to drink than just water.

She was convinced there weren't too many men like Jonas Steele, then quickly remembered there were six of them, four still single. But each was different in his own way, although when it came to women there were definite similarities.

When he led her straight to her car, she glanced up at him. "How did you know this car was mine? I didn't tell you what I was driving, and it's different from the last one I had when we worked together before."

He smiled. "I knew it was yours was because I saw you when you got out of it, although I didn't know it was you at the time. I recognized the legs later."

She stared at him, saw he was dead serious and couldn't help but laugh.

"What's so funny? "

If he didn't know… "Nothing," she said, shaking her head. She pulled the key from her purse. "Well, I'll be seeing you."

"I'll follow you."

She lifted a brow. "Why?"

"To make sure you get home okay."

She looked at him like he had a visible dent in his brain. "You don't have to do that. It's not like we've been out on a date or anything."

"It doesn't matter. We've spent the evening together

and it's late. There's no way I'll not make sure you get home. I wasn't raised that way."

She let out an exaggerated breath. "What if I get your number and just text you to let you know that I made it home?"

"Unless you deleted it, you already have my number from the last time we worked together. But texting me won't work. I removed that feature from my phone."

"You did? Why?"

He shrugged. "I was getting too many unnecessary messages."

"Yeah, I bet." She brushed a curl back from her face. "Look, Jonas, your wanting to make sure I get home safe and sound is thoughtful but truly not necessary."

"Your opinion, not mine. Ready to go?"

When she saw there was no use standing in the middle of the hotel's parking lot arguing with him, she opened her car door to get in. She then watched in her rearview mirror as he crossed the lot to his car. As she turned on the ignition, she shook her head. He had recognized her legs. Of all things.

She pulled out of the parking lot and another glance in the rearview mirror showed he was right on her tail. *Right on her tail.* That same heat she'd been battling between her legs all evening returned at the thought. Okay, she was an intelligent and sensible woman, but that didn't mean she couldn't get tempted every once in a while. Just as long as she didn't ever yield to such temptation, she was safe.

Still in the mood for jazz, she turned on the CD player in her car and the sound of Miles Davis flowed through, bringing back the mood that had been set earlier. Good music and the presence of a handsome man sitting at her table. It hadn't been a date, she reminded herself, although it had appeared as such.

It took twenty minutes to get home and she tried not to think of the man following her. Every time she would look in her rearview mirror he seemed to be staring back right at her. And when she pulled into her driveway she was surprised when he pulled right in behind her. It would have been fine if he had parked on the street.

Her throat tightened when he joined her on the walkway. "You don't have to walk me to the door, Jonas."

His lips curved into a wide grin. "Yes, I do."

She eyed him, one brow arching. Did he have an ulterior motive for wanting to walk her to the door? Was he hoping she would invite him in? Did she want to?

She wondered what kind of game he was playing with her now, and more importantly, why she was letting him. She'd given him her answer regarding working with him again—a decision she figured she would regret in the morning.

In a way she was already regretting it. But her sanity and peace of mind were more important and she was certain working with him again would rob her of both.

"Your key, please."

She blinked when his request jerked her back to the here and now. She looked up at him. They were at her front door. "My key?"

"Yes."

"Why would you want my key?"

"To see you properly inside."

Yeah. Right. He wouldn't be the first man who tried testing her, and she knew he wouldn't be the last. But then she also knew that this was Jonas Steele, a man who'd probably perfected his game. And for some reason he intended to try his game on her. Did she have something plastered on her forehead that said, *Try me?*

"Thanks, but I don't need you to see me inside, properly or otherwise," she said, using the key to unlock the door herself. "This is where we part ways."

"Do you really want to do that?" he asked, easing closer to her, too close for her comfort. His cologne was getting to her. His very presence was getting to her.

"Why wouldn't I? Besides, we both know I'm not your type."

He chuckled. "And what is my type?"

She blew out a breath, feeling herself getting annoyed. "Someone who enjoys playing your kind of games." She'd thought that she would, had convinced herself she could handle a man like him if she began thinking like he did, but she saw that wasn't working.

He inched closer. "And you don't enjoy playing my sort of games, Nikki?"

That answer was easy. "No, I'll pass."

"You're really not going to invite me in?"

He actually looked crushed, but she knew it was a put-on, just one of the many faces of Jonas Steele. He played whichever one worked at the time. "No. Sorry. Usually a woman invites a man inside when she offers him coffee, tea or something else to drink. I'm plum out of everything. I didn't make it to the grocery store this week."

He leaned against her door front. "We do pretty good on just water."

"I don't have any lemons," she said quickly

"We'll find our own pucker power," he said, easing a little closer to her. He had taken off his suit jacket and tie and was standing there, under her porch light, looking laid-back, cool and calm. And it didn't help matters when his gaze roamed over her. He was up to something and she felt she deserved to know what.

"Okay, Jonas, what's going on?"

"What makes you think something is going on? And what kinds of games do you think I like playing?"

Another simple answer. "Musical beds, for starters."

He nodded slowly. Then a smile touched his lips. "Are you worried about your fair share of my time in the bedroom?"

The man was impossible. Now she saw she'd done the right thing in turning down his offer for that job. "I wouldn't have been the one who needed to worry," she said snappily and regretted her words the moment they'd left her lips. Of course he would see it as a challenge. The notion was written all over his face.

"Umm, that would be interesting."

"Not if you can't even remember a kiss," she muttered under her breath and then wished she hadn't when he stared at her, letting her know he'd heard her.

"Oh, I definitely remember it, Nikki."

She waved off his words. "Whatever."

"Um, maybe we need to go inside and talk about that kiss."

She shook her head. "No, we don't. We can say our good-nights right here."

"Not until we talk. Evidently we aren't on the same page."

"Doesn't matter to me," she lied.

"It does to me. It won't take more than five minutes to clear this up."

There really was nothing to clear up, but she figured

she would be wasting her time trying to convince him of that. Besides, deep down she was curious about what he had to say. Men could talk their way in or out of anything. But what concerned her now more than anything was why he was coming on to her after all this time.

"I'm going to ask you again, Jonas. What's going on? Why are you trying to do me?" A girl couldn't ask any plainer than that.

He inched even closer. "Because the thought of doing you has been on my mind ever since that kiss."

She stared at him. Did he honestly think she would believe that? There was no way he could convince her that that kiss had meant anything to him. It wasn't like they lived in separate towns and it wasn't as if she was hard to find. Her best friend was married to his oldest brother, for heaven's sake.

Besides, if a Steele wanted a woman he strategized things to his advantage and went after her with no time wasted. Eighteen months had gone by and he hadn't made a move. They had run into each other at several functions and he'd deliberately gone out of his way to avoid her. She wasn't stupid.

She must have worn the look of disbelief well because he then said, "You don't believe me."

She shook her head. "No, I don't believe you. Good night."

He stuck out his hand to block her entrance inside. "What about another kiss? One for the road."

Nikki drew in a deep breath because deep down, she wanted another kiss. No joke. All she had to do was look at his mouth and remember the taste of it. Good Lord, how could she think of such things and especially with this man? The man who had a player's card with no expiration date.

"What would another kiss do, Jonas?"

"Prove you wrong."

Could it? She doubted it. But…

She studied his features. There was a look in his eyes that was more intense than the way he'd been staring at her in Mavericks. She let out a frustrating sigh. That's another reason she thought she wasn't cut out to be in the fast lane. A woman could get gray hairs trying to figure a man out. "A kiss and then you'll go away?" she asked softly, feeling her resistance to him slipping away.

"Yes. Scout's honor."

She stared at him for a moment and then said, "I'm taking you at your word." She opened the door and moved inside with him following quickly on her heels as if he thought she would change her mind.

Jonas closed the door behind him as both desire and tension stirred deep in the pit of his stomach. He glanced around. She had left a light burning on a table in the foyer, and he figured chances were she wouldn't invite him in to see the rest of the house, which was fine with him. All he needed was the area where they were standing.

She was in front of him, looking agitated and annoyed, ready for him to kiss her and get it over with. His jaw twitched as irritation filled him. First she turned down his job offer, and now she was trying to rush him off like he was a bother. And she even had the gall to tap her foot.

She tilted her head back and looked up at him. "Well?"

"Well?" he countered, moving a little closer to her.

"What are you waiting for?" she asked, lifting her chin.

"For you to get your mind in check."

Sighing, Nikki doubted that would happen. Her mind would never be fully in check when it came to Jonas. She really didn't understand what the big deal was. Why was he taking so long to kiss her? He was the one who suggested they do it again. She would have been perfectly satisfied with her memories.

"You have beautiful eyes, Nikki."

She blinked and her heart began beating a little harder when she noticed he had eased even closer to her. When had he done that? "Thank you. You have beautiful eyes yourself."

His lips curved into a smile as he took a step closer. Instinctively, she took a step back. He reached out and gently grabbed her around the waist. "Where do you think you're going?"

"Nowhere."

He towered over her, but his face was close, almost right in hers. His breath smelled of lemons and she recalled what he'd said about pucker power. "Why are you taking so long?"

"Nikki," he said in what sounded like an exasperated tone. "Some things you can't rush. Be patient. Besides, I'm thinking about a few things."

She cocked a brow. "What things?"

"Like how much I enjoyed kissing you the last time. How your taste remained on my tongue for days, months, and how no degree of brushing could get it off."

She looked stunned. "That's impossible. You left, almost knocking over my trash can in your rush to leave."

He reached out and lifted her chin. "It was either that or I stripped off your clothes and took you right there where you stood."

He spoke the words low and all but breathed them against her lips, making her pulse quicken and her heart rate increase. "I don't believe you," she whispered as a shiver of desire ran all through her.

"Then maybe I need to make a believer out of you."

He advanced. Instinctively she backed up again until she noticed the wall at her spine. She also noticed something else. He had braced his hands on the walls on both sides of her head, caging her in. When he shifted positions the lower part of him rubbed against her middle. He was hard. Extremely hard. Diabolically hard.

"Why is your heart beating so fast, Nikki?" he asked, moving his lips even closer.

"It's not."

"Yes, it is. I hear it. I can feel it."

She swallowed, thinking he probably could. When she'd decided to go ahead with the kiss she'd figured it would be an even exchange. It was something they both wanted. But now she had a feeling she would be paying a bigger price than he would.

She stared into his gaze and he stared back, but there was something in his look that gave her pause, made her heart, which was already beating like crazy, thump even faster. And was the floor actually moving beneath her feet?

"Place your hands on my shoulders. Both of them."

His words were whispered across her lips, and automatically she lifted her arms to comply. The air between them was electrified, charged. She didn't just place her hands on his shoulders; instinctively her fingertips dug into his shoulder blades. If he was bothered by it, he didn't let on. Instead his gaze moved from her eyes to her mouth and she watched as he gave her a soft smile.

She focused her attention on the shape of his lips and wondered about their texture. Their taste. And then before she could take her next breath, his mouth lowered to hers.

Chapter 4

Jonas felt as if he'd come back to a place he should never have left. Never had kissing a woman made him feel that way before. The memories he had of their last kiss hadn't done it justice. His lips felt like a magnet, fused to her in the most intimate way. The heat that had blazed to life the moment his mouth touched hers had his body quivering inside.

He was taking her mouth with a hunger that he felt all the way down to the soles of his feet. This was no mere kiss. This wasn't even about reacquainting their mouths. This was the forging of fires in the broadest sense of the word. He didn't want just to play on her senses, he wanted to dominate them. His mouth was relentless, untiring and filled with a hunger that had him devouring her as his tongue mated fiercely with hers.

A man with his experience could pick up on the

fact that moisture was gathering between her legs. The scent was being absorbed in his nostrils. He wanted to touch her there. Taste her there, like he was tasting her mouth. Mate with her there, the way his tongue was mating with hers. He was consumed by an urgency, an insatiable hunger.

His hands moved from the wall to grip her hips, then behind her to cup her backside. The soft material of her dress was no barrier against the hard erection he pressed against her. Her fingertips were pressing hard into his shoulders, eliciting pain and pleasure at the same time.

For him, kissing had always been a prelude to the next phase of sex. It was foreplay that he enjoyed, but he knew the prize was when he penetrated a woman, going deep and riding her hard. But with Nikki he had a totally different mind-set. His taste for her was relentless. Never had he craved kissing a woman so.

And to think she had assumed he hadn't enjoyed this the first time around. If only she knew the reason he'd left that day had had nothing to do with not enjoying the kiss but everything to do with enjoying it too much.

And now his insides felt as if they'd burst into flames and the only way to put them out was to take her to the nearest bed and lose himself. With that thought in mind he lifted her into his arms.

The feel of being swept off her feet caused Nikki's senses to return in full force. She pushed against Jonas's chest before easing out of this arms. There was no need to ask where he thought he was about to take her. He'd been headed in the direction of her bedroom.

And there was no need to ask how he knew just

where the room was located when he'd never set foot in her house before. Men like Jonas had built-in radar when it came to a woman's bedroom. She pulled in a deep breath, thinking that had been some kiss, definitively hotter than the last.

"Do you believe me now, Nikki?"

She glanced up, and like a magnet her gaze automatically latched to Jonas's mouth. Seeing the shape of his damp lips made her lick her own when she remembered why his were wet. Yes, she believed him. After the way he had devoured her mouth, she had no choice but to do so. And the thought that he had enjoyed the kiss as much as she had sent her into a head spin. He was fire and if she thought she could play with him without getting burned then she was only fooling herself. And her mother hadn't raised a fool. To keep her sanity, she needed to distance herself from him as soon as possible.

"You got the kiss so now you can leave." In reality he'd gotten a lot more than that. He'd snatched her common sense right from her, which was why she needed to hurry him out the door.

"Okay, I'll go, Nikki. But if you change your mind about coming on board for the Fulton project, let me know within the week."

She stared at him. Did he honestly think she could work with him now? Whenever she saw him she wouldn't think of work; she would think of kisses.

"There's no way I can work with you even if I had a change of heart, Jonas."

He took a step back and placed his hands in his pockets. "Why not? You're a big girl. I'm sure you can handle a one-night stand."

She frowned. There was no way she would consider such a thing. "That's not the point."

"Isn't it? You said you knew about my type so now let me tell you what I perceive as yours. Although you claim you no longer believe in that fairy-tale nonsense of everlasting love, you're still holding out for it. You want to believe that somehow your lucky number will get pulled and you'll meet a guy who wants to put a ring on your finger, marry you and give you babies. But my question to you, Nikki, is this. Are you willing to live your life and hold out waiting for a possibility? What if it doesn't happen? We both know the statistics. Chances are it won't."

He paused a second and to give her more food for thought, he added, "Just think of all the time you waste waiting for Mr. Right who just might not come at all."

She glared at him. "How can you be so cynical when your parents have been happily married close to forty years, and two of your brothers—who use to be die-hard bachelors—are now married?"

A crooked smile touched his lips. "Easily. I consider my parents' marriage one in a million, which means they beat the odds. And as for my brothers...the jury is still out as to whether their marriages will last. Don't get me wrong, I believe they love the women they married and the women they married love them. But a marriage is built on more than just love, so I'll wait and see if either of them will celebrate any five-year anniversaries."

She could only stare at him, not believing he said such a thing. She didn't know Eli and Stacey that well, but anyone who hung around Galen and Brittany long enough knew they were destined to share their lives together forever. How could he not see it? She knew the answer immediately. He didn't want to see it. He simply refused to do so.

"So there's no reason why you shouldn't enjoy yourself, Nikki. Have fun. If not with me then definitely someone else. But at the moment I'm thinking only of myself and the fun the two of us can have together. Why let life slip you by? You're nearly thirty, right?"

Now that was a low blow, Nikki thought. A man never brought up a woman's age. And before she could take him to task for doing so, he went on to add, "Don't get me wrong. You look good for your age. But time isn't on your side. Neither is it on mine. It happens. Life happens. So we might as well enjoy it while we can."

She crossed her arms over her chest and lifted her chin. She wondered if this was the game he ran on his women who eventually gave in to him. "Is that all?"

"No, but I figured that, along with the kiss, is enough for you to think about for now. However, if after all your reflections you still decide affairs aren't your thing, I still would like to work with you again. I'll even keep my hands and lips to myself and retain a strictly business relationship with you. Like I said at dinner, you're the best photographer around and I need the best for this project."

A smile curved his lips. "Good night and I hope to see you around."

Nikki blinked when the door closed behind Jonas. She then drew in a deep breath, wondering if she had imagined the whole thing. Had she and Jonas actually kissed again?

She touched her lips with her fingertips. They felt

sore and she knew why. This kiss had been more powerful than the last one. Jonas hadn't just kissed her, he
had devoured her mouth. And she hated to admit that
she had enjoyed it. Immensely. Slowly drawing air into
her lungs, she could still taste him on her tongue. Her
body was in shock mode with tingling sensations rushing through it. Every muscle was quivering, and she
was overheated with want and need that had her insides
sizzling.

She moved away from the wall thinking Jonas had
read her loud and clear. She wanted to be a bad girl
with a good-girl mentality. She even had Brittany convinced that she was a woman with no hang-ups about
engaging in casual affairs. The lie had sounded so true
that she had begun believing it herself. But Jonas had
shown her she was way out of her league.

Okay, he'd told her he was attracted to her, and the
kiss somewhat proved that he was. What he hadn't
told her was why he had kept his distance for eighteen
months.

She rubbed her forehead, feeling a humongous head-
ache coming on, but she knew what she had to do. Tomorrow she would call Senator Joseph's campaign
headquarters and accept the offer they'd made. The
sooner she got busy with her life, the sooner she could
put thoughts of Jonas out of it.

Jacketless, shirtless and horny as hell, Jonas let himself into his house. On the drive home he kept calling
himself all kinds of fool for kissing Nikki again. Why
was he a glutton for punishment? At least he didn't have
to wonder why he was so drawn to her.

There was something about her taste that even now

was causing an ache in his lower extremities. When had a kiss been so overpowering? So downright delicious that his entire body was revving up with thoughts of another one? And then another...

Besides that, there was something different about their date—and whether he wanted to admit it or not, what started out as a business meeting had ended up as a date. He had enjoyed her company more than any other woman's. Mainly because in addition to being a great conversationalist, she had a sense of humor. She had shared with him some of her and Brittany's escapades as teens growing up together in Florida.

What he needed to do was clear his mind and he knew the best way to do it. A way that worked each and every time. Taking the stairs two at a time he entered his bedroom and changed into a pair of jeans and a T-shirt, the perfect outfit for a late-night ride on his Harley.

A short while later he was in his garage, putting a band on his hair to hold the strands together before placing a helmet on his head. He straddled his bike, ready to hit the open road. Adrenaline flowed through every part of his body when he fired up the engine and took off like the devil himself was chasing after him.

He knew the route he was traveling. Could follow it with his eyes closed since it was the same one he always took whenever he rode his bike late at night. This was his favorite time for riding with a big beautiful dark sky overhead and stars sprinkled about. Usually he felt at peace, but on this particular night his mind was in turmoil. He definitely needed this ride.

He settled in his seat, drew in a deep breath and let the adrenaline flow. The sound of the thrumming engine had a calming effect, one he felt all the way down to his bones.

Now if he could only get Nikki out of his mind. A frown appeared between his eyebrows. Why even now, when he was out on the open road in the middle of the night, could he still inhale her scent? And why couldn't he get out of his mind just how she'd looked tonight in that outfit?

His frown deepened. How she looked tonight had nothing on her taste, which was something else he couldn't seem to get over. But he would. No matter what it took. Damn, hadn't he made that same resolution eighteen months ago?

The only reason he'd kissed her tonight was because he'd undergone a moment of temporary insanity. He was convinced that had to be it. And he was equally convinced that by this time tomorrow he would be back in his right mind and in some other woman's bed to make him forget. Hadn't that been what had helped him the last time? Yes, somewhat, but it hadn't taken care of the root of his problem.

He wanted Nikki in a way a man usually wanted a woman. In his bed. Whether he'd admit it or not, kissing her a second time had pretty much changed the dynamics of their relationship. She was now under his skin deeper than before.

Jonas looked ahead and saw the flashing railroad crossings go down. He expelled an agitated breath and brought his bike to a complete stop.

"If you straddle a woman like you do that bike then you're definitely a man who knows how to ride."

Jonas rolled his eyes before glancing at the very attractive woman seated behind the wheel of a canary-yellow Corvette convertible idling beside him. His gaze first appreciated the car and then the woman. The look she was giving him made him feel naked. Unfortunately for her, he didn't experience even the faintest hint of excitement from her intense perusal.

"Yes, I know how to ride and enjoy doing so," he responded, knowing neither of them was talking about his bike.

"Then maybe you need to follow me."

He thought that maybe he did, until he saw the ring on her finger. "And maybe you need to go home to your husband."

She pouted. "He's no fun."

Your problem, not mine. "I don't encroach on another man's territory."

"Um, that's a pity," she said sarcastically.

"Probably is." *Especially since tonight I'd love to ride a woman more than this bike.*

But as he took off when the railroad crossing arms went back up, he knew the only woman he wanted to ride. But he didn't want to think about it. He didn't want to think about her.

So he continued to ride as he tried to shut off his mind to any thoughts of Nikki Cartwright. About to take a curve, he leaned in, liking the feel of power beneath his thighs. It was a thrumming sensation he couldn't get anywhere else. The vibration of the bike's engine helped to lull him into a contented mood for the time being. He felt totally in sync with the road, the bike he was riding, and the entire universe. The feeling was totally awesome.

Jonas tried to recall the last time he'd had a woman on the bike with him. It had been a while since his back had rested against a pair of plump, ripe breasts or a woman's arms had been wrapped around him while she held on tight.

At that moment the image of the only woman he wanted to share a bike ride with loomed in front of him. And he was suddenly filled with arousal that had his erection pressing hard against his zipper. He drew in a deep breath and adjusted his body on the seat. As much as he wished otherwise, it was evident that Nikki would not be eradicated from his thoughts anytime soon. The woman was one sensual piece of art.

It was only when he came to a stop at a red light that he took in his surroundings. He was only a block away from where Nikki lived. What had possessed him to come this way when he lived in the other direction? What was this madness? He should be putting as much distance between them as he could. That kiss was proof enough that when it came to her he couldn't think straight.

And maybe that was the reason he should have a face-off with her once and for all. Granted, Nikki was a challenge to his sensibilities, but he refused to run in the opposite direction whenever he saw her, like he'd been doing for the past eighteen months. He would face her like a man and do what he knew he needed to do and be done with it.

Hell, the way he saw it, he would be doing her a favor. Like he told her, she was approaching thirty and it was time to put all that nonsense of a forever love out of her head. Being a romantic was one thing. Being a hopeless, incurable romantic was another.

He checked his watch. It was late, close to one in the morning. But there was someone he needed to call now.

Pulling to the side of the road, he killed his engine and removed his helmet. He took his cell phone out of his pocket to make a call.

"Hello."

"Stan. I figured you would still be up."

"Jonas? Kind of late for you to be calling. Is there a party somewhere that I'm missing?"

Jonas chuckled. "No. Just calling to collect a favor."

"Okay, buddy. I owe you so many of them I won't waste my time asking which one. Just tell me what you need."

"Your brother Jeremy is campaign manager for Senator Joseph, right?"

"Yes, that's right."

Jonas nodded. "Someone made a job offer to a photographer by the name of Nicole Cartwright. I want them to pull the offer."

"Pull the offer?" Stan asked, surprised.

"Yes."

"All right. I'll see what I can do."

"Thanks. I appreciate it."

Satisfied for the time being, Jonas returned the cell phone to his pocket and put the helmet back on his head. Firing up the bike's engine, he headed for home.

Chapter 5

"Senator Joseph's campaign actually withdrew their offer to hire you as a photographer?" Brittany Steele asked as she gazed across the table at her best friend.

"Yes," Nikki said, still somewhat annoyed at the call she'd received yesterday.

"Why?"

"They said something about reevaluating the budget. It was definitely bad timing since I had planned to call them to accept." Nikki glanced around Samantha's Café where she had met Brittany for lunch. A popular place to dine, the establishment was crowded.

She looked back at Brittany. "Now I need to look at other opportunities. Weddings, anniversary parties and family portraits are nice to do on the side, but they won't pay the bills."

"So what are you going to do?"

After taking a sip of her coffee, Nikki answered, "Not sure, especially since I turned down Jonas's offer."

Brittany raised an arched brow. "Jonas offered you a job?"

Nikki nodded. "Yes. It was a chance to work with him on that Fulton project. And he was going to pay twice as much as the Joseph campaign."

"Then why did you turn down Jonas? I would think being a part of that Fulton project would be a dream come true."

Nikki's cheeks warmed. There were certain things she had withheld from her best friend, and now it was time to come clean. "Do you recall that day we ran into each other when you first arrived in Phoenix and you were bidding on your mother's property?"

Brittany smiled as she cut into her salad. "Yes, that was over a year ago, but I remember. It was short of a miracle that we ran into each other after all those years."

"Yes, and that night we dined at Malone's and played catch-up on what's been going on with us over the past twelve years."

Brittany's smile deepened. "I was stressed out about Galen's outlandish proposal for my mother's property."

"Yes, well, I wasn't completely forthright about a few things."

Brittany stopped what she was doing and stared. "About what?"

"My relationship with Jonas, for starters."

Surprise lit Brittany's features and she set down her fork and knife by her salad bowl. "You and Jonas were involved?"

Nikki chuckled. "Only in my dreams. But when I

brought him up, I made it seem as if the two of us had merely worked together once or twice and hadn't gotten all that close."

"But you and he had been close?"

"Not sexual or anything like that. But we had kissed. The reason I didn't say anything was that I was too embarrassed to admit it, especially since it was a kiss that led nowhere. And one I took more seriously than he did. We were at my office one day and had gotten excited over this deal he'd clinched and got caught up in the moment."

Nikki leaned back in her chair. "Trust me. He regretted the kiss soon enough and made sure he kept his distance whenever we would run into each other after that. In fact, the first time we came in breathing space of each other again was at your wedding."

She could remember that day like it was yesterday. She had been one of the bridesmaids and he one of the groomsmen. She had avoided him like he'd been determined to avoid her.

"And I saw him again when I was the photographer at Eli's wedding," she said, stirring her soup. She shook her head. "It's funny we only seem to run into each other at weddings."

Nikki paused, remembering that day at Eli's wedding. She could have sworn more than once Jonas's gaze had been on her, but when she would glance over at him he would be either engaged in deep conversation with someone or looking someplace else. "I was surprised when I got a call from him three days ago asking that we meet to discuss a business proposition."

"The Fulton deal?"

"Yes. We met, he made the offer and I turned him down."

"Why?"

Nikki met Brittany's gaze. "Because I knew I would not be able to control myself around him…which leads to my next confession."

"Which is?"

"I'm not living in the fast lane like I led you to believe on that night. I gave you the impression that I'd given up believing in a knight in shining armor and that I was independent, empowered, a woman on the move. A woman who wanted nothing more than a casual affair with a man. I wanted to believe I was all those things and had convinced myself I could be. But…"

"But what?"

"I blew a big chance to prove myself with Jonas this week, which leads me to believe that I might not be as ready to move out of my comfort zone as I thought. Deep down a part of me is still programmed to believe in happy endings and everything that goes along with it—love, happiness and commitment. But then there's another part that knows such things no longer exist for most women and that I need to stop reaching for a fantasy and accept reality. I can't have it both ways."

She pushed her soup bowl aside. "So all that advice I gave you that night was all talk, and nothing that I would have had the courage to try myself."

A smile touched Brittany's lips. "All talk or not, it was good advice and if I hadn't taken it, I wouldn't have Galen." She leaned back in her chair and eyed Nikki squarely. "Sounds to me like there's a battle going on inside of you. Your head against your heart. Your head is filled with notions of how today's woman should act and the things she should want, versus the things that your heart—the heart of a romantic—wants. That old-fashioned happy ever after."

Brittany chuckled. "And don't you dare ask me which one you should listen to. That's a decision only you can make, and you'll know when it's the right one."

Nikki shook her head. "Not sure about that, and I might have muddied the waters even more. Jonas and I kissed again the other night."

The expression on Brittany's face showed she wasn't surprised. "And?"

"For me it was better than the first time, and there's no doubt in my mind that he enjoyed it as much as I did. But I know the score, Britt. Jonas is a bona fide player who doesn't have a serious bone in his body."

"And you want to become a female version?"

Nikki shrugged. "Not to that degree, but you know what they're saying. Good men are extinct, and more and more women aren't depending on a man for their happiness."

"*They're* saying. And just who are *they*?"

"Magazine articles, talk shows, reality shows, anybody you ask. Finding love, happiness and commitment is as unlikely as walking down the street and finding a million-dollar bill."

Brittany chuckled. "There aren't million-dollar bills."

Nikki giggled. "See there, another reason not to waste your time looking."

Brittany shook her head. "Seriously, in the end you have to do what makes you happy."

"But what happens if what makes me happy is something not good for me?"

"Then you'll know it and eventually reject it. In the

end, either your head or your heart will win." Brittany paused a second and then asked, "So what are you going to do about Jonas and that job offer? Is it too late to tell him you've changed your mind and want it after all?"

Did she want it after all? Nikki nibbled on her bottom lip. Nothing had changed since two nights ago. She still didn't feel comfortable working so closely with Jonas again. But in reality she realized that something had changed. She no longer had choices with her employment situation. She needed a job.

She was still attracted to him and it seemed he was attracted to her. But for how long? She couldn't forget his reputation when it came to women. "Not sure what I'm going to do yet. To go back and tell Jonas that I've changed my mind and will work for him is easier said than done. The issues I had with it then are the same issues I have now. And it wouldn't hurt if he wasn't so cynical."

Brittany laughed. "Yes, he's definitely that. I love my brothers-in-law, but they're hard-core players. However, look at Galen and Eli—so were they once. So maybe there's hope."

Nikki didn't know about the others but figured that hope was on the other end of the spectrum when it came to Jonas. However, at some point she needed to see it as his problem and not hers. She had allowed his way of thinking and acting to rain on her parade, and that wasn't fair. She should not have been afraid of taking that job for fear of how she would act based on his actions.

She sighed upon realizing she had turned down what could have been her big break because of him. Instead of taking his offer and taking him on in the process, she had given in to her fears and backed away.

She glanced up at Brittany and took a deep breath. "My financial needs outweigh my emotional ones right now. And you're right. It will be a battle between my head and my heart. I just hope I can survive the fight."

3 days later

"Mr. Steele, Nikki Cartwright is here to see you."

Jonas looked up from the document he was reading when his secretary's voice came across the intercom. *Finally*, he thought. It had taken Nikki almost a week to come calling, and for a minute he'd gotten worried that perhaps he'd misplayed his hand and there was some other job she had lined up that he hadn't known about. He tossed what was left of his Tootsie Pop in the trash can by his desk, leaned back in his chair and smiled. Evidently that wasn't the case.

"Give me a few minutes to wrap up this report, Gail, and then send her in," he said, standing to straighten his tie. He didn't have any report to wrap up. He needed the extra time to prepare himself mentally for the woman he couldn't get out of his mind. He sniffed the air; he inhaled her scent already.

He checked to make sure his shirt was neatly tucked into his pants while thinking that he would discount the fact it had taken manipulation on his part to get her here. After their second kiss, it had become extremely clear to him just how much he wanted Nikki in his bed, and at that point he had decided he would do whatever it took to get her there. Sleeping with her once should do it. He was convinced of it.

He was marveling over the brilliance of that supposition when he heard the soft knock on his office door. "Come in."

His gaze connected with hers the moment the door opened. He swallowed tightly and immediately thought he might need to sleep with her more than once. It would be breaking a rule, but some rules were made to be broken. "Nikki, this is a surprise." Like hell it was. He'd been expecting her. Hoping she would take the bait and decide she needed to work for him after all.

"I hope I didn't catch you at a bad time, Jonas. I thought about calling but figured it would be best if we talked in person."

"Sure, have a seat."

He watched her cross the room to the chair he offered, and thought she looked fresh in her jeans and pretty blue blouse. He liked how the denim fit over her soft curves. Seeing her in a dress that night had taken the guesswork out of what her legs looked like, and he hated that she'd covered them up today.

"You can have one of those," he said of the Tootsie Pops in a candy jar on a table near Nikki's chair.

"No, thank you. I don't normally have a sweet tooth."

He had to bite back from saying sweet tooth or not, what he'd tasted of her so far was simply delicious. He went to sit on the edge of his desk to face her, inhale her scent, recall the fantasies he'd had of her just last night. They'd been hot, lustful, erection-throbbing fantasies of him riding her. Her riding him. Oral sex. Can't-walk-the-next-day sex. When his stomach clenched he figured he better get his thoughts under control and out from under the bedcovers.

"So what can I help you with, Nikki?"

She began nibbling on her bottom lip, which meant she was nervous. He felt his erection throb, which meant he was horny. With effort, he pushed from his mind the thought of just what those two things might have in common.

"The other night you offered me the chance to work with you on the Fulton project."

He nodded slowly. "Yes, and you turned me down."

She looked good today, sexy as hell. Innocent and hot all rolled into one. There was something about that curly hair of hers and the way it crowned her face. It teased the primal maleness inside of him. And that errant curl that seemed to always be out of place, falling just so between her brows, was hammering something fierce below his belt.

"Yes, but later you said you would hold the offer for at least a week, in case I changed my mind," she reminded him.

He held back from telling her he didn't need reminding. He knew just what he said, how he'd said it and why he'd said it. It was right after deciding, that whether he liked it or not, eighteen months hadn't rid him of his desire for her and he would risk any feelings of vulnerability that bedding her would bring on. The main thing was to get her out of his system so things could go back to normal for him.

"Yes, I did say that. So, have you changed your mind, Nikki?"

"Yes. Does that mean the job is still available and you'll consider me for it?"

"Like I told you, I want the best and I consider your skill with a camera unsurpassed." That was the truth and had nothing to do with his plan to get her in his bed. The bedding part was a done deal as far as he was concerned.

"Thanks." She began nibbling on those lips again and there was silence between them. There was more she wanted to say, he knew, but she was hesitating.

"I take it that there's something else you need to clear the air about before you make your final decision." He couldn't let her sit there and gnaw her mouth off. He couldn't afford for her to do that, not when he had plans for that luscious-looking mouth of hers.

She sat up straight in her chair. "Yes, there is. We've kissed. Twice now."

He nodded, fighting back the urge to tell her that was for starters and didn't come close to all the other things he intended for them to do now that he'd made up his mind about a few things regarding her. "Yes, that's twice now."

"It can't happen again. You did say you're willing to keep your hands to yourself."

Yes, he had said that. But that didn't necessarily mean he'd meant it. "Is that what you want?"

He'd seen it. She hadn't been quick enough to disguise that flash that had appeared in her eyes. He knew what it meant so whatever she said now didn't matter one iota.

"Yes, that's what I want."

Yeah, right. "Okay, I'll give you what you want." And he meant every word. She was going to discover soon enough that a hands-off policy between them was the last thing she really wanted.

He pushed away from his desk. "So, are you going to work for me?"

When she hesitated, he lifted a brow and a smile

touched his lips. "What? Do you need me to put the strictly business policy in writing or something?"

She stood as well. "Of course not."

"Then what is it?"

"Nothing."

He tilted his head. "I think there is something bothering you."

She adjusted the straps of her purse on her shoulder. He couldn't resist breathing in her scent and almost groaned.

"No, I'm fine."

You definitely are. "If you're sure, we can shake on it for now and then Gail will have your contract ready in a few days. Like I told you there's a launch party to attend in Las Vegas."

She nodded. "I'll be there. I just need the itinerary."

"Gail will call you when that's prepared as well."

He crossed the room to her, refused to consider the very real fact that he hadn't been completely honest with her about everything and that she probably wouldn't like it one damn bit when she found out how he'd manipulated things to get what he wanted.

Jonas reached his hand out to her and she took it, and he immediately felt his body's reaction to the feel of her smaller hand in his. "Welcome aboard, Nikki. I'm looking forward to working with you again."

He knew she felt something as well, although she was struggling hard not to. She tried not to make eye contact with him. Tried not to glance down at their joined hands. "Thanks, Jonas."

When she began nibbling on her lips again he figured it was time to release her hand. "You still have my mobile number, right?" he asked.

"Yes."

"Use it to contact me if you have any questions. I'm attending a wedding this weekend in New York, and from there I'm flying out for Vegas." A smile touched his lips. "I plan to have a little fun in Sin City before work begins."

He saw another flash that flitted in her eyes before she had time to hide it. Um, was the mention of his fun time in Vegas causing her worry? Should he take that as a red flag that the forever-after side of her had a tendency to show every once in a while? Hell, he hoped not since that sort of thinking was a waste of time with him.

"Enjoy yourself."

His grin was mischievous. "I intend to."

She tilted her head slightly and the mass of dark curls hid one eye so he couldn't completely figure out what she was thinking. "We'll be in Vegas a few days before flying to Los Angeles," he said while leading her to the door. "That's where we'll board the *Velocity*. And from there our two-week adventure begins."

What he didn't add was how much he was looking forward to that time. He intended to work hard and play even harder. "Any questions, Nikki?"

She shook her head. "No questions. I'll see you in Vegas, ready to work."

Every muscle in his body reacted to the thought of them working closely together. In the conference room. In the bedroom.

Chapter 6

Nikki clutched her hand to her chest as she stared out the taxi's window. For as far as her eyes could see, there were tall elegant hotels, neon signs, glitter and glitz. Sin City. She could just imagine all the transgressions being performed and knew all of it wasn't at the slot machines. She shook her head. What had she expected from a state where prostitution was legal?

"Your first time in Vegas?"

She glanced up at the driver. Truth be told, it might be her last time as well. She was feeling overwhelmed. "Yes, and I doubt I've ever seen anything like it."

She figured there was no decline in the economy here, at least there shouldn't be. The casinos never closed. And just how many Elvis impersonators had she seen since leaving the airport?

"You haven't seen anything yet. Just wait until this

place lights up at night. That's when everything looks spectacular."

She could only imagine. Twice in the past she'd made plans to come to Vegas, but each time those plans had fallen through for some reason or another, leading her to believe there was a bad omen between her and this city.

Nikki didn't want to consider the possibility that her being here now didn't bode well, either. She had gotten a call from Jonas's secretary a few days ago letting her know there had been a change and she was needed in Vegas earlier than originally planned. In addition to rearranging her schedule, she had rushed to do some shopping to make sure she had all the appropriate outfits she would need beside her usual jeans and blouses. She couldn't help wondering what turn of events had made Jonas decide she needed to be here ahead of her scheduled time.

As the cab continued to whisk her along the Vegas Strip, a part of her tried downplaying her excitement in seeing Jonas again. She should really get over it—and him, to boot. Wasn't he the same man who'd kissed her twice already and then told her he planned to leave for Vegas a few days early to have fun—no doubt with other women? Not that she thought those kisses had meant anything to him, mind you. But it was the principle of the thing.

But that's just it, Nikki. Men like Jonas have no principles. When will you finally see that?

She let out a frustrated sigh. It's not that she didn't know it, because she did. It was her heart side—the one still filled with idealistic hopes and dreams—working against her, refusing to accept what her head already knew *but just refused to accept on most good days.*

She looked down at the camera around her neck and was reminded of the real reason she was here. It wasn't about Jonas. It was about her doing a good job and making a name for herself. If she didn't succeed at this project she would have no one to blame but herself.

But still…

And there was that *but* in there, although she wished otherwise. There was nothing wrong with enjoying herself while she was here, if time allowed. Her brother always said if you work hard then you should reward yourself and play harder. Truthfully, she couldn't recall the last time she'd had some "let your hair down" fun. Maybe it was about time she did.

Nikki settled back against her seat's cushion. She had a feeling that before she left Vegas she was going to have an eye-opener as to just how sinful this city really was.

Gannon Steele stared across the hotel room at his brother. "Now tell me again why Nikki Cartwright is arriving in Vegas earlier than planned?"

Jonas rolled his eyes as he continued to button his shirt. He wasn't surprised the youngest of the Steele brothers was questioning why he'd sent for Nikki to come to Vegas early. Gannon was pouting, disappointed that the two of them wouldn't be hanging together as originally planned. That meant Gannon would have to visit some of the Vegas hot spots on his own, including the Doll House, a gentlemen's club owned by one of Galen's friends, Quinton Hinton.

Gannon, who'd turned thirty a few months ago, was

determined not only to blaze a trail for himself, but also to follow in his older brothers' footsteps by doing the wild and the reckless. Over the years Gannon had heard about their outlandish escapades and exploits, and figured what was good for the goose was also good for the gander.

"I told you already. She needs to get set up, and I need to make sure Fulton knows we're on the job," Jonas replied.

"Yes, but her flying in means you'll be working and really, man, nobody comes to Vegas to work."

"I did, and you knew that when you followed me here, so stop whining."

Gannon frowned. "Hell, I'm not whining."

Jonas rolled his eyes. "Yes, you are, so get over it already or I'll send you back home to Mama."

Jonas chuckled when he saw Gannon's frown. Brother number six hated being reminded he was the baby in the family. Jonas loved his youngest brother, but at times he really wondered about him and hoped to hell he didn't end up being the worst of the lot where women were concerned. Their mother would never forgive them if he did. Gannon was still easily influenced by his older brothers and Eden had accused them more than once of corrupting Gannon's mind.

If only she knew. Gannon might be the youngest and he might be impressionable, but he could hold his own in ways Jonas didn't want to even think about. Back in the day there was no such thing as social media. And now Gannon had taken internet dating to a whole new level. Hell, he had even come up with his own form of speed dating.

"Checking out one of those brothels is on my to-do list today."

Jonas nodded. He wasn't surprised and figured that visiting one of those would probably make Gannon's day…and probably his night as well. He wouldn't complain if it kept Gannon busy for a while and out of his hair. "Sounds like a good plan. And I'll give Quinton a call to let him know you'll be dropping by the Doll House sometime later and to make sure you have a good time."

Gannon's face lit up. "Hey man, that will be great. I appreciate it."

Jonas chuckled. "Hey, that's what brothers are for."

It was only after Gannon left that Jonas took a moment to sit down, unwrap a Tootsie Pop and stick it in his mouth as he reflected on the real reason he had asked Nikki to come to Vegas early. As much as he assumed he would have fun in Sin City, he'd discovered that instead he had spent his time thinking about her, counting the days, the hours—hell, even the minutes—when she was to fly in. And for a man who was usually on top of his game, he hadn't been involved with any woman since the night they kissed. He hadn't a desire to do so. Hell, what was that about?

Instead of heeding these red flags, he took an even deeper plunge by summoning her earlier. At one point it was as if he couldn't get her here fast enough. He was tired of waking up from dreams in which she had a leading role and which had left him hornier and even more frustrated. He could only smile at the depth of his manipulations. He'd seen it as the only way to take care of those pent-up frustrations that had begun taking over his senses. If things went as planned, his photographer would be arriving any minute.

In all honestly, he had lied. There was nothing they needed to do before the launch party, but there was definitely something he needed to do. Bed her. Get her out of his system. And do it sooner than he'd anticipated.

He checked his watch. He would give Nikki time to rest up from her flight and then he would seek her out.

Nikki brushed back a curl from her face as she glanced around the spacious hotel suite. Decorated in the most vibrant colors and prints, it was simply beautiful. She hadn't expected a suite. A standard room in this hotel would have been enough considering the hotel's extravagance. But she had no complaints and liked the fact that Ideas of Steele was being more than generous.

She had a sitting room separate from the bedroom, which had a bed that was bigger than any she'd ever seen. *Leave it to Vegas,* she thought. But what really caught her eye was the flower arrangement on the coffee table. Thinking it was a gift from the hotel, she crossed the room and pulled off the card.

Nikki, welcome to Vegas. We need to have dinner later to go over a few new developments. I'll call you. Jonas

Her brow furrowed. *New developments?* Placing the card on the table she headed toward the bedroom to unpack, certain she would find out soon enough just what those new developments were.

A short while later, after she had unpacked and

taken a shower, she stood looking out the huge floor-to-ceiling window in the sitting room. Already she was anticipating nightfall when she would see the Strip light up. She figured she should have an awesome view from her suite on the thirtieth floor.

She tightened the belt of her bath robe—courtesy of the hotel—and was about to go back into the bedroom when the hotel phone rang. Crossing the room, she picked it up. "Yes?"

"Nikki, this is Jonas."

She drew in a deep breath. Why did he have to sound so darn sexy? And why did the fact that that sexy voice also belonged to a man with a sexy body and a drop-dead gorgeous face have her heart beating like crazy in her chest? She didn't even have to close her eyes to envision the tall, dark and handsome mass of sensual masculinity on her phone. Just once she would love to run her fingers through his wavy hair, nibble at the corners of his lips before sliding her tongue between them.

Feeling overheated and knowing those thoughts were out of line, she cleared her throat. "Jonas, thanks for the flowers. They're beautiful."

"You're welcome and I'm glad you like them. I felt it was the least I could do for having you come out sooner than we discussed. I appreciate your flexibility."

"No problem. You mentioned something about new developments."

"Yes. I'll cover everything over dinner. Is six o'clock okay?"

"Six will be fine. Do you want us to meet in the lobby?"

"No, I thought we could have dinner in my suite."

She paused and immediately the intimate setting

flashed right before her eyes and sent feathered sensations down her spine. She forced her heart to stop pounding while she tried to restrain her thoughts. The thought of just the two of them in his hotel room was—in addition to everything else—causing heat to form between her thighs.

"Nikki?"

Girl, get that head of yours out of the gutter. Can't you tell by the sound of his voice he's all about business and nothing else? He's gotten two kisses off you and figures that's enough, so chill. He hasn't been the least bit unprofessional since you and he agreed on your terms. He probably wants to have an early dinner with you so he'll have time for some hot date later tonight.

"Yes, I'm still here," she said, finally responding to her name

"Will dinner in my hotel room at six work for you? If not, I could squeeze some time in for us to go out if you prefer."

Squeeze some time in? Please. Don't do me any favors. "Dinner in your suite will work fine, Jonas. That way I can get out and tour the city later." She stayed on the line long enough to get his room number before hanging up.

She glanced at her watch. She had four hours and figured she might as well take a nap. After she had dinner with Jonas she would take a stroll down Las Vegas Boulevard. It was bound to be a long night and she wanted to be well-rested.

Jonas paced his hotel room while sucking on a Tootsie Pop. He glanced at his watch again. He had another fifteen minutes and he didn't know any woman who would arrive early to anything, so why was he tripping?

Oh, he had an easy answer for that one. He wanted Nikki. Now if the evening would only go according to his plans. They would enjoy dinner and then enjoy each other—all night long. He was no longer worried about the outcome of any type of vulnerability on his part. Since seeing her in Phoenix he had convinced himself he was dedicated to bachelorhood, and there was no woman alive who could make him think differently, no matter how deep his desire for her went.

Then what was with the flowers, Steele?

"So okay, I sent them," he muttered under his breath to the imaginary mocking voice he heard in his head. He had played on her romantic side in sending those flowers but didn't feel the slightest bit of regret doing so. When it came to women the only time he played fair was when she belonged to someone else.

So as far as he was concerned, the lines were free and clear with Nikki. A few months ago, without giving anything away, he'd gotten Galen into a conversation about her, figuring Galen and Brittany probably told each other everything. He'd been right.

Although Galen didn't know a whole hell of a lot, he was positive Nikki wasn't seriously involved with anyone. Jonas had figured that much out on his own after they'd kissed that first time. And the second time, he hated to admit he hadn't really thought about whether she'd gotten involved since then or not. Her dating status had been the last thing on his mind that night when he'd all but begged her for that kiss.

He paused in his pacing to toss the finished pop

in the trash. And speaking of that kiss—hell, not just one but both—he couldn't get it out of his mind. It didn't take much to remember the feel of her enticing curves plastered against him while he took her lips with a hunger that he could remember even to this day, at that very moment. His gut clenched and his heart began beating like crazy in his chest. There had to be a reason he wanted her so badly, and why even now his heart was racing while he waited for her arrival.

He was about to start pacing again when he heard the knock on his hotel room door. He checked his watch and saw Nikki was seven minutes early. His mother, who was the epitome of punctuality, was seldom early. She would use every single minute to make sure she was well together, as she would say.

Inhaling deeply he moved toward the door, feeling the way his heart was kicking with each step he took. He tried to prepare himself, figuring he was making a big deal out of nothing. Nikki probably wasn't wearing makeup—not that she needed any. More than likely she was wearing jeans—although he thought she looked good in them, too. And chances were she had her camera around her neck since he'd only seen her without it a few times.

He opened the door and swallowed deeply as his gaze ran all over her. She was wearing makeup, a skirt that showed off her beautiful legs, and instead of a camera, she had a beaded necklace around her neck.

She looked simply gorgeous.

Chapter 7

"You did remember we had a meeting, didn't you?" Nikki asked Jonas when he stood there and stared as if he hadn't been expecting her. He was wearing dark dress slacks and a crisp white shirt, as if he was about to go out for the evening.

"Of course. What makes you think otherwise?" he asked, stepping aside for her to enter.

"You're all dressed up."

His gaze roamed her up and down, then returned to her face. "So are you."

No, she wasn't really, she thought, glancing down at herself. Little did he know the few times she did get dressed up, she cleaned up pretty well. "I'm checking out the Strip after our dinner meeting."

He closed the door and leaned back against it. "You do that a lot, don't you?"

She lifted a brow. "Do what?"

"Go out alone. Why? I'm sure getting dates isn't an issue for you."

They'd had this conversation before so why was he bringing it back up again, she wondered. Evidently he'd forgotten their discussion. "I like male company, don't get me wrong, but once in a while I like just doing things solo. I don't have to impress anyone or—"

"Play the kind of games you think men like me are so good at playing," he broke in to say.

So he had remembered. "Um, yes, something like that." Not wanting to get into a debate with him about the tactics he used with women and just what she thought of them, she glanced around. "I thought my room was nice—thanks, by the way—but this one is even nicer. But that's expected since you're *the man*."

"Am I?"

She grinned. "Yes, my bank account will definitely proclaim such in six weeks."

He threw his head back and laughed. The sound was both surprising and heartwarming, sending hot shivers escalating up her body. In addition to the busy zipper on his pants, it seemed Jonas knew how to let down his hair and he had enough locks on his head to do it. "Glad to know I'm doing my part to stimulate the economy," he said when he finally stopped laughing.

She fought back the urge to tell him that he was doing his part in stimulating other things as well. Like that inner part of her that was feeling arousing sensations just from listening to his voice. And her eyes were appreciating the sight of him as well. His slacks covered muscled thighs, long legs and a trimmed waist, and his shirt couldn't conceal well-defined abs and broad shoulders.

She drew in a deep breath and then released it slowly. "Your note said something about a new development, which is why you wanted me in Vegas earlier than planned."

"Yes, we need to talk about that. Dinner will be here any minute."

She followed him to the sitting room, and when he gestured to the sofa, she sat down. Then she watched him ease his body into the chair across from her. He picked up a folder from the coffee table. It was then she noted the bag of Tootsie Pops. Evidently he liked the things.

"It's nothing major, just a change in how we're presenting *Velocity* this weekend," he said. "We're still providing the brochures as planned, but I've come up with something I think will add dimension to our presentation."

"What?"

"The use of JumboTrons, strategically located at different places in the ballroom, running simultaneously to give attendees an idea of what to expect when they board the *Velocity*."

She immediately envisioned such a thing in her head and could see it working to their benefit. "But will we have time to work on the video?"

"Yes, my videographer, Rick Harris, is in Los Angeles now, putting together everything on his end. It'll arrive on Friday. I'd like you and Rick to make sure everything is ready by Saturday night's launch party."

He paused a moment and then asked, "What do you think of that idea?"

"I think it's fantastic. Rick and I have worked together before on other projects and he's good."

Adding those JumboTrons really wasn't a big deal and wouldn't account for her having to drop everything and fly in to Las Vegas three days earlier than planned. There had to be more "new developments" they had yet to discuss. She tilted her head to the side and gazed over at him. He had unwrapped one of those Tootsie Pops and placed it in his mouth.

The muscles between her legs clenched at the way Jonas was sucking on the lollipop. You could tell he was getting sheer enjoyment out of doing so. And there was something about how the pop was easing in and out of his mouth, being worked by his tongue, leaving a sweet glaze all over his lips.

He caught her staring and held her gaze. "Would you like one?"

She swallowed. "No, thank you. Is there anything else to discuss?"

He shook his head and put the unfinished pop aside. "No, that's about it."

"You seem to like those," she said, motioning to the bag of Tootsie Pops on the table in front of him.

Jonas smiled. "Yes, they have definitely grown on me. They started out as a supportive measure from my brothers when I quit smoking some years back. They figured the pops would replace the cigarette. Basically they have."

He checked his watch. "Dinner should be here soon."

Nikki nodded. If the JumboTrons were the only new development then her coming to Vegas early made no sense, especially when Rick wouldn't be arriving until

Friday. That meant she had two whole days to do practically nothing.

She was about to point that out to Jonas when there was a knock on the door. He stood. "I'll get that. I think that's our dinner."

Jonas took a deep, steadying breath while watching Nikki leave to go to the powder room to wash her hands. He had seen the look in her eyes when she'd asked if there were any other new developments. She was an intelligent woman and was probably wondering why he'd sent for her three days before she was actually needed. Adding those JumboTrons was no big deal. She knew it as well as he did.

"Will there be anything else, sir?"

He glanced over at the waiter who had wheeled in the table set for two. "No, that will be all," he said, signing the invoice.

He was closing the door behind the man when Nikki returned. "Whatever it is smells good," she said.

Not as good as you smell and look, sweetheart, he thought, turning around and scanning her up and down. He really liked that outfit on her, admired the way the material clung to her hips and her rounded bottom and accentuated her curves. And then there were the shoes she was wearing. The sling backs did some serious business to her shapely legs.

He then recalled what she'd said earlier about walking the Strip after their dinner. Not by a long shot. Little did she know he had plans for her after they ate. Um, he could easily switch the timing of those plans to before dinner without much hassle. The food would keep and they would definitely have worked up an appetite for it later.

"I took the liberty of selecting something off the menu. I hope you don't mind. I understand you're a seafood lover and shrimp is your favorite."

"Yes, that's right. How did you know?

A smile touched his lips. "That's my secret."

He decided not to tell her he made it his business to know about any woman in whom he was interested. However, he would admit he had taken more interest in finding out things about her than any other woman before.

Before she could ask him to divulge those secrets, he said, "Now it's my turn to wash my hands. I'll be back in a minute."

Nikki watched Jonas walk away. All the Steele men had a sexy walk—even the old man—but she thought Jonas's was the sexiest. And the way his shoulders moved while the thick wavy hair flowed around his shoulders was eye-catching. She had never thought she would be attracted to a man who had more hair on his head than she did, but Jonas had proved her wrong.

He had also proved her wrong about something else as well—that she couldn't want him any more than she had before. And that surprised her, especially after that pep talk she'd given herself on the plane and most recently the one she'd had before stepping onto the elevator that had brought her to his penthouse suite. The look on his face when he had opened the door had reminded her of that night at Mavericks, when he had stared at her that same way.

She must be imagining things, especially since

they'd reached an agreement. And they had reached an agreement, hadn't they? He would be keeping his hands to himself. No more kisses, no more intense attractions or talk of an affair, right? Then why did she feel he was stripping her naked with his gaze each and every time he looked at her? And why was she stripping him naked with hers? Her mind was envisioning what he was packing underneath his slacks and shirt. And why did she want to see it for herself just for the hell of it?

She drew in a deep breath, not believing the way her thoughts were going tonight. But then why was she so surprised? Brittany had warned her about the battle— her head versus her heart. Her head wanted Jonas, the man, with all his flaws. Even if it was just to say she'd gotten a taste of the forbidden and was able to enjoy it and move on.

But her heart was singing another song—one of Love and Happiness—and intended to give Al Green a run for his money. Her heart didn't want her to waste her time on a man like Jonas, a man who could take that same heart, if given the chance, and break it. A man who would get what he wanted and then walk away without looking back.

Her heart wanted more. It felt it deserved more, and although there was no sign of a Mr. Right out there for her just yet, her heart didn't want her to give up too soon.

"Ready?"

She blinked upon realizing Jonas had returned. When she felt intense heat stir the lower part of her belly, she tore her gaze away from his, thinking of all the things she could be ready for. Those mesmerizing green eyes had an unnerving effect and were messing with her mind. They were hypnotic, spellbinding and luring her not to think straight.

"So are you going to stand over there, or will you join me over here, Nikki?"

The impact of his question had her staring at him. They were still talking about sharing dinner, weren't they? Then why were emotions she always downplayed around him suddenly forcing their way to the forefront? Confusing her mind? Suffusing her with heated warmth at the juncture of her thighs?

Nikki slowly crossed the room to where he stood beside the table. She had thought he would pull out the chair for her, and when he just stood there and stared at her, she felt her heart almost racing out of control. He moved and stepped closer, not just to crowd her space but to get all into it and take command. Hot shivers flowed through her.

And why was he wearing the scent of a man, a sensual aroma that was inebriating her senses? Her heart was being pushed to the background, where only her head was speaking, and what it was saying wasn't good. Definitely not smart.

Get real, girl! You claim you want to make the transition from a woman who believes in fantasies to a woman who realizes the real fantasies are the ones you make for yourself. There are no knights in shining armor, just rogues in aluminum foil. At least you know where this one stands and there won't be any expectations on your part. Cross over to the desire side by doing a smash and grab. Smash what has proved to be idealistic baloney once and for all, and grab what could be an experience of a lifetime.

She swallowed, hearing all the things her head was saying, but still, when he took a step even closer, her heart fought back and she couldn't stop the words. "If I remember correctly, things were going to be strictly business between us, Jonas."

A smile curved his lips. "Um, that's not how I remember things."

She narrowed her gaze. "And just what do you remember?" His scent was driving her crazy, breaking down her defenses even more.

He inched closer, and she felt him, his aroused body part pressed against her middle. Instead of recoiling from it, she felt fire rush through her veins and race up her spine. That same head that was trying to fill her mind with naughty thoughts began spinning. It was kicking out her common sense and replacing it with a whole lot of nonsense. Making her wonder such things as how it would feel to slide her fingertips along that aroused member, cup him in her hand, taste him in her mouth and—

"I distinctly recall a promise to give you what you wanted," he said, interrupting her thoughts and lowering his head down to breathe the words across her lips. "And I intend to push you over the edge, Nikki Cartwright, and make sure you want me."

And when he captured his mouth with hers, she knew she didn't stand a chance because she was a goner the minute he slid his tongue inside her mouth.

Chapter 8

Jonas had developed a taste for Nikki from their first kiss. That had to be the reason he was taking her mouth with an urgency that was stirring all kinds of emotions within him. It didn't matter that her mouth felt like pure satin beneath his or that her lips were a perfect fit. The only thing that mattered was the way they were connecting so intimately to his as he sank deeper and deeper into the warmth of her mouth.

Tangling with a woman's tongue had never driven him to the point where lust ruled his senses. The fire that had built up inside of him was blazing out of control, and that was the one thing he never lost with a woman. Control. And he knew at that moment there was no way he could regain it.

There was nothing he could do to stop the flow of adrenaline that was rushing through his body, drowning his pores and playing hell with his molecules. And his erection was throbbing fiercely, sending a sensual warning that if he didn't pull back now, there would be no pulling back later.

If he didn't ease his shaft inside of her, penetrate her deep while she moaned, thrust in and out and make her cream all over him, he would lose his mind. He wanted to make love to her so badly he could hardly stand it, and the thought of doing so sent shivers through him.

What he felt wasn't just desire, it was hard-core desire. And he refused to waste his time trying to figure out why. He'd done so for eighteen months and still didn't have a clue.

He continued to kiss her as if her tongue had been created just for him to enjoy. And he could tell she was enjoying it too from the way her fingertips were digging into his shoulders. Her moans sounded so starkly sexual they were tapping into his emotions, both physical and mental, and he knew of no way to stop them.

The need to breathe made him break off the kiss, and he stared up at her while every muscle in his body tightened in yearning. "I suggest that you tell me to stop now, Nikki, because if you don't, I plan to mate with you all over this place."

He paused a moment and then decided to add, "And just so you'll know, when I finish with you, the last thing you'll have energy for is a walk down Vegas Boulevard."

He'd been so brutally honest, but he felt that she deserved to know what she was up against. He had a fierce sexual appetite, and with her it would take a long time to be appeased. There was something about her that was tempting everything male inside of him. And there could only be one possible outcome.

Jonas watched the rise and fall of her breasts as she tried getting her breathing under control. He saw by the V-neckline of her shirt that she was wearing a pink bra. He couldn't help wondering if her panties were pink as well. That curiosity had him shifting his gaze back to her eyes and what he saw in them almost made it difficult to breathe.

Although she might never admit it to him or to herself, she wanted him as much as he wanted her. There was no if, and, or but about it. The eyes looking back at him were full of fire. As much fire as he felt thrumming through his loins right now. And at that moment, he planned on making good on what he'd told her. He intended to push her over the edge. Right onto her back with him on top.

He leaned in and slanted his mouth over hers again. His hands moved from her waist, slid down to cup her bottom and squeezed it gently before bringing it closer to the fit of him. Without releasing his hold on her mouth, he shifted to bring his hard erection closer to the juncture of her thighs, eliciting an automated sigh from deep within her throat. He liked the sound.

And he especially liked how she arched her back, bringing the firm tips of her breasts into his chest like heated darts, and sending shock waves of pleasure riveting through him. He felt hot inside and was burning in places that had never burned before. He moved closer, needing her curvaceous body even closer to his.

This time she was the one who pulled back from the kiss. But before she could draw in a quick breath he was unbuttoning her shirt as swiftly as his fingers could move to do so, trying like hell not to rip any in his haste. She hadn't told him to stop so he planned to make good on his threat. There was no way he could walk away from this, from her, even with all those red warning signs flashing him all in the face.

Without wasting time he went to the front clasp of her sexy, pink lace bra and unhooked it, freeing the most luscious-looking breasts he'd ever seen and soliciting a growl that erupted from deep in his throat.

His hands went still as he lifted his gaze from her breasts to her eyes. It seemed as if time stood still as their gazes connected, held, fused in a way that just wasn't rational. But at that moment, he couldn't break eye contact even if he wanted to.

Silence surrounded them and the air seemed electrified, charged, pricked with an element so sensual, the components were unknown to mankind. There was this unexplained and undefined chemistry between them. They'd gotten primed, ready, saturated in lust, and there was no turning back. No letting mere kisses suffice any longer. No more denying what they both truly wanted, although they should be fighting it. That was no longer an option. They wanted the real deal and wouldn't waste any more time getting it.

Nikki hadn't expected this, an odd surge of passion that splintered everything within her—every logical thought, every ounce of common sense. Instead she was feeling a burst of freedom that she'd never felt before and it was rejuvenating her all through her bones. She wanted this. She wanted him. She no longer cared that her head was winning the battle and her heart was losing this round. The main thing was that there was another war going on inside of her and it had nothing to do with logic, and everything to do with need.

And what she needed at that moment was to make love with Jonas. No matter how many regrets she might have in the morning, she needed him to touch her, make love to her all over the place just like he'd threatened to do. So she stood there and watched him. Waited with bated breath.

Now she understood the reputation he had attained. In the confines of the sauna rooms, ladies' clubs and sorority meetings, the feminine whispers discreetly echoed around town that when it came to lovemaking, bad-boy Jonas Steele had a finesse that could be patented. She'd never doubted it then, and she was seeing it in action firsthand now.

He slowly lowered his gaze to travel down her body, and she felt the heat of his green orbs on her breasts. Her hardened nipples seemed to tighten even more before his eyes. She felt it and knew he had to be seeing it.

"I need to suck on them, Nikki. I need to let my tongue wrap around them. I need to lick them."

His words broke the silence and suddenly the air oozed with need. A need that was unbearable and fueled by a lusty craving. Her gaze followed the masculine hands that reached up to push both her shirt and bra from her shoulders, bearing the upper part of her breasts to him. From the look in his eyes, he more than liked what he saw.

Before he could make a move she decided to play the Jonas Steele game by reaching out and all but snatching the shirt off his body, ripping buttons in the process and ignoring the fact that replacing the shirt would cost a pretty penny. At the moment she didn't care.

Nikki saw the tattoo on his stomach, a huge, raging bull. It was appropriate since he had the stamina of one. She was tempted to lick his stomach to soothe as well as tame such a fierce-looking animal. Then she would move lower and let her tongue wrap around him like he planned to do her.

Do her.

The thought of him doing her made the juncture of her thighs cream. And she felt the thickening moisture drench her panties. She tightened her legs together as sensations flared in her womanly core.

If he was surprised by the way she'd torn the shirt from his body he didn't show it. It seemed he was just as pushed over the edge as she was. And like her, he had inwardly conceded there was no turning back. No more discussions. From here on out there would only be action.

Her head had taken over big-time, filling her mind with thoughts of doing him, and acting out the part of the vixen she'd bragged to Brittany she was but had never truly been. She suddenly wanted to see if she could handle the role.

"You've done it now, sweetheart."

His words, laced with hot caution, spoken in that deep baritone of his, didn't scare her any. If anything they sent shivers of anticipation racing through her body at the same time they kicked her courage and confidence levels up a notch.

Before Nikki could dwell on anything else, Jonas reached out and pulled her to him in a way that had them tumbling to the carpeted floor, though he made sure his body cushioned her fall. Trying to regain the breath that had been snatched right from her lungs, she glanced down at him at the same moment she realized she was sprawled on top of him, her limbs entwined with his. She was shirtless and her skirt was hiked high enough she could feel air hitting her almost bare bottom. She felt her womanly core react to the hard erection pressing against it.

"Kiss me," he rasped before pulling her mouth down to his and immediately sliding his tongue between her lips. Sexual energy between them was surging out of control and she felt it in the sensual mating of their mouths.

Her senses were overwhelmed with the scent and feel of him at almost every angle. Their bodies writhed against each other, as if they couldn't get close enough, and his hands lifted her skirt even higher to palm her backside. His fingers traced a sensuous path along the crevice as if to verify she was actually wearing a thong. And then he released her mouth to latch on to a nipple, sucking it between his lips the way she'd seen him do that Tootsie Pop earlier.

Nikki moaned deep in her throat and felt her inner muscles contract with the sucking motion of his mouth on her breasts. He wasn't just trying to taste her, he was consuming her and propelling her body into quivers that rammed all through her. She had made love before, but never like this and never with this intensity or greed. And what frightened her even more was knowing there was pleasure still yet to be fulfilled. Areas yet to be discovered.

She moaned again when his mouth moved to her other breast, sucked another nipple between his teeth as if his very life depended on it. And now his hands were no longer torturing her bottom but had traveled to the front, eased between their connected bodies, slid underneath the waistband of her thong to begin toying in her now drenched feminine folds, stirring up the air with her scent.

He suddenly released her breast and gave her only a second to see the smile that curved his lips before he flipped her on her back so she was staring up at him. Before she could blink he had removed the shoes from her feet, and proceeded to jerk her thong and skirt down her hips and toss them aside, leaving her completely bare. Naked as the day she was born.

She held her breath as his gaze roamed up and down her body from head to toe, and she actually felt the hot path his gaze took and knew what areas it concentrated on before moving on to another. Then he was lifting her legs, hoisting them high up on his shoulders and bringing his face up close and personal to her bikini-cut feminine mound.

He leaned forward and she felt intense heat from his nostrils when he took his nose and pressed it against her, rubbed it up and down in her as if to inhale her scent as deep into his nasal cavity as he could. And then his nose was replaced with the tip of his tongue that jabbed through her folds, straight for her clit.

His mouth latched on to her, and then it was on. Every single rumor she'd heard whispered about him and his deadly steady, lickity-split, seemingly mile-long tongue was true. The man definitely knew how to give pleasure while he enjoyed the ultimate feast. Somehow he seemed to close his mouth in a way that made his jaws lock on her as his tongue greedily devoured her like it was a treat he'd developed a sweet tooth for, a craving he couldn't get enough of.

Never had she been sensually mauled this way before. Never had any man used his tongue to pleasure her to this degree. His tongue went deep, stroked hard, and she couldn't stop the moans as tension built within her, making her already electrified senses reel.

"Jonas!"

She screamed his name when her body fragmented into tiny pieces with the most intense climax she'd ever experienced. Instead of letting her go, he slid his hands beneath her, lifting her hips, pressing her more firmly to his mouth while his greedy tongue possessed her mega-stimulated mound. The sensations surging through her were over the top, off the charts, mind-boggling and earth-shatteringly explosive.

And before her heart rate could slow down, he quickly shifted positions and pulled her up in front of him, on her knees with her back to him. She heard the sound of him tearing off the rest of his clothes and ripping into a condom packet with his teeth.

Before she could recover from the orgasm that still had her mind reeling, her teeth chattering, he grabbed hold of her hips, spread her thighs and proceeded to slide his hard shaft into her from behind.

She continued to shudder as he began riding her, locking his hips to hers with every hard thrust. The sound of flesh beating against flesh as his skin slapped hard against her, his testicles hitting her butt cheeks, made her senses start reeling all over again. He glided his hands under them and cupped her breasts as he rode her. Each stroke into her body was long, sure and done with a purpose and not a wasted effort.

And when she threw her head back and tilted her hips at an angle to give deeper penetration, Nikki heard Jonas's deep groan before he frantically bucked against her body while using his hands to keep the lower part of her locked tight against him.

"Nikki!"

At that moment she didn't want to think of how many other names he'd screamed or that she would be added to the list. Another notch on his infamous bedpost. What mattered most at that moment was that they were in sync, connected with his engorged sex planted deep within her womanly core while her inner muscles clenched, relaxed and then clenched mercilessly again, draining him like he was draining her. He was once again showing her just how hot and explosive lovemaking could be, and she felt deep satisfaction all through her bones.

She came again as fire consumed her, raged out of control and compelled her to cry out his name once more as she enjoyed every last moment of the experience. And before she could fully recover, she felt him pulling her up off the floor and gathering her into his arms.

"Now I'll feed you and then we'll do this all over again in my bed."

And she knew at that moment he would make good on his warning that before he was finished with her they would do it all over his suite.

Chapter 9

The ringing of the hotel room's phone stirred Jonas from a deep and peaceful sleep. He slowly opened his eyes and squinted against the bright sunlight shining in through the window. It took a split second to recall where he was and why his body felt so achy. He couldn't stop the smile that touched his lips when the memories of the night before came flooding through his hazed mind.

He glanced at the spot beside him and saw it was empty. Except for the ringing of the phone there wasn't another sound. He didn't need to be told he was alone and his bedmate of the night before had vanished. Pulling up in bed, he reached out to answer the phone. "Yes?"

"Hell, I was about to hang up. What took you so

long to answer? I tried calling your cell phone all night. Where the hell were you?"

Jonas rubbed his hand down his face, frowning at all the questions Gannon was firing at him. "The reason it took me so long to answer the phone was because I was asleep," he growled.

"And the reason you couldn't get me last night was because I was busy." That was all his brother needed to know. There was no way he would admit that he'd been trying to screw Nikki's brains out. Which made him wonder how she had gotten out of the hotel room. After the intensity of their lovemaking, he was surprised she could still walk.

"Well, since you're up you can join me for breakfast. I can't wait to tell you about all that went on at the Doll House."

Jonas rolled his eyes. Gannon might be bursting at the seams, but personally, he could wait. Besides, he was very familiar with the gentlemen's club so nothing Gannon told him would come as a surprise. "I'm not up yet, Gan, so do breakfast without me. I need at least another three hours of sleep."

"Uh-oh. That means you scored last night. I have a feeling you didn't sleep in your bed alone and probably aren't alone now."

Jonas had no intention of appeasing Gannon's curiosity about his sexual activities, especially when they involved Nikki. "Goodbye, Gannon. I should be well-rested by lunchtime."

"I'm visiting that brothel today."

Jonas shook his head. "Make sure you have plenty of condoms."

"Dammit, Jonas, I'm not a kid. I know how to handle

my business, thank you very much. Just make sure you're handling yours."

Jonas blinked when the sound of Gannon's phone clicked loudly in his ear. He drew in a deep breath. Okay, the kid was thirty now, but old habits were hard to break. The five of them were so used to looking out for their baby brother they sometimes forgot he was now a man. And Jonas had to constantly remind himself that he was only two years older than Gannon. Two years but with a hell of a lot more experience.

He glanced around the room. One thing was for certain: Gannon was right, he needed to take care of his own business. And the first thing that topped the list was Nikki. The first order of business was to find out why he'd awakened alone in bed this morning. He was usually the one to decide at what point a woman left his bed and couldn't recall when it was ever the other way around.

But then he couldn't ever recall having sex with any woman with the intensity of last night's session. Nikki had drained him dry. He hadn't stood a chance against the contractions of her inner muscles. He had come more times than he could remember and had been putty in her hands. But then, she'd also been putty in his. He couldn't recall the last time he'd enjoyed getting between a pair of spread legs so much. And they hadn't been just any woman's legs. They had been Nikki's.

And then there had been his obsession with tasting her. He had gone down on her more times in a single night than he'd done all year. It seemed that once he'd tasted her, he hadn't been able to get enough. It was as if her clit had been created just for his mouth. At least his tongue had evidently thought so. Even now he was convinced the taste of her had lingered, and a part of him was glad that he could taste her again. He licked his lips and found her there. His curly-headed, jeans-wearing, tasty-as-hell fantasy girl.

He closed his eyes, not wanting to think of any female as being his fantasy girl. He hoped like hell that last night had effectively cleansed his desire for her from his system and that he wouldn't get hard each and every time he thought about her.

He frowned. If she was out of his system then why were shivers racing through him at the thought of seeing her and making love to her again? And why couldn't the memories go away? The memories of him on top of her. Her on top of him. Their bodies mating, moving together in an urgency that took his breath away just thinking about it. The feel of being inside of her, and how her inner muscles would clench him tight, while he took her with a hunger that bordered on desperation and greed.

He shook his head, trying to free himself of the memories and saw that he couldn't. The vision of her naked body, the intense look on her face when she came and the sound of her letting loose in pleasure were things he couldn't forget, so there was no use trying.

But he knew he eventually would forget when he moved on to another woman. He frowned at the thought that he didn't want another woman right now. He liked her well enough and there was no reason to move on. Surely one more night with her wouldn't hurt anything. A powerful force of pleasure rushed through him at the thought.

He would grab a few more hours of sleep and then he would get up, get dressed and get laid.

* * *

As the sunlight slashed its way through the curtains, Nikki lay in bed and stared up at the ceiling. Each time she moved she felt aches from muscles she hadn't used in years. But thanks to Jonas, she had certainly used them last night.

Granted she'd only made love but twice in her entire life—once in college and the other when she'd thought she'd met the man of her dreams four years ago, only to find out he'd shown interest just to make his old girlfriend jealous. She'd thought both times were okay, decent at best. However, what she'd shared with Jonas last night went beyond decent. In fact, there was nothing decent about any of it. They'd gotten downright corrupt. Never in her wildest dream had she expected to share something that naughty with any man. Did couples actually go that many rounds, try out all those positions even on a good night? She'd never experienced anything so amazing, so hot and erotic. And so spine-tingling sensational. Her dreams and fantasies hadn't come close to the real thing.

She remembered how she had checked out his body, studied all his tattoos. She had liked the fierce-looking bull on his stomach, but her favorite had been the Libra sign on his side.

She pulled in a deep breath thinking he had certainly given her fair warning. Nothing could have been closer to the truth. She wondered if other men had that much energy and enjoyed sex that much. And she knew that's what it had been, nothing but sex. He hadn't made love to her. She had made up her mind to stop equating sex with love.

So where did that leave her?

She knew the answer to that one. It left her right where she had lied about being for the past two years. She could remember the day she had looked herself in a mirror and decided to give up on marriage and babies and instead join the ranks of the single ladies. There was no man out there to put a ring on it so she'd decided to live her life, have fun and not have any regrets.

She closed her eyes to fight off the regrets. She really shouldn't have any. Any other woman would be smiling this morning from ear to ear. But then, any other woman probably would not have sneaked out of Jonas Steele's bed and fled to her own hotel room, where she'd slid into bed and eased her overly sore body beneath the covers.

Now it was morning and she was awake, her body still sore, and her heart fighting a losing battle against the memories stored in her head. And they were memories that made her blush just thinking about them.

After having sex that first time—on the floor of all places—Jonas had planted her naked body into the chair to eat dinner. And then he proceeded to sit across from her—naked as well—while they ate. He had carried on a conversation with her as if it was the most natural thing to share dinner with a woman in the nude.

Probably a natural thing for him, but it had definitely been odd for her. At least it had been at first. That was before dessert time when he had crawled under the table to where she sat, told her to spread her legs and then used his tongue on her like she was an ice cream cone, slowly licking her before plunging in deep with long, penetrating kisses. She had lifted the tablecloth to look down, observing the way his mouth was paying very special attention to that part of her, watching how he would flick his tongue left to right, right to left and then to the center before gently scraping against her clit with his teeth. Moments later, she couldn't help but lean back in her chair and stretch out her legs to spread them farther apart while he made her moan and groan. Never had she experienced anything so scandalous.

Nikki closed her eyes and drew in his scent, which wasn't hard to do since he'd left an imprint on every inch of her. She couldn't stay in bed all day. Besides, she knew from her workout classes at the gym that the best way to ease soreness out your body was to get a move on.

She glanced out the window. It was daytime now, but last night she had seen the brightly lit Strip from Jonas's hotel room. She had stood at his window. Well… actually, she had been leaning toward his window while he'd gotten her from behind.

Knowing if she continued to lie there she would eventually drown in all those tantalizing memories, she moaned at her sore body as she eased out of bed.

She would take a shower, get dressed and do what she had planned to do last night but had not gotten around to doing. She would walk the Strip.

"Just who do you keep trying to call, Jonas?"

"None of your business." Jonas frowned, putting his cell phone back in his pocket as he glanced across the table at his brother.

They were sitting downstairs in one of the hotel's restaurants waiting on the waitress to bring their food. He had slept five hours instead of the three, and would have slept longer if Gannon hadn't called, waking him up again.

Gannon smiled. "Yeah, right. You found another woman and you're trying to make a hit, aren't you?"

Jonas stared at his brother as he took a sip of his lemonade. Gannon would probably fall out of his chair if Jonas admitted he was trying to make a hit on the same woman from last night. He seldom did repeats and most people knew it. It wasn't in his makeup to spend time doing just one woman. Not when there were so many of them out there to do.

Instead of answering Gannon, he asked, "You've spent most of the time talking about the naughty happenings over at the Doll House. I noticed you didn't have much to say about your visit to the brothel."

"I haven't gone there yet. I got sidetracked with Nikki."

Jonas swung his head around so fast it was a wonder his neck hadn't snapped. He stared over at Gannon. "Nikki?" He was grateful Gannon had pulled out his iPhone to check messages, otherwise there was no way he would have missed what Jonas knew had to be an intense look on his face.

"Yes, Nikki," Gannon said, studying his phone. "You know, Brittany's best friend. Your photographer who flew in a couple days early because you needed her to start work." Gannon glanced up. "Well, I hate to tell you but she wasn't working today."

Jonas arched his brow, forcing his features to an expressionless state when he asked, "What was she doing?"

"Shopping. Walking the Strip. Having lunch. Shopping some more."

Jonas tilted his head to the side and stared at his brother. "And how do you know this?"

Gannon shrugged as he placed his phone back in his pocket. "I ran into her on the Strip and we spent some time together. I helped her carry her bags and later we had lunch together at The Glades."

Jonas frowned so hard he was certain anger lines appeared in his face. "You had lunch with Nikki?"

"Yes, and if you're getting mad because I woke you up to have lunch again, it was because I was still hungry. You aren't the only one who might have worked up an appetite last night. I met this woman at the Doll House and she was something else."

Jonas glared. Little did Gannon know that his anger had nothing to do with the fact that Gannon was making a pig out of himself by eating two lunches. His anger solely rested on the fact that he'd been trying to reach Nikki and hadn't been able to do so. Was she deliberately avoiding his calls?

"Did Nikki say what she would be doing after lunch?"

Gannon rolled his eyes. "Jesus, Jonas, give the woman a break. Do you really expect her to be on the time clock 24/7? When we parted she was on her way to do more shopping."

He simply stared at his brother knowing Gannon didn't have a clue as to his real interest in Nikki and that was a good thing. He picked up his water, took a sip and tried to ask as inconspicuously as possible, "So, how was she?"

"Who?"

Jonas let out a frustrated breath. "Nikki."

"Oh." Gannon then gave him a rakish smile. "She looked good as usual. Those tight jeans hug that rounded backside of hers like nobody's business."

Jonas frowned, not liking the fact that Gannon had been ogling Nikki's backside.

"Oops. I better not let Mercury hear me say that.'"

Jonas lifted a brow. "Say what?"

"Anything about Nikki's body." Gannon chuckled. "He told me at Eli's wedding that she was off-limits, so I can only assume our brother has the hots for her. He's probably already scored."

At that moment the waitress returned with their food and Jonas wondered if Gannon noticed the steam coming from his ears.

Jonas felt his jaw tighten as he stepped off the elevator onto the thirtieth floor. He hadn't been able to end lunch with Gannon quickly enough. The good thing was that Gannon had been in too much of a hurry to get over to that brothel to notice Jonas's bad mood. Or too busy helping himself to the steak Jonas had ordered but had been too pissed to eat.

He had tried calling Mercury, but according to his brother's secretary, he was in a meeting. But Jonas wanted answers and if he couldn't get them from Mercury, he would get them from Nikki. If she thought she was playing him and his brother against each other she was sorely mistaken. If she was involved with Mercury then why in the hell had she slept with him last night? The one thing the Steele brothers didn't do was share women.

He knocked on her hotel room door. Hard. Inwardly he told himself to calm down, but he was too angry to do so. If he had known something was going on between her and Mercury he would not have touched her. Dammit. Now he couldn't help but wonder when had she'd become involved with his brother. Had it been before or after their kiss eighteen months ago?

The door opened and he saw the surprised look on her face. "Jonas? Is anything wrong?"

He leaned in the doorway, drew in a deep breath and stared at her without saying anything for a moment. Then he silently asked himself why he was there. He had never run behind a woman, gotten upset when he couldn't reach one after a night of sex. It'd always been out of sight and out of mind for him. He'd found it so easy to move on to the next woman.

So why had he gotten so pissed at the thought he hadn't been able to reach her today? And why was the thought of Mercury having dibs on her eating away at his gut? He shouldn't even be here without first talking to Mercury to find out what was going on. But he couldn't wait. He had to see her. He had to know the truth.

"Jonas?"

"What?"

"I asked if anything is wrong."

The urge to reach out and pull her into his arms and kiss her was overpowering. He straightened and tightened his hands into fists at his side. He needed to know if she was involved with his brother. "Yes, something is wrong."

Instead of asking him what, she took a step back to let him into her hotel room.

Chapter 10

Nikki stared across the room at Jonas. He'd said something was wrong, which meant there could be only one logical reason for him to seek her out. Swallowing deeply, she asked, "Did Fulton not like the idea about using the JumboTrons?"

He stared at her for a second, and then instead of answering he rubbed his hand down his face. He then stared at her again and it appeared his green eyes had darkened in anger. "Well, is that it, Jonas?"

He shook his head. "Do you think I'm here to talk about JumboTrons, or that I'm here to discuss business period?"

She really didn't know how to respond to his question, or what answer he was looking for. So she asked a question of her own. "What other reason would you be here?"

He stared at her for a moment. "I slept with you last night," he all but growled.

She wondered what that had to do with anything. He was a Steele. He slept with women all the time. "And?"

"And you were gone this morning and I haven't been able to reach you all day."

She lifted a brow. He had tried reaching her? Why? "My phone battery was dead. I had it on the charger all day. So what's wrong? Why were you trying to reach me?"

He stared at her for a moment and then shrugged. "Doesn't matter now. I need to ask you something."

"Okay. What?"

"Why didn't you tell me that something is going on between you and my brother?"

She stared at him, wondering where he'd gotten an idea so ridiculous. She then recalled she had run into one of his brothers while walking the Strip and he'd offered to help her with the bags she'd collected from shopping. Afterward they'd had lunch together. Had someone seen them together and jumped to the wrong conclusions?

"Gannon was merely kind enough to help me carry a few packages," she said. "Then we—"

"I'm not talking about Gannon," he said in a low voice that was as hard as nails.

Now she knew he really had lost it. "Then what brother are you talking about?" she asked.

"Don't you know?"

"If I knew I wouldn't be asking," she responded smartly.

He paused a moment, narrowed his gaze and then said, "Mercury."

She expressed disbelief in her features. "Mercury! I barely know him."

"Are you saying the two of you are not involved?"

She placed her hands on her hips and glared at him. "That's exactly what I'm saying. Where did you get such a crazy idea?"

"He told someone you were off-limits."

"Then whoever he told that to must have misunderstood." She sighed, shaking her head. "You actually thought I'm banging your brother and still slept with you last night?"

"I honestly didn't know what to think."

Her frown deepened and she lifted her chin. "In that case, it's nice to know the kind of woman you think I am. Please leave."

Jonas stared across the room at Nikki suddenly feeling lower than low. It didn't take much to see she was pretty damn mad. And he could also tell his accusation had come as a blow. He could see the hurt in her face although she was trying like hell to hide it.

He drew in a deep breath when he thought of what he'd all but accused her of. He had listened to Gannon, who'd evidently heard Mercury wrong like she'd said. And instead of waiting to talk to Mercury about it first, he had stormed up here to Nikki's hotel room and confronted her about something that was undoubtedly not true. He couldn't blame Gannon for relaying false info. He could only blame himself for acting on it the way he had.

"I'm sorry," he said, knowing she had no idea the degree of his remorse. He had been quick to think the worst, mainly to disprove this theory that there was something about her that was different from other women he'd messed around with.

"Is there a reason you're still standing there?"

He met her gaze. Held it for a long while before saying, "I'm here because I can't think of being anywhere else."

She stiffened her spine and lifted her chin. "Then think harder while my door hits you in the back."

Boy, she was cruel, but no crueler than he'd been to her with his accusations. "You won't accept my apology?"

"Right now I don't want anything from you. Not even an apology." She paused for a second, drew in what he knew was an angry breath and then asked, "Do you know what your problem is, Jonas?"

Not waiting for him to answer, she said, "You want to judge every woman on the basis of your own sleazy behavior."

He couldn't say anything to that because maybe he probably did. And he wasn't even offended that she thought his behavior was sleazy. It had been described as worse on more than one occasion. Knowing there was nothing he could say or do to redeem himself at the moment, he crossed the room, and before reaching the door, he turned and looked back at her. The intensity of her glare had burned a hole in his back, he could feel it. But he would make it up to her.

Without saying anything else, he opened the door and walked out of it.

Jonas had made it to his room when his cell phone went off and he saw it was Mercury. He answered it in a frustrating voice. "Mercury."

"Hey, Jonas, Nancy said you called. Don't you have

enough to do in Vegas without trying to keep up with me? I hear Gannon visited the Doll House yesterday and that you missed all the fun."

Jonas frowned, not wanting to talk about anything with his brother but Nikki. "Look, Mercury, I want to know about Nikki."

"Nikki?"

"Yes, Nikki Cartwright. Did you or did you not warn Gannon she's off-limits?"

There was a brief pause, and then Mercury said, "Yes, I warned him off."

Jonas's stomach twisted, and it was like the breath had been sucked from his lungs. According to Nikki she and Mercury weren't involved. So did that mean Mercury was interested in her but she just didn't know it? "So you're interested in her?"

Mercury chuckled. "No."

"Then why in the hell would you tell Gannon she is off-limits?"

"Because she is. But I'm not the one who wants her."

Jonas's jaw hardened. "Then who the hell wants her?"

"You do."

"What?"

He could hear Mercury laughing. "Oh yeah, *you* do. I noticed it first at Galen and Brittany's wedding. You couldn't keep your eyes off her when you thought no one else was looking. And then at Eli's wedding when she was taking all those pictures, you were taking her in, angle by angle, every time that cute little body of hers moved around the room. You were all but salivating."

Jonas frowned. "I hate to burst that overimaginative mind of yours, but you're wrong."

"Umm, I don't think so, and now after this phone conversation, I know so. So the way I see it, telling Gannon and Tyson that Nikki was off-limits was actually doing you a favor. You can thank me for it later."

He heard the click as Mercury ended the call.

Nikki stood at the window looking out at the Strip, drawing in deep breaths and then expelling them slowly, tasting the anger still lodged deep in her throat. A part of her still couldn't believe it. The man who had passionate sex with her last night had stood in the middle of her hotel room less than ten minutes ago, all but accusing her of sleeping with one of his brothers? Just because he'd heard Mercury had said she was off-limits? Of all the nerve. If her career wasn't on the line she would pack up and return to Phoenix in a heartbeat.

But then again, when it came to Jonas, she never thought with her heart. She couldn't. She always thought with her head and that's where the trouble lay. Her head was trying to tell her he'd been more jealous than pissed, but with Jonas that didn't make any sense. He could have any woman he wanted. He'd certainly gotten her last night and big-time. And why had he seemed upset when he hadn't been able to reach her today? What was that all about?

She shook her head. Jonas, jealous over her? She chuckled, knowing nothing could be further from the truth. So they had shared lusty, heated, make-you-holler sex last night, through most of the night. For her it might have been a night to remember, but she figured for him it was business as usual.

When she recalled how he had stared her down, accusing her of being involved with his brother, she couldn't help but feel a resurgence of anger. But she needed this job, so the best thing for her was to do what she was being paid to do and leave everything else alone. Jonas fell in the category of everything else.

Okay, she would be a notch on his bedpost, but then he would be a notch on hers as well. Her notches may not get carved as often as his, but she could deal with that. What she couldn't deal with was an involvement with Jonas, so the best thing to do would be to keep her distance.

And that's what she intended to do.

Chapter 11

Jonas's gaze sought out Nikki the moment he walked into the launch party. She had her camera in hand, as she moved around the room and worked it like the professional photographer that she was. Even though she was only wearing a pair of silky-looking slacks and a matching blouse he thought she stood out over all of the women dressed in expensive designer gowns.

Although this was a working event for her, she looked just as elegant and refined as anyone else. And those slacks she was wearing showed what a curvy little backside she had, just as much as her jeans always did. Which was probably why several men were ogling her as she moved around the room, shifting, twisting and bending that cute rounded bottom all around, snapping one picture after another.

One man in particular was Curtis Rhinestone, a reporter for CNN. Jonas and he had attended college to-gether in Michigan and had been frat brothers. He could recall that back in the day while at the university, more than once he and Curtis had competed for the same girl. And now he didn't like the way Curtis all but licked his lips while staring at Nikki. It wouldn't take much for Jonas to cross the room and bust those same lips with his fist.

He drew in a deep breath wondering why it bothered the hell out of him to think of Curtis—or any other man for that matter—checking out Nikki. Why even now the temperature in the room seemed to have risen a few degrees since he'd seen her, and why while looking at her fully clothed he vividly recalled her naked. Beneath him…on top of him…

He took another sip of his drink. Why was he so fix-ated on her? Hell, she was just a woman. And he'd slept with more than he could ever count. But he'd always had the ability to move on without any problems. Why was moving away from Nikki causing him so much grief? Why couldn't he get a friggin' handle on those emotions she could so effortlessly stir within him?

"Well, if it isn't Jonas Steele."

Jonas looked up into the face of a woman by the name of Chastity Jenkins. He had met the PR firm owner while on a business trip to L.A. three years ago. He'd found her first name amusing since there was no part of her that came with a lock of any sort. It had been a one-night stand and that was all it was ever meant to be. He had made that clear in the beginning and at the end. So he had been surprised at the call he'd gotten a few months later saying she would be visiting Phoenix and preferred crashing at his place instead of a hotel.

As nice as he could, he'd told her he really didn't give a damn what she preferred, but staying at his place, even for a few days, wasn't going to happen. She hadn't liked his response and after expressing that dislike in a few choice words, she hadn't contacted him since.

"Chastity," he said dryly. "It's been a while."

She smiled up at him. "It wasn't my choice, Jonas."

No, it hadn't been her choice. Her comment let him know she still hadn't gotten over things. At least some-one hadn't. He glanced over at Nikki. She hadn't looked his way since he'd arrived, which meant evidently she had. The realization annoyed the hell out of him.

Chastity began talking, namely about her favorite subject. Herself. He really wasn't listening, only pre-tending he was since for the moment, he didn't have anything else to do.

Click.
Click.

Nikki moved around the room, taking pictures of one celebrity after another. This was her first assignment where so many famous people in the same place. And when it came to smiling for the camera they weren't shy.

She fought to ignore the kicking of her heart, which signaled Jonas was somewhere in the room. They had avoided each other for the past two days and that had been fine with her. They'd had their one-night stand—as brief and meaningless as it could get—and had moved on. The decision had evidently been a mutual one. But they did have to work together, so they couldn't avoid each other forever.

She twisted and bent her body, snapping one picture

after another and as if her camera was responding to the call of the wild…and the reckless: it unerringly zeroed on him. She sucked in a deep breath when he was captured within the scope of her camera's lens. Oh, God, he looked good in his dark suit with his hair flowing around his shoulders.

Her camera continued to snap away, as it moved all over him, from his expensive leather shoes to those fine-as-a-dime muscled thighs beneath his slacks. And it didn't take much for her to recall how those same thighs had held her within their tight grasp while riding her.

Her camera continued snapping, moving upward to Jonas's broad chest and the designer jacket he was wearing, to the handsome features that still haunted her dreams. They were dreams she couldn't restrict from her mind. She knew she was taking more pictures of him than any other person there tonight. It was as if she couldn't help it. And then as if he suspected he was the object of someone's attention, he shifted his gaze from the woman he was talking to and looked straight into the lens of her camera.

She swallowed deeply and her mind suddenly scrambled when she felt the full-fledged intensity of his stare directly on her. She forced herself to stay unruffled because she had no reason to lose her composure. She was merely doing her job. Besides, instead of looking at her, he should be concentrating on the woman he was talking to—the one with the heavily made-up face, over-the-top weave job, way-too-long French-tipped nails and blood red lips. She was talking a mile a minute, and all but demanding his attention. Would she be the one to share his bed tonight? The one who would be scratching his back this time? Getting the ride of her life? And should Nikki even care? Her heart began pounding viciously and she knew she cared although she shouldn't.

"Hey, you've been at it long enough. Shouldn't you be ready to take a break about now?"

She turned toward the deep, masculine voice and couldn't help but force a smile. It was the same guy who'd tried hitting on her earlier. He'd introduced himself as Curtis Rhinestone and said he worked for CNN. It was as if he'd singled her out since she had felt the heat of his gaze on her most of the night. He wasn't bad-looking. In fact most women would probably consider him downright gorgeous. She would too, if he could in some way hold a candle to Jonas. Unfortunately, he couldn't.

She lowered her camera, thinking she'd focused on Jonas too much already. She checked her watch. "You're in luck. Starting now I'm free for the rest of the night."

He smiled. "Good. I think it's time we got to know each other."

Out of the corner of his eye Jonas watched Nikki move around the room with Curtis and felt his anger rising. How dare Rhinestone try to take something that was his?

He drew in a sharp breath. When had he ever thought of any woman as his? No matter how many women he bedded, he'd never claimed one. What made Nikki different? What had there been about having sex with her that still had him breathless? He took a sip of his drink, his last for the night, as he continued to track

Nikki and Curtis while trying not to be too damn obvious.

"Excuse me if I'm boring you."

He shifted his gaze back to Chastity. Why was she still there, taking up his time? A better question to ask was why was he letting her? He knew the reason. He was allowing her to do so because she was so into herself she wouldn't notice that he was into someone else. At least he figured she wouldn't notice. Evidently he'd been wrong.

"You aren't boring me," he said, taking another sip of his drink.

"Then why are we still here? The last time we attended a party together we'd left within minutes."

She didn't have to remind him. They'd split the party in L.A. and he'd taken her up to his hotel room. He was just about to respond, explain that it had been three years ago, tons of women ago...especially one in particular. But then he saw Curtis lead Nikki outside on the patio and knew he had to put a stop to *that* foolishness once and for all.

"It was good seeing you again, Chastity. Now if you will excuse me..." Not waiting to see if she would excuse him or not, he walked off.

"It's a beautiful night, isn't it?"

The cool air hit Nikki in the face as she glanced over at Curtis. He was nice enough and for the time being, had taken her mind off Jonas, which was a good thing. Whether she liked it or not, the sight of Jonas and that woman who kept touching his arm, batting her false lashes up at him while giving him a toothy smile, had irked her. So when Curtis had suggested they step out on the patio, she had been more than raring to go.

She glanced around. They were high up on the fortieth floor, where she could see the brightly lit Vegas Strip with all the flashing neon signs. "So you're going to be a passenger on the *Velocity*?"

She smiled up at him. "Yes, and you will, too. Right?"

"Yes, I'm doing the coverage for CNN and looking forward to the next two weeks."

She took a sip of her wine. "So am I. Although I'll be working a lot of the time, I'll have time to relax and enjoy myself."

He smiled down at her. "And I hope I'll be someone that you'll enjoy your leisure time with."

Nikki wasn't caught off guard by his suggestion. In fact, she had been preparing herself for it. For the past twenty minutes he had been tossing out hints that he would love to spend time with her. The man sure didn't know the meaning of taking things slow.

"Are you sure you want to do that?" she asked.

"I'm more than sure. You're a very sexy woman and any man in his right mind would want to show you a good time."

In the bedroom, of course, Nikki thought. *Been there, done that just three days ago, and the memories are still too potent for me to even consider doing it with another man anytime soon...or ever.*

She was about to open her mouth, to tell him that she wasn't sure that was a good idea, when a masculine voice behind her spoke up.

"I don't know how that will be possible, Rhinestone, when she's with me."

Nikki spun around so fast she almost spilled her drink. She drew in a deep breath and watched as Jonas emerged from the shadows and strolled into the light. The muscle that was ticking in his jaw indicated he was angry, and if looks could kill both she and Curtis would be dead. What was his problem, and why had he made such an outrageous claim just now?

"Steele, I wasn't aware she was with you tonight."

Curtis's words jerked her from her dazed moment. What was Jonas trying to pull? She wasn't with him. He knew good and well that they didn't have that kind of relationship.

She was about to open her mouth to say just that when Jonas came to stand beside her and said in a voice with a hard edge to it, "Well, now you know."

Curtis met her gaze and gave her a chance to refute Jonas's claim. She would have if the vibes she was picking up off Jonas weren't infused with just any excuse to go upside the man's head. Did they know each other? Was something going on between the two men that she wasn't aware of? She decided the best thing to do for now was to put as much distance between the two men as possible before they came to blows. Based on their expressions, a fight wasn't far off. The friction between them appeared that intense.

When she didn't say anything Curtis turned his attention back to Jonas. The looked that passed between them verified what she'd assumed earlier. They did know each other, and there was something going on that she wasn't privy to, but at the moment felt caught in the middle of.

It was Curtis who finally broke the silence. "Then maybe I should back off."

"Yes, I would highly suggest that you do," Jonas said in what sounded like a low growl. "Now if you will excuse us."

And then he grasped her arm beneath the elbow and leaned close and whispered in her ear in that same low growl, "We need to talk."

She narrowed her eyes at him, and when Curtis walked off, leaving them alone on the patio, she snatched her arm back from Jonas and swirled to face him. "We most certainly do. I want to know what that was about."

Jonas stood staring at Nikki, not sure himself just what that was about. Never in his thirty-three years had he stood before a man and claimed a woman was with him. But a few minutes ago, he had done just that.

"Jonas?"

He drew in a deep breath and said the first thing that came to his mind. "I don't like him."

She frowned. "And you not liking him affects me… how? I believe he stated he wanted to show *me* a good time, not you."

His features suddenly hardened again and he leveled his gaze at her. "He's not getting near you, dammit."

She placed her hands on her hips. "Says who?" she snapped.

"Says me," he snapped back, advancing on her.

She didn't have the good mind to back up and his body pressed against hers. She felt crowded and it was at that moment her temper exploded. "And who the hell are you supposed to be? You're someone I slept with one time. And that's your famous motto—'one and done'—isn't it? Or have you forgotten? In case you have, then let me remind you. One and done, Jonas. And that one time doesn't give you any rights and *you* of all men wouldn't want them if it did. So what in God's name is your problem?"

He rubbed his hand down his face, inwardly acknowledging that he honestly didn't know what his problem was. The only thing he knew was that he wanted her again. Here. Right now. "You, Nikki Cartwright, seem to be my problem," he said in a low steely tone, seconds before grabbing her around the waist, lowering his head and sinking his mouth down on hers.

Chapter 12

Nikki saw it coming and had intended to resist. But all it took was for Jonas to take her mouth with a hunger that sent shivers all through her. Without letting up on her mouth, he drew her closer into the fit of his body, into the juncture of his thighs and right smack into the heat of the hard erection pressing against her.

His hands were no longer on her waist but had moved to her backside as his fingers skimmed sensuous designs all over her bottom while pressing her closer still. She released a tiny whimper from deep in her throat when his tongue seemed to plunge deeper.

Needing to touch him with the same degree of fervor, she placed the palms of her hands at the back of his neck and pulled him closer, locking her mouth even more to his. The silky, soft feel of his hair flowing her over hands as their mouths mated sent intense heat flaring through every part of her body.

Jonas had a way of making her feel both feminine and wantonly wicked at the same time, and there was nothing she could do but slide deeper into his embrace as he continued his sensual assault on her mouth. He was also assaulting her senses, battering them until he had her entire body trembling.

Then suddenly, she felt her legs moving, noted in the hazy part of her mind that he was walking her backward as the cool night air ruffled her curls. She wasn't sure just where he was luring her, but knew as long as he continued to plunder her mouth this way, she was game.

She heard the sound of a glass door sliding open and when he pulled her inside, she pulled her mouth away from his to glance around while drawing in several deep breaths. They were in a small room Ideas of Steele had reserved to store their equipment and supplies for the party.

Before she could say anything, reclaim her senses, he leaned forward and began brushing heated kisses around the corners of her lips. At that moment the only thing she wanted to reclaim was how he was making her feel. She didn't want to do anything but feel his warm breath against the contours of her mouth.

"I want you again, Nikki," he whispered softly before tracing the tip of his tongue along a path down the side of her ear. "I want you so damn bad. I'm going to burst out of my zipper if I don't have you."

Her heart began racing at his words, at the thought that he wanted her that much. But there was something she couldn't let go of and that was why they'd been at odds with each other over the past couple of days. He thought the worst of her. He thought she was someone capable of sharing brothers. And that was unacceptable to her.

She pushed back out of his arms. "I think we need to return to the party. Who knows? Mercury might have surprised us both and arrived in town and is there waiting for me."

He didn't say anything for a second, and then he reached out and took her hand in his, gently held it in his larger one. He stared down at her and met her gaze. "I told you I was sorry about that. It was miscommunication that I acted on without thinking. Don't ask me why I did it, but I did. I acted hastily and I regret it. Deep down I know your character is nothing but wholesome, above reproach."

He paused a moment, released her hand to rub the back of his neck and then said, "And what you said that day is probably true. I'm such a jaded ass that I overlook the decency in others at times. Again, I'm sorry."

"I didn't call you a jaded *ass*."

He chuckled. "No, actually you accused me of sleazy behavior and in my book it practically means the same thing." He got quiet and his expression became serious. "So, will you forgive me?"

She studied his features for a moment. "Will it matter to you if I do or don't?"

He stared at her, as if his gaze was touching every inch of her features, and she could barely breathe under the intensity. Then he finally said, "Yes, it will matter. I like you."

Nikki could only shake her head. Did he actually like her or like sleeping with her? They'd only done so once, but he wanted them to do so again. Tonight. And unfortunately, she wanted to make love with him again as well.

There was just something about the feel of being in his arms, having him planted deep inside of her, intimately connected to her, that made her insides quiver just remembering how it was between them. And it was a way she wanted to be with him again. But what about that "one and done" policy he was known for? Taking her again would be breaking one of his rules. She shrugged. He would be breaking it, not her. The thought of being his "exception" was sending spikes of pleasure through her and making her feel wild and reckless.

"I'm waiting for you to say that you accept my apology and that you like me too, Nikki."

She stared up at him and saw he was serious. There were sober lines etched under his eyes, slashed across his face, and she was tempted to smooth them away with her fingers. Instead, feeling bold, she leaned up on tiptoe and used the tip of her tongue to erase the lines.

Moments later she whispered against his lips, "I accept your apology and I do like you."

And then she went back to licking his sober lines away. Unable to stay mobile under her ministrations, he reached up and began running his fingers through the mass of curls on her head. The feel of his hands in her hair sent her pulse escalating.

And then when her tongue got inches from his mouth, licked his lips from corner to corner, he steadied her head to look at him and whispered, "You're welcome to come inside for a visit."

She did, easing her tongue into his mouth and that's when he crushed her to him and took over the kiss.

He could kiss her forever, Jonas thought as he plundered Nikki's mouth. This was heaven. At least it felt like it anyway. Like he'd told her, he wanted her and he wanted her bad. He wanted to suck on her breasts, lick them all over. Lick her all over. Taste her honeyed warmth again, a taste he hadn't been able to get over.

And then he wanted to make love to her, pump inside of her while her inner muscles clamped down on him. Pulled everything out of him. But he wasn't sure they had time to do all that now. If not now, definitely later. At this moment he would gladly get what he could.

All those thoughts made him slowly pull back from their kiss to look down at her. "Rick is handling things so don't worry about us being missing in action."

"You sure?"

He smiled. "Well, Curtis might miss you, but I won't be missed, trust me."

She chuckled against his lips. "You keep it up and I'm going to start thinking that you're jealous."

He knew she was teasing, but little did she know she had hit pretty close to home. He had gotten jealous. It wouldn't have taken much for him to rip Rhinestone in two. Instead of commenting on what she'd said, he reached out and took her hand in his. He leaned in and murmured against her lips. "Come here, I know just where I want to take you."

He'd said that literally and every cell in his body was ready, invigorated, fully charged. He pressed her hand lightly as he led her around a crate of boxes toward the east side of the room where another set of doors led to a private balcony.

They didn't have a whole lot of time, but he planned to relish to the fullest what they had.

Nikki drew in a deep breath the moment the cool air hit her in the face and shivers ran through her body. Jonas was standing directly behind her and she could feel his heat, his hard erection pressing against her backside. He reached his arms around her and held her around the waist.

"Look up at the stars, baby, and pretend it's just me and you out here in the universe," he whispered. "We are going to make the most of it with a very satisfying, mind-blowing quickie."

She glanced up at the sky. It was clear, with a full moon and twinkling stars. In a few days they would be up there in the sky, flying around in *Velocity*. The thought of them making love while up there sent ripples through her. She knew that she and Jonas would give new meaning to the mile-high club.

"I like this," he murmured close to her ear while his hand moved from her waist to cup her backside. "I like how you twist and bend it while stooping down taking pictures."

His touch felt good and anticipation ran through her when he slowly began easing her pants down her legs, followed by her thong. She stepped out of her shoes and glanced over her shoulder when she saw he had taken off his jacket and tossed it on a nearby bench. The sound of a packet being ripped open let her know he was putting on a condom. She heard the moment he unzipped his pants, and then she felt the long, hard heat of him touching the cheeks of that backside he said he liked so much.

"I love making out with you this way. The feel of being connected to you like this."

Nikki didn't think any man could arouse her the way Jonas did. With both his words and his actions. He liked to talk while seducing a woman and she liked hearing what he had to say. His words were blatant, erotic and usually provided an image that would take her breath away.

"Now for your blouse. We need to take it off as well."

She lifted a brow and under the moonlight she saw him smile. "I locked the door, baby, and this is a private balcony. Nobody is out here but you and me and what you see overhead."

"But you said it would be a quickie."

He took a step toward her, reached out and traced a path along the lacy hem of her blouse. "After the other night you should know that my quickies are also thorough."

He began unbuttoning her blouse as he held her gaze. "Besides, I don't care how quick I intend to be. There's no way I can penetrate you without tasting you all over first."

With the last button undone, her blouse fell open to reveal a black lacy bra. And with a flick of his wrist to the front clasp, the bra came undone and her twin breasts poured forth. "You won't need this for a while," he said, peeling the straps from her shoulders and easing them down her arms, before tossing the bra on the bench to join his jacket and the rest of her things he'd picked up and placed there.

She stood before him totally naked and she hoped everything he said was true. First, that with Rick in charge they wouldn't be missed at the party and secondly, that this was a private balcony.

"Do you know just how beautiful you are?"

She met his gaze and the awe in the depth of his green eyes—eyes that roamed up and down and zeroed in on certain body parts—made her breath catch in her throat.

That night they'd spent together he'd told her a number of times he thought she was beautiful. She had taken his words as those men would typically say to the women they sleep with. But there was a look in Jonas's eyes that made her think that perhaps he really thought so and he wasn't just feeding her a line.

Nikki knew she wasn't bad-looking, but she was far from a gorgeous babe. And she definitely wasn't the sleek and sophisticated type of woman Jonas's name was usually associated with. He probably just found the novelty of her amusing. Yes, that had to be it.

That thought didn't bother her. Things were what they were, and just as long as she kept on a straight head and did not put any more stock into this short, meaningless and oh, so brief affair—if she dared to call it that—then she would be okay.

Whatever other thoughts she wanted to dwell on suddenly flew from her mind when his tongue snaked out and licked around the areola before it wrapped around a nipple, slowly drawing it into his mouth. She could feel the aroused nub swell even more in his mouth. She closed her eyes and felt her inner muscles clench, and she tightened her thighs together to stop the ache starting to build there.

"Not so fast, baby," he said, reaching out and sliding his hand up her thighs to her center. "I want to feel how wet I can make you get."

She recalled how he would intentionally get her wet just to taste her. She had found out that oral sex was something he definitely enjoyed, and by the time he'd finished with her, she had enjoyed it as well.

She moaned the minute his fingers slid inside of her, moved around and plunged deeper as if seeking her moist heat. He touched her clit and began stroking it with his fingertips. Without missing a beat with his fingers, he released one breast and went to the other, giving it the same torment and pushing her even deeper into an aroused state.

He placed her back against the rail as he released her and she didn't open her eyes. She didn't have to. She knew he had lowered to his knees in front of her to make good on what he'd said he intended to do. And when she felt the tip of his hot tongue slide inside of her, locking on to the clit his fingers had tortured earlier, she couldn't stop the whimper that escaped her lips.

She wondered how a man's tongue could go so deep inside a woman. How did it know just what spots to hit to make her moan, whimper and groan?

He released her, leaned back on his haunches and held her gaze. "You like that?"

She drew in a deep breath, not once, but twice before she could answer. "Yes, and I see that you do, too."

He nodded slowly while he licked his lips. "Yes, but just with you." And before she could decide whether he was telling the truth or not, he grabbed hold her of thighs once again, leaned forward and plunged his tongue back into her depths.

She screamed when he began making circular motions with his tongue that had her grabbing his head to hold him there. Right there. How could he make the tip of his tongue feel so hot and find all her erotic places? Her G-spot was definitely taking a licking and then some.

And then suddenly, he did something with his tongue when it caught hold of her clit, wiggled in such a way that made her scream. Luckily the sound was muffled by the noise from the party. She clutched his head tighter to her and he clenched her thighs, locking his mouth to her as a way to let her know he didn't plan on going anyplace.

And only when the last orgasmic spasm flowed from her body did he unlock his mouth from her. She was still whimpering uncontrollably when he gathered her up into his arms and carried her over to the chaise longue. She kept her eyes closed, listening to his erratic breathing.

When she heard him removing his clothes, she drew in enough strength to open one eye and saw him moving toward her like she was his prey. Her gaze latched on to his aroused shaft embedded in a thatch of dark hair. It was so thick, so hard and so big the thought that he was about to use it on her sent sensuous shivers racing through her. She wasn't worried about not being able to fit it in, since she'd done it before. But then she had been pretty sore the next day. Um, maybe now was not the time to—

Before she could finish that thought, he reached out and effortlessly lifted her off the lounger. "Wrap your legs around me," he said in a deep, husky voice. As if he'd spoken to her body and her body alone, it complied and her legs wrapped themselves around him, crossing her ankles at his back.

"Mmm, I like your scent," he said, nuzzling her neck before licking it, then moving from the base of her throat up toward her chin.

"And I like yours," she responded, throwing her head back to give him better access to her neck and throat. This had to be the longest quickie on record. But she had no complaints, especially when she was on such a pleasurable receiving end. She would have to do something extra special to him the next time, and for some reason she had a feeling there would be a next time, at least until she was no longer a novelty.

She felt him spreading her thighs and when he eased the head of his manhood inside of her she couldn't help but moan. "Mmm, we fit perfectly," he said when he grabbed a hold of her buttocks and gripped them tight, pressing them closer into the curve of him.

She was convinced the head of his engorged penis had worked its way right smack into her womb. "What's next?" she asked, like there could be any other ending to what they were doing.

He smiled and she thought he looked so doggone handsome, the way his lips tilted at the corners, and the way that mass of wavy hair on his head made him look wild and untamed. "Now, I'll let your body know who I am."

She chuckled as she tightened her legs around him when he began walking. "I think you did that the last time. I could barely walk the next day."

A huge smile touched his lips as if he was pleased to hear that. She was tempted to pop him upside the head. But injuring him in any way was not at the top of

her list. She needed him to finish this. She desperately
needed him to finish this.

"Let's sit a spell," he said, easing down on the padded bench.

Sit? She raised a brow. Hadn't he planned to take
her against a wall or something? Evidently not as he
eased down on the bench, their bodies still connected
and facing each other.

"Mmm, now I can look at you," he said, staring into
her face. "I want to see you come."

"Do you?"

"Hell, yeah. And I want to see what I can do to you
to get you prepared."

No sooner had he finished his sentence, his hands
began rubbing her all over, starting at her thighs and
then lifting her legs to move down her calves.

He unwrapped her legs from around his back and
lifted them high on his shoulders. And their bodies remained connected during the entire process. "How did
you know my legs could get raised so high?"

He shifted a little to spread his legs as she sat straddling his lap. "Umm, I figured as much when I saw
how you moved around snapping pictures. Anyone who
moved the way you did has to have agility down to a
science. And you verified my assumptions the last time
we made love."

She didn't have to ask how she'd done that. It was
during one of those positions he'd sprung on her. She
had almost flexed her body into a bow to make sure he
didn't miss a thing.

Jonas intruded on her thoughts when he began mas-
saging her legs, kneading her knees and stroking her
calves. "You're tense," he said softly. "Relax."

Nikki looked at him. She thought she was relaxed. Maybe he'd gotten her eagerness mixed up with tension. "I'm fine," she said, when she really wasn't.

She was straddling his lap with her legs high on his shoulders while their bodies were connected…and she meant *connected*. If anyone were to see them now they would assume they were glued together, joined at the hips, thighs and definitely the reproductive organs.

"Wiggle a little bit closer."

She didn't think such a thing was possible, considering how close they were already. But she did so, which elevated her legs at a higher angle. "Oh." She felt it. Elevating her legs made her pelvis tilt in a way that stimulated her G-spot. She felt it, all the way to her toes. The sensations had her slanting her bottom for another sensual hit.

"Okay, let's not get carried away, Nikki."

She met his gaze and giggled. "I like you, Jonas."

He threw his head back and laughed. "You would now. But we've wasted enough time. I want to be looking in your face when you scream my name."

And without further ado, he began moving, lifting his hips off the bench as he began thrusting into her, holding her hips in place for every deep, concentrated stroke. She watched him the same way he watched her and saw the intensity in his features as he made love her, increasing the pace with hurried precision, going deeper and deeper, faster and faster with piston speed.

She screamed again when it became too much, the pleasure overtaking her, exploding inside of her and sending her entire body in a tailspin. And he didn't take his eyes off her. She held his gaze and saw when it got to be too much for him as well as he bucked, once, twice and a third time, gripping her thighs tight, hold-ing her body in place as he exploded inside of her.

He ground his hips against hers as a groan was ripped from his throat, but he kept thrusting and she came a second time, calling his name as he continued to rapidly stroke her pulsing flesh. And the erotic waves finally washed over her, cutting her loose from such an intense ride of pleasure. She leaned in and wrapped her arms around him while fighting to regain her breath.

"You are beautiful when you come," he whispered while gently stroking her back.

At that moment she didn't care if he was lying and all he'd seen was an ugly face. On two different oc-casions he had surpassed all her expectations in the bedroom. He'd proved the real thing was a heck of a lot better than fantasy, but mostly that maybe her head knew what it was talking about when it would tell her to enjoy today and put away the foolish ideas of yester-day.

"If we continue to stay connected like this, I'll be tempted to go another round," he whispered in her ear. The heat of his breath sent blood rushing through her veins.

Nikki knew he was telling the truth. The man had the stamina of a bull. Like the one tattooed on his stom-ach. She was a living witness to how many orgasms he could get and give in one night. She shifted and noted he was still hard, probably hadn't gone down. She looked at how her legs were hoisted up high on his shoulders and knew if she was going to get them down she needed his help. After all, he had helped get them up there.

"Will you help get my legs down?"

He smiled and she knew she'd made a big mistake. "Sure you want to go back to the party? Our contribution to tonight's affair is over by now."

He shifted positions a little and she felt just how hard he still was. "We need to go back," she said, not using too much of a convincing tone. But then how could she when he was still buried deep inside of her to the hilt and she was feeling him growing bigger and bigger. Her insides were already weeping in joy.

"No, we don't." And then he leaned forward and took her mouth and the only thing she could think of at that moment was that she hoped the noise from the party continued to drown out her screams.

Chapter 13

"So where were you last night, Jonas? I looked around the party and didn't see you anywhere."

Jonas paused in his packing to glance over at Gannon. "I was there, Gan. The only time I was missing was when I had to step out a few minutes for a bit of fresh air."

There was no need to tell his brother that air wasn't the only thing he'd left the party for. And it hadn't been for a few minutes. He'd been missing in action for a little more than an hour. After convincing Nikki to go one more round for the road, he had helped her redress before sending her back to the party ahead of him. He had remained behind to get his bearings and screw his head back on straight. He'd done neither. What he'd done was to remain on that padded bench, stretched out naked as a jaybird while staring up at the sky and remembering every vivid detail of their supposed "quickie."

He had closed his eyes at the memory of how good it had felt being inside of her, how her features took on a whole other look right before an orgasm hit her. He'd never seen anything so gorgeous in his life. Her gaze had held his, and his senses had almost gone on overload at the pleasure he'd seen radiating from her. All the while her inner muscles had clenched him, demanded from him something he'd never given any woman.

And that's when he'd come, exploding all over the place inside of her. Their union had been so explosive, so damn amazing, just thinking about it now had shivers running all through his body. When had mating with a woman done that to him? He should have been prepared for the strength of their lovemaking from the last time, but when it hit him again—that overpowering force that had practically transported him into another place and time—his mind, body and soul had been taken for one hell of a ride. It'd been one damn sexual transportation that had taken him to a whole new hemisphere, maybe another universe.

When he had returned to the party a while later, he hadn't had to worry about being missed. The place was packed. People were everywhere, wall-to-wall, with more trying to get in. He had looked around, but Nikki was nowhere to be found. He would have left the party in search of her if it hadn't been for Mr. Fulton, who'd wanted to talk his ear off.

By the time he'd been able to get rid of the man—who'd had one drink too many and was more than happy with how things had turned out—it was past three in the morning, and too late to go knocking on

Nikki's door. He figured she had to be as drained as he was. Instead he had gone to his own room, stripped naked for the second time that night and fallen in bed with Nikki's scent still clinging to him. Not surprisingly, he had been awakened by a phone call from Gannon, who'd reminded him he had a flight to L.A. that morning. For once he had appreciated his brother's call. Otherwise, he probably would have missed his flight.

"Jonas?"

He blinked when Gannon snapped his fingers in front of his face. He glared at his brother. "What?"

"Damn, man, where were you just now? I was talking to you and you zoned out like you were in another world and you had this downright stupid look on your face."

Jonas frowned as he zipped up his luggage. "You're imagining things." He checked his watch. "Look, I got to go. Thanks for coming and hanging out with me a few days on the Strip."

Gannon chuckled. "The visits to the Doll House and that brothel were worth the trip. Besides, other than those two days before the party, we really didn't spend time together."

Jonas nodded. And only because those were the two days he had been trying to avoid Nikki. "Yeah, but we had fun."

Gannon would be returning to Phoenix later that day. Jonas would be catching a plane to L.A. in time to board the *Velocity*. That's where he and Nikki would be meeting up again. She had an earlier flight, he knew, since she had a meeting with some Hollywood producer about a possible freelancing gig.

He couldn't wait to see her again. There was no reason to ask why. Didn't matter. The woman was so in his system. And what they'd shared last night out on that balcony beneath the moon and the stars was nothing short of spectacular.

He reached out to grab handfuls of his hair to bind it into a ponytail. He had decided at eighteen, much to his mother's dismay, that he would not let another barber do anything more than give him a slight trim. It hadn't mattered that his brothers had teased him mercilessly by calling him Samson. They still did on occasion.

"Have fun while traveling the globe, Jonas."

His thoughts went to Nikki, and he couldn't help but smile. "I'm going to try. What time does your plane take off?"

"Around two. I'm going back to the Doll House to hang out with Quinton. He's quite a character."

Jonas rolled his eyes. Yeah, that wasn't all Quinton Hinton was. A damn bad influence topped the list. Gannon was a grown-ass man, but still, he couldn't help warning his brother. "Don't get into any trouble, Gan."

He didn't particularly like the smile on his brother's face when he responded, "Trust me, I won't."

Nikki walked into the cabin she'd been assigned, still in a daze. She had read everything Jonas had given her on the *Velocity*, but never in her wildest dream had she seen anything so spectacular, magnificent and brilliant. It was as if she was on board the starship *Enterprise* for a taping of *Star Trek*. Everything she saw was not just state-of-the-art; it had to be part of the future.

Even this cabin, for instance, with an octagonal window that was right over the bed, giving her a sky view anytime she wanted it. There wasn't a lot of space, but it was used efficiently, right down to the bed that conformed to the person's size and weight. She'd heard the mattress was comprised of special fibers blended together that guaranteed a perfect sleep each and every time. Good, because she needed a good rest, she thought, yawning. She was still tired from last night.

She couldn't recall what happened without thinking about Jonas. The man was screwing up her head big-time, and her heart didn't stand a chance of getting any talking points into the mix. Each time her heart tried reminding her that Jonas was not her Mr. Right, her head would counter, *Maybe not, but he's definitely a hot and tantalizing Mr. Wrong.*

Deciding she needed sleep more than anything, she was glad the aircraft wouldn't be taking off for another three hours and that she wasn't due to make an appearance until the dinner meeting in another five.

Most of the other people who were on board—who'd been just as fascinated as she about the airship—were still walking around in awe. She had left the group to escape to her cabin the first chance she got. She knew Jonas was scheduled to be on board in a couple of hours, and she needed to pull herself together before seeing him again.

Although she didn't want to listen to her heart at the moment, she knew things couldn't continue like this. Did she really want to become some man's booty girl, a woman he could go to and get laid whenever he wanted? Granted, there was always something in it for her, but still. Didn't she want more? Besides, booty girls weren't the kind men wanted for wives.

And that's the point, Nikki, her head was saying.

*When are you going to accept that most men don't want
wives? If they did they would be knocking down your
door. You're everything any man would want, but that
never put you at the top of their list, so chill. Have fun.
Stop looking for Mr. Right because he's not out there.
Be smart and take what you can get. You don't need a
degree in psychology to know most men have issues
that you wouldn't want to be bothered with anyway,
so why are you so stuck in that forever-after mind-set?
Live today and let tomorrow take care of itself.*

Nikki drew in a deep breath and placed her hands
to her ears. She didn't want to listen to either her head
or her heart right now. All she really wanted was more
sleep and she was determined to get it.

Jonas glanced at his watch. Where was Nikki?
Granted the dinner meeting didn't start for another ten
minutes, but he wanted to see her now. He'd made it
to the L.A. airport just in time to catch the shuttle that
took him over to the gate were the *Velocity* had been
docked. Already the media were on it and the place
had been jam-packed. It was obvious everyone was in
awe of the huge zeppelin that Fulton intended to be the
first of many. But first, he had to make sure the *Velocity* was well-received, and it seemed from how things
were going so far, it was.

Fulton himself was hosting this dinner meeting, personally welcoming everyone on board. There was no
doubt he would wine and dine the media for positive
news coverage and already Jonas could tell the man had
them eating out of his hands.

Jonas glanced around the room, fought the urge to
check his watch again and frowned when he met Curtis

Rhinestone's gaze. He didn't trust him one bit. He had a feeling that although he'd managed to get Nikki away from the man last night, Rhinestone would still try and sniff behind her today, and if the bastard thought for one minute that Jonas would let him, then he had another think coming.

Getting agitated just thinking about it, he decided to move around the room, stretch his legs and appreciate the view. Unlike the others, this wasn't his first time aboard the airship, although this would be the first time he'd been in flight and so far it was smooth flying. He hadn't felt any turbulence, which was one of the *Velocity*'s strong points he would market. Because of the airship's structure it could easily hold its own, even in the most unruly of winds.

The last time he'd been on the *Velocity* had simply been an exclusive tour to see just what sort of marketing scheme he was getting himself into. Then, like now, he'd been truly amazed. There was no doubt in his mind that the *Velocity* would be a huge success. Already the naysayers were questioning the ship's safety and performance but he was certain by the end of this voyage everyone would see just what a remarkable airship this was. That was one of the reasons this trip was so important.

"I was wondering when you were going to get here, Nikki."

He turned at the sound of Curtis's voice and immediately felt his blood boil when Nikki entered the room and Rhinestone got all up in her face. Jonas was tempted to cross the room and smash the man's face in just for the hell of it, but he figured for now he needed to keep his cool. Working for Fulton was an opportunity of a lifetime and he wouldn't jeopardize it with drama. And what was pissing him off more than anything was that Rhinestone knew it.

He took a sip of his tonic water and studied Nikki. Even wearing her signature jeans and shirt she looked beautiful and he absolutely loved the soft-looking curls crowning her face. She had a camera in her hand, ready for business. But all he could think about at that moment was her, naked, straddling him while he thrust in and out of her, making out with her in a way he'd never made out with another women. Not with the same degree of passion, greed or urgency.

He suddenly felt a tingling in his fingers when he remembered them inside of her, stoking her heat, preparing her for his entry. Remembered how when he'd made it in he'd whispered naughty words to her, words that had made her blush while she had creamed some more. The warmth of her skin—whether it had been when their thighs had connected or when her legs had rested high on his shoulders—had wrapped him in a cocoon of sensuality he'd never felt before. She had done more than touch his body last night. She had somehow touched his soul.

Hell, how had that happened?

Had it occurred during those two days he'd tried to avoid her, only to go bonkers when he'd seen her again? Or had it been when they'd made out that night when she'd arrived in Vegas, right on the floor in his suite? For some reason he believed it had been that time when he'd kissed her, and then tried avoiding her for eighteen months. During that time he'd tried to convince himself she was just a woman and he had them anytime he wanted and whenever he wanted. What he hadn't counted on was her being different from all the others. He hadn't thought any woman capable of drawing out emotions in him, some of which he hadn't known he was capable of having. Like the need to do bodily harm to anyone who looked at her for too long.

Rhinestone glanced over his way with a smirk on his face. Jonas forced back the anger that tried rising to the top, well aware of the game the man intended to play. And if he thought he would play that game with Nikki then he was sorely mistaken.

Jonas inhaled deeply He refused to stand on the sidelines and let Curtis, or any man, make a move on Nikki. Curtis knew how he operated and until he made a public claim for a woman, the man wouldn't be backing off. And anyone who knew Jonas knew his hard and steadfast rule against ever doing such a thing. There were too many women out there to ever lay claim to just one.

He tried ignoring Rhinestone standing so close to Nikki. That resolve lasted all but two seconds. He placed his glass on the tray of a passing waiter and headed across the room after deciding it was time to break his own rule yet again.

Chapter 14

Nikki did the polite thing and nodded a few times while Curtis and another reporter conversed about how fascinated they were with the *Velocity*. She was surprised at the way Curtis had greeted her, especially after the obvious tension between him and Jonas last night.

She scanned the room, deliberately not allowing her gaze to wander where Jonas was standing. She'd seen him the moment she'd arrived and her heart had skipped a beat when he'd turned and their gazes had connected.

He was wearing his hair back in a ponytail and anytime he did so it only highlighted the angular lines of his face and showed a handsomeness that would take any woman's breath away. Dressed casually in a pair of jeans and a shirt, he was the epitome of masculine perfection.

She'd seen his frown when Curtis had stopped her. It was obvious he didn't like it. She really shouldn't care what he liked or didn't like because no matter how many times they came together, it was just for sex. He knew it as well as she.

"So what are your plans when we reach Beijing?" Curtis asked her, pulling her back into the conversation. "Surely you won't be expected to work while we're docked."

She opened her mouth to respond when a shadow crossed her path just seconds before a pair of lips brushed across hers in a kiss. Then a deep, masculine voice said, "Hello, sweetheart. I've been waiting for you and as usual, you were worth the wait."

For the hell of it, Jonas decided to brush a second kiss across her lips just to wipe the shocked look off her face. He stood by her side and wrapped his arms around her waist, ignoring the tension he felt flowing through her. He then turned to the two men and reached out for handshakes. "Rhinestone. Loggins. Good seeing you guys again. I hope you're enjoying yourselves."

He inwardly smiled at the way Rhinestone was recovering from a dropped jaw. The man was just as shocked as Nikki. He and Rhinestone weren't just fraternity brothers, they'd pledged on the same line. Kissing Nikki in front of everyone was a public claim to show their relationship was more than just casual. For Curtis to trespass on a fellow frat brother was a social taboo, a violation of the code of honor, something he wouldn't do.

"So how long have the two of you been involved?" Rhinestone asked, taking a sip of his drink and holding Jonas's gaze.

Jonas was quick with a response, which was a question of his own. "Why do you want to know?"

"Curious."

He was tempted to tell Rhinestone just what he could do with his curiosity, but instead said, "Long enough. Now if you gentlemen will excuse us, I think Fulton is ready for dinner to begin."

Taking Nikki's arm beneath the elbow, he led her to one of the tables in the room. He sensed her anger and knew she was holding her peace longer than he'd expected. Eventually she would let him have it but wouldn't do it here.

He leaned closer, considered her a moment and then asked, "You okay?"

She inclined her head and the gaze staring at him was filled with fury. "What do you think?"

He forced his lips to form a thin smile. "I don't know. That's why I asked. And no, I'm not trying to be a smart-ass."

"Then what are you trying to be?" she asked as they sat down at a table set for two. He'd deliberately chosen this one for privacy.

When they'd taken their seats, he leaned closer and whispered to her, his breath fanning the side of her face, "What I *intend* to be is the only man who's going to pleasure you on this air voyage."

Less than six hours later Nikki walked down the corridor that led to her hotel room. The *Velocity* had docked at the Beijing Airport without any problems.

Everything at the dinner party had gone well. Fulton had welcomed everyone on board and introduced his twelve flight attendants—males and females who looked like they had stepped off the covers of *GQ* and *Cosmo*. But she had to hand it to them, they had been true professionals and their customer service skills had been superb.

The meal they were served at dinner would rival that at any five-star restaurant. It was hard to believe they had dined while flying more than forty thousand feet in the air. Except for during takeoff and landing, they had been free to roam about the airship to enjoy the shopping boutiques, casino, library, game room and restaurant.

Jonas hadn't left her side the entire evening, clinging on to her like a grape to a vine. But she'd refused to indulge in private conversation with him. She ignored his air of possession whenever they conversed with others and got annoyed at how easily he would slide his arms around her waist and bring her closer to his side whenever another male got near, becoming territorial. When she hadn't been able to stand it anymore, she had feigned a migraine and gone to her cabin. He had offered to go with her to make sure she was okay, but she had turned down his offer and made it quite clear that she wanted to be alone. He'd called later to check on her, but when she answered the phone she had told him they had nothing to say to each other.

Reservations had been made for each passenger at several hotels in Beijing, where they would remain for three days on their own. She was grateful for that decision since she definitely needed to put distance between her and Jonas, even if only for three days.

As soon as the airship had docked, she had switched groups with another passenger and ridden off in a different limo from the one she'd been assigned. She felt good knowing Jonas had no idea where she was and wouldn't be seeing her again until they returned to the *Velocity* to continue their air voyage to Australia. As far as she was concerned, he could play his little game all by himself.

She rubbed her temple after entering her hotel room and closing the door behind her. What had she done in going along with Jonas's deception that they were involved in an affair? Sleeping with a man twice didn't constitute an affair, and considering his reputation, Jonas of all people knew that. So what if he'd transitioned from one-and-done to twice-is-nice? The only thing he'd accomplished was to gain triumph over Curtis, a man who evidently was his adversary. And he had used her to do it.

She glanced at her watch. It was in the middle of the day in Beijing, but her body was still in the Pacific time zone. She would sleep the day through and then tomorrow she would go out and do some sightseeing. By the time she returned to the *Velocity,* she would be able to handle the likes of Jonas Steele and set the record straight once and for all. They were not involved.

Jonas stared at the smiling flight attendant. "What do you mean Ms. Cartwright departed the *Velocity* a few hours ago?"

The young woman nodded. "Yes, sir. She requested a change in her itinerary and we were able to work something out with another passenger. She was in the first group that departed."

He drew in a deep agitated breath. He should have followed his mind and checked on her although she'd told him she wanted to be left alone. But he'd figured he would let her get some rest and then talk to her later. When she hadn't come out of her cabin for a while, he'd figured she had decided to grab a few more hours of rest, since they were the last group scheduled off the airship.

His gaze went back to the woman. "Then I'd like to know where she's gone since obviously she's no longer in my group and won't be staying at my hotel."

The woman's smile remained in place. "Yes, sir, but we can't divulge that information."

He of all people should know that. A high degree of privacy was one of *Velocity*'s strongest marketing points. He would have to use another approach. "Ms. Cartwright works for me and I need to get a message to her."

He knew before he'd finished talking that the woman wasn't buying it. She was one of the attendants who had worked the dinner meeting last night and had seen how he'd been all over Nikki. No matter what he said, the woman knew their relationship wasn't all business and if he couldn't find his woman then there must be trouble in paradise and she wasn't getting involved.

His woman.

Where had that thought come from? He shook his head. Damn. For the time being Nikki *was* his woman. He had pretty much claimed as much last night in a public display. And hadn't he made it clear to her that he intended to be the only man who would pleasure her on this voyage? Evidently she was still upset about last night and what he needed to do was talk to her as soon as possible. Hopefully, the two of them could reach some sort of an agreement.

"Do you not have her cell phone number, sir?"

"Yes, but I can't reach her." What he wouldn't say was that Nikki wasn't answering her phone.

"Sorry to hear that. Is there anything else, sir?"

He looked down at the woman, seeing she wasn't going to bend. He glanced down at her name tag. "No, Mandy, there's nothing else."

Jonas moved on as his mind began working. He'd always had ways of finding out whatever it was he wanted. One person who would know where Nikki had run off to was Brittany. However, he doubted his sister-in-law would tell him anything. He could turn to Galen to coax the info from his wife, but that would mean spilling his guts as to why he wanted to know. It was one thing to give a handful of strangers the impression he was enamored with a woman, but to give his brothers that same impression was another. He would never live it down.

That meant he would have to go to plan B and he had no qualms doing so. He had seen the way Mandy had ogled Rick last night and Rick's reputation as a ladies' man was just as bad as his. Jonas felt certain Rick could make more strides with Mandy than he had.

Rick owed him a favor and it was time for him to collect.

Nikki shifted in bed to drown out the insistent knocking at her hotel room door. Why was the cleaning service bothering her? Hadn't they seen the do-not-disturb sign on her door? "Go away," she called out before burying her head beneath her pillow.

When the knocking continued, she threw back the bed covers and stormed out of the bedroom to the door, pausing only to grab her robe off a chair. Customer service would definitely hear about this. She had wanted to rest for at least twelve hours. Jet lag was a bitch.

Nikki stopped halfway to the door when it opened. She crossed her arms over her chest, ready to take the person to task for disturbing her sleep. Her mouth dropped open when the person who walked across the threshold was not someone from housekeeping.

It was Jonas.

Chapter 15

"What are you doing here?"

After closing the door behind him, Jonas stood there, almost dazed, staring at her and thinking that with her curls tossed all over her head, bare feet and in a short robe showing a luscious pair of thighs, Nikki looked absolutely breathtaking.

She also looked absolutely mad. Furious was more like it.

"I asked what you're doing here, and what gives you the right to just come into my hotel room?"

He tossed his jacket on a chair. "I'm here to spend time with you. Someone from housekeeping heard me banging on your door, was fearful I'd wake up the whole floor, so she unlocked your door for me."

Nikki glared at him. "Wrong move on her part. I'm going to make sure she doesn't have a job much longer."

"Boy, you're mean."

"And you're leaving. Goodbye."

He shook his head and pushed his hair back from his face. He hadn't had time to bind it back after finding out Nikki's whereabouts. It hadn't taken Rick long to discover what hotel she'd gone to, and Jonas had caught the first taxi here. "I'm not leaving, Nikki."

"Fine, then I'll call security," she tossed over her shoulder as she headed for the phone.

"I wouldn't if I were you. Things could get pretty messy. More than likely your actions will generate gossip, fodder for the tabloids. I can see our faces plastered in the papers back home. Should be interesting reading."

She crossed her arms over her chest and stared him down. "You have more to lose than I do, Jonas. So what's it going to be?"

He crossed his arms over his own chest, stood with his legs spread apart and glared right back at her. "I'll tell you what it's going to be. You. Me. We have it out now, Nikki. You're still mad at me for what I did at that dinner party. Why? I thought women preferred knowing a man was interested in them. Last night I did something I've never done before, and that was to claim you as mine in front of everyone. So what's the problem?"

Nikki was convinced he really didn't have a clue. The man was so used to being in control, doing whatever the hell he wanted to do where women were concerned, that he thought *claiming* her was doing her a favor. Well, she had news for him. She didn't want to be claimed. She wanted to be loved.

Yes, yes, it was her heart talking again and she couldn't help it. The truth had hit her full force in the face at dinner. He had pampered her with attention, given her a taste of how things could be between them if they were in love. He hadn't left her side and had touched her easily, sliding his arms around her waist like it had been the most natural thing.

And every time he'd looked at her, although she'd tried to stay mad, her heart would leap in her chest, making her realize that without a doubt she had fallen in love with him. Though she had probably been in love with him for a while, at dinner she had opened her eyes and given in to her heart.

Giving in to her heart was one thing she could not abide. Admitting her love for Jonas had no place in this argument and there was no way he would ever know how she felt. There was no use. The man wasn't capable of loving a woman. That wasn't part of his makeup. He had probably figured out in that player mind of his that kissing her in front of everybody would entitle him to unlimited access to her bed. Well, she had news for him.

"I don't want to have it out with you, Jonas. I just want to be left alone."

"Do you?" he threw back. "I don't think so."

"I don't care what you think."

"Then maybe you should," he said, slowly moving toward her like a hunter who'd targeted his prey.

Nikki drew in a deep breath, convinced the man was mad. He was also sexy as hell. How could he not be when he was unbuttoning his shirt with every step he took? She backed up. "I don't want you, Jonas."

"Then I guess I'm going to have to change your mind about that."

She refused to back up any farther, deciding to stand her ground. She placed her hands on her hips and stared him down. "What is it with you Steeles? Why do you assume you can get any woman you want?"

He shrugged. "I can't speak for my brothers, but as for myself, the only woman I want is you."

She looked up at him. "Why?"

"I can give you a number of reasons. No woman can wear a pair of jeans like you do. Seeing your curvy bottom in them makes me hard each and every time. Then there are those soft curls on your head that frame your face. It's such a beautiful face."

His gaze went to her chest. "And then there're your breasts that fit perfectly in my hands."

His gaze shifted lower to the juncture of her thighs. He smiled. "The only thing I can say about *that* part is that I think I'm addicted to it. I love tasting it, touching it and getting all into it any way I can."

She lifted her chin. "Sounds all sexual to me."

"Probably because I'm a sexual kind of guy. But no matter how much I enjoy it, you're the only woman who has me wanting to come back for more, wishing there was a way I could stay locked inside you forever, make you a permanent taste bud on my tongue."

She knew it had to be a deliberate move on his part because her body was ripening with every word he said. Her panties were getting wet, her nipples felt sensitive against her robe and her lips were tingling. She should be fighting his assault on her senses, but she was getting pulled into a stream of mindless pleasure. The kind she knew he could deliver.

He slowly began advancing upon her again and she still held her ground, feeling the charged energy radiating between them that was breaking down her defenses, playing havoc with her senses one turbulent sensation at a time. She drew in a deep breath and filled her nostrils with his masculine scent and felt intense desire flood her middle.

"Why do you want to fight me, Nikki, when all I want to do is make love to you?"

His words were like ice water being dumped on a heated surface. She took a step back and narrowed her gaze. "You wouldn't know how to make love to a woman if it killed you, Jonas. All you know how to do is have sex with one. There is a difference."

He came to a stop in front of her. "Then show me how to make love. In fact I have a proposition for you. I propose that we enter into a private arrangement where for the rest of our trip on the *Velocity,* we don't have sex, but we make love."

She rolled her eyes. Those words just confirmed what she already knew. He didn't have an idea of what love was if he thought the arrangement he was proposing was possible. "Love isn't anything you can speak into existence. People can only *make* love when they are *in* love."

He reached out, wrapped an arm around her waist, drawing her closer. "In that case, let's pretend we're in love, then. You know that I don't love you and I know that you don't love me, but if it makes you feel better, we can pretend."

A part of Nikki couldn't believe he would suggest such a thing, but then another part of her did believe it. Although his parents were still happily married and he had two brothers who were also in happy marriages, Jonas just didn't get it, mainly because he'd never felt that emotion himself, and she wondered if he ever would. Who knew, maybe if he got a taste of it, he might like it.

She shook her head. Her thoughts were beginning to be just as insane as his, which meant her head was filling up with crazy ideas and ludicrous notions. Men like Jonas didn't fall in love. They didn't even know the meaning of it. But maybe if he were to pretend long enough…

There was that silly thought again. Besides, it wouldn't be any pretense on her part, so what would that do to her heart when he decided he didn't even like the pretend version? But then if she did enter into such a private arrangement with him, it would help her to move on and accept that the man she loved would never love her back.

She hadn't told anyone yet about the job offer she'd gotten from the L.A. producer who'd interviewed her before she boarded the *Velocity*. He'd been so impressed with her portfolio that he had called just minutes before the airship had taken off and made her a job offer as set photographer. The salary he'd offered had almost made her fall out of the bed in her cabin. And since he'd be directing a miniseries that would take three years of filming, it would be steady work for a long while.

The only drawback she'd seen at the time was moving from Phoenix to L.A. for those three years. But now, considering everything, the move to L.A. wouldn't be a drawback but a blessing. If she considered Jonas's offer of a private arrangement, the next two weeks would be all she would ever have before she left Phoenix to start a new life on the coast.

Jonas placed his finger beneath her chin so their gazes could connect. "So, baby, are you game?" he asked in a low tone, the depths of his green eyes holding hers. "Women are into this love thing more so than men, so if you want to pretend that you got me all strung out for you then that's fine. And just so we're clear, our arrangement ends when the *Velocity* docks back in L.A."

He moved closer still, so close his thighs were touching hers, and she could feel the hardness of his erection press against her stomach. And it felt so good resting there. So hot. So tempting.

"I can see you're hesitant. Maybe I need to give you something to help you make up your mind," he murmured, lowering his head to lick her lips.

"Something like what?" she asked, feeling her senses ooze away from her.

"Something like this."

He pushed the robe from her body and quickly removed her short baby-doll nightie as well. Then, as effortlessly as any man could do, he lifted her up off her feet and stood her naked body on the edge of the couch with her thighs spread apart.

"Jonas, I think that we—"

"Shh," he whispered, stepping back to remove his clothes and put on a condom although she knew she was on the pill. He then moved back to the couch to stand in front of her. "Bend your knees a little, baby, so I can ease inside you," he said in a deep husky tone.

She did as he asked and then glanced down to watch how the head of his engorged penis penetrated her flesh and slid deep inside of her. It fascinated her that something that large could fit inside of her so perfectly. Reaching out, he grabbed her hips to hold her body steady as he made the journey in. As deep as he could go. Then he reached out to lave her breasts with his tongue, licking all over the areola before sucking a turgid nipple into his mouth.

"You're starting to cream all over me and I like it," he said as he released her nipple. "It's hot and thick. Just the way I like to feel it. Just the way I love to taste it. But for now I want to pump you up. Give you reason to want to pretend we're in love."

And then the lower part of his body began moving as he captured her mouth, mating with it the same way he was mating with her womanly core. She moved to his rhythm as their bodies rocked and rolled, and she met his every thrust. And then he picked up speed and power, beginning to pound into her while he gripped her backside to hold her in place while he went deeper still, as if carving out his place inside of her.

"I can't get enough of you," he growled and she knew what he meant, mainly because she couldn't get enough of him, either. She widened her legs and the moment she did so, her senses spun out of control as he hit her G-spot.

She lifted her legs off the couch to wrap them around his waist as tight as they could get. He deepened the kiss and moved from the sofa to the nearest wall, where he pressed her back against the solid surface and continued to pound into her like the world would be ending tomorrow and he needed every thrust to count.

And they did.

Only with him was her body this sharp, keen, capable of feeling every single sensation he evoked. This was crazy. This was madness. And in the back of her mind she was reminded this was just sex. For him, yes, but not for her. He might be having sex with her, but she was definitely making love to him.

And then her body exploded under his forceful thrusts and she screamed his name as an orgasm ripped solidly into her, almost blinding her. It not only assaulted her body, it beat up on her senses. Whipped them to the point of no return. At that moment nothing mattered but this and how he was making her feel. She ignored that little chat from her heart that she deserved better. Instead she listened to her head. *You can't get any better than this.*

Jonas followed suit, roaring loudly on the heels of a deep masculine growl. He gritted his teeth while the lower half of his body continued to grind into her nonstop. He was pulling everything out of her and was still demanding more. And he was doing it in such a way that she felt every single movement. Never had she felt more connected to any man than right now.

She wrapped her arms around his neck and met his gaze. No words were exchanged between them. None was needed. And then their mouths joined again in a long, sensuous kiss.

Yes, she would agree to the private arrangement that he wanted, and when they returned to Phoenix she would be ready to move on with her life in another city.

It would be far away from the heartbreak she knew awaited her if she were to stay.

Chapter 16

"Okay, I give up," Jonas said, staring at the item on the serving tray that a waiter had just placed in front of them. "What is it?"

Nikki chuckled. "It's the carcass of the duck we had for dinner. The Chinese don't believe in letting anything go to waste so they fried it for us."

He arched his brow. "And we're supposed to eat it?"

"Yes."

He wiped his mouth and tossed his napkin on the table and leaned back in his chair. "I'll pass. I'm full already. What about you?"

She smiled over at him. "I'm full as well. Dinner was wonderful."

He would have to agree with her. The staff at their Beijing hotel had recommended this restaurant, and he had selected items off the menu that he recognized and had gone along with Nikki to try a few dishes he hadn't been familiar with and had enjoyed them as well. But he would draw the line with duck carcass.

Jonas studied Nikki as she sipped her tea, finding it hard to believe they'd spent the last two days together in perfect harmony. At first he had questioned his sanity in suggesting their private arrangement. To pretend to be in love with a woman had to be one of the craziest notions he'd ever come up with. But so far things were working.

He enjoyed watching her sleep and how her curls would fan her face and the soft snoring sounds she would occasionally make. And then in the mornings when she would wake up, he liked how she would smile up at him before reaching out for what had become their good-morning kiss. Of course that kiss would lead to other things.

"So, what will we do today?"

Her question pulled him from his thoughts and he glanced across the table at her. Her eyes were just as bright as her smile. "I'll let you decide today since yesterday's activities were my idea."

"Yeah, and you whined the entire time."

He looked offended. "I did not whine."

She leaned in closer across the table. "You did too, Jonas Steele."

He laughed. "Okay, maybe I did."

It had been his idea for them to climb the Great Wall of China, but halfway up he was ready to go back down. He hadn't known the place would require so much energy—energy he preferred using for other things like making love to her. Even now he was still overwhelmed by the power of what they shared in the bedroom. They were doing things the same way, but he could swear he was beginning to note a difference. A difference he couldn't quite put his finger on.

"In that case, since you're letting it be my decision, I suggest we take a cooking class."

He sat up straight in his chair. "A cooking class?"

She chuckled. "Yes."

He crossed his arms over his chest. "Why would I want to attend a cooking class? I have a woman who comes in twice a week to clean and cook enough food to last me all week. Then there are my weekly Thursday dinners at my parents' home. I don't need to know how to cook."

"I think it will be fun."

"Whatever," he said, taking a sip of his own tea. "I guess I'm game if that's what you really want to do."

Her smile brightened even more. "Yes, that's what I really want to do."

He smiled, enjoying the smile that curved her lips. "Okay. Where's my apron?"

With shopping bags in each hand, Nikki entered her hotel room and used her feet to shut the door behind her. All the passengers would return to the *Velocity* later that day and she had wanted to get some shopping in before the limo arrived to transport her and Jonas to the airport. Their next stop was Sydney, Australia, where they would be spending another three days.

Earlier that morning after making love, she and Jonas had toured a Chinese palaces and Tiananmen Square. Afterward, they'd shared lunch at, of all places, Friday's. Jonas had been tickled to see an American chain restaurant and insisted on going. She had invited him to go shopping with her in the afternoon, but he declined, saying he wanted to return to the hotel for a quick nap.

Nikki glanced at her watch. That had been three hours ago and from the soft hum of his snoring, it seemed he was still at it. Quietly placing her bags on the sofa, she tiptoed out of the sitting area into the bedroom. She leaned in the doorway and stared across the room at the man she loved.

His upper torso, not covered by the bed linens, was bare, as she was certain the rest of him was since he loved sleeping in the nude. She blushed when she recalled how he now had her sleeping in the nude as well, something she had learned was an enjoyable experience. Especially since Jonas had a tendency to wake up during the crazy hours of the night wanting to make love.

Nikki stepped into the room, closer to the bed. With his mass of hair all over the pillow, the man was pure temptation even while asleep. She drew in a deep breath. These would be the only days she would have with him this way, trouble free, filled with fun and excitement, and both beginning and ending with them connected in a way that took her breath away just thinking about it. It always felt good being wrapped in his embrace, held by him, hearing whispered erotic words that could make her come just listening to them.

She was about to move away from the bed when suddenly his hand snaked out and grabbed her around the wrist. She looked down at him and saw his eyes were open and the depth of his green eyes had her holding her breath.

His hold on her hand tightened when he continued

to stare at her. Then he said in a deep husky tone, "I want you, baby. And I want you now."

He pulled her into the bed with him, almost tore off her clothes, and it seemed within seconds after donning a condom he retrieved from the night stand, he was straddling her, easing between her legs, slowly penetrating her, deep and sure.

Gracious! Him inside of her felt so right. Why couldn't he see it? Why couldn't he feel it? Why couldn't he love her as much as she loved him? There were too many whys for her to concentrate on at the moment. Not when he was thrusting inside her so hard the whole bed was shaking.

"Come for me, baby. I want you to cream all over me," he said, breathing the words against her neck.

And she did, calling out to him while lifting her hips to take him in as far as possible. Their days were numbered, but she was determined to collect as many memories as she could.

"Brittany is pregnant?" Jonas asked, not believing what his brother Galen had just told him.

"Yes, and I'm so happy about it I can't stand it."

Jonas nodded, hearing that excitement in his brother's voice. And then he couldn't help but chuckle when he recalled what he'd suggested to his mother a few weeks earlier about hitting Galen and Brittany up for a grandchild. He could just imagine his mother's happiness and excitement as well.

"Have you told Mom yet?" he asked.

"No, we're telling her tonight when we go to the folks' place for dinner."

Jonas would give anything to be there to see the expression on Eden's face when they did. Expecting a grandbaby should definitely keep her busy and out of her single sons' business for a while.

"If you see Nikki, don't mention anything to her. Brittany wants to be the one to tell her. I think she's going to ask Nikki to be our baby's godmother."

Jonas nodded thinking Nikki would make a good choice for godmother. They had spent a lot of time together over the past two weeks, and he had been exposed to a side of her he hadn't seen before. He saw she was generous to a fault, liked to have fun and was loyal to those she considered friends. Like him she was close to her family, and like his, her parents had been married for a long time.

A part of him was trying to forget that tomorrow they would be returning home. At least he would. She mentioned that she had a meeting with someone in L.A. and wouldn't be back in Phoenix until the end of the week.

Jonas knew that everyone traveling on the *Velocity* could say that it had been one hell of a voyage and that they had had the experience of a lifetime. There was no doubt in his mind the reviews written by the media on board would be favorable, and it would be up to his staff to capitalize on the good publicity and roll out the marketing campaign that would guarantee a sellout as soon as *Velocity* took its next voyage.

He couldn't help but think of this one. After Beijing they had traveled to Australia, from there to Dubai and finally to Paris. They had covered four continents in fourteen days. Tomorrow they would leave Paris for L.A.

"Jonas?"

It was then that he recalled his brother's request. "Okay, I won't say anything to Nikki," he answered.

No one knew he and Nikki were involved other than those who saw them together on the airship. But he didn't care if the whole world knew it. The only thing was their affair would be ending soon so sharing the information was a moot point now.

Moments later he ended his call with Galen to walk over to the window and look out. This hadn't been his first visit to Paris and wouldn't be his last. He loved the place, with its elegant architecture, beautiful countryside and majestic castles. Everyone was staying at Chateau d'Esclimont, which was an hour outside of Paris. The place was simply breathtaking and nestled in the Loire Valley. He had discovered Nikki could ride a horse and the two of them had ridden two Thoroughbreds around the countryside. And then later they'd had a picnic near a picturesque lake.

Australia had been just as magnificent. It been somewhat strange knowing it was winter in the States and arriving in Sydney during the heart of their summer. He and Nikki had totally enjoyed themselves, taking a tour of the city and flying over the Great Barrier Reef. Seeing one of the seven wonders of the natural world had been totally captivating, something he would never forget.

And Dubai was certainly a place he would return to. There was nothing like sailing on the Persian Gulf and taking a camel ride across the desert. He couldn't help but smile when he recalled how Nikki had blushed profusely at the sight of camels mating. And then later that night, back in their hotel room, they'd done a little camel-like mating of their own.

He moved away from the window. The time he'd spent with Nikki was something he couldn't forget, either. She had brought something into the last two weeks that he hadn't expected. Namely, the kind of companionship he hadn't expected to find with any woman. She was someone he could talk to about anything, and he definitely enjoyed their conversations. Considering their rocky beginning, he was simply amazed at how well they got along. That didn't mean they agreed on anything, far from it. But they had a very satisfying way of compromising when they did disagree.

He was finding out that pretending to love a woman had its benefits, although he wouldn't want to do that with any other woman. Besides, he couldn't imagine any other woman agreeing to such a deal. But Nikki had. She had agreed to this private arrangement between them, and he didn't regret making it.

The only thing he regretted was that tomorrow things would come to an end. There was no doubt in his mind that he and Nikki would run into each other on occasion, but he would resume his life as he knew it and she would resume hers.

Yesterday he had viewed all the photographs she'd taken and of course he hadn't been disappointed. She had done an excellent job and he couldn't wait for the marketing campaign to move forward.

Once she emailed him all the photographs, her employment with Ideas of Steele would cease. He would pay her for her services and that would be it.

His hands shook when he tried pouring coffee from the pot in the room. After spending two such glorious weeks with Nikki, how was he supposed to get back into the swing of things without her? At that moment, the thought of becoming involved with another woman, going back to his "one and done" rule just didn't have the appeal it had once had.

Even worse, the thought of his manhood sliding between any woman's legs other than Nikki's, or his head being buried between any other woman's thighs, or his mouth mating with any other woman's, was leaving a bad taste in his mouth.

He put down his coffee cup and ran his fingers over his chin, feeling the stubble there. What in the hell was wrong with him? No woman had ever made him feel this way and, dammit, he didn't like it one bit. He needed to get ready to get his groove on once again, be the player he was. There were all those models, socialites and party girls who wanted to share his bed. He was certain any one of them could get him back on the right track, put his mind back in check. And put Nikki way in the back of it.

She'd been fun, enjoyable, but now it was time for them to move on, and they would because when the *Velocity* landed in Los Angeles, their private arrangement as they knew it would be over.

Tears of happiness sprang into Nikki's eyes. "Oh, Britt, that is so wonderful. Congratulations. I am so happy for you and Galen."

And she truly was. She knew Galen and Britt's relationship was solid and they loved each other very much. To Nikki, having a baby, one conceived in love, had to be the most rewarding thing that could happen to a woman.

"I can't wait until you get back. We're going to have to celebrate," Brittany cut into her thoughts and said.

Nikki agreed. "Yes, we will. I'll be back in the States later today, but I've got another meeting with Martin Dunlap before I come back to Phoenix."

"So you are going to take that job in Los Angeles?"

"Yes, I think it will be for the best. I'm at a place in my life where I need to make a change."

She drew in a deep breath. In less than two hours the *Velocity* would be leaving its docking station in Paris to return home. Everyone was on board and accounted for, and Jonas was in a private meeting with Fulton. She knew the man was pleased with how this trial voyage had turned out, and so far all the media coverage had been positive. She'd heard that people were already clamoring to get tickets for the next trip, which was scheduled in two weeks.

"I hate that we're going to be separated again, Nikki."

Nikki hated that, too. She and Brittany had lived across the street from each other while in their early teens, and when Nikki's military dad had received orders to move to another port, Nikki and Brittany had lost touch. They had found each other a year and a half ago when Brittany had come to Phoenix on business. She and Galen had met and the rest was history.

"We'll never be separate, Britt. I'll just be a plane ride away. Besides, now that you've asked me to be the baby's godmother, you'll be seeing me more than you think."

Brittany chuckled. "Yes, and I believe that one day you'll have all those babies of your own that you've always wanted."

Nikki wished that was true but wouldn't be holding her breath for that to happen. "Maybe. But in the meantime, I'll spoil my little goddaughter or godson rotten."

A short while later, after she ended her call with Brittany, Jonas returned to the cabin. After their decision regarding their private arrangement, they had begun sharing a cabin. They'd decided to use his since it had been the larger of the two.

He glanced over at her the moment he entered the room. He must have seen her red eyes, because he crossed the room and pulled her into his arms. "Hey, you okay?"

She nodded and looked up at him. "Yes, I just finished talking to Brittany. She told me about her and Galen's good news. She also told me that you were sworn to secrecy."

He chuckled. "Yes. That kind of news definitely made my parents happy. Galen and Brittany told them last night. I hear my mother is already buying out the baby stores."

Nikki could just imagine. She remembered how her mother had behaved when her brother and sister-in-law presented her parents with their first grandbaby.

Jonas stroking her back felt good. Being in his arms felt good as well. Boy, she was definitely going to miss this. Neither of them had broached the subject of what would happen when the *Velocity* arrived in Los Angeles. They didn't have to. It had been part of the agreement. He would go his way and she would go hers.

Of course their paths would cross in Phoenix from time to time. There was no way around it, and there was always the chance they might work together again. But the intimacy they'd shared would become a thing of the past. Their relationship would move from friends with benefits to just friends.

She pulled out of his arms and looked up at him. "I'm fine. How did things go with Fulton?"

"Great. He had a chance to look at the portfolio you put together and said you did a wonderful job. He told me to tell you that."

"Thanks." Their relationship was changing already. She could feel it. Although they had made love that morning, she had felt him beginning to withdraw. Her heart was breaking inside, but a part of her understood that that's the way things were to be. Nothing lasted forever, even if it was pretend.

Their gazes held and she felt the yearning stir within her as it always did. He had that effect on women. He certainly had that effect on her. But did they have time now? They would be docking in L.A. in less than four hours. There was a part of her that wished time could stand still.

"Nikki, I—"

She reached out and placed her finger to his lips. "I know and it's okay. I had a good time and I hope you did, too."

He nodded. "I did."

He pulled her back to him and lowered his head toward hers. She had gotten her answer. They would make love one last time. This would be their goodbye. And despite everything, she had no regrets.

Chapter 17

Three weeks later

"You're awfully quiet tonight, son. Usually you're the life of the party."

Jonas glanced up at his dad, a man whom he highly admired and respected. Over forty years ago Drew Steele had taken his small trucking company and turned it into a million-dollar industry that had routes all over the United States.

Another one of his father's accomplishments was always making time for his six sons, no matter how busy he'd been. And although he and his brothers would moan and groan about his parents' Thursday-night chow-down, where their attendance was expected, deep down they appreciated it as a way to stay connected, no matter how busy their schedules were.

Jonas forced a smile to his lips. "I'm fine. Besides, I decided to take a backseat to Gannon tonight since he seems to have a lot to say."

Drew chuckled. "Yes, I can see that." He paused a moment, then said, "I understand that the four-continent air voyage was a huge success and your company's marketing campaign was instrumental in getting it over the top. Congratulations."

"Thanks." Deep down he felt the credit should go to Nikki. Those photographs she'd taken had helped to introduce the *Velocity* into the market. His social media guru had taken Nikki's pictures and had done a fantastic job in incorporating them in the Ideas of Steele marketing plan.

Nikki.

He gazed down into his glass of wine wondering how she'd been doing. More than once he'd been tempted to pick up the phone to call her and ask. But each time he had talked himself out of doing so. Something was going on with him and at the moment he didn't have a clue as to what. All he knew was that as of yet he hadn't been able to get back into his game. Hell, the thought of kissing another woman had almost made him gag, and the thought of sharing a bed with one sent negative shivers through his body.

"And you sure you're okay?"

He met his father's gaze again. "Yes, I'm sure, but I'd like to ask you something."

"What?"

"That time when you and Mom were dating and you let her run off to Paris and almost lost her. Why did you do that?"

Over the years Jonas and his brothers had heard the

story of their parents' tumultuous love affair. They'd heard how Drew had refused to accept Eden as his fate and ended up pushing her away. By the time he'd come to his senses, she had left the States for Paris. Drew had freaked out at the possibility of losing Eden forever and had followed her and asked her to marry him.

His father met his gaze for a long moment and then said, "Because I was convinced I was not ready to love her or any woman. I honestly assumed I was above falling in love. I loved women too much to settle down with just one."

Jonas nodded. That pretty much sounded like the story of his life. "What made you see things differently?"

"I asked myself what I thought would be a simple question. Would my life be better without Eden in it? Was chasing women more important than making memories of waking up to the same woman, one who could connect to me on all levels? One who made me think about her when I should be working? One who made me think of having several little girls who would look just like her, even when I thought I didn't even want kids? When I finally was honest with myself and answered those questions, then I knew that whether I wanted to be or not, I was in love. And then I knew there *was* no way I could let her go."

Drew released a chuckle from deep within his chest. "Hell, I had it so bad for her and didn't even know it. I was pure whipped." He paused a moment, then threw in an extra piece of sage advice. "I believe a smart man not only recognizes when he's whipped but actually loves the thought of it, especially if the woman is worth it. There's nothing wrong with falling in love if it's a woman you can't live your life without."

Drew then glanced across the room at his wife, who was sitting down on the sofa talking to their daughters-in-law. "And for me, your mother is that woman. She always will be."

He then met Jonas's gaze again. "So if you're ever lucky to meet such a woman, whatever you do, please don't make the mistake your old man almost made."

Drew smiled then. "Come on. Your mom is beckoning us to dinner."

Jonas drowned out the conversation around him at the dinner table as he ate his food. Everyone seemed to be in a festive mood, so why wasn't he? Fulton had called today to congratulate him on an outstanding marketing campaign. Already voyages on the *Velocity* had sold out for the next six months and they were working on a waiting list that extended well into the next three.

However, what had really consumed Jonas's thoughts for the past three weeks hadn't been the success of *Velocity*'s marketing campaign. It had been Nikki. His Nikki. The woman who'd enticed him to push for a private arrangement with her for two weeks. It was an arrangement he still had memories about today. Never had a woman been so loving, so giving, so downright sexy.

Even now he could recall them dancing together in a nightclub in Sydney, him finally being talked into going shopping with her in Dubai, and the two of them viewing the Eiffel Tower in Paris. Their time together had been so ideal, so perfect. Exactly how it should feel for a couple who cared about each other.

Who had pretended to.

There were times when he was alone in his bed, at work or just riding in his car when he would remember and wish there was a way he could recapture those moments, a way he could book another flight on the *Velocity* and relive every single second. But he knew there was no way he could do that. So all he had was memories.

He felt an ache in the lower part of his gut just remembering all those sexy outfits she'd purchased on her shopping spree and how she would give him a personal fashion show, which ended with him removing every single item, stitch by stitch. Then they would make love all through the night and the early-morning hours.

Jonas glanced up when Tyson asked him a question about the *Velocity*. Moments later Eli and Galen asked him a few more questions. He knew his brothers had noted he was quieter than usual and were trying to draw him into the family's conversation. He appreciated their efforts, but he truly wasn't in a talkative mood tonight.

"So, Jonas, what happens if you get another big account like Fulton's and need a photographer?" Mercury asked.

Jonas frowned, wondering where the hell that question came from and why Mercury was asking. He glanced across the dinner table at his brother. "I'll do like I've always done and use a freelancer. Of course I'll approach Nikki Cartwright first. She's the best." Jonas then quietly returned to his meal.

"Yeah, but that won't be possible now that she's moving to L.A."

Jonas's head snapped back up and his green eyes slammed into his brother's. "What did you just say?" His tone had such a deadly and hard edge to it that everyone at the dinner table stopped eating and stared at him.

Mercury pretended not to notice Jonas's steely disposition when he answered with an insolent smile on his lips. "I said Nikki is moving to L.A. She got this job offer from some big-time producer and I understand she's moving away at the end of the month."

Jonas shifted his gaze from Mercury to Brittany, who was sitting at Galen's side. "Is that true?"

She nodded slowly. "Yes. I thought you knew."

Jonas drew in a deep breath. No, he hadn't known. For some reason he looked at his father, and when their eyes met, Jonas clearly remembered the conversation they'd shared before dinner.

He pushed his plate back and stood. "Please excuse me. I need to leave. There's some business I need to tend to."

Eden, who was completed dumbfounded, spoke up. "Surely whatever it is can wait, Jonas. You haven't finished dinner."

He shook his head. "No, Mom, it can't wait."

And then he headed for the door, only pausing to grab his motorcycle helmet off a table in the foyer on his way out.

Nikki couldn't sleep, but then that was the story of her life since she returned home. Too bad she couldn't get thoughts of Jonas out of her mind. She wondered if he ever thought about her with the same yearning and intensity that she thought about him. Probably not. The only good thing was that his name hadn't been linked with any woman in the tabloids since they'd gotten back, but she knew it was just a matter of time.

She thought about her move to L.A. Of course her parents and brother who lived in San Diego were happy with her decision, since that meant she would be closer to them. She hadn't lived in California since leaving home for college so perhaps the move would do her some good.

And then maybe she would be able to forge ahead with her life and forget about Jonas. Then she wouldn't have to worry about the possibility of running into him unexpectedly or worry whether he was with another woman. Not that it mattered, really. Just remembering all they'd shared was enough to shatter her these days.

And then there was another problem she'd encountered because of Jonas. Her body was going through sexual withdrawal. This time of night when she couldn't sleep, she would remember everything they'd shared, especially the time she'd spent in his arms, making love with him, using all those positions. And during those last fourteen days they *had* made love. She wondered if he'd been able to tell the difference. Probably not.

After a few more tosses and turns she finally sat up in bed. She clicked on a lamp and looked around. For the first time since she moved here she realized just how lonely this house was. Lonely and empty. Her bedroom was prettily decorated in her favorite colors of chocolate and lime green, and she'd hired a professional decorator to make sure things were just how she'd wanted them. But something was missing.

It really didn't matter now since she was moving away. Already her realtor had found a buyer so there was nothing or no one to hold her to Phoenix any longer. She would miss Brittany and their weekly lunch dates, but like she'd told her best friend, they were just an airplane flight away.

Galen had promised to call her the minute Brittany went into labor. More than anything she wanted to be around when her goddaughter or godson was born.

Since it seemed like sleep was out of the question for her at the moment, she slid out of bed and slipped into the matching robe to the baby-doll nightgown she was wearing. Both had been items she'd purchased while in Paris.

She had made it downstairs when she heard the sound of a motorcycle. One of her neighbors had recently purchased a Harley and she figured he'd taken it out for a late-night ride.

Nikki was headed for her kitchen to raid her snack jar. Thanks to Jonas she liked Tootsie Pops and always kept a bag on hand. Whenever she plopped one in her mouth she thought of him.

She stopped walking when she heard a knock on her door. Who on earth would be visiting her at this hour? She tightened her robe around her and went to the door, pausing to take a look out the peephole. Her breath caught in her throat when she saw her late-night caller.

She quickly entered the code to disarm her alarm system before opening the door. "Jonas? Why… What are you doing here?"

He was standing under her porch light in a pair of jeans, a T-shirt that advertised Ideas of Steele, and biker boots. In his hand he held his bike helmet. "Would it be okay if I come inside so we can talk?"

Although she had no idea what they had to talk about, she nodded and took a step back. "Sure. Come in."

Once he entered and closed the door behind him, she watched as he glanced around and saw the boxes already packed and sealed, ready to be picked up by the movers.

"I heard tonight that you're leaving town. I didn't know," he said.

She nodded. So he didn't know. Would it have mattered if he had? She doubted it. "Yes, I got a job offer in L.A."

"Why didn't you tell me you were moving away, Nikki?"

His question surprised her. Why would she tell him? It's not like they meant anything to each other. Those two weeks on board the *Velocity* had been nothing but a game of pretend that he'd initiated under the disguise of a private arrangement. She'd gone along with it because she loved him. And she had no regrets.

"Nikki?"

She met his gaze, suddenly feeling angry when she recalled how he'd started withdrawing from her the last day of their trip. They'd made love true enough, but she'd felt he was pulling back in ways he hadn't before. Now she placed her hands on her hips and lifted her chin to glare at him.

"I really didn't think you'd want to know, Jonas. We had an agreement and you made sure I understood the terms. I did. When we returned to Phoenix, things would go back to the way they were between us. So excuse me, but did I miss something?"

He blew out a long breath and rubbed his hand

across his face; then he looked back at her. "Yes, you missed something, and so did I."

She lifted a brow. "Really? Then please enlighten me because I have no idea what *we* could have missed."

"The fact that I have fallen in love with you."

His words took the wind out of Nikki's sail. She sucked in a deep breath, and it seemed that every muscle in her body tensed. She stared at him, saw his unreadable green eyes staring back at her. She slowly shook her head. "Impossible. You don't know how to love."

"I do now. You taught me, remember? For two weeks you taught me there's a difference between having sex with a woman and making love to one. I know that difference now, Nikki. I've always made love to you because I've always loved you. Since our first kiss, and possibly before it. But I fought it tooth and nail."

He paused a moment and then said in a low voice, "I probably would still be fighting it if I hadn't heard you were leaving. Once I heard I knew I couldn't let you go without telling you how much you mean to me. Just how much I love you."

Nikki closed her eyes, fearful when she opened them he would be gone and his presence would have been only a figment of her imagination. Evidently he'd read her mind, because when she opened her eyes, he said, "I'm still here."

Yes, he was still there, standing in the middle of her living room with his helmet clutched to his hand, his feet braced apart and his hair tied back in a ponytail. He looked like a rebel, a rogue, a man determined to defy the odds. A man who'd managed to claim her heart.

"Why do you love me, Jonas?" she asked, wondering if he really knew or if he only assumed he was in love with her.

"Why *don't* I love you?" he countered. "But to answer your question, I love everything about you. But I especially like how you handle your business. I admire that. And I love the way you make me feel when I'm inside of you, lying beside you in bed, or sitting across from you at a table. I think I fell in love with you that day we met at my office and you came in from the rain. I was so totally captivated by you then, but I tried denying it. And then that day we kissed in your office, I was so taken aback I couldn't think straight. That's why I tried avoiding you for eighteen months. You pulled out emotions in me that I wasn't use to feeling, and I was afraid that you would encompass my whole world. In fact, you do. My only question is how do you feel about me?"

She drew in a deep breath, fighting back tears and thinking only a man like Jonas would have to ask. Anyone else would have been able to see it on her face. "I love you, too, Jonas. I think I fell in love with you that rainy day as well, but I knew for certain how I felt while on the *Velocity*. But I thought loving you was a hopeless case on my part, although I wanted to use those two weeks to show you what love was about."

"You did, sweetheart. I know the difference between sex and making love. Each and every time I touched you, we made love."

"Oh, Jonas."

He placed his helmet on the table and then slowly crossed the room and pulled her into his arms. "Just so you know, me loving you is not about making any demands. More than anything I want you to follow your dream. Move to L.A. if you have to, but I'll be coming with you. I can set up a satellite office and work from just about anywhere."

Nikki's eyes lit up. "You would do that for me?"

"I would do that for *us*. I don't want to be away from you. I got used to having you around on the *Velocity,* and I've been miserable these past three weeks without you."

He paused a moment and then said, "And I need to be completely honest about something, confess to something I did just to keep you around me."

She lifted a brow. "What?"

He reached out, captured her finger and wrapped his bigger one around it. "That night you turned down my job offer I took measures into my own hands."

"How?"

"By playing a favor card. I called a guy I knew whose brother is closely tied with Senator Joseph's election campaign. I had him renege on your job offer."

She stiffened in his embrace. "You did?"

"Yes. I did."

She didn't say anything for a minute, just stared at him. The multitude of emotions revealed in his eyes nearly took her breath away. Even then he had wanted her and had even been willing to play dirty to get her. But she would have to admit that the end result had been worth it.

"I hope you know doing something like that is going to cost you," she said, making sure he heard the lightness in her voice when she began seeing a wary look in his gaze.

"Hmm, what's the charge?"

She paused as if thinking about it and then said,

"You're going to have to love me for the rest of your days."

He drew her closer. "Baby, I had planned on doing that anyway."

And then Jonas lowered his mouth to hers, kissing Nikki with the hunger he had only for her and no other woman. Only with her did he want to feel free, be loved and give love. Only with her did his emotions rise to the top. And only with Nikki was he not afraid to want more than what he'd been getting. He wanted commitment. He wanted to abolish his one-and-done policy and replace it with one-and-only, because that's what Nikki was to him.

He broke off the kiss and swept her off her feet and into his arms. "I need to make love to you. And just so you know, I haven't touched another woman since you. I couldn't because they weren't you and I didn't want anyone else."

He leaned down and kissed her again. When he released her lips, he asked, "Let's go to the bedroom?"

He slowly carried her there, kissing her intermittently along the way. When he reached her bedroom he placed her down in the middle of her bed. He glanced around. "Nice room."

She looked him up and down and smiled. "Mmm, nice man."

He chuckled and likewise, let his gaze travel all over her. "Nice woman."

And then he began removing his clothes, and she watched as he removed every single piece. He then moved back to the bed and with a couple flicks of his wrists, he had removed the robe and gown from her body.

"You're pretty good at that, aren't you?" she said when he'd gotten her naked.

"Only for you, sweetheart," he said against her throat before trailing a path with his tongue past her ear. "And there is something else I'd like to ask you."

"What?" She was barely able to get the word out before his hand lowered between her legs and he quickly moved to the honeyed warmth he knew awaited him there.

"Will you marry me?"

It seemed she had stopped breathing, and he leaned back and stared into her face. She returned his stare and he knew what she was doing. She had to see the sincerity of his question in his features, in his eyes, in the lips he then eased into an earnest smile.

He saw the single tear that fell from her eye before she smiled and said, "Yes, yes. I'll marry you. I'd almost given up hope that I would find him."

He lifted a brow. "Find who?"

"My knight in shining armor." She chuckled. "Little did I know he would be riding a motorcycle instead of a horse, but I'll take him any way I can. My Mr. Wrong became my Mr. Right. I love you so much."

"And I love you, too."

And then he was kissing her again, pulling her into his arms while their limbs entwined. And then he eased over her, slid between her legs, lifted her hips and stared down at her while he penetrated her. He'd never tire of looking down at her while they made love.

"Damn, I miss this. Damn, how I miss you," he said in between deep, languid thrusts. He didn't intend to rush. Instead he made love to her with the patience of a man who had all day and all night. He wondered if she noticed the difference in their lovemaking and figured eventually she would. She wrapped her legs around him and, lifting her hips off the bed, met his thrusts, stroke for stroke.

"Oh Jonas, I miss this, too," she said, as her inner muscles clenched him hard, trying to pull everything out of him.

He threw his head back and screamed her name at the same moment she screamed his. He gripped her hips tightly, needing as much of a connection with her as he could get.

And that's when he knew she felt him, felt him in a way no other woman had felt him before. He was exploding inside of her, christening her insides with his release.

Her shocked eyes looked up at him with delight when she realized he hadn't put on a condom. He didn't intend to use one ever again. This was the woman he would marry, and he wanted babies with her. No other man who would be her babies' daddy. With her he would share everything.

Moments later, when they were both spent, he slumped down in the bed and gathered her into his arms. They would sleep, wake up and make love, sleep and then make love some more. Later. Tomorrow. They would talk and lay out a strategic plan to tackle how they would make things work with her new job in L.A. They were and always would be a team.

"You forced me to realize I wanted the very things I thought I would never desire, Nikki," he whispered, emotions clogging his voice. "But I can see so clearly now and I know what I want, sweetheart. More than anything I want you."

And then he leaned down and slanted his mouth over hers, knowing this was the beginning, and for them there would never be an end.

Epilogue

A beautiful day in June

Nikki glanced around the ballroom that was filled with over five hundred guests who'd come to witness one of Phoenix's most notorious bachelors tying the knot. It had been the kind of wedding she'd always dreamed of having, with her mother and her mother-in-law working together. Her dream had come true.

She glanced across the room at her husband, who was talking to his father and some of his cousins. There were a lot of Steeles, more than she'd known existed, and now she was a part of the family. She and Jonas had decided to alternate living in L.A. and Phoenix. His idea for a satellite office had been a good one.

"You're such a beautiful bride," one of Jonas's female cousins, Cheyenne, the mother of triplets, told her, pulling her back into the conversation. They were standing there talking with Brittany and two more of Jonas's female cousins from Charlotte. Brittany was showing already, and she and Galen had found out a few months ago they would be having twins. Everyone in the Steele family was excited at the thought of multiple births again.

"Thanks." And she felt beautiful, because of Jonas. When she had walked down the aisle to him at the church, it was as if the two of them were the only ones there. The gaze that had held hers spoke volumes and had sent out several silent messages, ones that only she could decipher. That was a good thing. If anyone else had read his thoughts, they would have been scandalized.

"Ladies, I need to borrow my wife for a minute."

She glanced up when Jonas suddenly appeared by her side, sliding his hand into hers. He looked devastatingly handsome dressed in his white tux with his wavy hair flowing about his shoulders. His green eyes were sharp when he glanced down at her. "We'll be leaving in a few minutes and I thought we should say goodbye to our parents before we took off."

She beamed up at him. "Okay."

As a wedding gift, Mr. Fulton had given them the honeymoon suite on board the *Velocity*. They would remain in Dubai for two weeks and would return to the States on the *Velocity* when the airship came back through, making its rounds.

Halfway over to where their parents stood, Jonas stopped and pulled her into his arms and kissed her. She ignored the catcalls and whistles as she sank closer into her husband's embrace. When he finally released her, she smiled up at him. "And what was that for?"

He grinned. "I thought it was time for me to make another public claim. You're mine and I want the whole world to know it."

Nikki was filled with intense happiness. Her head and her heart were no longer at battle. Now they were on the same page, reading from the same script and the writing said *Jonas loves Nikki. Nikki loves Jonas. And they will live happily ever after.*

* * * * *

THE BOYFRIEND
ARRANGEMENT

ANDREA LAURENCE

One

"You have got to be kidding me!"

Sebastian West scanned his proximity card for the third time and yet the front door of BioTech—the biomedical technology company he co-founded—refused to open. Seeing his employees moving around inside, he pounded his fist on the glass, but all of them ignored him.

"I own this company!" he shouted as his secretary walked by without making eye contact. "Don't make me fire you, Virginia."

At that, she came to a stop and circled back to the door.

"Finally," he sighed.

But she didn't open the door as he'd expected. Instead she just shook her head. "I'm under strict orders from Dr. Solomon not to open the door for you, sir."

"Oh, come on," he groaned.

She couldn't be moved. "You'll have to take it up with him, sir." Then she turned on her heel and disappeared.

"Finn!" he shouted at the top of his lungs, pounding on the glass with angry fists. "Let me in, you son of a bitch."

A moment later Sebastian's former college roommate and business partner, Finn Solomon, appeared at the door with a frown on his face. "You're supposed to be on vacation," he said through the glass.

"That's what the doctor said, yeah, but since when do I take vacations? Or listen to doctors?" The answer was never. He certainly never listened to Finn. And as for vacation, he hadn't taken one in the decade since they'd started this company. You couldn't be off lying on a beach and also breaking barriers in medical technology. The two were incompatible.

"That's the whole point, Sebastian. Do you not recall that you had a heart attack two days ago? You're not supposed to be in the office for a minimum of two weeks."

"A mild heart attack. They didn't keep me in the hospital for more than a few hours. And they're not even sure I really had one. I'm taking the stupid pills they gave me, what more do you want?"

"I want you to go home. I'm not letting you in.

I've had your badge deactivated. I've also sent out a memo that anyone who lets you in the building will be terminated."

So much for piggybacking through the door behind someone else. He did have a laptop, though, if he could get Virginia to bring it out to him. That wouldn't technically be breaking the rules if he worked from home, right?

"I've also had your email and remote access accounts temporarily suspended, so you can't even work from home." Finn was always remarkably good at reading his mind. He'd been able to do it since they were in college. It was great for working together. Not so great for this scenario. "You are on mandatory medical leave, Sebastian, and as a doctor, I'm sorry, but I'm going to enforce it. I can handle things for two weeks, but I can't run this company with you dead. So get some R and R. Take a trip. Get a massage. Get a hand job. I really don't care. But I don't want to see you here."

Sebastian was at a loss. He and Finn had started this company after school, pouring their hearts and souls into technology that could make people's lives better. He was the MIT engineer and Finn was the doctor, a winning team that had developed advanced technologies like prosthetic hands and electric wheelchairs controlled by a patient's brain waves. That seemed a noble enough cause to dedicate his life to.

But apparently a decade of trading sleep and vegetables for caffeine and sugar had caught up with him.

Of course he didn't want to die; he was only thirty-eight. But he was close to a breakthrough on a robotic exoskeleton that could make paraplegics like his brother walk again.

"What about the new prototype for the exo-legs?"

Finn just crossed his huge forearms over his chest. "Those people have gone a long time without walking. They can wait two more weeks while you recover. If you keel over at your desk one afternoon, they'll never get it. As it is, I'm having a defibrillator installed on the wall outside your office."

Sebastian sighed, knowing he'd lost this fight. Finn was just as stubborn as he was. Normally that was a good match—they never knew when to take no for an answer. But that wouldn't benefit him in this situation. He knew the doctor's orders, yet he'd never once imagined that Finn would enforce them this strictly. He'd just thought he'd work ten-hour days instead of the usual eighteen.

"Can I at least come in and—?"

"*No*," Finn interrupted. "Go home. Go shopping. Just go away." With a smug expression Finn waved at him through the glass and then turned his back on his business partner.

Sebastian stood there for a moment, thinking maybe Finn would come back and tell him he was just kidding. When it was clear that Finn was deadly serious, he wandered back to the elevator and returned to the lobby of the building. He stepped out onto the busy Manhattan sidewalk with no real clue as to where he was going to go. He'd planned to take it easy for a few days and head back to work today. Now he had two full weeks of nothingness ahead of him.

He had the resources to do almost anything on earth that he wanted. Fly to Paris on a private jet. Take a luxury cruise through the Caribbean. Sing karaoke in Tokyo. He just didn't want to do any of those things.

Money was an alien thing to Sebastian. Unlike Finn, he'd never had it growing up. His parents had worked hard but as blue collar laborers they'd just never seemed to get ahead. And after his brother Kenny's ATV accident, they'd gone from poor to near destitute under the weight of the medical bills.

Scholarships and loans had gotten Sebastian through college, after which he'd focused on building his company with Finn. The company eventually brought money—lots of it—but he'd been really too busy to notice. Or to spend any. He'd never dreamed of traveling or owning expensive sports cars. Honestly, he was bad at being rich. He probably didn't even have twenty bucks in his wallet.

Stopping at a street corner, he pulled his wallet out of his back pocket and noticed the leather had nearly disintegrated over the years. He'd probably had this one since grad school. Maybe he should consider getting a new one. He had nothing better to do at the moment.

Up ahead, he spied Neiman Marcus. Surely they sold wallets. He made his way across the street and over to the department store. Sebastian stopped long enough to hold the door for a group of attractive women exiting with enough bags to put a kid through a semester or two of college. They looked vaguely familiar, especially the last one with the dark hair and steely blue eyes.

Her gaze flicked over him for a moment and he felt it like a punch to his gut. His pulse pounded in his throat as he tried to unsuccessfully swallow the lump that had formed there. He didn't know why he would have such a visceral reaction to the woman. He wanted to say something but he couldn't place the woman and decided to keep his mouth shut. Half a second later she looked away, breaking the connection, and continued on down the street with her friends.

Sebastian watched them for a moment with a touch of regret, then forced himself into the store. He made a beeline for the men's department and quickly selected a wallet. He wasn't particularly choosy with that sort of thing. He just wanted black leather and a slim profile with enough room for a couple cards and some cash. Easy.

As he found a register open for checkout, he no-

ticed a strikingly attractive brunette ahead of him.
Sebastian realized she was one of the women he'd
just seen leave the store a few minutes before. The
one with the blue-gray eyes. He wished he remembered who she was so he could say something to her.
They'd probably met at one event or another around
town—Finn forced him to go to the occasional party
or charity gala—he couldn't be sure, though. Most of
his brain was allocated to robotics and engineering.

Not all of it, though. He was red-blooded male
enough to notice her tall, lean figure, long, chestnut
hair, big blue eyes and bloodred lips. It was impossible not to notice how flawlessly she was put together.
She smelled like the meadow behind his childhood
home after a warm summer rain. Deep down inside
him something clenched tightly at the thought.

What was it about her? He told himself it was
probably nothing to do with her, exactly. The doctor
had told him to refrain from strenuous physical activity—*Yes, that includes sexual relations, Mr. West*—
for at least a week. It had been a while since he'd
indulged with a lady, but maybe since it was forbidden, his mind was focusing on what it couldn't have.

Why was he so terrible at remembering names?

As Sebastian got closer to the counter, he realized the woman was returning everything in her bag.
That was odd. If the register was correct, she'd just
purchased and immediately returned about fifteen
hundred dollars' worth of clothes. He watched as

she slipped out of her leather coat and shoved it into the empty department store bag, covering it with the packing tissue so you couldn't see inside.

His chronic boredom was temporarily interrupted as she piqued his curiosity with her actions. "Excuse m—" he started to say.

She turned suddenly and slammed right into his chest, forcing him to reach out and catch her in his arms before she stumbled backward on her sky-high heels and fell to the ground. He pulled her tight against him, molding her breasts to his chest until she righted herself. He found he really didn't want to let go when the time came. He was suddenly drunk on her scent and the feel of her soft curves pressing into his hard angles. How long had it been since he'd been this close to a woman? One he wasn't fitting a prosthetic to? He had no clue.

But eventually he did let go.

The woman took an unsteady step back, pulling herself together with a crimson flush blooming across her cheeks. "I am so sorry about that," she said. "I'm always in such a hurry that I don't pay attention to where I'm going."

There was a faint light of recognition in her blue-gray eyes as she looked up at him, so he knew he was right about meeting her somewhere before. "No, don't apologize," he said with a wry smile. "That's the most exciting thing to happen to me all week."

Her brow furrowed in disbelief.

Perhaps, he mused, he didn't look as boring as he was.

"Are you okay?" she asked.

He laughed off her concern. She was tall for a woman, especially in those stilettos, but he didn't really think she could inflict damage to him. "I'm fine. I'm just glad I was able to catch you."

She smirked and looked down self-consciously. "I suppose it could've been worse."

"You actually look really familiar to me, but I'm horrible with names. I'm Sebastian West," he said, offering her his hand in greeting.

She accepted it tentatively. The touch of her smooth skin gliding along his sent an unexpected spark through his nervous system. He was usually focused on work, and other pursuits, like sexual gratification and dating in general, typically took the back burner. But with one simple touch, physical desire was moved to the forefront.

Unlike their brief collision, this touch lingered skin-to-skin, letting him enjoy the flickers of electricity across his palm. The connection between them was palpable. So much so that when she pulled her hand away, she rubbed it gently on her burgundy sweater as if to dull the sensation.

"You do look familiar," she agreed. "I'm Harper Drake. We must've met around town. Perhaps you know my brother Oliver? Orion Computers?"

That sounded familiar enough. "He's probably

pals with my friend Finn Solomon. Finn knows everyone."

Harper narrowed her eyes for a moment, looking thoughtful. "That name sounds familiar, too. Wait… are you involved in some kind of medical supply business?"

Sebastian's brows rose in surprise. That wasn't exactly how he'd categorize what he did, but the fact that she remembered that much stunned him. And, to be honest, it pleased him just a little bit.

"You could say that." He grinned.

Harper beamed. She was pleased to finally place this guy in her mind. When she'd caught a glimpse of him earlier, he'd grabbed her attention. He'd looked so familiar when he'd held the door for her that she was certain she'd known him from somewhere. Unfortunately, Violet being so hell-bent on running up the street to pick up Aidan's wedding present had meant she couldn't stop.

Once she'd split from her best friends, Lucy Drake, Violet Niarchos and Emma Flynn, she'd stealthily circled back to Neiman Marcus to return everything she'd just bought. She couldn't have that weighing down her credit card for long. She hadn't expected to run into the familiar man again. Certainly not literally.

Real smooth, Harper.

"Okay, well then, I think it must've been one of the hospital benefits this past winter."

He nodded. "I do think I went to one of those. Finn tries to get me out every now and then."

Sebastian West didn't have a face she could forget, even if she lost context. He had a strong jaw, a nearly jet-black goatee, eyes just as dark, and a crooked smile that stirred something inside her. No, she'd remember him for sure. If she had a type, he'd be it.

It was a shame he wasn't one of the rich CEO guys her brother associated with all the time. She didn't mean to be shallow, but meeting a guy with his act together financially would certainly benefit her current situation. It would also make her feel a little better about how things would be handled once it all changed on her birthday.

The last seven years had been one long, hard lesson learned for Harper. One in the value of money the spoiled little rich girl she'd once been had never really experienced before. She would be the first to admit that her father had basically given her everything she'd wanted. After her mother died, he'd spoiled her. And continued to spoil her until he'd no longer had the resources.

Harper had never imagined that the well would run dry. When it had, she'd made a lot of necessary adjustments in her life. At least secretly. It was embarrassing enough that she'd blown all the money she'd inherited when she'd turned eighteen—especially since she was an accountant—she didn't need anyone else knowing about what she'd done.

After falling from the top of the world to her current spot near the bottom, she'd earned a whole new appreciation for money and for the people who were good at managing it. And soon, when she had money again, she intended to be very careful about how she handled it. That included triple-checking every guy she dated. Not that she intended to date Sebastian...

"Well, I'm glad we bumped into each other today," Sebastian said with a sly grin.

Harper chuckled. As her gaze broke away from Sebastian's for a moment, she saw Quentin—her ex, of all people—walking toward them. Grabbing Sebastian's arm, she turned them both toward a display of men's shoes, hoping maybe Quentin hadn't seen her. "I'm sorry," she muttered under her breath. "I'm trying to—"

"Harper?"

Damn it.

Harper turned to face the ex-boyfriend she'd done her best to avoid for the last two years. She stepped away from Sebastian, leaning in to give her ex a polite but stiff hug. "Hello, Quentin," she said in a flat, disinterested tone she knew he wouldn't pick up on. He never did.

"How have you been?"

Lonely. Anxiety-riddled. "I'm great. Never better. How about you?"

"Amazing. I actually just got engaged."

Engaged? Quentin was engaged. The one who didn't want to commit. If Harper hadn't already been feeling crappy about being the last single friend in her social circle, this moment would've been the straw that broke the camel's back. She pasted a fake smile on her face and nodded. "That's great. I'm happy for you."

Quentin didn't notice her lack of sincerity. "Thank you. Her name is Josie. She's amazing. I can't wait for you to meet her. I think you two would really get along."

Harper had to bite her tongue to keep from asking why his ex would have any interest in hanging out with his fiancée. "I'm sure we would."

"So, Harper…" Quentin said as he leaned in to her. His arrogant smile made her shoulders tense and the scent of his stinky, expensive cologne brought to mind nights with him she wished she could forget. "Will I be seeing you at Violet's wedding? It's the event of the year, I hear. I can't believe she's flying all the guests to Dublin for it. And renting out a castle! It's wild. Maybe I should've dated her instead of you." He chuckled and she curled her hands into fists at her sides.

"I am going," she said with a bright smile she hoped didn't betray her anxiety over the upcoming trip. "I'm one of her bridesmaids."

"Are you going alone?" Quentin cocked his head

in a sympathetically curious way that made her hackles rise.

Why would he assume she was going alone? They'd been apart for two years. He'd moved on. Surely she could've found someone to replace him by now. She hadn't, but she could've. "No. I'm not going alone. I'm bringing my boyfriend."

The minute the words passed her lips she regretted them. Why had she said that? Why? He mentions a fiancée and she loses her damn mind. She didn't have a boyfriend. She hadn't even committed to a house-plant. How was she supposed to produce a boyfriend in a couple days before the trip?

Quentin's eyes narrowed in disbelief. "Oh, really? I hadn't heard you were dating anyone lately."

Harper was surprised that he'd been paying attention. "I've learned to keep my private life private," she snapped. After their messy, public breakup, it had been another lesson hard learned. She hadn't even considered dating for six months after they'd ended due to the trauma of the whole thing.

"Well, who's the lucky guy? Do I know him? I look forward to meeting him at the wedding."

A name. She needed a name. Harper's mind went completely blank. Looking around the department store, her gaze fell on Sebastian as he perused a nearby display of dress loafers.

"You can meet him now. Sebastian, honey, could

you come over here for a minute? I'd like you to meet someone."

Sebastian arched his brow inquisitively at Harper as she mouthed the word "please" silently to him. He wandered over to where she was standing. "Yes, *dear*?"

"Sebastian, this is my ex, Quentin Stuart. I've mentioned him, haven't I? Anyway, I was just telling him about the two of us going to Ireland for Violet and Aidan's wedding."

Quentin stuck out his hand to Sebastian. "Nice to meet you, Sebastian…?"

"West. Sebastian West." He shook Quentin's hand and quickly pulled his away.

"Sebastian West as in BioTech?"

"Actually, yes."

Harper didn't recognize the name of the company, but then again she didn't know much about Sebastian because they weren't really dating. She remembered a brief discussion at a party about him working in medical supplies and how he didn't get out very much. She'd figured he'd sold wheelchairs and hospital beds or something. Maybe she'd been wrong. Quentin wasn't the type to waste brain power on remembering things that didn't impress him.

"Wow, Harper. Quite the catch you've got in this one." An uncomfortable expression flickered across his face and quickly disappeared. "Well, I've got to run. I was on my way to meet Josie and I'm already late. I'll see you two lovebirds on the plane to Dublin. I look forward to speaking with you some more, Sebastian."

Harper watched Quentin walk out of the store. Once he was gone, her face dropped into her hands. She just knew she was bright red with embarrassment. "I am so sorry," she muttered through her fingers.

Sebastian surprised her by laughing. "Want to tell me what that was all about?"

She peeked through her hands at him. "Um... Quentin is my ex. It was a messy breakup, but we still hang in the same social circles from time to time. When he asked about my date for the wedding we have coming up, I panicked. I told him you were my boyfriend. It's a long story. I shouldn't have dragged you into that, but he put me on the spot and you were standing right there." She gestured toward the display and shook her head. "I'm an ass."

"I doubt that," Sebastian said, a twinkle of laughter still in his dark brown eyes.

"No, I am. I've made the whole thing ten times worse because now I'm going to show up at the wedding without you and he's going to know I lied. And I just know he's going to show up with his beautiful, new fiancée and I'm going to feel even more like crap than I already do."

Harper knew she should've just owned that she was single. How bad would that have been? To just

state proudly that she'd been dating and not interested in settling down or settling on the wrong guy.
She was almost thirty, but that was hardly the end
of the world. In fact, *her* thirtieth birthday couldn't
come soon enough. It brought a twenty-eight-million-
dollar payout with it that she was desperate to get her
hands on.

"Don't worry about what he thinks," Sebastian
said. "He seems like a schmuck."

"I'm no good at the boyfriend thing. I have ques-
tionable taste in men," Harper admitted. "It's probably better that I just make up boyfriends instead of
finding another real one."

Sebastian nodded awkwardly. "I'm glad to help.
Well, I hope the wedding goes well for you."

"Thanks." She watched him leave. But with every
step he took, the more panicked she became. She had
no easy way of contacting this guy once he walked
out the door. She didn't want to let him get away
quite yet for reasons she wasn't ready to think about.
"Sebastian?" she nearly shouted before he got out
of earshot.

He stopped and turned back to her. "Yes?"

"How would you like to go on an all-expenses-
paid trip to Ireland?"

Two

Sebastian didn't know what to say. He'd never had a woman offer him a vacation, much less a woman he hardly knew. Actually he didn't have women offer him much of anything. It was impossible when he never left the lab. The only woman he was ever around on a daily basis was his assistant, Virginia, who was in her late fifties and married.

"Um, run that by me again?"

Harper closed the gap between them with an apologetic smile on her face and a sultry sway of her hips. So many of her features were almost masculine in a way, with piercing eyes, sharp cheekbones and an aquiline nose, but there was nothing masculine about her. Her dark brows were arched delicately over eyes that were like the stormy seas off Maine where he was born.

He imagined a similar maelstrom was stirring inside her to make an offer like that to a complete stranger. Surely she could find a romantic interest if she wanted one. But he was willing to say yes to almost anything she offered when she looked at him that way.

"My friends are getting married in Ireland next weekend. They're flying everyone there, plus putting all the guests up in a castle that's been converted into a hotel. It wouldn't cost you anything to go but some leave from work. I'm not sure what your boss is like, since this is short notice, but I was hoping you would be interested."

"In going to Ireland?"

She nodded. "With me. As my boyfriend. I just introduced you to Quentin as my boyfriend and said you were going, so he's going to expect you to be there."

His brow furrowed. Her boyfriend. For a week. In Ireland. What could go wrong? Absolutely everything. Pretending to be her lover could be complicated. But what could go right? His gaze raked over her tall, lean figure with appreciation. Everything could go very right, too.

Wait—*crap*—he wasn't supposed to be "active." Just his damn luck. "Just to be clear—are you wanting or expecting you and me to…um…"

"No!" Harper was quick to answer with wide eyes. "I mean, not for real. We'd have to pretend to be a couple around everyone else—kiss, be affectionate, you know. But when we're alone, I promise it's strictly hands off. I'm not that hard up. I just can't go to this thing alone. Not after seeing Quentin and finding out he's engaged. I just can't."

Sebastian blinked his eyes a few times and tried to mask some of his disappointment. He wasn't sure if he could stand being around her, touching her in public and then just flipping the switch when they were alone. The doctor wanted him to, but he wasn't the best at following doctor's orders.

This day had done well to throw him off his game. First, getting locked out at work with mandatory vacation and now this. A beautiful woman wanted him to travel with her to Ireland for free and pretend to be her lover. That just wasn't business as usual for him. He wasn't entirely sure what to say to her. It seemed foolish to say yes and downright stupid to say no.

"I'll pay you two thousand dollars to go. It's all the money I have in my savings account," Harper added, sweetening the pot as she seemed to sense his hesitation.

She was serious. Her insecurity struck him as odd considering how confident and put together she seemed. He wasn't sure why this was so important to her. There must be more to the situation with her ex than she was telling. "Aren't your friends going to wonder where I came from? You've never spoken about me before and suddenly I'm your wedding date?"

Harper waved away his concern. "I'll take care of that. My friends have been so wrapped up in their own lives lately they'd probably not notice if I did have a boyfriend. They certainly haven't mentioned that I don't have one."

"And why is that?" Sebastian couldn't stop himself from asking. But if he was going to pretend to be her boyfriend, he needed to know if there was something about her that repelled men. From where he was standing, he didn't see a thing wrong with her. She was beautiful, well-spoken, poised and polished. Aside from the slight hint of desperation in her voice, she seemed like quite the catch. There had to be something wrong with her.

She shrugged and sort of fidgeted before responding, showing the first sign of vulnerability, which he was glad to see. "Like I said, I don't have the best taste in men. Things haven't worked out with anyone I've been attracted to since Quentin and I broke up."

"You can't find a decent man to go to dinner with you, but you trust me enough to travel across the ocean with you, share a bedroom and make out in front of your friends?" There was a flaw in her logic here. "I could be crazy. Or a criminal. Or married. I could attack you in your sleep or steal your jewelry. The possibilities are endless."

Harper scoffed at his trepidations. "Honestly, I take that risk on every date I go on in this town. Have you seen the guys on Tinder lately? No…you probably haven't." She chuckled. "I know you have a job, you smell nice, you're handsome and you went along with my lie just now, so you're easygoing. You're already a head and shoulders over every date I've had in the last six months. If you don't want to go, or can't, just say so. But don't turn it down because you're concerned about my blatant disregard for my own welfare or poor sense of judgment. My friends are already well aware of that flaw in my character."

"No, I can go. As of this morning my schedule is amazingly wide open for the next two weeks." That was an understatement. But was this what he should spend his time doing? He didn't exactly have a more tempting offer.

"Do you find me physically repulsive?"

Sebastian swallowed hard. "Not at all. To the contrary, you're the most beautiful woman I've laid eyes on in a very long time."

Harper's eyes widened a touch at his answer, but she quickly recovered with a sly smile curling her lips. It must have boosted her confidence because she moved a step closer to him, closing the gap until they were nearly touching. "Do you think you'd have trouble pretending to be my lover? Or have a problem kissing me?"

Every muscle in Sebastian's body tightened as

she spoke. The warmth of her body and the scent of her so close caused an instant physical reaction that would answer any of her questions if she bothered to notice. He balled his hands into fists at his sides to keep from reaching for her. He'd craved the sensation of touching her again since the moment he'd let her go after the collision.

He shook his head stiffly. "No. I think I can manage that."

Harper's gaze never left his. "Okay, great. Are you opposed to a free trip to Europe? You have a passport, right?"

"I have a passport, yes." It had no stamps in it, but he had one. Finn did most of the travel around the world, schmoozing on behalf of their company. Sebastian kept his nose in his paperwork and schematics, but Finn had made him get a passport anyway.

"Okay. Then I see no reason why you shouldn't say yes."

Neither did he. Why was he making this so hard?

It really was a simple thing. He had no reason not to go. All he had to do was walk around Ireland with this stunning woman on his arm. He had no intention of taking her money, but a trip would be a nice distraction without any work on his plate for the next few weeks. What else was he going to do? Finn was right that he could help more people healthy than dead, but taking a break was hard for him. Being a couple thousand miles from his work would make it easier.

"When do you leave for the wedding?"

"Monday afternoon."

"It's Friday morning. Three days? Are you serious? Won't your friend think it odd that you're suddenly adding a guest to her wedding on such short notice?"

"Not really. I RSVP'd for two. I just needed to find my plus one."

"You're cutting it awfully close. Desperate?"

"I prefer to think of it as optimistic."

"Three days…" he repeated. Something about this whole situation struck him as insane, but there was a fine line between insanity and genius.

"So does your silent resignation mean you're at least considering coming with me?" Harper grinned wide, her whole expression lighting up with excitement.

It was hard for him to turn her down when she looked at him like that. He wanted her to keep looking at him that way for as long as possible. "Well, yes, I am. I'm just not sure I'll make a very good boyfriend, fake or otherwise. I'm kinda out of practice."

"I'm not worried about that." Harper leaned into him and wrapped her arms around his neck in an unexpectedly intimate way. His whole body stiffened as she pressed against him. "You know what they say."

Sebastian took a deep breath and tried to wish

away the sudden rush of desire that coursed through his veins as she stood close. It seemed wrong to react like this to a woman he'd just met, despite how easily she was able to coax it out of him. "What's th-that?" He stuttered in his response, something he hadn't done since elementary school. She had managed to get under his skin so quickly.

"Practice makes perfect."

He nodded. "I've heard that."

Harper frowned, lowered her arms and looked down to where his hands were tensely curled at his sides. She took them in her own and moved each one to rest at the curve of her hips. "Relax, Sebastian. I'm not going to bite. We've got to be a lot more comfortable touching each other if we're going to convince anyone we're really together."

He splayed his fingers across her denim-clad hips and pressed the tips into the ample flesh there. With her so close, he wanted to lean down and kiss her. Her full, pouting lips and wide, innocent eyes seemed to plead for it. Indulging seemed like the natural thing to do. She felt good against him. Perhaps too good for the middle of Neiman Marcus. There was definitely not going to be a problem faking attraction with Harper. The problem would be pretending that the attraction wasn't real when no one was watching.

"I'll go," he blurted out, almost surprising himself.

Harper stiffened in his arms, looking up at him

with a smile that was hesitant to believe him. "Are you serious?"

Sebastian nodded. "Yes, I'm serious. I'll go to Ireland with you as your fake boyfriend."

With a squeal of excitement, Harper hugged him tight. Before he could prepare himself, she pressed her mouth to his. He was certain it was supposed to be a quick, thank-you peck, but once their lips touched, there was no pulling away.

Sebastian wasn't imagining the palpable sexual energy between them. The way Harper curved against his body and opened her mouth to him was proof of that. He wanted to take it further, to see how powerful their connection really was, but this was neither the time nor the place, so he pulled away while he still could.

Harper lingered close, a rosy flush highlighting her cheeks. "Listen, I've got to go. Would you care to walk me to my apartment? I don't live far."

"I can't." He wanted to—quite badly—but he got the feeling it was an invitation better declined at the moment if they were going to spend the next week together. Things could get weird before they even left.

Harper pulled away just enough to let a chill of air rush in where the heat of her body had been. "Why not?"

He picked up the wallet he'd set down on a display when he'd spoken with Quentin. "I still have to buy this."

A light of amusement lit her eyes. "You're so literal. I can wait while you check out."

It would be so easy to say yes. He took a deep breath and thought up another valid reason. "I also have some things to take care of if I'm going with you on Monday."

Harper pouted for a moment before she nodded and covered her disappointment with a smile. "Okay. Well, I'm going out with my girlfriends tomorrow, but how about we get together on Sunday night? We can get to know each other a little better before we get on the plane."

"At your apartment?"

"A bar is probably a better idea. Being you're a stranger and all, right?"

He breathed a sigh of relief. He could avoid temptation in a bar. Once they got to Ireland, he wasn't so sure. "That sounds good."

"Give me your phone."

Sebastian handed over his cell phone and Harper put her information into his contacts.

"Text me so I have your information, too. We'll get together Sunday."

With a smile and a wave, Harper handed over his phone and disappeared from the store. Sebastian watched her walk away and, with every step she took, was more and more convinced that he was making a big mistake.

* * *

"I know that we're leaving Monday and I should probably be packing or getting ready, but I really needed one last girls' night before we go." Violet eased back into the sofa cushions with a large glass of wine in her hand. "Why didn't any of you tell me how stressful weddings could be?"

"Well, Oliver and I eloped, so it wasn't stressful at all," Lucy said. "Besides, in the end it's just a party. Now, nine-month-old twins…that's stressful."

Harper chuckled at her new sister-in-law's observation. The twins—Alice and Christian—were little darlings, but the minute they started walking, she got the feeling they would be tiny tornadoes of destruction. Especially Alice. She was a little spitfire, like her namesake, their great-great-aunt Alice.

"No one said you had to fly all your friends and family halfway around the world to get married," Harper pointed out, taking a sip of her wine. "You could've had a ridiculously expensive and over-the-top affair here in Manhattan like Emma did."

Emma came into the room with a frown pulling down the corners of her flawlessly painted rose lips. "My wedding was not over the top. It was small and tasteful."

Harper arched an eyebrow and laughed. "You may have only had thirty people there, but I'd hardly classify it as small and tasteful."

"I had a beautiful reception."

"You had an ice vodka luge," Harper challenged.

Emma twisted her lips and sighed. "That was Jonah's thing. He insisted." She settled beside Violet on the couch. "And it would've been ten times bigger if my mother'd had her way. You saw what she did with my baby shower. But seriously, don't stress too badly about the wedding, Vi. It's in Ireland. In a castle! It will be beautiful, I promise."

"It will," Lucy chimed in. "You've got an amazing wedding planner who has it under control. The best in the city. All you need to do is show up and marry the love of your life. That's easy."

Violet smiled. "You're right. Aidan has told me the same thing a dozen times. I just can't stop stressing out about every little detail. In a week from today I'll be Mrs. Aidan Murphy! Have I forgotten something?"

"If you have, it doesn't really matter. As long as both of you show up, say I do and sign your license with a qualified officiant, you'll be married at the end of the day. Everything else is just details," Emma said.

Violet nodded. "You're right. I know you're right. I just need to say it until I believe it. What about you guys? Are you packed and ready to leave yet?"

The women around the coffee table nodded. "Everything is ready. Just a few more things to throw in the luggage before we go. We're leaving the twins with Oliver's dad," Lucy said. "That's the biggest stressor for me. I haven't been away from them since they were born, but there's no way I'm flying overseas with twins at that age.

"Knox is older than the twins, so I'm hoping he does okay on the flight. It will be his first," Violet explained. "I couldn't leave him behind, though. It seems wrong to marry his father without having him there."

"Of course. I'm sure he'll do great. Georgette is staying with my parents, but they'll have her nanny with them, so I'm not worried." Emma turned to Harper. "What about you? Are you ready to go? At least you don't have men and kids to wrangle before the trip. I almost forget what it's like to just have to worry about myself."

"Yep," Harper said. She took a deep breath and prepared herself to tell the story she'd come up with after talking to Sebastian. Her intention was to tell them as little as possible, but she knew she had to fill the girls in on her new beau before the trip. They were the only ones who would really care. If she sold the story to them, everyone else would take it at face value.

Including Quentin. Hopefully. If he didn't buy it, there was no point in continuing the ruse. This whole ridiculous scheme was designed with the sole purpose of making him believe she had someone in her life. That she wasn't pathetically single and still pining for him. Because she was anything but pining. She was glad to have Quentin out of her life. He was just too egomaniacal to see her single status as anything other than a reflection of her wishing they were still together.

Selling it to her friends wouldn't be so easy, though.

"I've got the dress, the passport and…uh…the boyfriend all ready to go." She said the words quickly and then waited for the inevitable response.

Emma, Violet and Lucy all paused as anticipated and turned to look at her. The questions came too fast and furiously for her to respond to any of them.

"What?"

"Your boyfriend?"

"Am I missing something, here?"

Harper winced and nodded when they finally quieted down. "Yeah, um, his name is Sebastian." She got up to refill her wine and stall the conversation a moment. She was going to need some alcohol to get through this conversation. When she came back into the room from the kitchen, the girls were sitting frozen in place with expectant looks on their faces. "He's the guy I've been seeing for a few months."

"Months?" Violet wailed. "You've been seeing a guy for *months* and didn't think to mention it to us?"

"You guys have all been busy with your own lives. Babies, weddings…" Harper explained. "And, to be honest, I didn't want to jinx it. It wasn't that serious at first and I got tired of mentioning guys to you all and then we didn't get past the third date. Things were going well, so I wasn't ready to talk about him yet. Just in case."

"And now you're ready to talk? 'Cause you're sure as hell going to give us every detail," Lucy sassed.

Harper shrugged. Not really, but the time had come to spill some information if she was going to pull this off. "I guess I have to if I want to bring him on the trip."

"I noticed you RSVP'd for two, but you left off the guest's name," Violet said. "I was wondering what that meant."

"Yeah, I was hopeful that things would work out for him to come," Harper continued to lie, noting that after pretending she had money for a decade, pretending to have a boyfriend wasn't as hard as she'd thought it would be. "But if it fell apart between us, I thought I might bring a friend. Or no one. But things are great and so Sebastian is coming. I'll give you his information to add to the travel manifest."

"I'm eager to meet him," Emma said. "And intrigued. You haven't really had much luck dating since you and Quentin broke up. Where did you two meet? He's not one of your Tinder finds, is he?"

"Oh, no. Those were a mess. I actually met Sebastian at one of the hospital fund-raisers this winter. The one raising money for the orthopedics center, I think." That, at least, wasn't a lie. They had met there. They just hadn't started dating. "He works with medical equipment. He can tell you more about all that. Anyway, we hit it off and he asked me to dinner. Things have just sort of progressed from there."

"Wait," Violet said, sitting at attention on the sofa. "We were all at that fund-raiser. Do we know him? Sebastian who?"

"Sebastian West." Harper was suddenly nervous that maybe they did know him. She and Sebastian hadn't gotten together to talk yet, so she ran the risk of getting caught not knowing something obvious about him if any of the girls knew who he was. Quentin had recognized his name and company, so it was a possibility.

Thankfully none of them perked up at hearing his full name. "I doubt any of you know him. He spends more time working than socializing. He's super smart. I'm excited for you all to meet him." She grinned wide and hoped she was selling her story.

"We're all excited," Violet echoed as her eyes narrowed at Harper in suspicion. "I can't wait for Monday."

Harper took a large sip of her wine and nodded with feigned enthusiasm. "Me neither."

Three

Sunday evening Sebastian arrived at the bar a full fifteen minutes before he was supposed to meet Harper. He wasn't particularly anxious about their meeting, but he couldn't stand just sitting around his apartment any longer. He'd sat there for the last two days trying to fill the hours. Without work, he found he had far too many minutes on his hands.

He'd spent as long as he could packing and preparing for the trip. He'd taken his clothes and his tuxedo to the cleaner. He'd carefully collected his toiletries and underthings, but that had taken only a few hours out of his newfound free time.

Sebastian had tried reading a book. He'd watched some television. Both had bored him after a short while. By Sunday afternoon he'd had nothing to do but pace around his apartment and wish away the hours. He wasn't sure how he'd get through the next two weeks if he hadn't met Harper and had this trip to Ireland fall into his lap. He might just go insane. How was that supposed to improve his health? Mentally weak but physically strong? What good was that?

When his watch showed it was almost time to meet Harper, he'd rushed out the door. He'd taken a table in a quiet corner, ordered himself a gin and tonic with lime—ignoring doctor's orders—and awaited her arrival with his notebook open to read over some notes. He carried it almost everywhere he went, writing down ideas and schematics when they popped into his head. He'd learned the hard way that he could lose the spark of inspiration if he didn't immediately capture it.

This way he was still waiting, but at least he was out of the house and potentially doing something productive in the meantime. Thankfully, Harper showed up a few minutes later. She was looking attractive and fashionable once again with layered lace tops and a long sweater over skinny jeans. Today her dark hair was pulled up into a bun, highlighting the line of her neck and her dangly earrings.

Sebastian was once again struck by the fact that this woman should be able to find a boyfriend easily. He didn't understand why he was even there pretending to be one. Then again, the same thing could probably be said of him. Life was complicated sometimes.

"Thanks for coming. And thanks for doing all of this," she said as she settled into her chair across from him.

"No problem. Would you like a drink?"

"Just water for me," she said with a polite smile. It surprised him. A glass of wine or a martini seemed far more her speed. He didn't question it, however, and waved down the bartender for her water.

"Are you packed and ready to go?" she asked.

"Mostly. What about you?"

"The same. I feel like I'm not ready, although I can't imagine what I haven't packed yet."

"Don't forget the slinky lingerie," Sebastian said. The sudden image of Harper wearing some kind of silk-and-lace chemise came to his mind and made him immediately regret his words. He didn't need that vision haunting him over their next week together.

"What?" Harper's eyes were suddenly wide with concern.

"It was a joke," Sebastian soothed. And that's what he'd intended it to be, even if a part of him wouldn't mind if she threw a nice piece or two in there.

"Oh," she said, visibly relaxing. Apparently the idea of being his girlfriend for real was not nearly as appealing to her as it was in his own mind. "Yeah, no, I'm packing the ugliest pajamas I've got."

"Flannel footie pajamas with a zip front?" he asked.

"Yep. I'll be dressed as a giant pug dog."

Interesting. "Trapdoor for convenience?"

"No, just a front zipper, but they do have a tail and a hood with puppy ears and a nose I can pull up."

"Excellent. Since pugs aren't my thing, I'm sure the sight of you in that dog outfit will squelch any misplaced attraction that might arise between us."

"Perhaps I should buy you one, too. I saw one that was basically a poop emoji costume."

"Not Spider-Man or Deadpool? You went straight for the poop emoji?"

"Yeah, sorry."

They both laughed for a few moments and the tension dissipated between them. Sebastian was relieved. He didn't want either of them to be uncomfortable. It would make the week ten times longer than it would be already.

"So tell me everything I should know about you," Harper began. "I'm your girlfriend, after all, so I need to know all the important things."

Sebastian tried not to wince at the thought of talking about himself. He hated doing that. He tried to think of what he would share with someone if he were really dating them, but he found he didn't know the answer to that, either. "I'm from Maine. A small coastal town called Rockport, specifically. I went to MIT. Technically, I'm a mechanical engineer, but I've branched out quite a bit after college."

"I thought you worked for a medical supply company."

Sebastian frowned. That was probably his fault. He liked to keep the details of his work vague. "Not exactly. BioTech is a medical research and development company. My partner Finn and I develop new medical technology."

"Your partner? You mean you don't just work there?"

"Eh, no. We started the company together out of college. I own it."

Harper frowned, wrinkles creasing her forehead. "Are you serious? I offered you every penny I had in savings to go on this trip and you're the CEO of a company? You probably make more in an afternoon than I do in a paycheck."

Sebastian held up his finger in protest. "You offered me the money. I never said I would actually take it. And I'm not going to, of course."

"So you're rich. Why didn't you say something? Like when Quentin asked about your company?"

At that, Sebastian shrugged. "I'm not the kind to flaunt it. Finn is the face of the company. I'm the mad scientist behind the scenes. I'm happy with the anonymity. I've seen how being well-known and wealthy has complicated his love life and I'm not interested in that."

"In a love life?" Harper asked with an arched brow.

"In a *complicated* love life. Or, hell, maybe a reg-

ular one. I work too much for any type of relationship to succeed."

"But you're going to drop everything and go with
me on a trip to Ireland on short notice?"

Sebastian sat back in his chair and sighed. It would
be easy to tell her that he'd had a heart attack and
was on mandatory vacation, but he didn't want to. He
didn't like people knowing his business, especially
when it changed how they perceived him. Whether
it was knowing he was rich, or sick, or used to be
poor…it didn't matter. He liked private things to stay
private. "When you're the boss, you can do what you
want," he responded instead.

She shook her head. "I can't believe you didn't
say anything until just now. What if I hadn't asked?
Would you have waited until someone recognized
you on the plane and I looked like a fool for not
knowing my boyfriend is a millionaire?"

"Of course not! I would've told you. And you're
one to point fingers, Harper. You're keeping plenty
of secrets yourself."

She straightened in her chair and narrowed her
gaze at him. "What is that supposed to mean?"

"I saw you walk out of Neiman Marcus with your
friends. Then you ditched them and came back ten
minutes later to return everything you'd bought.
What is that about? It's not buyer's remorse, I'm
pretty certain."

Harper's lips twisted in thought as she considered her answer. "I'm trying to save money."

Sebastian looked at her with a pointed expression on his face. There was more to it than just frugality, of that he was sure. He'd done his research since they'd met. Her family owned Orion Computers. She lived in a really nice apartment on the Upper East Side. But she only had two grand in her savings account? That didn't add up in his mind.

His silence prompted her to keep talking. "I'm having a bit of a cash flow shortage. I'm embarrassed about it, so I haven't told anyone, even my friends and family. Until I get things straightened out, I'm trying to be smart about my money, but I have to keep up appearances."

"Like blowing a fortune on designer clothes and then immediately returning them?"

"Yes."

"Don't they notice you never wear them after you buy them?"

She shook her head. "You need a map to get through my closet. Things disappear in there, never to resurface."

Sebastian nodded thoughtfully. "Sounds like a complicated charade to keep up. Pretending to have a boyfriend should be a piece of cake."

"Well, thankfully it's a short-term thing. I should be back on my feet soon and then no one needs to know I lied about it. And as for you and me...well,

I'm sure we will have a sad, but not unexpected, breakup not long after we get back from the trip. Not so soon as to be suspicious, but we can't wait too long or people might start inviting us to things as a couple here in town."

"Sounds tragic. I'm already sad."

Harper looked at him with a smile. "I'm enjoying your sarcastic sense of humor. We might actually be able to pull this off."

"I think so, too. Of course, over time I think you're going to become too clingy for me and we're going to want different things from our relationship."

She groaned. "Ugh. You sound like Quentin. Don't do that or we'll have to just break up now."

Sebastian laughed. "So since we're going to be around that guy, should I know what happened between you two?"

Harper winced at the thought. "That is a story that would require something stronger than water to talk about."

"A cocktail then? My treat," Sebastian added. He waved over the bartender. It wasn't until then that it occurred to him she might be drinking water out of necessity, not desire.

"That's sweet of you. A Cosmo, please."

Once the man returned with the dark pink beverage, Harper took a sip and sighed. "We were together for three years and we've been broken up for two. We met at a party and we really seemed to hit it off.

Things went well between us, but I noticed that it didn't seem to be going anywhere. We'd stalled out at the point where most people take the next step."

"He didn't want anything serious?"

"I thought we were already serious, but I suppose that was my mistake. I was thinking we were on track to get engaged, moving in together…do all the things that other couples around me were doing. But he was always working. Or said he was. He's an attorney and kept insisting he had to put in the long hours if he was going to make partner. I thought it was because he wanted to build a solid future for us, but the truth was that he was perfectly content where we were."

"He was seeing other women."

"Bingo. While I was officially his girlfriend in the public eye, I found out there were three of us he was keeping on the hook. He used long hours at work as his excuse to run around town with different women, and I didn't even question it. I don't know if he couldn't decide and thought that he'd eventually know which one he wanted, or if he just liked keeping that many balls up in the air at once. But eventually I found out about the others and broke it off. When I confronted him, all he said was that he just wasn't ready for a commitment."

Sebastian frowned. "He told you the other day that he's engaged now, didn't he?"

Harper's posture deflated slightly in her chair and he found he hated that. He wanted to punch Quentin in the face for taking such a beautiful, confident woman and leaving her broken.

"Yes," she said softly. "He's bringing her on the trip. You see why I can't go alone? I just can't face him and his fiancée in the state I am in. I'm almost thirty. I'm happy with my life on most days, but I have to admit that I'm not at all where I expected to be at this point. I'm sure everyone else looks at me and thinks I'm the sad, single one in the group."

Sebastian understood. He knew what it was like to be judged by people. While Harper had worked hard to keep up appearances, he'd simply buried his head in his research and tried to block out the rest of the world. It had served him pretty well. Eventually, though, he'd known his avoidance mechanisms would fall apart. His had fallen apart when he'd hit the floor in cardiac arrest. Hers might all come crashing down when her delicately structured pyramid of falsehoods took a hit. He hoped he wouldn't be the reason it fell.

"I will strive to be the imaginary boyfriend you've always dreamed of having someday."

"You go up first," Sebastian said as they stood on the tarmac together. "I prefer to sit in the aisle seat if you don't mind."

Harper nodded and climbed the steps ahead of him to board the private plane. The minute she stepped on and turned the corner, she realized the Boeing Business Jet that Violet's father, Loukas Niarchos, had chartered for the flight wasn't going to be like any plane she'd been on before. Instead of a first-class cabin, she found herself walking through a lounge with a bar, seating areas with couches and swivel chairs, flat-panel televisions and a variety of tables. To the left there was a doorway leading to an executive office where she could see Loukas already chatting on the phone, his laptop open.

A flight attendant greeted them with a smile and directed them through the lounge into the next room to the right. There they found what could be either a conference room or a dining table that sat twenty for a meal. Each chair was plush camel-colored leather with a seat belt if it was necessary. Harper got the feeling the kind of people who chartered flights on this plane wouldn't tolerate turbulence.

"This is like being on Air Force One," Sebastian muttered into her ear as they walked through a narrow hallway past a fully appointed bedroom suite, two full-size bathrooms with showers, and a galley kitchen currently manned by two more smiling flight attendants. "Is this how you're used to traveling?"

Harper shook her head. "No. I'm used to boring old first class unless I'm traveling with family on the Orion corporate jet. That's nice, but it only seats eight. And there's no bedroom. Or office. Or cocktail lounge. My family is normal rich, not filthy rich."

Sebastian chuckled and nudged her forward.

"Good. I don't think I could handle a filthy-rich girl-friend. I'm glad this is a first for us both."

At that point, the plane finally opened up into a traditional seating area. Appointed like a large, first-class cabin, there were six seats in each row. They were in sets of two, divided by two wide aisles. Each seat had its own television screen, blanket, pillow, and controls that allowed its occupant to lay fully flat for sleeping on the overnight flight. A flute of champagne and a chocolate-covered strawberry stenciled with the letters *V&A* in edible gold awaited each guest at their seat as well as a handwritten card in calligraphy with each person's name.

Violet was certainly out to throw a memorable wedding, if nothing else.

They'd been assigned row thirteen of sixteen, seats A and B, so she made her way down the right aisle through the crowd of familiar faces. They were nearly the last to board, so the area was bustling with activity as guests settled in. Quentin hadn't been kidding when he'd said this wedding was the event of the year. People salivated over the idea of receiving a coveted invitation, but the guest list had been kept down to less than a hundred by virtue of the plane and the wedding venue.

Even then, Harper still knew almost everyone on the plane. A few friends and family of Violet's fiancé, Aidan, were unfamiliar to her, but there were far more of Violet's circle than anyone. She smiled and waved politely as she pressed on, even when she saw Quentin in the back row on the far left. He was sitting beside an attractive brunette who seemed a little young for him, but Harper was trying not to let her bitterness color her opinion.

"Here we go," she said as she stopped at their row. Emma and Jonah were seated across the aisle from them in the center section, and Harper could see Emma was already heavily appraising Sebastian from her seat. She tried not to focus on that, instead stowing her bag and her coat in the overhead bin to clear the aisle for others to board.

"Introductions!" Emma said before Harper could even slide into the row to sit.

She pasted on a bright smile and turned their way. "Sebastian, these are my good friends Jonah and Emma Flynn. I work for Jonah's gaming software company, FlynnSoft. You guys, this is my boyfriend, Sebastian West."

Jonah stuck out his hand and the two men exchanged a firm handshake. "Good to meet you both," Sebastian said. "Harper has told me how much she enjoys her job at FlynnSoft. I'm sure that reflects well on you, Jonah."

She tried not to look impressed and instead turned toward her seat. It wasn't until that moment that she noticed a small, white envelope on the window seat. She picked the envelope up and settled in so Sebastian could take his place at her side. She looked around, wondering who might've put it on her seat, but no one seemed to be looking or paying any attention to her. There weren't envelopes like this one on the other seats. Just one for her, with her name written on the front in nondescript block letters.

While Sebastian put his bag in the overhead bin, Harper opened the envelope and pulled out the single page inside. It was handwritten, and relatively short, but it delivered a huge impact.

I know your little secret. If you don't want everyone to find out the truth and risk your big inheritance, you'll do exactly what I say. Once we arrive in Ireland, you'll go to the bank and withdraw a hundred thousand dollars. Then you'll leave it in an envelope at the front desk of the hotel for "B. Mayler" by dinnertime tomorrow. Miss the deadline and I'm going to make a big problem for you, Harper.

She read the words a dozen times, trying to make sense of it all, but there was no way to make sense of what she was seeing. Her heart was pounding in her ears, deafening her to anything but the sound of her internal panic. The fantastic plane and everyone on it faded into the background.

This was blackmail. She was being blackmailed. How was that even possible?

Harper had been so careful about her secret. Aside from sharing some of it with Sebastian yesterday, no one, not her closest friends or family, knew the truth. Not even her brother or father knew about her financial difficulties. She'd kept it quiet for over eight years, working hard to make ends meet until the next payment came and she didn't have to fake it any longer. Sebastian had been the first to question her curious behavior, and it hadn't seemed to hurt to share a little information with him considering her birthday was right around the corner.

But someone had found out her secret, and that was a big problem.

Her grandfather on her mother's side of the family had set up a thirty-million-dollar trust fund for both her and her brother when they were born. It included a two-million-dollar payment on their eighteenth birthdays followed by a twenty-eight-million-dollar payment on their thirtieth birthdays. Harper's thirtieth was only a few weeks away now. She could see the light at the end of the tunnel. She should be coasting to the finish line, but her foolish youthful behavior had put everything at risk.

After her father ran into financial troubles with his gold-digging second wife, her grandfather had added a new provision to the grandchildren's trusts—if it was discovered that they had been financially irresponsible with their first payments, there would be no second payment. Ever-responsible Oliver had had no problem managing his money and had made his own fortune many times over. He hardly needed the second payment by the time his thirtieth birthday came around. But not Harper. By the time the provision was added, her frivolous lifestyle had already helped her blow through most of the first two million.

When she found out about the addendum, she'd realized she had to keep her situation a secret. Her grandfather couldn't find out or she'd risk the money she desperately needed. That second payment would put an end to her charade. She wouldn't have to eat ramen noodles for weeks to pay her massive building fee at the beginning of the year. She wouldn't have to return everything she bought and scour the thrift stores for designer finds to keep up her facade of a spoiled heiress. Harper wouldn't blow this new money—she wasn't a naive child any longer—but it would be nice not to have to pretend she had more than two grand in her savings account.

Thankfully that two thousand dollars she'd earmarked for Sebastian could stay put. It was all she had aside from her FlynnSoft 401K with its stiff withdrawal penalties. Where was she going to come up with a hundred thousand dollars by tomorrow? In a month, easy. But now…it was an impossible task.

"Are you okay?"

Harper quickly folded the letter closed and shoved it back into the envelope. She looked over at Sebastian, who had settled into his seat and buckled up. "I'm fine," she said. "Just reading over something."

"You look like the plane is about to crash," he

noted. "You're white as a sheet. Since they haven't even closed the cabin door yet, I was concerned."

"Flying isn't my favorite thing," she lied, and slipped the note into her purse. "Even on a fancy jet like this. My doctor gave me some pills and I hope to wake up in Ireland before I know it."

"Sleep? And miss a minute of this luxurious travel?" Sebastian picked up his crystal champagne flute. "Shall we toast before you slip into a drug-induced coma?"

Harper picked up her drink and fought to keep her hand from trembling with nerves. "What should we drink to?"

"To a safe, fun and *romantic* trip," he suggested with a knowing smile.

"I'll drink to that." She gently clinked her glass to his and downed the entire flute in one nervous gulp. Sebastian arched a curious eyebrow at her, but she ignored him. She needed some alcohol, stat, before that note sent her into hysterics.

Turning away from him, she fastened her seat belt, sat back and closed her eyes.

"You'll be fine," he soothed. "You're surrounded by friends and family. I'm here to hold your hand through the whole flight if you need me to. You don't have a thing to worry about."

Normally he would be right, and if her nerves were over flying, it might be helpful. But she couldn't feel safe and relax knowing that one of the people on this plane—one of her very own friends and family—was her blackmailer.

This was going to be a long trip.

Four

"What a great room!"

Harper followed Sebastian into their room at the hotel, grateful to finally be there. The flight itself had been uneventful once they'd taken off. She'd taken the pills with another glass of champagne—probably not the best idea—and woken when the wheels touched down in Dublin. Even if she'd had the money to pay her blackmailer, she hadn't had the chance to stop at a bank and get it. Two chartered luxury buses had picked them up at the airport and transported everyone on the nearly three-hour drive through the Irish countryside to their final destination of Markree Castle. The castle and its sprawling grounds had been renovated into a hotel and the entire location had been rented to house their group and host the wedding and reception.

Sebastian had looked out the window on the bus, contentedly taking in the lush green landscape as it went by, but Harper hadn't been able to enjoy it. Every person who'd passed by her was run through a mental checklist of potential guilt or innocence. She supposed that was the most unnerving part of it all. This wasn't just some random internet criminal who'd dug up some dirt and tried to make a dime off her. It was someone she knew. Someone she trusted. She couldn't quite wrap her head around that.

Like she didn't already have enough to worry about on this trip. She eyeballed Sebastian as he sat on the bed and gave it a test bounce. It wasn't a large bed—a double perhaps—which would mean close quarters at night. Harper hadn't thought much about that when she'd concocted this plan. A lot of hotels in Europe had twin beds and that was what she'd expected. Just her luck that they'd end up with a room obviously appointed for lovers. Lovers who wanted to be close all the time.

She'd have to thank Violet for hooking her up, she thought drily.

The room was small but well done. There were towels twisted into swans in the bathroom, rose-scented bubble bath on the edge of the claw-foot tub, candles, lace curtains, red foil-wrapped heart chocolates on their pillows, a velvet love seat by the fireplace… Were this any other trip with any other man, Harper would be thrilled with the romantic vibe. It might help set the mood for their romantic ruse, but at the moment, pretending to have a boyfriend seemed pretty unimportant. Now she wished her only problem was being single.

As it was, it felt like the universe was just screwing with her.

"What's wrong with you?"

Harper turned toward Sebastian with a frown. "What do you mean?"

He watched her, stroking his dark goatee with thought. "I mean, you've been acting funny since we got on the plane to come here. I thought it was nerves, but it's been hours since we landed and you seem as distant as ever. We're in Ireland. Everyone thinks we're an adorable couple. You should be happy. What's going on?"

It was just her luck that her fake boyfriend would be so in tune with her emotions. Quentin wouldn't have noticed, but he was rarely concerned with anything but himself. She opened her mouth to tell him that she was fine, but his movement stopped her.

Getting up from the bed, he crossed the room and stood directly in front of her. He was close enough to reach out and touch. It took everything she had not to fall into his arms and let his strong embrace protect her from the outside world. But that felt a little too forward for their current situation.

Instead he stood close, without touching, looking deeply into her eyes. "And don't tell me it's nothing," he added. "My mother carried the weight of the world on her shoulders but would always insist that everything was fine. It was something then and it's something now. I know it when I see it."

Harper wanted to tell him. She needed to tell someone. Maybe he would know what to do, because she sure as hell didn't know how to handle this situation. She'd never been blackmailed before. Pulling away from him, she grabbed her purse off the entryway table and withdrew the small envelope from inside it. She handed it to Sebastian without a single word of explanation.

Sebastian's gaze flickered quickly over the note. By the time he was finished, his mouth had fallen into a deep frown of displeasure. Combined with his dark hair and eyes, something about his usual easygoing demeanor seemed to shift to almost wicked. Like she'd angered Bruce Banner. She almost expected his eyes to glow red with fury when he looked up at her. Instead she found them unexpectedly soft with concern. He was irate, but not with her.

"Where did this come from?" he asked, holding the note up.

"It was on my seat when we got on the plane. That's all I know." Harper wrapped her sweater tighter around her, as though it would help. She wished she had something more to go on, but she didn't. It was on generic white stationery and written with a block print text that anyone could do. There was nothing to give any kind of hint about who had left it there.

"Why didn't you say something to me?" he asked.

"When? When we were trapped on a plane for eight hours with eighty other people—one of whom was probably the blackmailer? They were likely watching me, waiting for my reaction to finding their little love note. So I didn't give them the satisfaction of panicking. I took my pills and went to sleep like it was nothing. But it's not nothing. I'm worried sick about this whole thing. Thankfully you're the only one to notice."

Sebastian looked over the note again before handing it back to her. His mouth tightened with irritation, highlighting the sharp, square lines of his jaw and the dark goatee that framed it. "So you suspect it's one of the wedding guests? Not the flight crew?"

Harper shrugged and tore her gaze from the tempting curve of his bottom lip. She wanted more than anything to focus on that. To lose herself in Sebastian's kiss and forget about the mess she was in. She got the feeling he wouldn't mind indulging her with a little distraction. But this wasn't the time. Blackmail was serious business.

"I'd never seen any of the crew before. We were one of the last couples to board, so almost any of the guests could've put it on my seat. As you've read, I'm supposed to leave the money at the front desk, so it has to be someone that's still here in Sligo with us. I'm sure the flight crew is back in Dublin."

She sank onto the bed, clutching the note in her hand. Where she hadn't allowed herself to really react on the flight, now, in the privacy of their hotel suite, she felt herself starting to emotionally unravel. "What am I going to do, Sebastian?" she asked with eyes squeezed tightly shut to trap the tears. She hated to cry.

She felt the bed sag beside her and Sebastian's comforting warmth against her side. "The way I see it, you've got three options. One, you pay the blackmail. That will keep your secret under wraps, but you're giving the blackmailer the upper hand. I don't know what you're being blackmailed for, but at any time they could demand more money to stay quiet. You'll never really be free of the blackmailer's hold on your life. But that's a risk that might be worth taking. Only you can answer that question."

She knew paying the blackmailer wasn't the best choice, but it was the one she'd take if given the chance. Unfortunately that wasn't an option for her. "I couldn't pay it even if I wanted to. I told you before that I was in a tight spot financially. It's possible that given some time I could go to a bank and get a loan with my apartment for collateral. But they want it tonight. By dinnertime. That's just impossible, especially considering we're in the middle of a remote estate in the Irish countryside. Even in Dublin, I couldn't have pulled it off."

"Okay," Sebastian said after listening to her logic. "The second option would be to call the police. Blackmail is illegal. They could take prints off the card, perhaps leave a dummy package at the desk for the culprit to pick up and then arrest them. You'll run the risk of the secret being exposed in the process, but they'll get their punishment."

Harper shook her head. She didn't want cops involved. Not in this situation. It would be bad enough for her to lose her inheritance and for everyone to find out what she'd done. She didn't need her story being in the newspapers, too.

"What's option three?" she asked.

"Option three is to expose the secret yourself and take their power away."

She could do that, but it would be a twenty-eight-million-dollar decision. Just the thought made her stomach start to ache with dread. She was stuck between a rock and a hard place. "I... I can't. It will ruin everything I've worked so hard to achieve."

Harper felt Sebastian's arm wrap around her shoulders. She couldn't resist leaning into him and resting her head against his chest. It was soothing to listen to the beating of his heart and enjoy the warmth of his embrace. It had been a long time since she'd had someone in her life to hold her like this. To listen to her when she had worries on her mind. She knew she had been lonely, but she didn't realize how deeply she'd felt it until this moment.

"Harper," Sebastian said after a long silence with her in his arms. "I have to ask this. Whether or not you answer is up to you, but it's hard for me to help you when I don't know. What could you have done to be blackmailed for?"

She knew the question would come eventually. Harper dreaded having to explain her youthful stupidity to anyone, but for some reason it was worse to tell Sebastian. He was successful, like her brother. He never would've made the mistakes she'd made. But she needed to tell someone. To have one person on this trip she could trust. He was the only one she could eliminate as a suspect since he couldn't possibly have left the note on her seat.

Harper sighed heavily and buried her face into his chest to avoid speaking for a little while longer. She pressed her nose to his collar and breathed in the spicy scent of his cologne and his skin. It was easy to stay there and pretend that everything would be okay for a little while longer.

"I'm a spoiled little rich girl," she said at last.

"Tell me something I don't know," Sebastian responded unexpectedly.

Harper sat up sharply and frowned at him.

"I'm kidding," he said. "Please continue. I'm just trying to keep things light."

Harper slumped over and sighed. "My brother and

I originally had trust funds set up for thirty million dollars each. When my mother died, my grandfather decided that, without her guidance, it might be better to break it into two payments. A small, two-million-dollar payment when we turned eighteen, followed by the rest when we turned thirty."

"Makes sense. An eighteen-year-old is more likely to blow all the money and have nothing to show for it."

"Exactly. And, basically, that's what I did. My father had given me everything I could ever want. When I went off to college, I continued to live that way, just on my own money for a change. When I started to run low, my father pitched in. But then he ran into his own financial problems and I was on my own."

"I don't hear anything that's blackmail worthy. Did you spend all the money on drugs or something?"

"Of course not! I spent it on shoes. Clothes. Trips. Makeup. Designer handbags. Expensive meals. Nonsense, really, but what I'd always been used to. And, no, nothing was criminal. Embarrassing, but not criminal. I went to Yale for a finance degree and yet I was a fool with my own money. No…the problem came after my father got a divorce. My grandfather was worried that our dad had set a bad example and added an additional requirement to the trust to keep us in line—if we blew the first payment, we wouldn't get the second."

"Does he know what you did?" Sebastian asked.

"No. Most of the money was long gone before he even added the stipulation, but I'd transferred the funds into my private accounts so no one had any insight into my finances. But someone has found out. And if I can't magically come up with a hundred grand, it's going to cost me a cool twenty-eight million instead."

Sebastian's blood was boiling. He was pretty sure his doctor wouldn't be too pleased that his relaxing vacation time had been overshadowed by drama of the worst kind. He could hear his pulse pounding in his ears as he marched down the stone hallway of the castle.

Harper was still in their room, spinning in circles and attempting to unpack her luggage. He'd stepped out to give her some privacy and to get a little air. The truth was that he didn't want her to know how angry he was over her whole situation. After her confession, she might mistakenly think he was angry with her and he was anything but.

Instead he was feeling remarkably protective of Harper. It was almost as though she really was his girlfriend. With her curled up in his arms, it was hard for him to remember this was all a sham. It certainly felt real. Maybe too real for the first day of the charade.

Before he'd left the room, he'd promised to keep

her secret, with one caveat. If he found out who her blackmailer was before she did, he couldn't promise her that he wouldn't cause some trouble for the jerk. She might not know that Sebastian had grown up on the wrong side of the tracks, but he had and, at a moment's notice, the scrappy kid who'd used his fists to defend himself could come out. Whomever was putting Harper through this hell deserved a black eye. Or two.

Even as Sebastian headed down the staircase to the main lobby, he could feel his hands curl into tight fists. He was strung tight, clutching his notebook under his arm and ready to fight at the slightest provocation. He hadn't been sure where he was going when he'd left the room, but he found himself loitering around the front desk. Perhaps the culprit would be there, waiting on a payment to be dropped off.

He was in no mindset to work, so he set aside his notebook, grabbed a copy of the local paper and settled into a large wingback chair by the fireplace. Despite being early summer, it was Ireland and that still meant cool weather, especially given they were near the northwest coast. The fire offered a comfortable, draft-free place to sit in the stone behemoth of a building.

Sebastian glanced over the words in the paper, but he was focused more on the comings and goings. There were few at this hour of the afternoon. It was likely that many had fallen prey to jet lag and were napping in their rooms before the welcome dinner. Most of the people he saw in the lobby were wearing the uniforms of the hotel staff.

After about thirty minutes, out of the corner of his eye, he noticed someone approach the front desk. He turned his attention fully to the man standing there, realizing almost immediately that it was one of the few people on the trip he actually knew—Harper's ex, Quentin.

That made sense. Harper had mentioned that she'd been short on cash basically since college and she'd only dated Quentin a few years ago. If they'd been at all serious, there had to have been signs of her difficulties. Sebastian had noticed it in minutes. Quentin, of all people, should have been able to tell if Harper was broke. If not, maybe she'd confided in him and forgotten about it. And perhaps he might also know that her financial luck was about to change. It made sense. But would he be bold enough to try to get a piece of it?

Quentin stood nervously waiting at the counter for the desk clerk to return and, after a brief exchange Sebastian couldn't hear, turned and headed back toward the elevators empty-handed. He glanced around the lobby as he walked, an almost agitated expression lining his face. And then his gaze met with Sebastian's pointed glare.

He knew he could turn away. Try to appear more subtle in his appraisal. But at the moment, Sebastian

didn't care if the bastard knew he was watching him.
Let him know they were on to his sick game. Let him
check the desk twenty times tonight. He was going
to be disappointed. No matter what Harper wanted
to do, she was right about one thing. There wasn't
going to be any way to pull a hundred grand out of
thin air in a foreign country.

It might even be a tricky thing for Sebastian to do
and he had ten times that much cash in his checking
account at any given time. Banks simply didn't like
handing over that much money. There were too many
checks and balances, wire transfers, international
calls and such before they parted with it. Perhaps if
they were in Monte Carlo where people parted with
larger amounts in the casinos on a regular basis, but
rural Ireland? Not likely. If Quentin was behind this
blackmail plot, his timing was crappy.

Quentin quickly broke their connection with an
anxious biting of his lip and turned his back to wait
for the elevator. Within a few seconds it opened and
he disappeared without looking back in Sebastian's
direction.

Sebastian was so engrossed in watching his mark
that he didn't notice someone approaching his chair.

"May I join you?"

He turned and recognized Harper's older brother
standing there. Oliver and his wife, Lucy, had been
introduced briefly to him on the bus, but they really
hadn't had time to talk aside from some basic pleas-

antries. Sebastian expected that he had questions for the new boyfriend. Any brother worth his salt would when his little sister was involved, even if she was a grown woman. "Please, have a seat. I'm just trying to stay awake until dinnertime, so I could use some company."

Oliver chuckled and settled into the other wingback chair. He had a cut-crystal lowball glass in his hand filled with some ice and a dark amber liquor. "I know how that is. International travel messes with your internal clock. I'm hoping to eat a huge dinner, have a couple drinks and pass out at a reasonable hour. Whatever that is. I'm not sure if Harper told you, but Lucy and I have nine-month-old twins. Our sleep schedules haven't been reasonable in quite some time."

"I can imagine. I wouldn't be surprised if the two of you did nothing but sleep when a wedding event wasn't taking place." Sebastian hadn't noticed any children on the flight but Violet and Aidan's toddler, so he presumed they were all back in New York with their nannies and their grandparents. Sounded like the perfect getaway to relax, nap and have some alone time together.

And yet he was downstairs with Sebastian instead.

"Lucy is actually napping right now. I told her not to because it would screw up her sleep, but she told me to mind my own business and go downstairs." Oliver chuckled and sipped at his drink. "They're a sassy group of women, my sister included. I never thought I'd be roped into all of it, and yet here I am. Do you know what you're getting yourself into, Sebastian?"

He smiled. He was pretty sure he was in over his head when he'd agreed to go on this trip and she'd kissed him in the department store. "If I didn't, I'm getting a good feel for it on this trip," he said. "It's been quite the experience so far and it's only the first day here. Being the odd man out allows me to sort of observe from the fringes, which is fine by me. To be honest, I don't spend a lot of time with people. Certainly not like this. My business partner, Finn Solomon, is the outward face of our company. I spend most of my time sketching out plans or tinkering with my latest ideas in the lab at work."

"I used to be that way. When I inherited Orion from my father, the company was a mess. Apple was king and PCs weren't cool anymore. Especially those old tower dinosaurs everyone had at work or in their closets. I sacrificed a lot of my personal life sitting with my engineers, trying to brainstorm new computer products that would make us competitive again. Now, of course, we're back on our feet and I'm able to shift my focus to other more important things, like Lucy and the twins. Say, have you been married before?"

Let the prying begin. Nice segue. "I haven't. I suppose I've been more focused on building our company, so I've never married or had any children."

Oliver nodded thoughtfully. "You know, all of Harper's friends have recently settled down and had children. After Violet and Aidan get married this weekend, Harper will be the only single one left."

"She's mentioned that."

"I suppose she feels some pressure to follow suit."

Sebastian narrowed his gaze at Oliver. "You're asking if Harper is barking up the wrong tree with me since I'm a thirty-eight-year-old workaholic bachelor?"

Oliver simply shrugged and sipped his drink. "Is she?"

"I suppose I'm getting to the age where I need to take the idea of a family more seriously, but until Harper, it hadn't really crossed my mind. I'm not opposed to it, no, but it simply hasn't been in the cards for me yet."

Her brother listened thoughtfully and nodded. "I was the same way until Lucy blew through my life like a hurricane. I didn't think I was ready for marriage or children, either, but she changed everything. It was like my eyes were suddenly opened and all I could see was her and our future together. Is it like that with you and my sister?"

That was something Sebastian didn't think he could lie about. It was easy to pretend to date and to be attracted to Harper because he was attracted to her. But to love her? To envision their future to-gether? That was different and he had no doubt her brother could spot it if he fibbed. "It's only been a few months, but I think we're definitely getting to a more serious place. I care for your sister," he said.

And he did. He didn't want to see her get hurt, be it by him or Quentin or whomever that sleazy blackmailer was. That meant he cared a little, even for a woman he hardly knew. It was hard not to when he'd been drawn into her world and her problems so quickly. If Lucy was a hurricane, perhaps Harper was a tornado, plucking him from a wheat field and sucking him up into the swirling drama of her life.

"Listen, I don't want to do that stereotypical brother thing where I threaten you not to hurt my sister and wave around my shotgun. It's kind of cliché and not that effective, if Quentin is any evidence of that. I also don't own a shotgun. But I will say that you're the first man my sister has seriously dated in quite a while. I'm happy for you both, but I'm also nervous. She's kept this relationship quiet and the fact that she's suddenly announcing it to the world means she's feel-ing more comfortable with her feelings for you, what-ever they may be. My sister is all sarcasm and sass on the outside, but all that is there as a barrier to protect the fact that she's really a marshmallow on the inside. She gets hurt easily."

Sebastian listened carefully. Even though he knew this relationship wasn't real, he took her brother's words to heart. He'd already been a witness to Harper's softer side—the side that was nervous about what other people thought of her and the part that was tied in knots over her secrets being exposed. She definitely had a soft underbelly. To be honest, seeing that part of her had endeared her to him more than he realized. She wasn't just the snarky single friend living the footloose and fancy-free life in Manhattan. She was more than that. Much more. And it made Sebastian curious to unearth more of her hidden layers.

Oliver glanced down at his watch and sighed before finishing off his drink. "Well, I'm glad we could have this little chat. I'd better head upstairs and wake Lucy so she has time to freshen up before dinner. I'll see you and Harper there in a little while."

"We'll see you later," Sebastian said with a wave. He watched Oliver disappear from the lobby and glanced back over at the hotel front desk. He hadn't been watching it for at least fifteen or twenty minutes. Anyone looking for the package of blackmail money could've come and gone and he'd missed it while chatting with Oliver.

Frustrated, he folded up the newspaper and decided to follow Oliver's suit. It was almost time for the welcome dinner in the great hall and he could use some time to change. With a sigh, he picked up his notebook and headed for the staircase to find Harper to report on what he'd seen, carefully leaving out her brother's little chat.

As far as he was concerned, Quentin should be at the top of the suspect list and he was going to keep an eye on him.

Five

Since everyone was tired, the welcome dinner was short and, for that, Harper was relieved. Aidan and Violet said a few words, thanked everyone for coming, and every couple was given a gift bag. Inside were some useful essentials: a schedule of activities, a map of the property and some authentic Irish chocolates.

Harper had difficulty focusing on any of the food or conversation. Her eyes kept running over each guest, wondering which one was expecting to be a hundred grand richer before bedtime. No one was watching her, no one was acting odd, and yet she could feel someone's eyes on her. Her gaze flicked over to Quentin. He seemed a little out of sorts tonight. He fidgeted with his food and didn't engage anyone, even his fiancée, in conversation.

After Sebastian had mentioned seeing her ex go by the front desk, it had confirmed her suspicions that he might be behind this. He was the only one who made sense. He knew a little about her situation, or he had back when they dated. The question was whether or not he needed money badly enough to use it against her. She didn't know. A hundred grand wasn't a lot in the scheme of things. All she knew was that she hated being in the same room with him. She wanted to escape upstairs as soon as she could.

At the same time, as they got up to leave the great hall, Harper realized she was also dreading going back to the suite with Sebastian. When he'd returned to the room before dinner, she had thankfully already dressed for the evening. She'd been in the process of curling her hair in the bathroom as he'd entered their room. He'd gone about changing his clothes, paying no attention to the fact that Harper was in the next room with the door wide open.

She'd tried not to stare in the mirror at him as he'd walked around in his navy boxer briefs, laying out his outfit. She'd told herself that it was surprise, not desire, that had caused her to study his mostly naked body so closely. She'd expected the mad scientist to be soft through the middle from long hours at the lab and less-than-ideal eating habits, but he wasn't. His body was long and lean with hard muscles that twitched beneath tanned skin that extended far below his collar line.

How did he get a body like that working in his lab for long stretches of time?

"Ye-ouch!" she'd hollered, pulling her attention back to the blazing-hot curling iron where it belonged. She'd sucked at her burned finger and focused on finishing her hair, even when he'd come into the bathroom still in his underwear. He'd bent over the sink to splash water on his face and beard, then combed his hair back and was done. Men had it so easy.

"Could you put on a robe or something?" she'd finally asked. Despite her best intentions to ignore him when they were alone, she was sure to burn off a chunk of hair if he kept walking around mostly naked.

Sebastian had seemed startled and mildly insulted by the request at first, but had quickly retrieved one of the resort robes and covered up.

She'd thanked him and the tension between them eased. They'd finished dressing, gone down to the great hall and sat together throughout the meal, engaging in polite conversation with those around them. They'd smiled, leaned into each other, shared bites of food and were as lovey-dovey as they could stand to be until they were finally released for some welcome rest.

Now that she'd had an eyeful of what he was hiding under his suits, Harper wasn't sure how well she would sleep tonight. Not lying a mere inch or two from Sebastian for hours on end.

They bypassed the elevator and walked slowly and silently up the staircase together to their suite. About halfway up, Harper felt the brush of Sebastian's fingers against her own. She looked down and put her hand in his when she realized he was intentionally reaching for her. He was right. They should be holding hands. She couldn't let any awkwardness that happened behind closed doors impact the show they were putting on for everyone else.

If only touching him didn't unnerve her the way it did. His hand was large and warm, enveloping hers in a way that made heat radiate up her arm. By the time they reached their room, her blood was humming through her veins and she felt as if the silk pussy bow that tied at the collar of the Fendi blouse she'd chosen was about to choke her. She also felt flush in the otherwise cool castle. That could only be Sebastian's doing.

He let go of her hand long enough to open the door and let her step in ahead of him. He followed behind, pulling the door shut and fastening the privacy latch.

Harper wasn't the only one who was oddly overheated. As she untied the bow at her neck, she watched Sebastian slip quickly out of his suitcoat and tug his tie loose. She found her eyes drawn to the hollow of his throat as he unfastened his collar and continued down the line of buttons until a touch of dark chest hair was exposed.

Suddenly the thought of pressing a kiss against that part of his neck appeared in her mind. The warm scent of his skin, the stubble brushing her cheeks, the rhythmic thump of his pulse against her lips... An unwelcome tingle of desire surged through her whole body, making her belly clench and her breasts ache with longing in the confines of her bra.

When her nervous gaze met his, she found a questioning look in his eyes and a room that was abruptly very quiet. "What?" she asked before turning away to focus on kicking out of her pointy-toed heels.

Sebastian just shrugged and sat in a chair to pull off his shoes. "You were staring at me, that's all. I was waiting for you to say something. Did I get some shepherd's pie on my shirt?" He looked down at the pristine gray shirt.

She wished he was a mess. Maybe then she could ignore the building attraction between them. Instead, he'd been the perfect companion so far. Perfect aside from being too attractive, too nice and too supportive. A soft, pasty midsection would really help her control her libido right now, but she knew that what was under that shirt was anything but. "No. I just... got lost in my thoughts, I guess."

It was then that, with them both in states of partial dress, they found themselves at an impasse. Harper didn't know what to do next. She certainly wasn't about to tell him what was on her mind. If she stood there any longer, he'd continue to undress like before. She supposed she could gather up her pajamas and take them into the bathroom to change like this was a sleepover with a group of shy ten-year-old girls. Perhaps that would give him time to change privately, as well.

She turned to where her luggage was sitting open and started riffling through it. Thankfully she'd thought to pack pajamas that were less than intriguing. She had passed on the dog onesie—it was too bulky—but had chosen something just as unappealing. There was a piece of nice lingerie for show, but the rest was purely practical in nature. They were flannel, for the potentially cold Irish nights, and long-sleeved, to keep any glimpses of exposed skin to a minimum.

"Here," he said.

Harper turned her attention to Sebastian in time to see him deliberately taking off the rest of his clothes. "Um, what are you doing?" she asked, clutching her pajamas to her breasts for dear life as she realized what was happening.

"I'm getting this out of the way." He shrugged off his dress shirt and stepped out of the suit pants that had pooled at his feet. "We can't spend this whole week tiptoeing around each other and if you keep burning fingers on your curling iron while you sneak peeks at me, people are going to start asking questions. We're sharing a room. Sharing a bed. It doesn't matter what does or doesn't happen in the bed—we need to be more comfortable around each other. You said so yourself when we first agreed to this whole thing." Standing in nothing but those same navy boxer briefs, Sebastian held out his arms. "Take a good look. Get it out of your system. It's just the standard equipment."

Harper watched with confusion and curiosity as he displayed himself to her. His equipment was anything but standard. Her gaze flickered from his defined biceps to the chest hair across his pecs to the trail that ran down his stomach to the gray waistband of his briefs. She was tempted to glance lower, but he turned, giving her a look at his muscular back and curved rear end, as well.

"Well?" he asked with his back to her.

"Why are you so tanned?" she blurted out to her own embarrassment.

He turned around to face her with a smile. "You're staring at my ass but your only question is why I'm tanned?" He shrugged, unfazed by her question. "Okay, well, my apartment building has a rooftop pool. I swim a lot. It's one of my stress relievers. It's not enough, apparently, but it's what I do. I'm not big on going to the gym. It's boring."

"What do you mean it's not enough?"

Sebastian's lips twisted for a moment in thought and he shook his head. "Nothing. There's not enough stress relievers in the world when you're in my line of work, that's all." He looked down at his chest and back at her. "Seen enough?"

Harper nodded nervously.

Sebastian mirrored her nod and sought out a pair of lounging pants from his bag. He tugged them on and looked at her with a wry grin. "Now when you talk to your girlfriends about getting me out of my pants, you don't have to lie."

Harper smiled, still fiercely holding her pajamas as though they were a protective armor. It felt silly after that to hide in the bathroom to change, but was she brave enough to do it out here?

"Your turn."

Her gaze met his. "What?" she said with obvious panic in her voice. Did he honestly expect her to parade around mostly naked because he had?

He held up his hands to deflect the blowback. "I'm just kidding Harper. Relax."

Harper held in a nervous twitter of laughter at his joke. "Oh."

"It's nothing I haven't seen before, anyway," he added. "I'm sure it's nice and all, but I'm not about to hurt myself while I stare at you."

Harper didn't know if she should be relieved or offended. He'd told her before that she was beautiful, but at the moment he seemed as though he couldn't care less about catching a glimpse of her naked body. Maybe he was using reverse psychology on her, she couldn't be sure, but she had the sudden urge to take off her clothes and prove him wrong.

Against her better judgment, she went with the surge of bravery and decided to put him to the test. "That's good to know," she said. She set her pajamas on the edge of the bed and pulled her blouse up over her head. She paid no attention to Sebastian as she straightened the straps of her cream-satin bra and unzipped her pencil skirt. She let it pool to her ankles, bending slowly to pick it up off the floor and to give him all the time he might need to see her cream thong and firm ass. She'd spent a lot of hours in the gym working on that butt and he damn well better be impressed by it.

She wanted to turn and look at him. For some reason, she wanted to see naked desire and need in his eyes. She knew it was there—she could practically feel his gaze on her body. But she didn't dare look at him. She wasn't sure what she would do if she found what she was looking for. Would she act on it? Ignore it? As it was, they would both spend tonight aching for something they couldn't have.

Harper decided not to turn in Sebastian's direction. It was enough to know that he hadn't moved from his spot since she'd started undressing. She forced herself to step into the plaid pajama pants. She unbuttoned the flannel top and readied it to put on before reaching back to unfasten her bra. Before she could slip it from her shoulders, she caught a blur of movement from the corner of her eye and a moment later the bathroom door shut hard. The shower came on not long after that.

So much for being comfortable around each other and getting it out of their system, she thought. Harper continued to put on her pajamas with a grin.

It was only the first day and she could already tell this was going to be a miserably boring trip.

It was not at all what she had envisioned when they'd been invited to the glamorous overseas wedding of Violet Niarchos and Aidan Murphy. Yes, sure, they'd flown on a snazzy chartered plane and were sleeping in a private Irish castle, but watching the Queen of England snore into her teacup would be more exciting than hanging around this rotting pile of bricks with a bunch of blowhard billionaires.

She'd heard the wedding coordinator talking to her assistant on the plane about the week's itinerary. It sounded like one boring event after another with no end in sight. The week promised "highlights" like a round of golf for the gentlemen, a tea party for the ladies and shopping excursions into the sleepy village by the sea.

Couldn't they have at least stayed in Dublin for a night? Every person who walked past her in the hallway was worth a bloody fortune and yet hadn't the slightest clue how to have any fun with their money.

If not for the little blackmail scheme she was running, the whole trip would be a waste of her time. So far, even that had proven fruitless as far as money went, but it had been something to do. Watching Harper squirm under the pressure of blackmail was nice, but it wasn't what she really wanted.

That spoiled little princess needed to shut up and pay up. She could afford it. It was one tiny fraction of the fortune she was set to inherit from her dear old grandfather. Harper hadn't worked for or earned that money. It was to be dropped in her lap just because she'd been born into a family that handed down multi-million-dollar trust funds just as easily as other people passed hazel eyes and freckles down to their children.

She might not have all the money now, but she would have it soon. In the meantime, Harper could easily get her hands on it. She could borrow it from one of her rich friends, her brother…even her new boyfriend was loaded. Basically anyone on that flight could hand over the cash without blinking. Harper just needed the right motivation to ask.

Harper didn't deserve twenty-eight million dollars. She didn't even deserve the twenty-seven million, nine hundred thousand that would be left after she paid the blackmail.

She deserved it. She needed it.

And she was going to get it before the week was up.

That was the longest night of Sebastian's life.

As it was, he'd stayed in the bathroom far longer

than was necessary. After he'd showered and tried to take the edge off, he'd meticulously brushed and flossed his teeth, rinsed with mouthwash, washed his face…anything and everything he could do to kill time and wipe the image of Harper's near naked body from his mind.

She might as well have been naked. That tantalizing little thong left almost nothing to the imagination and with the creamy color that nearly matched her skin, the rest of it just blended away. He'd tried to play it cool. Act like the mature adult he thought he was when they'd started this little game. He'd gritted his teeth, tried to think of the most un-arousing things he could, and even closed his eyes for a moment or two. But he hadn't been able to keep his gaze away for long. When she'd moved to take her bra off, though, he'd known he'd had to go.

It was that or… No. That hadn't been an option.

Theirs was a fake relationship. Despite all the handholding, embraces and canoodling they did in public, it was all fake. They weren't in love. They hardly knew one another. When he'd signed up for this, he'd thought it wouldn't be that hard to pretend to be Harper's lover. Now he wanted it for real so badly he could hardly draw in the scent of her perfume without gaining an erection.

By the time he'd come out of the bathroom, almost all the lights were out and Harper had been in bed. She'd been lying on her side with her back to him, so he'd been able to get into bed, turn off the nearby lamp and go to sleep without having to face her again.

At least that had been the idea. Instead he'd spent most of the night tossing and turning. He'd felt anxious. Squirmy. Filled with nervous energy that he couldn't shake. He should have been exhausted after staying up all day to adjust to the time change, but it hadn't mattered. All Sebastian's body cared about was the warm, soft female lying mere inches from him.

He remembered seeing the light of dawn through the curtains right around the time he was finally able to doze off. The next thing he heard was the shower running. When Harper emerged from the bathroom—fully dressed, thank goodness—she sat in the chair and rifled through the welcome bag they'd received the night before.

"What's on the agenda today?" he muttered into his pillow with a gravelly, sleepy voice.

"Today they've chartered a bus into the nearby town of Sligo if anyone wants to go shop or sightsee. It leaves at ten, after breakfast is done."

"And when is breakfast?"

"About fifteen minutes from now."

Reluctantly, Sebastian pushed himself up and swung his legs out of bed. "I'll be ready in ten," he grumbled as he stumbled into the shower and turned on the water.

He quickly washed his hair and body, cleaned up his goatee, and was ready to go in ten minutes, as he'd predicted. He was wearing a more casual outfit for a day in town, so the jeans and polo shirt had come together quickly. Harper was dressed more casually, as well. When she stood to leave, he couldn't help but notice her skinny jeans were like a second skin. They clung to the delicious curve of her ass and thighs, bringing back flashes from the night before that were not breakfast appropriate.

"Is something wrong?" she asked.

If he didn't want to embarrass himself, yes.

"No," he said and reached for a windbreaker in the closet. "I was just considering a jacket." He folded it over his arm and carried it in front of him as they headed downstairs to eat.

"Miss Drake?" a voice called out as they reached the lobby and headed toward the great hall.

They both stopped, turning their attention to the front desk where a clerk was looking their way. The woman had an envelope in her hand that looked eerily familiar.

Sebastian's empty stomach started to ache with the feeling of dread. It was a similar envelope to the one Harper had received on the plane. He wasn't sure why that surprised him. She hadn't met last night's blackmail request, so another note had arrived. He hadn't been in the lobby to see who had left it there. When he'd mentioned seeing Quentin loitering around the

desk the night before, Harper hadn't seemed surprised, which had just reinforced his idea that he was
the suspect to watch.

"I have a message here for you, ma'am," the clerk
added in a thick Irish accent.

Harper knew what it was, too. They walked together to the front desk and she took the envelope
from the woman's hand. It had her name written on
it in the same nondescript block text. "Thank you,"
she said.

"Did you happen to be working when they left the
note? To see who left it?" Sebastian asked.

"No, sir. I just started my shift. The previous clerk
said it had been left at the desk early this morning
while she was setting up the coffee station. She didn't
see who left it, either. Is there a problem?"

"No," Sebastian said with a reassuring smile.
"Thanks so much." He turned back to Harper, who
was looking at the envelope with a face almost as
white as the parchment. "Let's take that back upstairs," he suggested. "Breakfast can wait."

She nodded blankly and let him lead her out of the
lobby. He glanced around, looking for someone loitering curiously in the area, but it was mostly empty.
A couple he didn't recognize was looking at magazines in the corner, but there was no one else there.
They were all likely in the great room gathering for
their first authentic Irish breakfast.

Back in the room, he escorted Harper over to the love seat and sat beside her.

"You know, with everything else going on last night, I almost forgot I was missing the deadline. This morning, the thought hadn't even crossed my mind. How could I forget about something like that? And then I saw the envelope in her hand and I remembered what a mess I was still in. Now I don't want to open it," she said.

"Why not?"

"Because…it's not going to be good. He's going to be angry because I didn't pay the blackmail money. There's one of two things in this note—a second chance to pay or notification that my secret is as good as public knowledge by now. I could walk into the dining hall and everyone could know the truth about me."

"You won't know which it is until you open it."

With a sigh, she ran her finger under the lip of the envelope and ripped it open. She pulled out another small card, identical to the first, with the same block-style text inside. Harper held it up to read aloud.

"It seems your payment got lost in the mail, Harper. Yesterday was a tiring day of travel, so I'm going to be kind and give you another opportunity to give me what I want. This time, to make it easier, make it one hundred thousand euros in an envelope at the front desk by noon tomorrow. Don't disappoint me again."

Harper's hand dropped into her lap with dismay. "Great, now the price has gone up. When I looked at the exchange rate yesterday, it was in the euro's favor. He's now asking for something in the neighborhood of a hundred and twenty thousand dollars in the name of 'convenience.' I mean, why not?" She giggled, bringing her hand to her mouth just in time to stifle a sob. "I couldn't pay the hundred grand, so two days later, naturally, I should be able to pay that and more."

Sebastian wrapped his arm around Harper's shoulders and pulled her tight against him. She gave in to the embrace, burying her face in his chest and holding on to him. He hated seeing her upset. He wasn't a very physical person by nature, but if he got his hands on her blackmailer, he wasn't sure what he would do. At the moment he wanted to choke the guy until tears ran down his cheeks like Harper's did.

"What am I going to do?" She sniffled against his polo shirt. "He's not going to go away. I don't have the money. I don't know what to do, Sebastian."

He sighed and stroked her hair as he tried to come up with an answer. He wasn't sure there was a way out of this that wouldn't be painful somehow. "Do you trust any of your friends enough? Lucy or Emma maybe? Your brother perhaps?"

"Trust them enough for what?"

"Enough to ask them to help you with this. To

give you the money. Just a loan until you get to your birthday and can pay them back."

Harper pulled away and shook her head. She wiped the tears from her cheeks, leaving black smudges of mascara that he wanted to reach out and brush away.

"I can't do that. I just can't."

"You don't think they'd give it to you?"

"No, they would. Each and every one of them would in a heartbeat," Harper explained. "That's why I can't ask. I'm not going to abuse their friendship like that. Besides, they'd want to know what it was for. They'd worry that I was in some kind of trouble."

"Aren't you?" he asked.

"Yes, but not trouble I want any of them to know about. This whole thing is so embarrassing. Really, even if I wasn't at risk of losing my inheritance, I wouldn't want anyone to know about the financial trouble I'm in. I'm an accountant. It just looks so awful."

Sebastian gently stroked her back, considering his options in this situation. Initially he hadn't been in favor of paying the blackmail, but this wasn't going to go away. This person was going to get the money or ruin Harper's life in the process. "What about the bank?" he asked.

She looked up at him, confusion creasing her brow. "What do you mean?"

"What about seeing if the local bank would lend

you the money? When we go into town today, we can stop at a bank and see what options you have."

"Not many," she said. "Without collateral, getting that much money would be nearly impossible. If by some chance they did agree to loan me the money, it would be at an outrageous interest rate."

"Not necessarily," Sebastian said thoughtfully. "What if I cosigned?"

Harper sat back against the arm of the love seat and looked at him with an expression he couldn't quite read. "Are you serious?"

He shrugged. "Yeah."

"That's really sweet of you to offer, Sebastian, but I can't ask you to do that. It wouldn't be right."

"Why? I have no intention of paying a dime of the money back. It's all on you. And if you don't pay it when your inheritance comes through, I'll see to it that there are unpleasant consequences for you, if it makes you feel better about it."

She blinked a few times as though she were trying to process his offer. "You'd really do that for me?"

"Of course," he said. "You're my girlfriend. Don't you think the blackmailer would think it suspicious if you couldn't come up with the money somehow and yet your boyfriend is a millionaire?"

Sebastian wasn't sure what the reaction would be, but he certainly wasn't expecting her to throw herself into his arms. Before he knew what was happening, Harper's lips were pressed to his once again. Just like at Neiman Marcus, she was enthusiastically thanking him with her mouth. Unlike at Neiman Marcus, this time there wasn't a crowd of onlookers to keep the kiss PG-rated.

If he was honest with himself, he'd been wanting this kiss since that one had ended. Not one of the quick pecks she gave him when they were out in public, but a real kiss. One where he could taste the cool mint-toothpaste flavor on her tongue and let his hands roam until they discovered that under today's long-sleeved T-shirt she was wearing a lace bra.

The kiss intensified as his palms cupped her through her shirt. Harper moaned softly against his mouth and moved closer to him on the love seat. It would be so easy to pull her into his lap, whip the shirt off her head and bury his face between the creamy breasts he'd only glimpsed the night before. But he wouldn't. Not now.

As much as he didn't want to, Sebastian forced himself to pull away. This wasn't the time or place for this to happen. If he and Harper ever transitioned from a fake relationship to a real one, he didn't want it to be because she was emotionally compromised or felt indebted to him.

He rested his forehead against hers as he took a cleansing breath and chuckled to himself.

"What's the laugh for?" she asked.

"I was just thinking that I would've offered to co-sign yesterday if I'd known I'd get that kiss in return."

Harper grimaced and shook her head with mock dismay. "Let's get back downstairs. We don't want to miss the bus to Sligo."

Six

"Wipe that anxious look off your face."

Harper clutched her purse to her chest and frowned at Sebastian. "I can't help it," she argued. "I don't like walking around with this much cash."

"You're not walking through downtown Manhattan. You're riding a bus with friends through the Irish countryside. We'll be back at the castle in a few minutes. No one on the bus is going to mug you, I'm pretty sure."

She could only sigh and shake her head, diverting her attention out the window to the passing scenery. Ireland was a beautiful country with rolling, emerald hillsides, misty valleys and wild, gray seas. She wished she was able to enjoy it. Harper had always wanted to go to Ireland but never managed to make the trip before. But now that she was here, all she could think about was the twenty-five thousand euros in her Birkin purse and the bastard she was about to give it to.

"Maybe B. Mayler is on the bus. Ever think of that? Maybe he followed us into town."

Sebastian turned to look over his shoulder at the people on the bus. "I doubt it. Besides, he wouldn't need to steal it from you. You're about to give it to him outright."

He was probably right. She hadn't seen Quentin on the bus or in town. She half expected to see him sitting in the lobby when they arrived, waiting with baited breath for her to leave the package at the front desk, especially after Sebastian had seen him at the desk the night before. She hated to tell Quentin that he was going to be disappointed.

Twenty-five thousand euros. Not a hundred thousand. That was all the bank would give her even with Sebastian's signature on the loan. If they'd had more time...if she'd had better credit, more collateral...if Harper'd had ties to Ireland... Their reasons for limiting the amount of the loan had gone on and on. She supposed she should be happy to have gotten this much. She was a quarter of the way there. Maybe it would keep the blackmailer happy until she could get more.

Looking into her purse for the twentieth time,

Harper checked to make sure the bundle of bills was still there. It was in a white envelope, labeled as directed, and included a note that explained this was all she could get until she returned to the United States. She intended to leave the package at the front desk as they went in. Then, maybe, she would be able to take a deep breath for the first time since she'd spied that envelope on her plane seat.

Or perhaps not.

As they pulled up the curved gravel driveway of Markree Castle, she closed her bag to make sure the envelope wouldn't fall out. Sebastian stayed close by her side as they exited the bus and walked into the hotel.

Despite their situation, it was nice to have him be there for her. He hadn't signed up for any of this drama when he'd agreed to come on the trip as her boyfriend. He'd been promised a free vacation and instead he'd been roped into a blackmail plot. And yet he hadn't complained. He'd been her sounding board, her shoulder to cry on and, at the moment, her personal bodyguard. Harper didn't know how to thank him for everything he'd done so far. If she'd come on this trip alone, she wasn't sure what she would've done.

They stopped at the desk long enough for her to hand over the package with instructions for the desk clerk. She slipped it into a blank mail slot on the back wall and went to answer the phone as though it was nothing to her. Harper supposed it was. Just something left for a guest. Who would imagine it was filled with thousands of euros in cash?

"Let's go upstairs," Sebastian suggested. "We need to get away from the desk so he can come pick it up."

Harper didn't argue. She just took his arm and let him lead her away. It felt good to cling to him, to have the strong support of his body against her own. It meant so much to have him there for her. It had been a long time since she'd had that in her life. When so much of her day-to-day existence was a lie, it was almost impossible to let people in. Even her best girlfriends, the people who knew her better than anyone, didn't know the whole truth about her.

As they stepped inside their room and he closed the door behind them, she realized how lonely she had been. Even when she had been with Quentin, something had been missing. She was holding part of herself back from everyone, never letting anyone completely in.

But Sebastian knew all her secrets. And he was still there with her. At least for now.

Harper didn't expect him to stay around after the end of the trip. He had a life to return to and so did she. But they had the here and now together and, for her, that was enough. She just needed to feel like she wasn't going through this by herself. She wasn't lonely when he was around. She didn't have to pretend to be someone she wasn't. It was such a relief to be able to let her guard down and just relax into who she really was for the first time in forever.

She turned to look at Sebastian. His large, dark eyes were watching her from across the room the way they always did. He constantly seemed to be in silent study of the world around him. Of her. Perhaps it was the engineer in him, taking things apart and putting them back together in his mind. Figuring out how things worked. What made them tick. What made her tick. The idea of him instinctively knowing just how to push her buttons was enough to make her need to slip out of her suddenly too warm jacket.

He was one of the most intense men she'd ever encountered. And now, in this moment, she wanted to lose herself in that intensity.

"Sebastian."

It was all she said, yet she knew her tone conveyed so much more to him than just his name. He bit thoughtfully at his full bottom lip as his gaze narrowed at her. At last, he started moving toward her at an unhurried pace. Their gazes never broke away from one another as he came nearer. And even when he was close enough to reach out and pull Harper into his arms, he didn't touch her. He just studied her, taking in every inch from her dark ponytail to the cobblestone-scuffed deck shoes she'd worn into town.

This was her move to make. Their relationship was set up with parameters she'd defined. If they were going to cross a line, she had to be the one to do it. And that was fine by her.

Her lips met his before she could lose her nerve. Their kiss this morning had been proof that there was more between them than just some arrangement. Excitement and gratitude had overridden her good sense then, but the kiss had been about anything but saying thank you. The current running beneath the surface was one of mutual attraction, undeniable chemistry... they had just been holding back out of respect for the agreement they'd made. This relationship was supposed to be all for show, right?

But all that went out the window when he looked at her the way he did. Touched her the way he did.

"Make me forget about all of this," she said in a desperate whisper against the rough stubble of his cheek.

Sebastian didn't hesitate to give her what she'd asked for. Within seconds her shirt was over her head. His hungry mouth traveled down her chin and throat to bury in the valley between her breasts. He nipped at her delicate skin with his teeth even as he unclasped her bra and cast it to the floor.

The sensations were so overwhelming, all Harper could do was close her eyes and try to take it all in. His hands moved quickly to cover her exposed breasts. She groaned as her tight, sensitive nipples grazed his rough palms. His fingertips pressed into her flesh, squeezing and kneading her breasts.

The moment he drew one tight bud into his mouth, Harper's head fell back and she cried out to the ceiling. His silky, hot tongue bathed her skin, sucking hard and then biting gently with his teeth until she gasped. She gripped his head, trying to pull him closer as she buried her fingers in the dark waves of his hair. She couldn't get close enough.

Then he pulled away.

Sebastian stood fully upright for a moment, his hands encircling her waist. He held her steady there as his dark eyes studied her face. He seemed to take in every detail, from the curve of her lips to the scar across her brow where she'd fallen out of a bunk bed as a child.

Harper suddenly felt self-conscious as she stood there, topless and exposed to his scrutiny. What would he see if he looked that closely? She wanted to turn off the lights, to cover up, pull away before he found something he didn't like about her body.

Then he shook his head and said, "Beautiful," under his breath and she tried to put those worries aside to be the beautiful woman on the inside that he saw on the outside.

With his firm grip on her, he pulled her across the wooden floor to their four-poster bed. He pushed her back until she was sitting on the edge. Harper eased back just as he moved forward, planting his left knee and fist into the soft mattress beside her. Hovering over her, he used his right hand to trace faint circles across her stomach.

It both tickled and turned her on at the same time. She tried hard not to squirm under his touch, but her body couldn't stay still. She ached to move closer and pull away all at once. Then he moved down and brushed his fingers over the button of her jeans. With a quick snap, they were undone and he pulled the zipper down to the base. He probed under the fabric, tracing over the lace that protected her center.

Harper gasped as he grazed her most sensitive spot once, twice, then a third time, more forcefully, making her back arch up off the bed.

Sebastian's gaze fixed on her. Ever the engineer, he studied her expressions and her every reaction to his touch. With a satisfied smirk, he eased back and hooked his fingers beneath her jeans. He slid them over her hips and down her legs, throwing them to the floor.

His hands replaced the denim, sliding back up her legs and gliding over every inch of her skin. His mouth followed in their wake, leaving searing kisses along the insides of her ankles, calves, knees and inner thighs. When he reached her panties, Harper expected him to pull them off like he had with her jeans. Instead he grasped the side with his fist and tugged hard until the pieces came off in his hand. He threw the torn strips of fabric away.

"That's much better." With nothing else in his way,

he pressed her thighs further apart and leaned in to lap his tongue over the newly exposed flesh.

The sensation was like a lightning bolt through her core.

"You're buying me new panties," she gasped. "Those were twenty-five dollars and I can't afford to replace them."

"Fine," Sebastian said. "I'll buy. You three pairs. For every one. I destroy." With each pause in his speech, his tongue flicked over her again.

"Are you planning to rip them all?"

"It depends." He spread her legs wider and moved his mouth more furiously over Harper until she was once again squirming beneath him.

"Depends on what?" Harper gasped and gripped the blankets beneath her in tight fists.

"On whether or not they get in my way."

Harper made a mental note to keep her nicer panties in her luggage. That was her last coherent thought.

At that moment Sebastian slid two fingers inside her. He thrust them deep, positioning the heel of his hand to grind against her clit. His whole hand started moving and she began to unravel. The combination was like nothing she'd ever felt before. She found herself yelling out, gasping and crying, even long before her release. The sensations were almost overpowering.

Her orgasm came fast and furiously. She wasn't prepared for how hard the pulsating waves would pound her body. She shuddered and rocked against his hand, shouting with the power of her release until it had nearly zapped all her strength. It took all she had to reach down and grab his hand, pulling it away from her. She couldn't take any more. Not quite yet, at least.

Harper closed her eyes and collapsed against the mattress. Her skin was pink and flushed, the butterflies still fluttering inside her. She swallowed hard, noting her raw throat as she gasped for breath. She wasn't entirely sure what she'd expected from Sebastian, but it hadn't been that. She'd never experienced an orgasm like that in her life. It was intense. Overwhelming. Amazing. And as soon as she recovered, she wanted to do it again.

Sebastian's weight shifted on the bed and she heard him walk into the bathroom. She opened her eyes when she heard him come back in. He had gotten rid of his clothes and replaced them with his pajama pants.

Bending down, he scooped her into his arms and placed her properly onto the bed. He crawled in beside her and tugged the blankets over them both.

Harper was surprised. She didn't think they were finished. She was great, of course, but she thought for sure that he would want some for himself. Maybe he didn't have protection with him. She'd have to be sure to correct that before they got together again.

Instead, he rolled onto his side and wrapped his

arms around her, pulling her into the warm nook of his body. It was unexpected, but perhaps exactly what she needed.

"What are you thinking about?" he asked.

"Not a damn thing," Harper said. She could barely string together a coherent sentence at this point.

"Good. Mission accomplished," he said.

"You know what I've noticed?"

Sebastian clung to consciousness long enough to make a thoughtful sound in response to Harper's question. "Mmm?"

"I've realized that I really don't know anything about you, but you know everything about me."

The question was enough to jerk him from the comfortable nap he'd almost settled into. Apparently the post-coital bliss he'd induced in her was short-lived and her mind was spinning again. With his eyes wide open now, he sighed. "That's not true. We met up before the trip and talked about each other for the cover story."

Harper snuggled against his chest and let her fingers twirl through his dark chest hair. "Yes. We talked about a few things, but you were pretty light on details. You know all my deepest, darkest secrets and all I know is that you went to MIT."

"There's not much more about me to tell," he said. It was a lie, but the one he preferred people to believe. "I had a very boring, uneventful life before I went to college and met Finn. Then we started a business, invented some stuff and got rich in the process. My life is still boring, I just have more money. Unlike you, there's no secret dramas, no trust fund stipulations, no blackmail plots. You're not missing out on much with me, I promise."

Now it was Harper's turn to make a thoughtful sound. Eventually she stilled and her breathing became soft and even against his chest. Of course, she had riled him up and fallen asleep, leaving him lying in bed with a brain no longer interested in sleep.

Part of him felt bad about lying to Harper mere minutes after giving her an orgasm. She had been brutally honest with him about her life, but that was out of necessity, not out of a willingness to share her past with him. He'd been sucked into her blackmail plot or he was certain she wouldn't have told him, just like she hadn't told anyone else. He was just there. And he was okay with that. She just shouldn't expect him to reciprocate.

It wasn't because he had huge skeletons in his own closet. His uncle Joe had gotten a DUI for driving his riding lawnmower to the gas station drunk to get more beer. That was the closest his family had come to brushes with the law. No scandals. No secrets. They were just the one thing that he couldn't be once he'd found himself dropped into the world of Manhattan society against his will—poor.

Harper had been angry with him initially for not

telling her that he was rich. It was her presumption that he wasn't—he hadn't said anything either way. He typically didn't. Sebastian wasn't the kind to present himself like the usual power-hungry Manhattan CEO, so most people wouldn't think he was, much less believe him if he insisted otherwise. Finn was the suave one: well-dressed, well-spoken, well-traveled. He reeked of money and prestige. No one ever questioned that he was the president of BioTech.

Sebastian flew under the radar and he liked it that way. He didn't like the way people changed around him when they found out he was rich. All of a sudden people acted like he was more important and things he said were more interesting. He'd go from being mostly ignored to receiving invitations to play racquetball at the club. He didn't play racquetball and had no intention of starting. It was all perception. His wealth shaped how people saw him.

And the same would be true if his rich friends found out he'd come from a dirt-poor background.

At the moment he was sleeping under the same roof as some of the most powerful business owners and billionaires in Manhattan. When he'd been introduced as one of them, they'd welcomed him with open arms. He was good enough for Harper, he owned his own company…he must be good people. But would they respond differently if they knew he was fifteen years removed from what they considered to be poor white trash? That his parents would be living in the same trailer he'd grown up in if he hadn't bought them a house with his first million?

Harper had money troubles of her own, but even at her poorest, she had more money than his family'd had growing up. He'd had to bust his ass to earn scholarships and get through college to build a career and wealth of his own. None of it had been given to him by his daddy or grandpa or anyone else.

While he'd been sympathetic to her plight when she'd told him about blowing her first two-million inheritance, a part of him had winced internally at the thought of it. Finn had some family money that helped them get started, but it was nowhere near enough. What could Sebastian have done if someone had handed him two million to get BioTech off the ground? They could've gotten a decent facility up and running instead of working out of a garage the first year. They could've gotten their first major product into production years earlier.

And she'd blown it on purses and shoes.

Harper had obviously grown up a lot in the years since she'd made those mistakes. She'd not only managed to support herself, but do a good enough job at it that no one questioned that she wasn't still rich. But with that big balloon payment looming in her future, he had to wonder if she would be back to her old habits.

It would take longer to blow through twenty-eight million, but she could still do it. Then what? There would be no third payment to bail her out again unless some rich relative died.

Or she married well. To a rich CEO perhaps?

Sebastian sighed and looked down at Harper as she slept peacefully on his chest. He didn't want to think that way about her. She hadn't seemed at all like the typical Manhattan gold digger. But she certainly had seemed a lot more interested in him once she'd realized he was rich and not just some wheelchair salesman. Yes, he could easily revive the glamorous lifestyle she had once lived. Since things between them had accelerated so quickly, a part of him worried about her motivations.

She'd been completely in love with that creep Quentin only two years ago. A guy who might very well be blackmailing her right now. She herself had said she didn't have the greatest taste in men, and choosing Quentin certainly seemed like a style over substance choice in his opinion.

That said, she genuinely seemed attracted to Sebastian. She hadn't asked anything of him, even though they both knew he could pay off that blackmail and put an end to it all. If it would ever end. She'd barely agreed to let him cosign the loan. And yet part of him was still concerned about what Harper was after.

He didn't mind getting physically closer to her. He was happy to. Holding her warm, soft body in his arms was one of the best things to happen to him in a long time. He actually wished he could've taken this afternoon further, but he knew putting the brakes on when he had was the right choice for now. He'd felt his heart racing uncomfortably in his chest as she'd come and had decided he needed to stop there. He'd promised to help her forget her problems and he'd done that.

The doctor had told him he would know if he was feeling well enough to indulge. It had been almost a week since his attack, so hopefully that would be soon. But that was about as far as he was willing to go with Harper. At least for now. There were too many unknowns, too many balls in the air for him to let this fake relationship develop past much more than a simple vacation fling.

Once they were back in New York, he would return to his lab, she would inherit her fortune and they'd likely go their separate ways. He didn't have time for a relationship and she wouldn't need his help any longer. Things would fall apart. So planning for the worst, Sebastian intended to keep his distance.

Seven

This was too easy, really.

Although she was hardly a criminal master-mind—she'd never committed a crime in her life before this trip—this wasn't proving that difficult. All she'd had to do was tell the woman at the desk that she needed a new room key. The overly trusting employee had made a new one for her without question or identification and handed it over. After all, they were all friends and family here for a wedding. Certainly a trustworthy crowd…

Then all she had to do was wait. Today's itinerary included a trip to a few tourist destinations of interest, including a local abbey and a ruin of another old castle. She'd feigned a migraine and stayed at the hotel while everyone else loaded into the buses to go.

Once she was certain they were good and truly gone, she made her way to Harper's room. The door opened right up, revealing the relatively tidy space. She took her time looking around at the antique furniture and heavy velvet drapes. The room was much nicer than the one she was staying in, but she wasn't one of the bride's best friends like Harper was.

After the courier she'd hired picked up the package at the front desk and brought it to her in the castle's east gardens, she'd been certain her plan was a success. Then she saw the note inside and counted only a quarter of what she'd been expecting. It was a lot of money to be sure, but not enough.

Harper seemed to think that she was the one in control of this situation. That she could just not pay, for whatever reasons she could come up with, and everything would be okay. That was not the case. That meant taking her threat up a notch.

She'd only intended to leave a note in the room. She'd wanted to invade Harper's space and unnerve her by showing what she could do if she wanted to. But once she was there, she realized she had an opportunity to make this a more lucrative visit and create a huge impact at the same time. She opened the largest piece of luggage and dug around inside. Most of the clothes were hanging in the closet, so all that was left in the bag were some intimates and a Louis Vuitton jewelry roll tied up with a leather cord. Bingo.

She unrolled the bundle, looking over the neatly organized pieces of jewelry in the different pockets. A few looked like nice costume jewelry, but in one pouch she pulled out a pair of diamond stud earrings that were at least one carat each. She slipped them into her purse, following with a necklace with a fat, pear-shaped sapphire pendant. Last, she pocketed a diamond-and-ruby tennis bracelet and an aquamarine-and-diamond cocktail ring. All nice, but somehow she'd expected more from Harper. Maybe she'd left her pricier pieces at home this trip.

In the other piece of luggage, Sebastian's she assumed, she found a fancy pair of gold-and-emerald cufflinks in a velvet box and an old pocket watch. She wasn't a jeweler, but she knew enough to estimate that she'd made up for a good chunk of the money Harper had shorted her. It was a start, at least. She'd have a jeweler back in the States appraise her haul later.

Harper seemed to think there was no way she could come up with the money, but she just wasn't putting her mind to it. Just flipping through the clothes in the closet, she spied a couple designer pieces that would fetch a pretty penny on Poshmark. The Hermès Birkin purse she was carrying the other day would, too. There was a waiting list to get one of those bags. Even the case she kept her jewelry in was worth at least a couple hundred dollars.

Harper had a lot of expensive things. There wasn't a single designer piece in her own closet, but then again, she wasn't pretending to be rich. Having these things was all part of Harper's ruse. Of course, if she could get her hands on stuff this nice just to fake out her friends and family, she could get the money, too.

Part of her wanted to blow the top off Harper's whole lie just to expose how shallow she was. What a horrible thing it was to be poor! She was just trying to make it by until that next big payment from granddad, then everything would be okay again. In their lifetimes, most people would never see the amount of money she'd already blown, never mind what she was set to inherit later.

There were worse things than being poor in this world. Perhaps being shallow? Being a liar? Maybe even a thief? She laughed at that thought. She didn't look at this as theft. She was just an instrument of karma in this scenario. If she got a tiny piece of the pie in the process, that was just a bonus.

She turned around and looked at the tidy, elegant room. Housekeeping had already come for the morning and left chocolates on the pillows. It hadn't been a part of her original plan, but she decided on the spot that it could use a little redecorating. Just to make the place look lived in, of course.

When she was out of breath and the room looked

like it had been hit by a tornado, she took the white envelope out of her pocket and left it on the nightstand.

She had officially turned up the heat on Miss Drake.

They'd spent a long afternoon touring the Irish countryside and Sebastian had enjoyed it. It was a quiet, peaceful country to just sit and soak in the atmosphere. A good choice for a vacation location and he was sure his doctor would approve. Outside Dublin, most of the towns were small and laid back. No honking taxis and aggressive panhandlers. Just old historic sites and friendly people, all with stories to tell.

Despite the peaceful scenery, having Harper in the seat beside him on the bus had the opposite effect. The nearness of her kept his pulse fairly high. Every now and then he would get a whiff of her perfume. She would lean in to him to say something, touch his knee and playfully kiss him. At this point, the lines of their relationship were so blurry, he didn't know if she was really kissing *him* or if it was all for show. Though if people were suspicious of their relationship, it was a little too late to care. The wedding was tomorrow. They would be back in the US before long.

So did she mean it?

Sebastian tried not to overthink it. Instead he turned back to his notebook and worked on a sketch he'd started at the abbey. It seemed an odd place to get inspiration for medical equipment, but there had been a statue in the museum that was wearing some kind of armor. The shape of how it fit to the knight's leg had got him to thinking about prosthetic and robotic legs in a whole new way. That was all it had taken for him to lose all interest in old churches and to turn his focus back to work.

"You're not even listening," he heard Harper say.

Snapping out of the zone, Sebastian looked up. "What?"

"You're a million miles away. Did you hear a word I said?"

He shook his head sheepishly. "I didn't. I was focused on my work."

"I thought so. What is that?"

He sighed and looked at the rough sketch. It would take a lot of refinement for the doodle to become a cutting-edge piece of equipment, but it was a start. "One day, it may be BioTech's latest design for a robotic prosthetic. This one is for the leg."

She looked at the sketch thoughtfully. "Is that the kind of thing you usually work on?"

He shrugged. "It varies. Our very first product, the one that put us up with the big boys, was a prosthetic arm. Looking back at it now, it seems like such a crude design, but it changed everything for patients at the time. Lately we've been using 3D printing to develop custom fits for patients. Insurance wouldn't pay for something like that, so most people couldn't afford a customized fit until now. That's made a huge difference in comfort for people who've lost limbs."

"Do you work a lot with soldiers?"

"Yes. We also work with accident victims or people born with various birth defects. That's only part of what we do there. My latest project is for paraplegics. If I can get a successful prototype finished— one that can be produced affordably enough—it could change the lives of thousands of people that are wheelchair bound. This sketch is part of that."

There was a long silence and when Sebastian turned to look at Harper, he realized she was staring at him, not his sketches. "What?" he asked.

She smiled and reached out to brush a chunk of dark hair from his eyes. "I've never seen you like this."

"Like how?" He looked down to take inventory of himself self-consciously.

"I've never experienced your passion for your work. I guess I thought you were just another guy making a buck on medical research, but you really seem to care about what you're doing. Your work is amazing."

"Thank you," he responded awkwardly.

It always made him uncomfortable when people gushed at him about his research. He didn't do it for the feel-good factor. He did it for people like his brother who faced a lifetime lived with physical limitations. If he could finish the exo-legs, it meant he would have accomplished his biggest dream. Seeing his older brother walk again would mean he'd finally succeeded. The money, the success, the praise…it was all nice, but that wasn't what he wanted. He wanted to see the look on his mother's face when she saw her oldest son walk across the room unassisted. To him, that was worth sacrificing most of his life. Unfortunately he'd pushed too far and almost sacrificed all of it.

"So what inspired you to go into this line of work?" she asked.

He'd been waiting for that question. That was a slippery slope in conversation and Sebastian wasn't ready to go there. Not with reporters and not with Harper. He had a prepared answer for those times, however. He'd done several interviews and never wanted to bring his brother or his past into the discussion. It wasn't because he was embarrassed to talk about his brother's accident or his family situation. It was more that he wanted to maintain their privacy as well as his own. He didn't need the headline claiming he was a "rags to riches" success driven by his poor brother's tragic accident. That simplified the story far too much.

"I was always interested in robotics and engineering," he began his practiced story. "When I met up with Finn, he was in medical school and we got the idea to combine our specialties and start a company together after graduation. It was easy to develop a passion for the work when you see how it can impact people's lives."

"I imagine it is. I'm a corporate accountant for Jonah's company. There's no passion there, but I'm good with numbers so I got a finance degree. We're a video game company, though. It's hardly important work."

"It's important work to the people that love to play those games. Every job is critical in a different way. Finn says I'm a workaholic, but when you're doing something that can change someone's life, how do you justify walking away from your desk for a moment? Especially for something as trivial as a vacation?"

"I guess it's about balance. You don't want to burn out. But look—here you are on a vacation. Sounds like that's a big step for you."

Sebastian chuckled to himself. She had no idea. "It is. I haven't been out of my labs this long since we started the company ten years ago."

"So how were you able to do it now?"

He tensed in his seat. What was he going to say? A doctor-enforced break? Not the answer he wanted to give. He was supposed to be a successful guy. He didn't want to show weakness to Harper or any of the other people on this trip. Like a pack of wild animals, they could easily turn on the weakest member. He didn't want to give any of them the ammunition to come for him. Not his background, not his health, not his fake/real relationship with Harper. If he let out too much about himself, he might be the next one blackmailed.

"You gave me no choice," he said with a laugh. "A beautiful woman walks up to me in a department store, asks me out and offers me a free trip to Ireland. How can any red-blooded man pass that up?"

Looking up, Sebastian noticed they had reached the hotel. He was relieved to end the conversation there. "Looks like we're back."

Everyone gathered their things and shuffled back into the hotel. The arrival couldn't have been better timed. He was more than happy to stop talking about himself. All he wanted to do now was to go upstairs, take a hot shower and get ready for dinner. Tonight they were hosting some kind of authentic Irish dinner show at the castle with traditional music and dance. It sounded interesting enough.

"I'm ready to take off these shoes," Harper said as she slipped her key card into the door. She took two steps and stopped short, sending him slamming into her back.

"What's wrong?"

Harper pushed open the door and revealed the mess that had once been their hotel room. Their things were scattered everywhere. Furniture was overturned. It was awful.

"Don't touch anything," he said. "We've been robbed."

"Don't touch anything?" Harper asked. "What are we going to do? Call the police?"

"That was my thought."

Harper walked into the room and picked up a familiar white envelope sitting on the nightstand. "Think again. If we call the cops, the blackmailer will expose me for sure."

With a sigh, Sebastian slammed the door shut and walked in to survey the mess. "So what does it say? I take it he wasn't pleased by the partial payment."

"It says that he's taken a few things to make up for the missing money. That was just a punishment, though. He still expects a hundred and twenty thousand dollars before the wedding reception ends." She looked up with despair in her eyes. "What about the twenty-five thousand euros he's already got? It's like it didn't even count. That or he's just jacking up the fee every time we miss a deadline." She dropped her face into her hands. "This is never going to end."

Sebastian walked over and sat beside her on the mattress. "It will end. He can't string this along forever. You're going to turn thirty and once you inherit, there's nothing to hold over your head. Or he exposes you and there's no money to be had. But it will end." He wrapped his arm around her shoulders. It wasn't the best pep talk he'd ever given, but it was something.

He didn't know what else to say as they sat and looked at their destroyed hotel suite. It must have taken quite a bit of time to do it, but given they'd been gone for hours, the blackmailer had had all the time in the world.

"Did you bring anything valuable?" he asked.

"Just a few things. Mainly pieces I was going to wear to the wedding." Harper got up and sought out her overturned suitcase. "My jewelry roll is gone. Oh, wait…" She spied it in the corner and picked it up. She poked through a couple pockets and shook her head. "He got all the good stuff. That sapphire necklace belonged to my mother," she said, tears shimmering in her eyes.

Sebastian cursed and stood to go to her. "We can call the cops. We don't have to mention the blackmail. You'll need the report for your insurance claims."

"What insurance?" she chuckled sadly. "You're talking like I have the money to insure all this stuff. I don't. It's gone. It's all just gone. Probably forty thousand dollars' worth of jewelry, easy. Did you bring anything?"

Sebastian hadn't really thought about his things. He hadn't previously been a target of the blackmailer, but he supposed if they wanted money, they'd get it from anywhere. "Not much," he said. Looking around, he found the box with his cufflinks for his tuxedo. It was empty. Figures. The only other item he had with him was his grandfather's pocket watch, but it wasn't worth anything. He carried it for sentimental value.

He dug around in his stuff, flinging pillows out of the way, but found that it, too, was gone. He turned a chair right-side up and sat with a disgusted huff.

"What did he get?" Harper looked at him with wide eyes of concern.

"My great-grandfather's pocket watch," he said. "He was a train conductor. It's not worth a dime to anyone but me. I can't believe the bastard took it."

Harper groaned. "Oh, no. I'll replace anything you lost once I get my money," she offered. "I know I can't replace your grandfather's watch exactly, but I'll do whatever I can. I'm so sorry to have dragged you into this whole mess."

"It's not your fault," Sebastian said. "But we've got to find a way to put an end to it all. Maybe I just need to give you the money."

"Sebastian, no," she said, crouching at his knee. She looked up at him with a dismayed expression. "I can't ask you to do that. You've already done too much."

He shook his head. "I don't want to pay him. He doesn't deserve the damn money, but it might be the only answer we have. But if we do pay him," he said with angrily gritted teeth, "I want all our stuff back."

"So what do we know about this Josie?" Lucy asked in a hushed voice over a delicate china plate of tea sandwiches.

They were at Violet's bridal tea, a ladies-only

event. All the men, Sebastian included, had gone to play a round of golf, followed by some day drinking that would likely run until the rehearsal dinner. This was one of Harper's first real opportunities to sit with her friends without Sebastian or the other guys since they'd arrived in Ireland.

Violet was at another table near the front, being adored by all the ladies in attendance, leaving Harper, Lucy and Emma to sit in the back corner and gossip as they often did. They all shrugged in response to Lucy's question, Harper included. She didn't know, or really care much about Quentin's new fiancée. She had bigger, more pressing worries, but she was interested in why the others were so concerned.

"I hadn't met her before the trip, but I had heard about her through the grapevine. To hear it told," Emma said as she gripped her teacup, "the engagement was quite the surprise to everyone. Given his current situation, I think a lot of people felt that Quentin might have chosen a woman with a fatter bank account and better connections. As far as I know, Josie is a broke nobody. She's a secretary for a financial firm or something. Not exactly what I was expecting. Of course, all that could've happened after he proposed and then he was stuck with her."

Harper perked up in her seat at Emma's story. "Given his current situation? Stuck? What do you mean by 'all that'?"

Emma and Lucy shared knowing glances before

turning back to Harper. "We hadn't said anything because bringing up Quentin in conversations always seemed to put you in a bad mood."

"Yes, well, talking about someone's ex is hardly a way to perk up their day. Unless it's bad news. Is it bad news?"

Lucy nodded. Her dark eyes lit with excitement. "Apparently he was cut off by his dear old dad."

Harper sat back in her seat, her jaw agape. That certainly was news. Quentin was an attorney, but he was a long way from being the successful hot shot he pretended to be. Most of his money had come from his family. When they were dating, she recalled him getting a ten-thousand-dollar-a-week allowance from his father. He'd been twenty-eight at the time, giving Harper a run for her money when it came to being spoiled.

"He's the low man on the totem pole at his law firm," Harper said. "Without his allowance, he would be in big trouble. He couldn't afford his apartment, his car…he certainly couldn't afford the giant engagement ring I've seen her sporting, either."

"Exactly," Emma said.

"Do we know why he got cut off?" Harper asked.

Lucy shook her head. "I haven't heard anything specific, but you know he had to have done something his dad really wasn't happy about to get cut off."

"So why would someone in his position propose to a woman that won't be any help with that situation?

There are plenty of rich, single women in Manhattan that he could've chosen instead. He could've even come crawling back to you," Emma said.

"Not likely," Harper said. Quentin knew Harper didn't have any money or he might've tried. She couldn't tell the others that, though.

"What's so special about her?"

"I don't know. He loves her, maybe?" Harper replied with a sarcastic tone.

"Love? Quentin? Come on, now." Emma snorted. "If he was capable of that, he would've married you years ago. Maybe she's from an important family or one of his clients' children. No, my bet is that his father disapproves of the engagement and cut him off when he found out Quentin proposed. Unless she's got more to offer than meets the eye, I think he's searching for his relationship escape hatch. Once this wedding is over, he's going to drop her like a rock to get back in daddy's good graces. You just watch."

"Why would he propose to a woman his father didn't like?" Lucy asked. "Could she be pregnant?"

The three turned to where Josie was seated sipping tea. Her dress was fairly tight, showing no signs of a baby belly. "I doubt it," Harper said.

"I wonder if he just wanted to be engaged to someone at the wedding to make Harper jealous and it ended up backfiring on him."

Harper turned to Emma and frowned. "That's silly. Who would make up a fake relationship just to make someone else jealous?" The irony of the words were not lost on her.

"Maybe not jealous. Maybe he just didn't want to come here and face you on his own."

"He hasn't even spoken to me the whole trip. I doubt he's given me much thought at all."

"Well, you may be right, but I think it gives him the perfect motive to pick a random girl to be his fiancée for a few weeks."

Harper lifted her teacup and sipped thoughtfully. Being cut off by daddy also gave her the one piece of the puzzle she'd been missing—the perfect motive for Quentin to blackmail her.

Eight

Sebastian was exhausted from a day golfing with the others but keen to get back to Harper to tell her everything he'd overheard during the trip. Between eighteen holes and half a dozen beers, mouths had loosened among the gentlemen. In addition to getting to know them all better, he'd picked up some stock tips, improved his swing and gotten some more dirt on her ex, Quentin.

As the bus pulled up in front of the castle, he spied Harper walking out toward the east gardens. When they unloaded, he trotted off after her, catching up just as she reached the intricate hedges that outlined the borders. She sat on a stone bench that overlooked the formal pattern of flowerbeds in bright summer colors that contrasted with the lush green of the grass.

"Harper!"

She turned and looked over her shoulder at him. She was wearing a pretty, pale pink, eyelet sundress with a matching sweater. "Hey there, Arnold Palmer. How did the golf go?"

He strolled the rest of the way toward her to catch his breath. He needed to do more running, apparently. "Awful," he said as he dropped down beside her on the bench. "I couldn't tell them I'd never played before, so I had to fake it and claim I was rusty from working too much."

"You've never played golf? What kind of CEO are you?"

Sebastian chuckled. "The kind that doesn't take clients out to schmooze on the greens. That's Finn's job. I work. But I have played golf. Just not this kind. I'm used to the windmills and the alligators that swallow your ball if you putt it into the wrong hole."

"Miniature golf. You've played Putt-Putt. Yeah, I'd say that's a little different."

"I'll tell you, though. Once I got the ball near the hole, I was an excellent putter. Just took me five swings over par to get that close."

Harper winced and laughed. "Wow. Lose any money?"

He shook his head. "I'm not that stupid. There was no way I was betting on my game. I did offer Quentin a wager, though. I bet him a thousand dollars that he'd shank his next ball into a sand trap."

She arched her brow curiously. "And?"

Sebastian reached into his pocket and pulled out a roll of hundred dollar bills. "I think I jinxed him. He basically shot it straight into the sand dunes and couldn't get out. Completely rattled the guy. I didn't feel guilty about it, though. If he's your blackmailer, then this thousand may have come from the money you paid him yesterday. If that's true, then I'm glad to steal some back." He handed the cash over to Harper.

"What is this for?" she asked, looking at the bills uncurling in the palm of her hand.

"For whatever." He shrugged. "It's not my money, so you can light cigars with it for all I care. Pay it to the blackmailer. Pay it on the loan. Get a really expensive manicure. Save it for a rainy day. Whatever you want. Just spend it knowing that I took it from Quentin. That should make it all the sweeter."

Harper closed her fist around the money and nodded. "It will," she said before slipping it into the little wallet pocket of her cell phone case. "Anything else interesting come up this afternoon?"

"Lots of man talk. Mostly bluster without substance. It got a little heated about the Yankees once alcohol got involved. The groom's face turned as red as his hair when someone said something about the Mets being a better team. I was smart enough to stay out of that. I don't know enough about sports to comment intelligently."

"Really? You didn't play sports in school?"

Sebastian frowned. "No. That wasn't my thing," he said. He supposed it might've interested him if he'd had the time. Maybe the swim team. But the fees to participate in school sports had been too high and all his free time had been taken up by working to help support his family. He hadn't had the typical frivolous youth, but Harper didn't know that. "I did learn something interesting about Quentin, though."

Harper turned toward him on the stone bench. "Me, too. But you go first."

"Okay. While we were talking, someone mentioned that Quentin was in some legal hot water. Apparently he'd tried to flip some real estate and used shoddy contractors to save money. The people that bought the place took him to court and the judge sided with them, awarding them a settlement to correct some of the repairs. Guess for how much?"

"A hundred thousand dollars?"

"Bingo."

"That is interesting. It certainly gives him a reason to come after me for exactly that much money. Especially after what I learned about him at the tea party."

"What's that?"

"His father cut him off, financially. We're not sure if it's because he disapproves of the fiancée, or maybe because of his legal troubles, but he isn't getting any more money from his father. I can tell you that's huge. He's probably hurting for cash right now. Even that thousand-dollar loss to you today likely stings."

Sebastian only shrugged. "He should've turned down the bet, then. He's too cocky to think he will lose."

"That is Quentin for you. Looking back, I know I dodged a bullet with that one."

"I'm sure you did. For all your dating angst, I hear you're quite the catch. All the gentlemen I spoke to think rather highly of you," Sebastian added with a smile.

Harper blushed with embarrassment and pushed a stray strand of dark hair behind her ear in an endearing way. He liked the way she was wearing it today. It was down in loose waves, almost like wild morning-after hair. It made him think about how it had cascaded across the pillows the other afternoon as he'd pleasured her. When he'd touched it, it had felt like silk between his fingertips. He wanted to touch it again.

"Do they now?" Harper said. "What did they say?"

"Well, they all congratulated me for winning you over. They said you were an amazing woman and that I would be a fool to let you slip through my fingertips."

Sebastian knew their words to be true before the

men had confirmed it. Harper, however, seemed dumbfounded by the whole conversation.

"Really?"

"Yes, really."

"Even Quentin?"

Sebastian nodded. "Even Quentin. I don't know if it's all part of his game or not, but he said there were times when he knew he'd made the wrong choice letting you go."

Harper gasped. "I can't believe it."

"I don't know why. You're smart, beautiful, funny, sweet…"

"Quit buttering me up."

"You tend to lie a lot, though," he added with a smile. "Of course, they don't know that. They did mention that you have expensive tastes and might be costly to keep, but that you were worth it."

Harper laughed aloud at the final observation. "That sounds more like I was expecting to hear. How funny. Who knew golf with the boys could be so enlightening?"

It certainly had been for him. He'd already been dreading the end of the trip and their run as a couple, but his chat with the other men had made him wonder if maybe he shouldn't push harder for something more with Harper. Something beyond the physical. He'd been worried about letting himself get too close, but perhaps in time it might be possible. If he let himself do it. If he could take a step back from his work and allow life to take its place. Balance had never been his strength. He was balls-to-the-wall, all or nothing. Here, a relationship was easy because work wasn't interfering. Back home, the relationship would interfere with his work.

And that was only if Harper was open to the possibility. Now that he'd filled her head with compliments about how great a catch she was, he might not be what she wanted. He was a great stand-in for a boyfriend in a pinch, but would she want him once they were back in the States again? Maybe only if her grandfather cut her off.

"I guess the men's golf game is just as big a gossip cesspool as the ladies' tea," Harper said with a smile. "Did my brother say anything embarrassing?"

"Not much. He'd already said his peace to me a few days ago. The first day we arrived, actually."

Harper's eyes got big as she stiffened on the bench. She put her hand on him, squeezing his forearm. "What? No. What did he say?"

Sebastian chuckled. "Nothing too embarrassing, just basic big-brother stuff. I think he was just worried about you. He wanted to make sure my intentions were honest. He gave me a little insight into you, too."

"Like what?"

"Like, I'm not telling you," Sebastian retorted.

"So unfair. You've got all the insight into me and you're this puzzle box I can't get into." With a sigh, Harper pushed up from the bench.

"Where are you going?"

"Back inside to get ready for the rehearsal. I'm a bridesmaid, you know."

Sebastian stood with her. Before she could get away, he wrapped her in his arms and pulled her close to him. "I forgot to say how nice you look today."

Harper smiled. "Thank you. You don't need to lay it on so thick, though. I don't think anyone is watching us out here together."

She seemed to think that every word, every caring gesture, was part of the game when it wasn't. How was he supposed to know if anything she said or did with him was genuine? That orgasm was genuine enough, but everything else? He couldn't be sure. Perhaps the idea of something real between them was a bridge too far.

But for now, he was going to go with it.

"I don't really care," he said, dipping his head and capturing her lips in a kiss.

As rehearsed, Harper marched down the rose-petal-strewn aisle in her lavender bridesmaid gown clutching a bundle of purple-and-cream roses with dark purple freesia and ranunculus in her hands. She was the last of the bridesmaids, with the rest of the wedding party already waiting up front with the minister.

Today, the Markree Castle gallery was acting as the chapel where the wedding was taking place. The long hall was lined with wooden paneling and pale blue-green walls. As she made her way down the long stretch of chairs that lined the aisle, she looked up to the pitched wood-beam ceiling and the intricate stained-glass windows that adorned the far end of the chapel, taking in their beauty.

Turning to the left, she lined up with Emma and Lucy to await the arrival of Violet in her wedding finery. She glanced over at the groomsmen across the aisle. They all looked handsome in their black tuxedos and lavender ties. Even little Knox had a matching tux. Aidan had managed to comb his wild red hair into submission for the special occasion. He was practically beaming with his eyes laser-focused on the back of the hall for the arrival of his bride.

The musical crescendo started and all the guests stood. The doors opened and Violet stepped through on the arm of her father. Even knowing what the dress looked like on Violet, Harper still felt the magnificence steal her breath as everything came together so beautifully.

The Pnina Tornai gown from Kleinfeld's was a beautiful but relatively plain gown from the front, allowing Violet's beauty to shine. It was a strapless, white ball gown with a crystal belt and corset top that molded to her perfectly. Her neck was as long and graceful as a swan's with her hair up and a simple diamond-and-pearl choker at her throat. In her hands, she carried a magnificent hand-crafted brooch bouquet made of silk rosettes in different shades of purple and covered in Swarovski crystal pins in two dozen different styles. Dripping from the teardrop-shaped bouquet were strings of pearls and strands of crystals.

But that was just the beginning. Harper heard the gasps of the guests as Violet passed and the back of the dress was revealed. That was where the beauty of the gown shone. From the waist down, the dress was a waterfall of large, silk roses that cascaded to the floor several feet behind her. The moment Violet had put on the dress at the bridal salon, they'd all known it was the one. Few other dresses could stand up to the grand venue like this one could.

As she looked out, Harper spotted Sebastian in the crowd. He'd chosen to sit on Aidan's side since he had fewer guests attending.

He was looking incredibly dapper in his tuxedo. He claimed he hardly ever wore it, but it fit perfectly and suited him well. The only thing missing were his cufflinks that had been stolen. She had gone that afternoon to Oliver's room and borrowed a pair, claiming Sebastian had forgotten to pack his own.

Unlike everyone else in the church, whose eyes were on Violet, Sebastian's eyes were on Harper. When he realized she had turned his way, he smiled and gave her a wink before looking over to Violet with the others as she stepped up to stand beside Aidan.

Harper handed her bouquet off to Lucy so she could straighten Violet's train and veil. Once they were perfect for pictures, she took the very heavily jeweled bouquet so Violet could hold Aidan's hands during the ceremony.

Once the service began, Harper looked down at the beautiful arrangement in her hands and the reality of the moment finally hit her. She was the last of her single friends. Practically, she'd known that. Violet and Aidan had been engaged for a while as they'd planned the event, so it's not like it had snuck up on her. But until that moment, she hadn't allowed herself to really grasp what it meant.

She was on the verge of thirty, hardly an old maid, but seeing the last of her friends pair off made a wave of sadness wash over her. Why hadn't she found someone like they had? She should be happily engaged and ready to start her life with someone, and yet here she was, basically bribing a man just to pretend to be her boyfriend at the wedding.

Her gaze drifted back to Sebastian. He was sitting in the chair, listening attentively to the service. She was so thankful he was there with her for this. Yes, it was because she had asked him to be, but she wondered what would've happened between them if things had gone differently. If he had asked her to dinner instead of her asking him on this trip…if there had been no wedding and they'd decided to go for drinks after they'd met at the store…would they have become real lovers instead of ones just for show?

In that moment she wished they were in a real relationship. Not just because she didn't want to be alone, but because she found she really cared for Sebastian. He was smart, handsome, thoughtful and kind. He was there for her when she needed someone. There was a part of her that was extremely susceptible to being treated the way he treated her. That part of her wanted to fall head over heels for him.

The other part didn't know where they stood.

Yes, they had crossed the line of their fake relationship that afternoon in their room, but their ruse had muddied the water. Was their attraction real or did they just think they were into one another because they spent all day flirting and pretending to be a couple? She was pretty certain that her draw to Sebastian was authentic. The moment she'd laid eyes on him outside Neiman Marcus, she'd been attracted to his dark eyes and strong jaw. She'd wanted to know more about him instantly.

Honestly, after spending a week together, Harper found that she still wanted to know more about him. Mainly because he wasn't opening up to her the way she'd hoped. In all their conversations there had been plenty of chances for him to tell her about his childhood or where he'd grown up. His time in college. Anything outside of work. But that was really all he spoke about. His work was his life.

She knew Sebastian was passionate about his job, but she couldn't help but feel that there was more to him that he wasn't sharing. Intentionally. That worried her. Not because he was keeping potentially damaging secrets that would run her off, but because he didn't think he could open up to her.

If he didn't think he could share with her, what would happen once they returned to New York and didn't have a wedding packed full of events to get through? Would he call her? Would he want to kiss her again? Or would he return to his lab and disappear into his tools and toys the way he had before the trip?

She didn't know the answer. And that uncertainty scared her. Perhaps because no matter what the answer was, she knew it was already too late for her. Those dark eyes and that crooked smile had already captured her heart.

Maybe it wasn't being the last single friend that was troubling her today. Being single hadn't really ever bothered her before. Maybe it was knowing that, yes, she wanted a romantic moment like this for herself, but that she wanted it *with Sebastian*. She wanted him to be the man to whom she recited her vows to love, honor and cherish. She was upset because she knew deep down that she would never have this moment with him.

The loud sound of applause jerked Harper out of her thoughts. She turned to the altar in time to realize that the wedding ceremony had ended. Aidan and Violet were sharing their first kiss as husband and wife.

"Ladies and gentlemen, may I present for the very first time, Mr. and Mrs. Aidan Murphy!"

Violet turned to Harper to get her bouquet and face the crowd of wedding guests. Harper moved behind the bride to straighten her dress and veil one last time before Aidan scooped up Knox in his arms and they marched down the aisle as a family. Once they departed, she took her bouquet from Lucy.

Lucy followed the bouquet with a tissue she'd tucked away in her bra. "Here," she said, despite fighting tears of her own. "Don't mess up your makeup before the photos."

It wasn't until that moment that Harper realized she was crying. But it wasn't because of the beautiful service—it was because she knew she was right about her future with Sebastian. She dabbed her eyes, took a deep breath and pasted a smile on her face for the cameras.

No matter what, she still had a wedding reception to get through.

The new Mr. and Mrs. Aidan Murphy walked down the aisle together, holding their adorable toddler. Both of them were beaming with happiness and it took everything she had to not scowl at them as they went by. She put a fake smile on her face and clutched her program as the rest of the wedding party followed in their wake.

First was tech heiress Emma and her rebellious, gaming CEO husband, Jonah. The two of them were so beautiful together that she already hated their daughter. She was still a baby, but she would no doubt grow up to be a Victoria's Secret Angel or something. Behind them was the formerly poor but incredibly lucky Lucy, who'd managed to inherit half a billion dollars from her boss, then married her boss's nephew, Oliver, with his computer empire. She wished she'd had that kind of luck, but she'd learned she had to take control of her own destiny.

Last down the aisle was Harper on the arm of a groomsman that must be a friend of Aidan's because she didn't know him. She'd only studied the people with enough money to matter on this trip. This guy didn't matter. None of these people really did. Once she got her money, she was pretty sure she'd never see the likes of most of them again. That is, unless she uncovered another scandalous tidbit to make some more money off of them.

The guests at the wedding stood and started filing out of the gallery toward the dining hall for the cocktail reception. After thirty minutes of that overly romantic ceremony, she needed a drink. Maybe two. Or four by the time dinner rolled around. This was going to be a long night.

They were headed back to the States soon and she

could feel time was running short. Time in Ireland. Time with all of these people. Time to execute her plan and make off with the money she needed.

The blackmail payment was supposed to be at the front desk before the reception ended, but she wasn't holding her breath. Every other deadline had passed with disappointment. Why would this one be any different?

She wanted her money. She didn't want to have to pull the trigger and expose Harper. That wouldn't do either of them any good. No, Harper was being obstinate, insisting she couldn't pay when they were surrounded by people who could just write a check for that amount if they wanted to. Harper only had to ask. But she wouldn't.

Harper was going to ruin things for her. So that meant that she had no choice but to ruin things for Harper.

Nine

Sebastian spun Harper on the dance floor and then pulled her tightly against him. Dinner had been excellent, but he couldn't wait to take Harper out for a spin. He wasn't much of a dancer, but it was the only socially acceptable way he knew of to hold her body against his in public.

"You really look beautiful tonight, Harper. Have I said that yet?"

"No," she said with a smile, "but thank you. You should know, though, that I'm just a bridesmaid, so I can only be pretty. At a wedding, only the bride can be beautiful. It's the rules."

He leaned in to her and the scent of her floral perfume tickled at his nose, putting his nerves on high alert. It made him want to pull her closer. Or better yet, to tug her off the dance floor and head upstairs to their hotel room. His medical restrictions on sexual activity should be over now. He'd take it slow just in case, but he needed to indulge in Harper at least once before all of this came to an end.

Sebastian pressed his lips to the outer shell of her ear. "Well, don't tell Violet, but I think you're the most stunning woman here tonight. I don't care who the bride is. You take my breath away even when you're wearing that ugly purple dress she picked for all of you."

When he pulled away, he could see Harper blush before she glanced down to look at her dress with a critical eye. "You don't like my dress? I like it. I mean, I like it for a bridesmaid's dress. I wouldn't wear it to the Met Gala or anything, but it's pretty enough."

He didn't know what one would wear to the Met Gala, but he was pretty sure this pale purple frock with flowers on the shoulder wasn't it. "To be honest, I think you would look much prettier without it."

Her brow arched in suspicion. "I think you just want me to be naked."

Sebastian shrugged. "If you want to look your best, my vote is for naked."

"Just like a man," she groaned. "No respect for the power of fashion."

That was true. For all his money, Sebastian didn't

know one designer from the next, nor did he care. He'd be just as happy buying all his clothes at Target, if Finn would let him. He was more about function than style most days. He couldn't even tell you the name of the designer he was wearing right now. It was someone important. Finn had made sure of that. But without slipping out of his jacket to look at the name sewn inside, he had no clue.

What he did know was that the tuxedo was getting hot. Or maybe it was dancing so close to Harper that was overheating him. Looking around, he spied a door that opened onto a courtyard.

"You want to get some air? It's getting a little warm in here."

Harper glanced around the room for a moment and nodded. "Sure. I think we still have a little time before they cut the cake."

Sebastian took her hand and led her off the dance floor. They made their way around a few tables before they reached the door that opened up to the courtyard. Out there, half a dozen small bistro tables and chairs had been set up. Each table was decorated with a floral arrangement and a flickering pillar candle protected from the breeze with a tall hurricane glass. At the moment, no one was outside, giving them some privacy.

He stepped over to the stone wall that separated the patio from the gardens beyond. It was a clear, cool night with a sky full of stars. He couldn't imagine this many stars existed if he lived in Manhattan his whole life. He'd only seen this many on nights in Maine as a kid. Even so, it hardly held a candle to the beauty of the woman standing beside him.

He hadn't just been flattering her earlier, it was the truth. It would be so easy in a moment like this—with candlelight highlighting the soft curves of her face and stars reflecting in her eyes—to let his guard down and fall for Harper once and for all. The music and the moonlight seemed to be conspiring against him tonight, wearing down his defenses. This week was supposed to be relaxing and yet he'd spent the entire trip fighting with himself.

He hadn't expected any of this when he'd agreed to come to Ireland. Yes, he'd thought he would spend a few days holding hands with and kissing a beautiful woman overseas. He'd never imagined that he would be tempted to take their fake relationship seriously and open up to her. That he might look forward to returning to New York and spending time with her instead of rushing back into his lab at the first opportunity.

If he had, he might not have taken the trip. His work was at such a critical point. Could he risk taking time away to build something serious with Harper? He wasn't sure.

"Ahh, this feels good," Harper said. "Normally it would be cold, but it got so hot in the ballroom."

"Maybe it's all the champagne," Sebastian offered.

"Or maybe it's the pressure," she said with a sigh.

"Pressure? What kind of pressure?"

Harper leaned her elbows against the patio wall to look out at the garden. "The reception will be over soon and my time is running out. That means the blackmailer is going to realize he isn't going to get any more money out of me. He won't have any choice but to expose my secret. I wonder how long he'll wait. Will he reveal the truth tonight? Wait until the morning and ruin my flight home? Maybe wait until we're back in New York and have something printed in the paper so everyone, not just the wedding guests, finds out? I wish I knew how it would happen so I could brace myself for it."

Sebastian had been enjoying the romantic evening with Harper and pondering a future with her, and all the while her mind was on her troubles instead of her company. Perhaps he'd better put those thoughts aside before he regretted them. "And here I thought you might be enjoying the wedding reception."

She shook her head sadly and straightened up. "I wish I could. This was supposed to be a great trip and a special wedding for one of my best friends. Instead it's been nothing but a waking nightmare where everyone has Irish accents. I really just want to get on the plane and go home so I can get started dealing with the fallout."

Sebastian took her hand in his. She felt so small and delicate in his grip when she was speaking in such a defeated tone. "You're going to be okay, you know."

"What do you mean?"

"I mean that no matter what happens, you're a strong, independent woman. You've made the best of your situation before and you'll continue to make the best of it, regardless of what the blackmailer does. He might feel like he's in control of your fate, but he's really not. How you handle your situation is entirely up to you."

Harper studied his face for a moment and nodded. "You're right. And I think I'm going to start handling the situation right now." She turned away from him to head back into the reception.

Sebastian reached out and grasped her wrist before she could get away. "Wait. What are you going to do?"

She took a deep breath and straightened her spine. "I'm going to confront Quentin and put an end to this."

"Quentin? May I speak with you privately for a moment?"

He hesitated, looking at his fiancée before whispering into her ear and nodding to Harper.

Harper hadn't had any discussions with Jessie or Josie or Jamie—whatever her name was. She wasn't interested in chatting with her ex-boyfriend's new fiancée. It was hard enough to look at the glittering diamond rock on her ring finger and not think about the bare finger on her own hand. The only difference lately was that when she imagined a man down on one knee proposing, there was only one face that came to mind.

And it sure wasn't Quentin's.

He finally disentangled himself from his fiancée and followed Harper out into the hallway. "What's this all about, Harper? Josie doesn't really like me talking to you, to be honest. The sooner I'm back in the reception, the better off I'll be."

Harper couldn't care less about Quentin's fiancée and her jealous streak. "This won't take long. All I want to say is that I can't give you any more money, Quentin."

She'd hoped that her blunt confrontation would catch him off guard and he might give something away. Instead he stopped short and narrowed his gaze at her. "What are you talking about, Harper?"

She crossed her arms over her chest. "Oh, cut it out. I'm tired of playing these games, *B. Mayler*. I've given you all the money I can get my hands on right now. You've stolen jewelry from my room and that will have to suffice until—"

"Wait," Quentin said, holding up his hands. "I haven't stolen anything from your room. I don't even know where your room is in this place. And what money? Seriously, Harper, I have no idea what you're talking about."

Her ex's tone gave her pause. It was a sincerely

confused voice and it matched the expression on his face. "You're being sued, right? And your dad cut you off, didn't he?"

A ruddy blush of embarrassment came to his cheeks. "How did you hear about all that?"

"It's a small world. But I know it's true, so don't pretend you don't need the money."

"Sure, I could use some money. I wouldn't have dropped fifty grand on Josie's ring if I knew my dad was going to cut me loose a few weeks later. He doesn't like Josie, but I'm sure he and I will work that out. And the lawsuit is no big deal. My attorneys are handling it. But I don't know what my problems have to do with you."

"You're going to stand there and tell me that you're not the one that's blackmailing me?"

"What? No, I'm not." His eyes widened in concern and he leaned closer to speak in a softer voice. "Someone is blackmailing you?"

The concern in his voice might as well have been a punch to the gut. Harper didn't know what to say or do, but the truth was plain as day when she looked into his clueless face: Quentin was not her blackmailer.

So who the hell was?

"You know what? Just forget I said anything," Harper said. "Go back inside before Josie gets upset."

Quentin hesitated for a moment and then nodded, silently returning to the reception hall.

Harper was relieved to see him go without a fight, but the relief was short-lived.

From the very first blackmail message, she'd been fairly certain that Quentin had been behind it. He was the only one with the slightest inkling of her financial difficulties. When they'd dated and she'd finally opened up about her problems, he'd actually coached her on some financial planning. They'd even used the same financial advisor. But no one else, until she'd told Sebastian, had known.

Maybe she was fooling herself. Maybe everyone saw through her ruse and was too kind to say anything. They just let her carry on as though no one was the wiser. If that was the case, then anyone could be the blackmailer.

Harper stood at the entrance to the reception hall and watched everyone enjoying themselves inside. Violet and Aidan were cutting the cake while a crowd gathered around them. Flashes from cameras and the *awws* of bystanders drew everyone to the corner where the towering confection was on display. A few people were sitting at their tables, chatting and sipping their flutes of champagne.

Some people she knew better than others, but who was capable of blackmailing her? Of ransacking her room and stealing both her and Sebastian's things? She didn't even know where to begin looking for a new suspect.

"Miss Drake?"

Harper turned her attention to the waiter who had come up beside her. He had previously been carrying a silver tray of champagne flutes, but now his tray held nothing but the miserably familiar white envelope.

"I have a message for you," he said. "It was left at the front desk."

Of course it was. "Thank you," she said with a sigh and accepted the letter. She supposed she should open it and see what the latest threat entailed. The money was due by the end of the reception. There was only an hour or so left in that and she was pretty sure that both of them knew she wasn't paying it. So what was the point?

She slipped the envelope into the front of her bra to read later. Maybe. What did it matter in the end? She wouldn't have the money. Unless the blackmailer was bluffing the whole time, her news was going to come out sooner or later.

When she'd first told Sebastian about the note she'd received on the plane, he'd told her that one of her courses of action would be to expose the truth before anyone else could. To take the power back from the blackmailer. At the time, the idea had been out of the question. She would be throwing everything out the window if she did that. Now she wondered if that hadn't been the best policy all along. Perhaps if she spoke to her grandfather and explained her situation, he would understand. Or not. Perhaps he would cut her off and that twenty-eight million would vanish into thin air.

So what?

It seemed like a ridiculous thought to have. It was a life-changing amount of money. She'd been scraping by for years waiting for the day that money would arrive. But now that she stood there, she realized that things hadn't been so terrible. She had managed just fine. She had a good job at FlynnSoft that paid well and offered amazing benefits like a gym, a no-cost cafeteria and coffee shop, and insurance for minimum premiums and co-pays. Her beautiful, large apartment was paid for. The fees and insurance were high, but she paid them every year without fail.

No, she didn't have all the latest fashions. Her high-end pieces were either relics from her previous spending days or lucky thrift store finds. She had learned over the years how to get by without keeping up with the Joneses. If she told the truth about her situation to her friends and family, the pressure to shop and spend money with them would likely go away. No one had ever treated Lucy any differently when she'd been the poor one in the group. After she'd inherited half a billion dollars and married Harper's rich brother, she was still the same old Lucy.

Perhaps she could be the same old Harper. Just a little less flashy. She'd spent the last eight years just trying to get to her thirtieth birthday when perhaps she needed to be happy that she had made it all this time on her own. If she wasn't pretending to be something she wasn't, she could make changes to make her life easier. Maybe she could sell her flashy apartment for something more reasonable, then pocket the profit into savings. She could sell some of her designer clothes that she never wore anymore.

The realization that she didn't need her grandfather's money was a profound one for her. Suddenly it was as though a great weight had been lifted from her shoulders. She didn't know who her blackmailer was, but she was about to stick it to them. The one thing they couldn't have counted on was the spoiled heiress Harper Drake having the nerve to go it on her own.

Straightening her spine, Harper marched into the reception hall with a feeling of purpose. Cake was being distributed and the happy couple was sharing a piece at their table near the front. The band was playing a soft instrumental piece and the dance floor was empty for the moment. This was her chance.

She snatched a flute of champagne from a passing server and climbed the steps of the stage. Several people had made toasts to the couple from this perch earlier. Violet had only had bridesmaids since she said she couldn't choose a maid of honor from her three best friends. Harper could easily be the next one from the wedding party to make a toast to the happy couple.

The stage band saw her approach and eased out of the song they were playing so she could offer her good wishes to the bride and groom. She nodded and waved to them, taking the microphone from the stand and walking to the edge of the platform.

"Hello, everyone. I'm Harper Drake and I've known Violet for many years. Our families knew each other growing up, but we really got close when Violet and I went to Yale together and joined the same sorority. Pi Beta Phi sisters forever!"

The crowd laughed and applauded. "It's true. There, I made best friends for life. Not just Violet, but also Emma and Lucy, who is now my sister-in-law. Over the last few years, I've seen each of these beautiful, smart, wonderful women find love and happiness. I could not be happier for all of you. And tonight, I want to raise a toast to Violet and Aidan. May your lives together always be as magical as the fairy-tale wedding where it started."

She raised her glass and the room applauded and joined her in the toast. Harper didn't leave the stage, however. She waited for the applause to die down and continued. "Tonight, in this room, are some of the most important people in my life. So I wanted you all to hear the brief announcement that I'd like to make. No—I'm not engaged or pregnant, so let's just get that out of the way," she said with a smile. "I actually want you all to know that I've been lying to you.

"Every day for the last eight years or so, I have gotten out of bed and lived a lie. I have carried on with my life as though nothing has ever changed, but the truth is that I am broke. Flat broke. It seems silly in retrospect to lie about something like that, but my pride got in the way. No accountant wants to be seen as a poor money manager and that's what I was. I was spoiled rotten and when the well ran dry, I didn't know what to do."

Harper sipped her champagne and took a moment. Her eyes stayed focused on the tapestry on the back wall. She feared that making eye contact with someone might make her start to cry and she didn't want to do that right now.

"You're probably wondering why I'm up here telling you this. It's because someone found out about my lie—someone in this very room—and they've been using it to blackmail me. You see, if my grandfather found out I wasted all my money, I would lose the rest of my inheritance. So they've harassed me throughout this entire trip. They've taken thousands from me I couldn't afford to give, ransacked my hotel suite and stolen family pieces that can never be replaced. They've demanded money that I can't pay. And I won't ever pay it because my inheritance is basically out the window at this point.

"So I'm up here tonight to tell all of you the truth and to apologize for misleading you. And also to tell my blackmailer, whomever he or she is, that they can kiss my ass. Thank you."

She put the microphone back in the stand and made her way off of the stage as quickly as possible. She had done what she'd had to do, but she wasn't sure if she was ready to face the backlash yet. The room was unnervingly quiet, but eventually the band started to play again.

"Harper!"

She heard someone shout her name, but she didn't stop. She couldn't stop. She just wanted to get out of the ballroom as quickly as she could.

Harper made it out of the party and down the hallway before she felt a warm hand clamp down on her wrist. She stopped, spinning on her heel to find Sebastian standing behind her.

"Let me go, please," she said. "I just want to go back to our room."

He looked at her with his big, dark eyes and nodded. "That's fine. But you're not going without me."

Ten

Alone in their suite, they took their time getting undressed. There was no sense of urgency pressing them on. Tonight, she knew, they were going to savor the moment. It was their last night together and an emotionally heightened one after everything that had just happened downstairs.

"Unzip me please," she asked, presenting her back to Sebastian and lifting her hair.

He had already slipped out of his jacket and tie. He approached her, gently taking the zipper and sliding it slowly down her back. Harper could feel his fingertips grazing along her spine as he traveled down to the curve of her lower back. His touch sent a shiver through her whole body. She closed her eyes to savor the sensation of his warm breath against her skin.

His large, firm hands cupped her shoulders, pushing the one floral strap down her arm. With little effort, her dress slipped to her waist and then pooled at her feet in a puddle of lavender chiffon.

She heard his sharp intake of breath and realized he had discovered her lavender lace boy shorts. She had strategically chosen them for several reasons. First, was how they would wear beneath the dress. Second was that the cut highlighted the curve of her butt nicely. And last, they were replaceable when Sebastian tore them.

She felt his fingers grip the clasp of her strapless bra and then it fell to the floor with the rest of her clothes.

"Looks like you dropped something," he said.

Harper glanced down at the floor and realized that the note from the blackmailer she'd tucked into her bra had fallen out. She bent to pick it up and held it thoughtfully in her hand. "Another love note," she said.

Without hesitation she walked across the room to the fireplace and tossed it inside. The flames immediately started to blacken and curl the corners, then the whole thing was engulfed in the orange blaze. Although she hadn't intended it to be a symbolic gesture, it felt like one now. Consequences be damned, she was done with her blackmailer.

"Now, enough of that interrupting my trip." Harper turned back to Sebastian and approached him. She started unbuttoning his dress shirt, feeling immediately calmer and content as her hands ran over the chest hair hidden beneath it. "I don't want to think about anything but you and me right now."

She pushed his shirt over his broad shoulders and then wrapped her arms around his neck. Her lips sought his out tentatively. When they met, she molded against him, pressing her breasts into the hard wall of his chest to get as close to him as she could. "Make love to me tonight," she whispered against his mouth. "I want you. All of you."

Sebastian kissed her tenderly and then pulled away. There was a hesitation in him she didn't understand, but she shoved her doubts away when he said, "Whatever you want, darling."

His words made her smile. She hooked her fingers into the loops of his pants and tugged him over to the bed. Harper sat on the edge, bringing his waist to her eye level. There, she unfastened his belt, unbuttoned and unzipped his tuxedo pants, and slipped them down with his briefs.

She reached out for him then. He was hard and ready for her without even touching. She wrapped her fingers around his soft skin and stroked gently until she heard him groan. She moved faster, leaning in to flick her tongue across the tip.

"Harper!" Sebastian nearly shouted, grasping her

wrist to still the movement. "Wait a minute," he said. "Before we… I don't have anything."

Harper leaned over to the nightstand and pulled a small box of condoms out of the drawer. "I picked these up when we were in town one day."

After their last encounter, she'd wondered if not having protection had put the brakes on things and she hadn't wanted to run into that problem again.

The breath rushed out of his lungs all at once. "Oh, thank you," he groaned. With that worry off his mind, Sebastian seemed to become more engaged. He pressed Harper back against the pillows and covered her body with his.

She loved the feel of his weight holding her down, the scent of his cologne and skin teasing her nose, and the heat of him warming her chilled body. His lips and hands were all over her, leaving no inch of skin unloved as he moved lower and lower down her body.

His fingers brushed over the lace barrier between them. To her surprise, he eased them from her hips and tossed them to the side. "I like those," he said when he caught her surprised expression. "If I ruin them, you can't wear them again."

Harper laughed, but the sound was trapped in her throat when his fingers dipped between her thighs and stroked her center. Instead it came out a stran-gled cry as he knowingly teased the right spot. When his finger slipped inside her, Harper's inner muscles clamped down and both of them groaned aloud.

"I wanted to take my time with this," he said, shaking his head.

She reached for the condoms and handed him the box. "We can take our time later. I want you right now. I'm ready."

"So am I." He didn't hesitate to tear open the box and grab one of the foil packets from inside. Within seconds Sebastian had the latex rolled down his length and in place.

Harper shifted her legs to cradle him between her thighs and slid her hips lower.

He leaned forward, bracing himself on his elbows.

Harper lifted her knees to wrap them around his hips, but he stopped, leaning down to kiss her instead. "Thank you," he whispered.

"For what?"

"For this week. I know I was supposed to be helping you, but I needed this time away almost as much as I need you. So thank you for that." Sebastian kissed her again and this time he pressed his hips forward and entered her, ending any further conversation.

Harper gasped against his lips as Sebastian filled her. She gripped his face in her hands and kissed him hard even as he eased back and surged forward into her again. She was surprised by the stirring of pleasure deep inside her. It wasn't something she expected based on past experience, but there was something about the way he moved. A tilt of his hips, maybe, that made every stroke more amazing than the last in a way she couldn't even describe. It was just like Sebastian to have mastered the mechanics of sex.

It was so intense, she had no choice but to close her eyes and hold on. She clung to his bare back and lifted her hips to meet his every advance. Her cries grew louder and louder as her release built inside her and she couldn't hold back any longer. She shouted his name as the dam broke and the rush of pleasure surged through her.

He thrust harder then. Previously his movements had been controlled and measured in a way that was distinctly Sebastian. He seemed to be taking his time and yet ensuring every stroke made the maximum impact. As her orgasm started to fade, she realized the calculated Sebastian was giving way to a man on the edge.

He thrust hard, again and again, until he finally stiffened and groaned in her ear. He held perfectly still for a moment, his eyes squeezed tightly shut. Then he collapsed beside her on the mattress, his breath ragged with strain.

Harper curled up against his side, resting her head on his chest to listen to his heartbeat, which was faster than she expected. They lay together like that until both his breathing and his pulse had slowed to normal. At that point, he seemed to relax.

He wrapped his arm around her and placed a kiss against her forehead.

"Everything okay?" she asked, lifting her head to look up at him.

"Yes, we're good," he said. "Great, actually."

Harper chuckled and lay back. "I'm glad. I've been fantasizing about this moment all week."

"Really?" Sebastian laughed. "I'm sorry to make you hold out so long. I figured you had other things on your mind. Speaking of which, you were really amazing tonight."

"Well, thank you. I aim to please."

Sebastian swatted her bottom playfully. "That's not what I meant. I was talking about the reception. It took a lot of guts to get up there and take control of your situation. I was really proud of you."

"Oh," she said in a sheepish tone.

"What prompted it? You went to talk to Quentin and the next thing I know, you're on stage."

"I spoke with him, but it was apparent that he wasn't involved. That scared me. I had no idea who I could be dealing with and I decided it wasn't worth hiding any longer. You had been right from the beginning—exposing myself was the only way to take back my power. But I don't want to talk about that anymore. It's taken up this whole trip and I want to put it behind me. Tonight I'd rather talk about you for a change."

She felt Sebastian stiffen in her arms at the mention of talking about him. "Please," she added. "Tell me something I don't know about you. Like why you decided to go into medical technology. What inspired you? And I don't mean whatever practiced answer you put together for the company web site. The truth. What happened?"

He'd spoken about combining his engineering skills with Finn's medical expertise before and it seemed a winning combination, but there was still more to it. She could tell. No one dedicated themselves to their work like that without a reason. A personal reason.

Sebastian sat thoughtfully for a moment. The silence was long enough for her to worry he might not answer. But then he began.

"I was a shy, nerdy sort of kid. I liked to tinker. My older brother, Kenny, was more outdoorsy. He was always riding his bike or skateboarding. He stayed active."

Harper felt anxiety start to tighten her shoulders. She should've anticipated that this conversation wouldn't be a cheerful one. With his type of work, inspiration likely came from some kind of tragedy. She wanted to kick herself and yet, in the moment, was so grateful he was sharing, she would happily listen to any story he told.

"His best friend in high school ended up getting a four-wheeler for his birthday one year. My brother had graduated from high school at that point and he and a couple friends had gone camping somewhere to ride the ATV and hang out for the weekend. I don't know the details of what happened, but Kenny ended up rolling the four-wheeler. He was wearing a helmet, thankfully, but the ATV landed on top of him and crushed his lower spine. They were so deep in the woods, they couldn't land a helicopter out there to get him, so they had to carry him out on a gurney until they could reach an ambulance, which drove him to a place where the helicopter could pick him up."

Harper grasped his hand in the dark as he spoke, squeezing it tightly.

"The accident severed his spinal cord. He was eighteen and doomed to be a paraplegic for the rest of his life. I saw the toll his accident took on him and on my family. It was my hope that doing the work I do, someday I could develop something that would help him. One of the projects I've worked on for years has been a mechanical exoskeleton that would allow Kenny to walk again."

"That sounds amazing."

"It does. But so far, it's been the one thing that has eluded me. I have the technology together. I have a prototype that works in the lab. But my goal is to create something anyone can afford. Not just for rich people or ones with good insurance. That is going to take more time. That's why I work so much. For Kenny. And all the other Kennys in the world."

Harper had asked the question and now she knew

the answer. In that moment she almost wished she hadn't. Now she knew just how important his work was to him. It was personal. It was his first love. Unlike Quentin, who used his work as a cover for affairs, Sebastian was truly a workaholic. It made her wonder if that meant there would never be any room in his life for anything—or anyone—else.

It was then that she realized that she was fighting a losing battle with him. No matter what happened between them, she could never fully have Sebastian in her life. She would be better served by keeping her feelings to herself and moving on once they arrived home.

There was someone out there for Harper. Someone who would love her, treat her well and let her be the most important thing in his life. Unfortunately that man just wasn't Sebastian West.

"Ladies and gentleman, welcome to New York. The current time is nine thirty in the evening."

Sebastian perked up in his seat after the wheels hit the ground and the pilot announced the long flight was finally over. He wished he'd been able to sleep on the way back and have it go as quickly as flying over, but that wasn't the way it worked.

Instead he'd spent most of the flight watching the television in the lounge with several other wedding guests. Harper had been…quiet…since they'd left Ireland. He wasn't sure what was wrong. Things had to be looking up. The blackmailer was out of business, they didn't have to pretend to be dating any longer, they were back home…life could return to normal.

Even Sebastian was relieved to know he only had a few days left on his leave before he could get back into the office. He might not burst through the door like usual, but he had a lot of exciting sketches in his notebook and he was ready to get to work on the prototypes as soon as possible.

Perhaps Harper wasn't interested in things returning to normal. Going home meant facing the consequences of her actions with her grandfather. Even Sebastian had to admit that he wasn't quite ready for their fake relationship to come to an end. But she hadn't voiced any interest in continuing. Perhaps he had read too much into their physical connection.

They were two of the last people off the plane. Most everyone had their drivers picking them up in black, luxury sedans, so the parking lot of the small airport emptied quickly. By the time they collected their bags and went out to where they'd parked, Sebastian found it was just the two of them.

"So now what?" he asked, setting down his luggage beside his car. Although he rarely drove it in the city, he had a blue BMW that he traveled back and forth to Maine in from time to time.

Harper set her bag down and sighed. "I've got an Uber coming to get me."

"That's not what I meant," he said. "I meant with us."

She crossed her arms over her chest in a defensive posture she'd never taken with him before. "I don't know. The week is over. Thank you very much for being my boyfriend on the trip. You were very… thorough."

"Thorough?" He couldn't keep the irritation from his voice. "Is that what you call it?"

"What else would you call it, Sebastian?"

There was a tone in her voice that he couldn't pinpoint. He wasn't sure if she was daring him to admit that it was more than just for show or not. Did she want him to profess his undying love and beg her to be his girlfriend for real? Or did she just want him to lay out his feelings so she could stomp on them? The way she'd pulled away from him today made him unsure.

"I sure as hell wouldn't—"

"Your time is up, Miss Drake," a woman's voice interrupted him.

Both Harper and Sebastian turned their attention to the shadowy figure standing in the dark, empty parking lot outside the airport.

The person took a few steps closer into the beam of an overhead light and Sebastian could finally make out who was standing there.

He didn't know her name, but he recognized the woman as Quentin's fiancée. And more importantly, she was aiming a gun at Harper.

Without thinking, he took a step forward and put his arm out to shield Harper. "What the hell are you doing pointing a gun at people?" he asked.

"Josie?" Harper asked from over his shoulder. "What's going on?"

"Surprised?" The woman smiled but it came out more like a smirk. "I bet you didn't suspect little old me for a second, did you? Of course not. You haven't given me a second thought this whole trip. I wasn't important or rich like the rest of you. I was just the disposable arm candy."

That was true. Sebastian had hardly paid any attention to the younger woman who'd always seemed glued to Quentin's side. To be fair, he hadn't really known many of the people on the trip, but Josie had been a silent, ignorable presence. Harper hadn't even known the woman and she knew everybody.

If that was true, how had Josie managed to get hold of such personal, private information about Harper?

"You're the one blackmailing me?"

"Guilty," Josie said without moving the gun a centimeter. It was still fixed on Harper, even if it had to go through Sebastian to get there.

"I don't understand," Harper said, pushing his arm out of the way. "How did you find out about my trust conditions? Did Quentin tell you?"

Josie shook her head. "All Quentin provided me was access to you. The rest I got on my own. If you'd bothered to speak to me this trip, you might've discovered that I work for your financial management firm. I know everything about you, Harper, including the provisions of your trust. I just knew a spoiled diva like you would've blown it. It only took a little digging to find out what I needed to know. Honestly, it was too easy."

"Why would you do this to me, Josie? I've never done anything to you."

"Aww, it wasn't personal, Harper. It's just about the money. It could've just as easily been any one of you."

"It was personal to me. Ransacking our room? Taking my late mother's necklace, his grandfather's watch—that was personal. I've spent the last week tied in knots because of you. And for what? Just some money?"

"You say that just like a rich person. You've gotten good at fooling everyone. Yes, I just did it for some money. That's enough for most people, although I have to admit I haven't gotten much cash out of the deal. I've spent this whole trip trying to get my point across with you, but nothing seems to be working. I've threatened you, stalked you, raised the price, promised to expose you, and here I stand with mere pennies of what you owe me."

"I don't owe you anything. Nobody owes you a damn thing. Everything you've gotten was taken by force."

"And everything you've gotten was given to you on a silver platter. All you have to do is give me the money and I'll be on my way."

"You of all people know that I won't have any money until after my birthday. How can I pay you what I don't have?"

Sebastian wished he could think of something to do. Like some smooth kung-fu move to kick the gun out of Josie's hand and then wrestle her to the ground. But he was an engineer. At best, he could outthink her. If he could get his heart to stop pounding so loudly so he could focus.

"Like you couldn't get it if you needed it with all your rich and powerful friends. Violet spent more money on the rehearsal dinner alone than I was asking for. To tell the truth, I feel like I've been accommodating. I doubt there are many other blackmailers out there that would've given you as many chances as I have, Harper. But I'm done being nice. I need the money and I need it now."

"Why would I pay you another cent?" Harper asked. "It's all over, Josie. It's been over since the wedding. Everyone knows my secret. You can't blackmail me with it anymore."

She nodded. "That's true. That's why I brought along the gun. This isn't so much a blackmailing anymore as an armed robbery. I want my money."

"Why do you need money from me? You're marrying Quentin. His family has plenty of money. A hundred thousand is nothing to them."

"And I'm nothing to Quentin," Josie replied with narrowed eyes. "It turns out he was just using me to make you jealous. He proposed and brought me on this trip just because he knew it would bother you. He never expected daddy to cut him off in the process. Now that the trip is over and he sees you're in love with someone else, he's dropped me like a rock and gone crawling back for forgiveness. So the money is more important than ever, actually."

Sebastian watched the heated discussion continue to volley between the two women. He curled his hands into fists at his sides as frustration and anger built inside him, but he felt an unpleasant tingling sensation running down his left arm. It forced him to shake out his hand in the hope it would go away.

It didn't.

The women continued to talk, but he found he couldn't focus on their words any longer. He felt the panic start to rise in him. Yes, Josie was holding a gun on them, but this was a different kind of panic. A familiar one. He was getting dizzy as he tried to focus on the two small figures standing in front of him. He reached out for Harper to steady himself before he stumbled.

"Sebastian!" Harper said in a startled voice. "What's wrong? Are you okay?" she asked.

He wanted to answer her but he couldn't. His chest

was suddenly so tight he could barely breathe, much less speak. As the vise tightened harder on his rib cage, he realized that this wasn't just some random panic attack. This was another heart attack—a stronger one than last time.

The doctors had warned him to take it easy. And he'd tried. He'd done as best he was able and yet here he was—looking into the eyes of the woman he loved and wondering if it was for the last time. Was it done? Had he lost his chance to say all the things to Harper he'd been too afraid to voice? Could he say enough in time?

"I love…" He gasped and hunched over, unable to finish. His hand slipped from her shoulder and he heard her scream as his knees buckled beneath him.

Blackness enveloped Sebastian and he was unconscious before he hit the hard pavement.

Eleven

"Harper?"

Harper sat up from a dead sleep, making the best she could out of the recliner in Sebastian's hospital room. Still groggy, she wiped an unfortunate bit of drool from her chin and looked around. That's when she realized that Sebastian was awake.

She leaped from the chair to stand at his bedside. "You're up," she said with a smile.

"I guess. I feel like I've been hit by a truck." He brought his hand up to his face, dragging all his IV tubes along with it. "What happened? Where am I?"

Harper was surprised but relieved that he didn't remember the last few days. It had been a roller coaster of tests, bloodwork, scans and, finally, a stint placed in one of the arteries to his heart. He'd been out of it most of the time. Harper had just sat by his bedside waiting for the next bit of news from the nurses and doctors caring for him.

"You had a heart attack at the airport," Harper explained. "You've been in the hospital for a couple of days."

Sebastian frowned as he looked around, taking inventory of his body. "Why does my wrist hurt?"

"That's how they went in to put a stint in your chest."

He put his hand against his chest and shook his head. "Wow."

Harper sat on the edge of the bed. She'd been filled with a mix of emotions over the last few days that she'd never expected—and never wanted to experience again. First was the fear of being shot by a vengeful and bitter Josie. She'd never anticipated being confronted with a weapon like that and had hardly known how to respond. When Sebastian collapsed, Harper had reacted and rushed to his side, forgetting all about Josie. She wasn't sure how long her blackmailer had stood there with the gun, but eventually Harper looked up and Josie was gone. Apparently she hadn't wanted to hang around for the fire department and ambulance to arrive.

Since then, she'd hardly given that situation any thought. The fear of suddenly losing Sebastian before she could tell him how she felt had taken its place in her mind. All the way to the hospital, she'd sat in the back of the ambulance, racked with guilt at thinking she'd put him in a dangerous situation that had almost killed him. Then days of anxiety waiting for the results of all his tests.

Finally, and most recently, she was angry.

That was the most surprising emotion, but the one she couldn't shake. The night before, the doctor who had been treating Sebastian had come in with another man he introduced as Sebastian's cardiologist. They'd spoken to her about his ongoing condition like it was something she was aware of. They'd discussed how this was more serious than his previous attack. Two weeks away from the office wouldn't be enough this time.

As they'd continued, it became harder for her to keep a neutral expression on her face. Harper hadn't wanted them to know she had no idea what they were talking about. But the more they'd talked, the more things about Sebastian had started to fall into place.

Like why the workaholic could drop everything and take a trip to Ireland. He wasn't *allowed* to work. Not after his last heart attack had driven him to the floor of his lab less than two weeks ago.

Two weeks ago he'd had a heart attack and he hadn't said anything about it. He'd acted like nothing happened and got on a plane with her to Ireland. The truth of it made her mind spin. What if something had happened in Ireland? That castle had been out in the middle of nowhere, literally hours from Dublin. How long would it have taken to get him to a hospital with a state-of-the-art cardiac care unit?

If he had told her, at least she could've known to watch for the signs. Or when he'd collapsed, she would have known what it was and been able to tell the 9-1-1 operator and the EMTs he had a heart condition. As it was, she'd just sat helplessly, crying and saying, "He just collapsed," over and over in despair and confusion.

Talking to his business partner hadn't made her feel any better. Finn was listed as his emergency contact and medical power of attorney, so he'd been called into the hospital the minute they'd arrived. He was the one who had authorized the tests and cleared it with the hospital for Harper to stay even when she wasn't family. She was indebted to Finn for that alone, much less the information he'd shared with her while he was there.

"The doctors said you're going to be okay. But you've got to take it easy. You'll probably be discharged tomorrow. Finn has set up a nurse to stay with you at your apartment."

"I don't need a nurse," he argued.

"Finn says, and I agree, that you lost your ability to make decisions in this arena when you had that second attack. You're not going into work. You're getting a nurse to make sure you're taking all the medications and eating well. You're supposed to register for a cardiac rehabilitation program to help you rebuild your stamina and design an exercise regime to keep this from happening again. You have to do it all, to the letter, or you're going to have another attack. You might not bounce back the next time."

Sebastian opened his mouth to argue with her and then stopped himself. "Okay. You're right."

Harper had practiced what she'd wanted to say to him a few times in her mind. She wasn't sure it would come out right, but she had to try anyway. "It's been a long couple of days in this hospital, Sebastian."

"I bet. Weren't you wearing that outfit on the flight home?"

Harper looked down, but she knew he was right. She hadn't gone home. She had ventured down to the gift shop for a toothbrush and some other toiletries to get her through, but other than that, she hadn't left his side. Their suitcases and everything in them had been left behind at the airport where they'd run into Josie. In the ambulance, she'd called Jonah and he'd gone back to pick up their things for them. He and Emma had offered to bring her whatever she'd needed, but she hadn't wanted to be a bigger imposition than she'd already been.

"It's been even more stressful for me because it came out of the blue. Young, healthy thirty-eight-year-old men do not just drop to the ground with a heart attack, Sebastian."

She watched as his jaw tightened. "I didn't think it was important."

"Important?" she cried. "You didn't think it was important to tell me that you were recovering from a heart attack? That you were supposed to be recuperating? I didn't need to know that because *it wasn't important*? We had sex, Sebastian. That could've killed you."

Sebastian sighed. "I didn't want you to treat me like I was fragile. I'm not fragile. The sex didn't kill me. Not even close. And if that woman hadn't tried to kill us, I probably wouldn't even be here right now."

"That's not what the doctor said. He said that you were supposed to schedule a heart catheterization while you were off from work to check for arterial blockages. Not only did you not schedule it, you left the country instead. You could've died, Sebastian. Right there at my feet. And I wouldn't have had the slightest clue as to what was happening to you or why because you didn't tell me."

"I thought I had it handled. I didn't want to worry you when you had your own problems to deal with."

"If it were only that, I might buy it. But it's more than just your heart condition, Sebastian. Yes, you kept something so important a secret from me, but you haven't opened up to me about anything else, either."

"I told you about my brother."

She nodded. "Only as it pertained to your work

and your inspiration. You never share anything about your past, your feelings. You just won't let me in."

That was the crux of it: how could he possibly care about her—really, truly care about her—if he was shutting her out like this?

It was then she realized that maybe this was a problem of her own making. This wasn't supposed to be a real relationship, despite how far they'd gone off the rails. They weren't supposed to confide in each other, get physical and fall in love. She was the one who'd broken the rules and fallen for him. She'd poured her heart and soul out to him and gotten nothing in return. So this was really a mess she'd made. She couldn't be mad at him for sticking to their agreement. He didn't love her. And she had to be okay with that.

But she didn't need to stay around and witness the evidence of her foolishness any longer. If she stayed, she would say something she would regret and she didn't want to agitate him any more than she already had when he was in this fragile state.

"Where are you going?" he asked as she stood and scooped her purse up from the floor.

"I'm going home."

"Why?"

Harper stopped and looked at him one last time. "Because the wedding is over," she said. "Thanks for pretending to be my date this week. I couldn't have gotten through it all without you."

He sat up in the bed and reached for her. "Wait. Are you coming back?"

She moved toward the door, finally shaking her head. "Why would I? Now I know you're going to be okay. You're in good hands. Goodbye, Sebastian." She slipped out the door before he could respond.

Dashing down the hallway, she rushed into the nearest elevator to keep from changing her mind.

"Mr. West, you have a visitor," Ingrid called from the living room.

Sebastian had heard the phone ring a few minutes earlier and assumed it was the front desk. They were the only ones who called the house line. That meant he either had a delivery coming up or a visitor. He'd already received some flowers from his parents and a plant from work, so he'd figured there might be a guest coming upstairs. He had gotten out of bed, put on some real clothes and straightened his disheveled appearance in anticipation of company.

Looking in the mirror was rough. His goatee was getting long and the rest of his beard was starting to fill in with coarse, almost black hair since he hadn't shaved since in Ireland. He needed a haircut, too, as the dark waves were getting wild and fighting his comb to stay standing straight. His eyes were blood-shot and he was bruised and scabby from the elbows down from the hospital using him as a human pin cushion.

It really was a lost cause. A brush through his hair and a swig of mouthwash was the best he could do on short notice. He wanted to look somewhat put together just in case it was Harper.

He'd had a couple visitors since he'd gotten home from the hospital—his family had even driven down from Maine to see him—but the only person he really wanted to see was Harper. So far, she had eluded him.

He made his way down the hallway to where his home health aide, Ingrid, was waiting on him. She smiled and gestured to the couch where someone was sitting. It was Finn.

Damn.

"Don't get too excited to see me," Finn said in a dry tone. "I wouldn't want to put too much strain on your heart."

Sebastian made his way over to his recliner next to the couch and settled into it.

Ingrid brought them both bottles of sparkling water and then disappeared into the kitchen to give them some privacy.

"Sorry," Sebastian said. "I was hoping you were someone else."

"Harper, perhaps?"

"Yes." There was no sense in trying to deny it.

"Has she been by to see you since you left the hospital?"

"No." It had been several long, lonely days without her smiling face and sassy attitude.

Finn frowned at his partner. "That seems odd. Are you sure that she's okay? She wouldn't leave your side for a moment at the hospital."

Sebastian didn't remember most of his time at the hospital, but knowing she'd been there, so dedicated to making sure he was okay, made him feel better. He'd never had someone like that in his life before. And yet he'd managed to ruin it the moment he'd woken up. "Yes, well, once she determined I was okay, she left and said she wasn't coming back. I was just being optimistic that she'd changed her mind."

"What did you do?" Finn said in his usual accusing voice.

Sebastian shrugged it off. "I suppose I deserve that," he admitted. When things went wrong around the office, it was typically Sebastian's doing. He'd overload the breaker and cause a building-wide blackout. He'd set off the smoke alarm with his latest project and sent everyone marching out to the street while the fire department searched the building. Honestly, there were times where he wondered why Finn wanted to be his business partner. Or even his friend. But sometimes you had to overload the breaker to achieve greatness.

"She was sick with grief when I saw her at the hospital the first time. That woman loves you and cares about you very much. If she isn't here with you this very moment, you screwed up pretty badly."

"Okay, yeah, I screwed up," he said. "I didn't tell her about…well, anything. Including my heart condition. She said I was shutting her out. I guess I was."

"Why would you do that? She's by all accounts an amazing woman. I know her family, too. You don't drive a woman like that away when she loves you, Seb."

"I don't know why I did it. I guess it's just all I know how to do. I'm not a relationship guy. I'm an engineer. A pioneer in medical technology. I don't know how to be that and a man in a serious relationship. Is it even possible to be both at the same time?"

Finn chuckled and shook his head. "You'd better figure it out or you're going to be a lonely old man. I can't have you coming to my house for the holidays every year for the rest of your life. Eventually you're going to become our creepy uncle Sebastian."

"You're the one that invited me to your family Thanksgiving," Sebastian pointed out in a bitter tone.

"Of course I did. Otherwise you would've been at the office working. Or sitting at home eating who knows what with a plastic fork. If you're going to shake up your life, you've got to make a lot of changes."

Sebastian was used to his fair share of lectures from Finn—it was one of the side effects of working with a doctor—but for the first time in his life, he was actually listening to what his partner had to say. "Okay, fine. Fix me, Yoda. I'm a ball of clay in your hands. Turn me into a pastier, hairier but more charming version of you."

Finn ran his palm over his shaved head and twisted his lips in irritation. Fortunately he was used to Sebastian after years of working together. They were very different, but they complemented each other well. Sebastian's inventions wouldn't have been nearly as successful without Finn there to guide and market them. And Finn probably would've settled into some nice, boring dermatology practice on the Upper East Side if he hadn't had Sebastian pushing him to do more important things with his life.

"You've got to take better care of yourself, for one thing."

Sebastian couldn't help rolling his eyes. "Thank you, Dr. Obvious. But not all of us can be hunky Shemar Moore look-alikes with chiseled abs and muscular thighs like tree trunks."

"You think looking this good is easy?" Finn quipped. "It takes a lot of work. I'm at the gym five days a week. While you're getting junk food delivered to the office, I'm drinking protein smoothies or bringing in grilled chicken breast and kale salad for lunch. Life is a series of choices. You've just got to make better ones."

"You sound like my nutritionist," Sebastian grumbled. He'd already met with her and had his first cardiac rehab appointment. Basically he'd just walked on a treadmill while they'd done an EKG and monitored his blood pressure. It would get harder from there. As for the nutritionist, she'd decided to sign him up for a meal delivery service while he was recuperating. There was going to be a lot of lean protein and vegetables he couldn't recognize in his future.

Finn crossed his muscular arms over his chest. "I might know what I'm talking about, Sebastian. I *am* a doctor, you know."

"I know. And listen…" Sebastian leaned forward and rested his elbows on his knees. "For all my blustering, I am taking this all to heart. I know this is serious and I'm changing. I want to change. At this rate, I won't live long enough to be your kids' crazy uncle Sebastian, and I know that. I've always had this drive in me and succeeding was more important than anything else, including my own health. But you were right."

Finn held up his hands to halt the discussion. "Wait. Repeat that please. I want to cherish it."

Sebastian smirked at his partner. "You were right, Finn! Anyway, I'm trying to be serious for a moment here. My work is important, but I'm not helping anyone if I'm too sick to continue. I can't sacrifice my life, my health or my relationships to make my inventions a reality. There's more to life, and I realize that now. I realized it the instant I hit the ground."

He shook his head, thinking back to that night as

he'd stared down the barrel of Josie's gun and felt his chest tighten like a rubber band was wrapped around him. "It was the scariest moment of my life. As I went down, I looked at Harper and realized what was happening and how serious it could be. My life could've been ending. In those few seconds, all I could think of was that I'd never told Harper that I loved her. I was going to die and she was never going to know. I tried, but then I passed out."

Finn listened silently, a pained expression on his face. "That sounds horrible. Why didn't you tell her the first chance you got at the hospital? It might've changed everything for the two of you."

"I don't know. I've kicked myself over how that whole thing played out. I was so disoriented at first and before I could get my bearings, she was laying into me about keeping secrets. I instantly went on the defensive and then she was gone. But she was right, I wasn't telling her things. I have so much I need to share with her. But I need to start with how much I love her. That's the most important part."

"Wow," Finn said. "It's true. You've really fallen hard. I can see it in your face when you talk about her. I wasn't sure I'd ever see the day you looked up from your notebook and noticed someone other than a client. And to fall in love… If you can fix this, you might beat me to the altar. Maybe I can be your kids' crazy uncle Finn."

"Shut up," Sebastian groaned. "You've got women

lining up outside your apartment. If you could just pick one to keep, you'd be married in no time."

Finn laughed. "Probably so. If you're serious about wanting to marry Harper, maybe I'll catch the garter at your reception. You never know what can happen then."

Sebastian's expression instantly sobered. "I am serious about marrying her. I'm serious about all of this. I want to get my health in order so I can go to her and feel confident that I'm not selling her damaged goods. Then I want to tell her how I feel and, hopefully, she feels the same way. If she does, I'm going to propose right there on the spot. Time is too precious to waste. I don't want to give her the chance to slip away from me again."

"If you're really planning to propose, I know a good diamond guy. I could give him a call and have him bring some pieces here to the apartment."

That was a relief. Sebastian didn't even know where to start when it came to that. He couldn't name the four Cs if his life depended on it. "Set it up. I've still got to talk to her father and ask permission, but I want to move forward on everything. I want it all in place when the time comes."

"Sure thing." Finn picked up his phone and typed in a few things. "I'll have him text you."

"Perfect. It feels like everything is falling into place. I just have one more little thing to do first."

"What's that?" Finn asked.

"I have to figure out where Harper lives."

Twelve

"Come in."

Harper took a deep breath and turned the knob that led to her grandfather's study. She had been fearing—dreading—this moment since she was twenty-two years old. Now here she was, a woman of almost thirty years, and she felt as nervous as ever.

It was easy to be brave in Ireland when she'd been thousands of miles away from the consequences of her poor choices. With Josie having disappeared and the blackmail behind her, Harper knew she had to face her grandfather and the reality she'd avoided all this time. She had to tell him she was broke. Odds were that he'd probably already heard the news by now, but she'd wanted to tell him in person as soon as she had the chance.

"Afternoon, Grandpa."

The elderly man looked up from his desk and smiled at the sight of his only granddaughter.

"Harper! What a surprise! You're looking lovely, as always. For a moment I thought it was your mother standing there. You certainly have come to look so much like her as you've gotten older."

Harper gave him a hug, ignoring the tears in his eyes as they both thought about the woman who'd been taken from them too soon. As she sat, Harper realized that she was older now than her mother had been when she died. It was hard to believe. Life could be so unfair sometimes. It made Harper feel foolish for wasting all her emotional energy on such silly things when her mother had been facing her own death and leaving her children behind at the same age.

"To what do I owe this visit?" his asked. "I didn't expect to see you before your birthday. The big one is coming, isn't it?"

Harper smiled and nodded. "Yes, I'll be thirty."

"I suppose you'll have a big party to celebrate with your friends. Blow some of that inheritance on expensive champagne?"

She winced and shook her head. Considering everything that had happened over the last week, she hadn't planned anything. Turning thirty was depressing enough. Add that she was now going to be single and broke going into her thirties and she couldn't gather up much reason to celebrate. "Not exactly. That's why I came by to see you today. I needed to talk to you about my trust fund."

"Can't wait until the end of the week for the money?" he asked with curious gray eyes. "I suppose I could loan you a few dollars until then."

"No, Grandpa," she said, reaching out to stop him from pulling out his wallet. "I'm not here to borrow money. I'm actually here because I needed to tell you something."

His brows went up in surprise and he eased back into his leather chair. "Okay. What is it, Pumpkin?"

She took a deep breath, trying to figure out how she was going to tell him the truth. Pumpkin had screwed up. She'd thought that losing out on the money would be the hardest part, but she was wrong. Telling her grandfather what she'd done was far worse. The sun had risen and set on Harper as a child as far as he was concerned. He would be so disappointed.

"I'm broke, Grandpa."

He narrowed his gaze at her, visibly trying to piece together what she meant by that. "Broke, you say?"

"Yes. I've been keeping it a secret all these years because I was embarrassed and I didn't want to lose the rest of my trust fund. But I'm coming clean. I blew all the money when I was in college and I've been faking it ever since."

"So all these years…you never once asked for money. Your father didn't have any. How did you get by?"

Harper shrugged. "Like everyone else. I worked hard. I saved every dime I could instead of blowing it like I would've in the past."

"But no one knew the truth? Not even your brother?"

"No, I didn't tell anyone. Not Oliver, not Daddy. I didn't want anyone to know, especially you."

"If that's the case, why are you telling me this now, Pumpkin?"

Now it was her turn to frown. "Because I should be honest. You added the provision that said if I mismanaged the first payment, I wouldn't get the second. And I blew it. I wanted—no, needed—to tell you the truth, so you can have your financial manager do something else with the money. I've forfeited my share."

Her grandfather reached for the candy bowl on the edge of his desk. He grabbed a soft caramel and handed a second one to her. For as long as she could remember, he'd always had caramels in his study. He unwrapped the candy and chewed it thoughtfully. Harper could only hold on to hers. She was waiting for his response. The rebuke. The disappointment. For him to announce that he was donating her inheritance to a charity.

But he didn't. He just chewed his caramel and watched her. Finally he said, "Something else is wrong. What is it?"

"You mean aside from throwing away twenty-eight-million dollars?"

He nodded. "That's just money. Something else is bothering you. Something more important."

Sebastian. Could that be what he saw? "I've just had a rough week, Grandpa. Nothing has been going my way, be it my love life or anything else. Someone tried to blackmail me and they stole Mama's sapphire necklace when I didn't pay them in time. The guy I love lied to me and I don't know what to do. Really, losing the money is just the latest thing to come up. I'm not having a big birthday celebration. I don't feel much like celebrating."

"Tell me about this man. You said he lied to you."

She nodded. "He kept me in the dark about so many things in his life. I worry that he can't open up to me. Why would he keep things from me?"

"Why would you keep your friends and family in the dark about your own situation, Harper? I imagine you'll find the answers to your questions about your gentleman in your own motivations."

"I was embarrassed. I didn't want anyone to know I could be so stupid. They might treat me differently." As she said the words aloud, she realized her grandfather was probably right about Sebastian and his secrets. Would she have treated him differently if she'd known he was physically fragile? Perhaps. Was he embarrassed that he'd let his drive get in the way of his health? Probably.

Since they'd started out as a week-long fake romance, there'd been no reason for him to tell her those things. Honestly, if she hadn't been blackmailed, she wouldn't have confessed her own truths to Sebastian. Why would she expect him to do the same?

They had a lot to learn about each other. A week wasn't nearly enough time to peel back all the layers and expose the secrets shared with only the most intimate of partners. She'd overreacted out of fear, she knew that now. Seeing Sebastian lying on the ground surrounded by EMTs...the sirens, the wires, the shouting... It had been all so unexpected, so scary. Josie and the gun hadn't been important anymore. All that had mattered was Sebastian.

She'd almost lost him in the moment and she hadn't understood why. Then she'd turned her back on him and walked away—losing him for certain—just for doing the same thing she'd done her whole life.

She was a fool.

"Harper, why do you think I added that provision to your trust?"

She turned back to her grandfather and shook her head. "To scare me straight? I was a spoiled little diva. I'm sure you didn't want me to make the same mistakes as Daddy did."

"That's a little harsh," he said. "You just didn't know what it was like to go without. You didn't grow up poor, like I did, so you didn't have the appreciation for it. That wasn't your fault. But you have it now, don't you?"

Harper chuckled bitterly. "Most certainly. I kick myself every day for wasting what I had. I think about what I could've done differently. If I'd been smart or industrious like Oliver…"

"You don't have to be like your brother. He's one of a kind, and so are you. Let me ask a different question. If you were to have a second chance and someone handed you that two-million dollars over again, what would you do?"

She didn't even have an answer at first. "That's hard to say, Grandpa. I'd probably go wild and prepay my co-op fees and utilities for the next year. Stick the rest in the bank for a rainy day."

Her grandfather's old, weathered lips curled into a smile. "Okay then." He reached across his desk for his cell phone.

Harper was confused by his response. "Okay what?" she asked.

"Okay, it's time to call my estate manager and discuss releasing the rest of your trust fund."

"What do you mean, *release it*?"

He reached out and patted her hand. "Happy birthday, Harper. I'm satisfied that you've grown into the mature, responsible woman I've always known you could be. And as such, you're about to be twenty-eight-million dollars richer. Now go find this man you're in love with and plan a proper birthday celebration."

Sebastian walked into the lobby of Harper's building as though he were approaching the X on a treasure map. Finding where she lived hadn't been an easy task. To ask for it from her friends was to admit he'd never been to her home before—an incredibly suspicious fact considering they were dating. But without any other options, he'd had to confess the truth about their fake relationship to Emma when he'd hunted her down at FlynnSoft. But it was only when he'd told her that he was hopelessly in love with Harper, for real, that she'd given him the address for Harper's building.

He was in the process of signing in at the front desk when he heard a voice from over his shoulder.

"She's not home."

Sebastian paused and turned to find Harper standing behind him with a full bag of groceries in her arms.

"That's a shame," he said. "I really wanted to talk to her about something important."

Her blue-gray eyes searched his face for a moment. "Something important, huh? Well, maybe I'll let you up and you can wait for her. I'm sure she'll be interested in hearing what you have to say for yourself."

Ouch. Okay. "I'd really appreciate it."

Harper smiled and headed toward the elevator with him in her wake.

Sebastian hadn't been sure what kind of reception he would receive after the way they'd parted at the hospital. So far, it had been pretty neutral, but he was going up to her apartment. She could've just turned him away. That was something.

Running into his arms and kissing him would've been another option, but he may not deserve that. He had a lot of apologizing to do before hugs and kisses would be on the agenda. Her semi-frosty reception proved that much.

When they stepped into her apartment, Sebastian got his first real dose of what Harper's life was like. It was a nicer place than he had—a remnant of her old life—decorated with some familiar and inexpensive IKEA pieces. As she set her groceries in the kitchen, he noticed a nice bottle of champagne and a couple pouches of ramen noodles. He supposed she had learned balance over the years.

Sebastian hovered awkwardly at the entrance of the kitchen as she put away her groceries. He was waiting for the invitation to talk, but she hadn't given him one yet. He wanted to sit and look her in the eye, not try to apologize while she was distracted with chores.

Finally she folded the paper sack and looked at him. "Do you want a drink? I want a drink."

"I'm not really supposed to," he admitted. He really wanted one—it would ease the tension—but he was working on a new healthy lifestyle. Day drinking two weeks into the plan would doom him to failure. "Some water would be great, though."

She eyed him for a moment before she nodded and pulled two bottles of water out of the fridge. She handed him one and pointed to the wall. "Let's head into the living room. People always congregate in the kitchen and I hate that."

Sebastian backed out of her way and followed her lead into the open and airy living room. She had comfy couches, a few nice pieces of art he recognized and a decent-size, flat-screen television on a shelf. There was a wall of books on one side of the room and a wall of windows on the other. From where he was, he could spy a glimpse of green—Central Park—a few blocks away.

"Have a seat," she said as she settled onto the couch.

He opted for the oversize chair just to her right, facing her. Their knees almost touched as they sat, but he kept his joints to himself for the moment, no matter how badly he wanted to touch her. "Thanks for talking to me, Harper."

She shrugged and opened her water. "The last time I saw you, you were on death's door. I was hoping to hear you were doing better."

"I am," he said proudly. "I've been going to cardiac rehab three times a week and they've started me on a new lifestyle program that will make me more mindful of what I eat and how much rest I get. It's made a huge difference already."

Harper listened to him talk but nothing more than a casual interest lit her eyes. "I'm glad to hear that."

"Me, too. Going forward, I know I can't let my work overtake my life. I want more than a career and a string of patents under my belt. I want a life, too. A wife. Maybe a family."

That got her attention. She sat more upright in her seat, her brows knitting together in thought. "That's a big change for a workaholic bachelor. What's going to keep you from losing yourself in your work again and this time ignoring your new family instead of just your health?"

She didn't think he could change. "I'm not going to ignore you, Harper. I couldn't possibly."

"I didn't mean me," she said. "I just meant in general. Old habits die hard. Like keeping secrets. Trust me, I know."

"I'm sorry I lied to you. It wasn't that I didn't trust you with the different aspects of my past. I was just... embarrassed. You understand that, don't you?"

"Of course. But I told you everything, Sebastian. You told me almost nothing."

"If you hadn't been blackmailed by Josie, would you still have told me? Or was it only out of necessity?"

The self-righteous expression on her face softened a little. Her gaze dropped to the cap of her water bottle as she fidgeted with it. "And then I find myself clutching your unconscious body in the middle of a parking lot, screaming. When the ambulance arrives, I can't tell them your medical information. I can't say if you have a history of cardiac problems. I know literally nothing. You could've died and there was nothing I could do to help."

"I shouldn't have put you in that position. I never dreamed it would happen again or I would've said something."

Harper nodded. "I understand we started off with the whole fake relationship thing, but that's over. The wedding trip is over and now this is real life, Sebastian. Real feelings. We're not playing a game any longer. I need to know the truth."

"About what?"

"About *everything*. I want to know everything you've been keeping from me before I can consider continuing this relationship."

"Right now? You just want me to lay out my whole life story right now?" He had an engagement ring burning a hole in his pocket. He was desperate to hear her say yes and move forward, but Harper wasn't having it.

She sat back against the couch cushions, making herself visibly more comfortable. "Do you have somewhere you need to be, Sebastian? Work, perhaps? It's a Saturday, but who knows with you."

"No," he insisted. "There's nowhere I need to be but right here, right now. I'll tell you whatever you want to know if it will make you feel more comfortable in loving me. Because I love you, Harper. I've never let myself love a woman before. I'm not sure I'm going to do things right, but I can't help how I feel. I'll do anything you want me to if it means you'll tell me that you love me, as well."

Harper's jaw dropped at the first mention of the word "love" and stayed there until he was done speaking. "Well, why don't you start from the beginning? You've never said much about your family or where you grew up. Just about your brother's accident."

Sebastian nodded and sat back in his seat, ready to tell her whatever she wanted to know.

"I grew up poor," he said. "And so we're clear, not the kind of poor you've been. I mean dirt poor. Oldest-trailer-in-the-trailer-park poor. I never owned a new pair of shoes until I went to college and bought them myself. Until then, every bit of clothing I'd ever had was my brother's hand-me-down. My parents did everything they could to get ahead in life, but there was always something on the next horizon ready to knock them back down.

"When my brother and I were old enough, we worked to help make ends meet. Kenny worked at the burger place near our high school. I liked to tinker and helped my dad with fixing the car and such, so I ended up working at a shop that fixed old lawnmowers and small engines. If I could, I'd mow people's lawns after I fixed their mowers, too, for extra cash. Every penny went to my parents. For a while, we were doing okay. My dad got a promotion, my brother graduated from high school and started working full time. Then he had his accident."

Harper was watching him speak so intently, he wondered if she was even breathing. He shook his head and sighed. "We had insurance, but Kenny fell off the plan when he graduated. He didn't have any at work yet, either. There was a little coverage from the owner of the ATV, but it wasn't nearly enough. He spent my entire senior year in hospitals and rehabilitation centers. The bills were crippling. My mom had to quit her job to stay home and take care of him, making it worse."

"How awful," she whispered.

"I was determined to do more than just rebuild lawnmowers my whole life. I wanted to make something of myself so I could help my parents and my brother. That's what drove me. I worked as much as I could after his accident, and the only money I ever kept for myself was enough money to apply to MIT and take my entrance exams."

"How are they now?" Harper asked.

Sebastian finally found a reason to smile.

"They're great. With my first million, I bought my parents a real house in Portland that was near the doctors and specialists Kenny sees regularly. It's nice, but not too big for them to maintain, and it's fully wheelchair friendly so my brother can get around. I bought them an accessible van and I send them money every month to help take care of things. My dad continues to work out of pride, but he should be retiring in a few years."

Harper smiled and reached out to put a hand on his knee. "I'm glad to hear it."

"We've all come a long way. It took a lot of hard work to get there. I don't regret it or the toll it took on my health to get there. I just know I need to do better going forward."

"I can understand why you did what you did. To start with nothing and build a company like yours is amazing. I bet you look at someone like me, who squandered a fortune, and resent the hell out of it."

Sebastian shook his head. "I don't. Everyone comes from a different place, but that makes them who they are. You made your mistakes and you grew from them. You owned them. I'm not sure I'd be strong enough to stand up and do what you did at the wedding. Even with the money I've made, giving up almost thirty-million dollars is heartbreaking."

"Well, actually, it turns out that I didn't."

He frowned at her. "What do you mean?"

"I spoke with my grandfather. I came clean about the whole thing. He decided I'd learned my lesson and gave me the money anyway. That's why I bought the champagne. Today is my birthday. My grandpa wanted me to throw a big party but I wasn't ready for all that after what happened in Ireland. I thought I might have a little celebration by myself. Would you like to join me?"

Sebastian smiled. "I would." He wouldn't have more than a sip since he was trying to be good, but he would certainly toast to her birthday.

They got up and went to the kitchen where she poured two champagne flutes. Back in the living room, they sat, this time both of them on the couch together.

"Happy birthday, Harper," he said, raising his flute. "I'm glad I was able to be here today to celebrate with you. I wasn't sure if I would have the chance to tell you that. Or any of the other things I said to you today. Thank you for giving me the chance."

Harper smiled and clinked her glass against his. "Thank you. This isn't how I imagined my birthday, but it couldn't have been better, really. I've learned a lot about myself the past few weeks. Without Josie trying to blackmail me, I might not have realized that I could get by on my own. Or that I didn't need money and fancy cars to define me. I also wouldn't have realized how important you are to me, too."

Sebastian's heart stuttered in his chest and this time it had nothing to do with his clogged arteries. He set his untouched drink on the coffee table. "I'm sorry I didn't know it was your birthday today. I would've brought you a present." He reached into his pocket. "Instead, all I have is this."

Her gaze locked on the blue box and her jaw dropped once again. "What…" Her voice trailed off.

"I told you before that I love you, Harper. And that I'm ready to find some balance in my life. But what I left out was that I want to find that balance with you. Just you. Life is too short to hesitate, and I can't risk losing you again."

Sebastian slid off the couch onto one knee and opened the box to display the emerald-cut halo ring inside. "I promise that I won't keep secrets from you anymore. I promise I will never make my work seem more important than you or our family. You are the most important person in my life, Harper. I never knew I could love someone the way that I love you. Please do me the honor of being my wife, Harper Drake."

He looked at her in time to see her eyes flood with tears. "Yes," she whispered with a smile that spread from ear to ear.

Sebastian slipped the ring onto her finger and squeezed her hand in his. They stood and she leaped into his arms. He pulled her tight against him and kissed his fiancée for the very first time.

This was the start of their future together. A future he almost didn't have, but that he would cherish with Harper for as long as he could.

Epilogue

"Merry Christmas, everyone!"

Harper heard the commotion at the door and rushed out of the kitchen to see who had arrived. She was excited to host her first Christmas with her family and Sebastian's family all together.

Sebastian was hugging his mother as she came through the door. His father was right behind her with arms full of presents. And in the back was Kenny. *Standing*.

With the help of Sebastian's exoskeleton proto-type, his brother moved in a slow but steady pace through the doorway with a wide grin on his face. He looked almost as happy as Sebastian himself.

Nothing could match his excitement. This was the culmination of his dream. The best Christmas gift he could ever give his family. She knew watching Kenny walk across the room and sit by the fireplace unaided was the greatest present Sebastian could ever receive.

It was his sketches from Ireland that made the difference. He didn't realize it at the time, but once he returned to his lab, Sebastian had a breakthrough. She could tell it pained him to come home at a reasonable hour each night when his mind wanted him to keep pushing, but his goal had still been achieved in the end.

The two families were introduced and everyone gathered with drinks and appetizers in the living room. Harper was just about to return to the kitchen for more eggnog when Sebastian caught her eye.

He reached under the tree for a gift and gestured for Harper to follow him down the hallway to their bedroom. "I wanted to give you this now," Sebastian said once they were alone.

"Now? It's only Christmas Eve."

"Please open it."

Harper sighed and accepted the beautifully wrapped present from her fiancé. He'd already given her such a beautiful engagement ring, she felt guilty accepting a present from him. She opened the golden foil lid and found a collection of sparkling items wrapped in tissue paper.

A sapphire necklace. A ruby tennis bracelet. Diamond earrings. An aquamarine cocktail ring. Emerald cufflinks. An old pocket watch.

It couldn't be.

Harper's eyes grew wide as she looked down at the gift and back up at Sebastian. "This is my mother's jewelry. And your things, too. Josie stole all of this. How on earth did you get it back?"

Sebastian grinned even wider than he had when his brother had successfully walked through the front door of their apartment. "Well, it turns out that our little blackmailer went after someone else to make some cash. Instead of paying, they went straight to the police. All these items were found in her apartment when she was arrested. The cops contacted me last week because the jewelry matched the description in the police report we filed."

She picked up the pocket watch and looked at it in wonder. Harper had thought she might never be able to replace this special piece for Sebastian. "They said they couldn't find Josie."

"Apparently that wasn't her real name. But after she tried to blackmail Quentin—"

"My ex, Quentin?" she interrupted in surprise.

"Yep. When he got the threatening letter, he remembered what happened to you and led the cops straight to her door. Turns out her name is Amanda Webber. I hope she looks good in orange."

Harper smiled and handed Sebastian his great-grandfather's watch. "Merry Christmas, my love."

"Merry Christmas, Harper."

* * * * *

AN INTIMATE BARGAIN

BARBARA DUNLOP

For my husband

One

The last time Zach Rainer felt this level of anxiety, he was walking out of a Texas group home on his eighteenth birthday. Twelve years later, there was more than just his future at stake.

He'd been navigating the Interstate since dawn in his three-year-old Jaguar convertible with nothing but a stale truck stop sandwich and six cardboard cups of coffee to keep him going. His business partner, Alex Cable, had insisted the road trip from Texas to Colorado would clear his head. Zach should have known better. Thinking didn't solve problems, action did.

Now he checked himself into the Caspian Hotel in downtown Lyndon, Colorado, and accepted his key to an eighth-floor room. While he pocketed his credit card, his attention was drawn to the mezzanine level that overlooked the atrium lobby. Sharply dressed men and glittering ladies circulated at the top of a grand, curving staircase, while chamber music sounded around them.

He put the room key in his pocket and left his bags with the porter. Tugging the sleeves of his travel-worn blazer, he took the friendly clerk's advice and started for a sports-bar down the hall. The woman had assured him it would be a lot less crowded there. Though, given his wrinkled shirt and day's growth of beard, he was guessing she thought he'd fit in better with the sports bar crowd. Not that he cared about making any kind of impression. He was too tired and too hungry to worry about anything more than a hot meal and a long night's sleep.

Tomorrow morning, he'd drive up into the hills behind Lyndon to the Craig Mountain Brewery and take stock of the place. Craig Mountain was the weak link in DFB Incorporated, the microbrewery conglomerate that he and Alex had grown over the past twelve years. At the same time, Craig Mountain had suddenly become the potential salvation of the entire corporation and the hundreds of jobs that went with it.

At the end of the hall, he entered the dimly lit bar through a lighted archway. He blinked to adjust his eyes, then he zeroed in on an empty table across from the wide-screen television. A basketball game was playing, the announcer's words scrolling in closed caption across the bottom of the screen, while an eighties rock tune came through speakers high in the corners of the room.

It was Lakers versus Celtics. Neither were teams he followed, but watching the action would help his mind rest up for tomorrow. Production at Craig Mountain was currently ten thousand barrels per year. In order to save DFB, he needed to triple that in the next six months.

As he rounded the polished bar, his attention was snagged by a startlingly beautiful, auburn-haired woman. Perched on a leather chair, she was alone at a table and looked seriously out of place in the casual atmosphere. She wore a low-cut, black cocktail dress with spaghetti straps over her smooth shoulders. It clung to her body in a drop waist, then layered out into a full skirt, ending at midthigh.

Her graceful, lavender-tipped fingers were wrapped around the martini glass in front of her. She was obviously deep in thought, her attention fixed on a spot on the far wall. The flickering light from the television highlighted her compelling hazel eyes. They were streaked with gold, mesmerizing and undeniably sexy. Her hair was pulled back in a wavy updo, a few loose strands artfully arranged at her temples, brushing against dangling crystal earrings.

Zach's feet came to an automatic halt, and he couldn't seem to stop himself from gaping at her beauty. She glanced up and caught him, drawing back in surprise. He knew what she must be thinking, and immediately opened his mouth to apologize.

But to his surprise, she smiled and nodded a greeting.

Zach might be exhausted and starving, but he still had a pulse. He wasn't about to walk away from a reception like that.

"Hello," he offered, seizing the opportunity to ease closer to her table.

"Getting away from the crowd?" she asked, her deep red lips curving into a friendly, open smile.

He nodded. "They told me it would be quieter back here."

"Well, a different kind of noise anyway," she acknowledged with a wry glance at the speakers.

Zach had to grin at that. "Not my favorite, either."

"At least the crowd is thinner."

"Agreed," he replied.

"My face was about to crack from all that smiling."

"You're smiling now," he pointed out, taking the final couple of steps that brought him to the chair opposite her. He rested his hand on its back.

"I guess I am." She tipped her head quizzically, and her beautiful, golden eyes narrowed. "I don't remember meeting you at the reception."

Zach knew he was about to be outed as a stranger. He also knew he had about two seconds to figure out a way to prolong the conversation. He boldly pulled out the chair and slid into it.

"That's because you didn't meet me." He took a stab in the dark. "Are you a friend of the bride?"

"What bride?"

Damn. Okay, that was a huge miss. And he couldn't think of anywhere else to go but the truth. "I confess. I wasn't at the reception."

"You mean you're not here to celebrate Mayor Seth Jacobs' election victory?"

"I am not," he admitted, holding her gaze.

She squinted with suspicion. "You have anything against Mayor Jacobs?"

"I do not. I've never met the man."

Her face relaxed at that. Her shoulders drooped a little, and she leaned back into the big, brown leather chair.

Zach knew he was about to get his marching orders. Too bad. He'd have loved to sit here and get to know this woman, even if it did mean forgoing the burger and fries he'd promised his empty stomach.

"So you don't know who I am?" she asked.

"I'd like to," Zach immediately put in.

She chuckled. "While I'd prefer it if you had no earthly idea."

He didn't miss a beat. His tone went low and intimate as he propped his elbows on the lacquered tabletop and leaned toward her. "I can live with that, too."

She rested her own elbows on the table, leaning forward, a playful glint now lurking in her expression. "I wasn't offering to date you."

"I didn't think you were." He quickly backed off. Okay, he'd hoped she was. But a guy could hope without penalty.

"Are you lying?" she asked him.

"I am not."

She contemplated him a moment longer. "I take it you're not from Lyndon."

"No, ma'am."

"Passing through?"

"Essentially." He hoped he wouldn't have to stay long. He hoped tripling production at Craig Mountain proved to be a straightforward proposition, that he could leave the brewery manager with instructions for expansion then get himself back to his corporate headquarters in Houston. He'd left Alex to hold down the fort during a very critical time.

Her sexy fingertips drummed lightly against the table. "So, we could do this?"

"Do what?" He found himself hoping all over again, but he sure wasn't going to presume a second time.

"Have a casual conversation about nothing that matters. You don't know me. I don't know you."

"Absolutely," he agreed without hesitation. He could talk with her, or do absolutely anything else that she wanted.

Someone entered the bar through the archway, drawing her attention. She tracked the progress of a fiftysomething man as he headed for the bar. After a few seconds, she seemed to relax. She turned back to Zach.

"Waiting for someone?" he couldn't help asking.

She emphatically shook her head.

His second guess would be that she was avoiding someone. He took a chance on his instincts. "You want to get out of here?"

She seemed to contemplate his words for a long, slow moment. "Yes," she finally answered. "I believe I do."

He gestured with a tilt of his head. "I saw an exit door at the far end of that hall. We can probably make a clean getaway."

"What makes you think I need a getaway?"

He leaned across the table again, dramatically lowering his voice. "You're acting like someone who needs to lie low for a while."

She matched his posture once more. "You make me sound like a felon."

"Are you a felon?"

She fought a grin. "Would it matter?"

"No," he answered honestly. With her looks and sense of humor, it truly would not.

She chuckled low, drew back and rose from her chair, retrieving a small, black clutch. "Then let's do it."

He stood with her. She moved past him, and the exotic scent of jasmine teased his senses.

He inhaled appreciatively then affected a Chicago-gangster drawl. "Act natural, Doll-Face, and stick close to me."

She matched his tone. "Right beside you…Lucky."

He couldn't help grinning to himself as they crossed the bar. He lowered his voice. "You want I should score us a getaway car?"

"We're only half a block from Main Street," she stage-whispered in return. "Plenty of hideouts there."

They ducked into the hallway then hurried for the back exit. Zach pushed the heavy, steel door open, and they crossed the threshold into the late-summer night. The door clanged shut behind them.

"A clean break," she breathed, pressing her back dramatically against the brick wall.

"Stick with me, Doll-Face," he rumbled in return, making a show of checking both directions on the quiet street. "I don't see any gumshoes hanging around."

"Good to know. But I'm more worried about constituents."

"Constituents?" He played dumb. "You mean the feds?"

She shifted away from the wall and started down the short block toward Main Street, her high heels echoing on the pavement. "I mean the good people of Lyndon. I don't want anyone to recognize me."

"So I'm hiding you from the entire town?" he asked with mock incredulity.

"Only from the people I know."

"How many people do know you?"

"Several thousand."

He fought what seemed like a natural urge to fold her hand into his. "You don't make things easy on a guy," he grumbled instead.

"You seem pretty good at this," she responded, glancing up. "You sure you're not a real criminal?"

"I'm a businessman." As soon as the words were out of his mouth, he realized they made him sound like a character from *The Godfather*. "A legitimate one," he added. But that wasn't much better. "I don't have so much as a parking ticket," he finished, hoping he hadn't scared her off.

"What kind of—" But then she determinedly shook her head. "Nope. I don't want to know what you do."

The wind had picked up, lifting the loose strands of her hair. He resisted an urge to reach out and smooth them back. "Can we at least trade first names?"

She hesitated, a look of consternation crossing her face. Then, just as quickly, she grinned. "Call me Doll-Face."

He paused as they reached the curb, half turning to offer a handshake. "Call me Lucky."

She glanced at his hand briefly, then reached out to wrap her delicate fingers over his rough skin. "Hello, Lucky." Her sweet voice seemed to touch a place deep inside him and settled there.

He let their handshake lengthen, having absolutely no desire to let her go.

Abigail Jacobs didn't usually flirt. She rarely had the inclination and, lately, she certainly hadn't had the time. But tonight was different. Her life was about to take a dramatic U-turn, and she didn't want to face the change just yet. Joking with Lucky was keeping the future at bay.

After tonight, she'd no longer be Abigail Jacobs, sister and campaign manager to mayoral candidate Seth Jacobs. She wouldn't be running the campaign office, picking up the phone to call business owners and reporters. She wouldn't polish speeches, organize events, manage budgets and head off crises. Tomorrow morning she'd pack away her dressy clothes, turn in her office keys, give up the leased Audi and leave Lyndon City in a dusty, ranch pickup truck.

Growing up, she'd loved her ranch life, the freedom, the fresh air and open spaces. But somewhere along the way, the city had sunk its hooks in her, making her wish for things she couldn't have. With her sister Mandy recently engaged to their former neighbor Caleb Terrell, and similarly, her other sister Katrina engaged to Caleb's brother, Reed, her father and mother in Houston working on his stroke recovery and her brother Seth now the mayor of Lyndon, she couldn't abandon her other brother, Travis, to manage the ranch alone.

Like it or not, the ball was ending, and tomorrow morning Cinderella was going back to the dust and manure of the real world.

"Hungry?" asked Lucky beside her, his coffee-colored eyes warm in the glow of the streetlights.

"Sure." It had been quite a while since Abigail had eaten. In a rush this morning, she'd skipped breakfast, and she'd been too nervous to eat all day. When the polls finally closed at dinnertime, the entire team had waited with bated breath for the vote count.

Of course, there'd been food at tonight's victory party, but there she'd been too busy fielding congratulations and questions about her future plans to eat anything. She'd told everyone she was looking forward to going home to the family ranch. After about the hundredth lie, she'd made her escape to the hotel sports bar.

"Steak?" Lucky asked with a nod toward the glowing red sign for Calbert's.

She shook her head. "Too many people I'll know in there."

"Thai?" he suggested, zeroing in on a smaller, lower-key restaurant a few doors down.

"How about a burger from the drive-through?"

Bert's Burgers, half a block down in the other direction, catered mostly to a teenage crowd. Much as they'd tried to get out the youth vote, Abigail doubted anyone under the age of twenty-one would recognize her.

"We don't have a car," Lucky pointed out.

"We can walk to the drive-through and take the burgers down to the lake."

He arched a skeptical brow. "You sure?"

She nodded.

There were some picnic tables on the lawn by the beach. The election party fireworks finale was planned for later on the waterfront. But it would take place on the wharf at the opposite end of the bay. This time of night, their only company in the picnic area would be the mallard ducks that slept in the marsh.

"Not much of a date," he noted as they took advantage of a break in traffic to cross in the middle of the block.

She couldn't help smiling at that. "This is a date?"

"Not in my book."

"So why are you worrying about the aesthetics?"

They stepped up on the sidewalk on the other side of the street.

"Because you're wearing a two-thousand-dollar dress, and I'm buying you a burger and fries."

"Who says you're buying?"

"I'm from Texas."

She smacked her hands dramatically over her ears, signaling her unwillingness to learn where he was from. "La, la, la, la—"

He playfully pulled one of them away. "You can already tell that by my accent."

"Just because you grew up in Texas doesn't mean you live there now."

"I do."

"Quit breaking the rules," she warned him.

"There are rules?"

"Yes, there are rules. We agreed."

"Well, the rule in Texas is that a gentleman always buys a lady's dinner."

"This is Colorado."

They came to a halt beside the drive-through window, and he peered up at the lighted menu board. "And this isn't exactly dinner."

A teenage girl in a navy-blue-and-white uniform, her hair pulled back in a ponytail revealing purple beaded earrings, slid the window open. "What'll you have?"

"A mountain burger," Abigail decided. "No onions, extra tomato and a chocolate shake."

"Same for me," said Lucky, extracting his wallet. "But I'll take some fries with that."

Abigail decided not to press the issue of payment. What point would she be making? That she was an independent woman? That this wasn't a date? Date or not, she doubted a five-dollar dinner would make any man feel entitled to so much as a good-night kiss.

Not that she'd necessarily mind kissing Lucky. She found herself stealing a glance at his profile while he handed the girl a twenty. He was an incredibly attractive man. As tall as her brothers, easily over six feet. He had gorgeous brown eyes, thick, dark hair, full lips, a straight nose, with a square chin that was slightly beard shadowed. He wasn't cowboy. She'd call it urbane. With an edge. She liked that.

"Cherry turnover?" he asked, turning to catch her staring.

She quickly blinked away her curiosity. "No, thanks."

"We're good," he said to the girl.

The cashier rang their purchase through the register, handing him the change, while another employee appeared with a white paper bag of food and a cardboard tray holding two milk shakes and paper-covered straws.

Lucky took the bag in one hand, the milk shakes in the other. "Lead on."

"You want some help?"

"I've got it."

"Texans don't let women carry things?"

"No, ma'am."

Abigail couldn't help wondering what he'd think of her hauling hay bales and lumber, and hefting saddles back at the ranch. Then she compressed her lips, determinedly banishing the image. That would be her life tomorrow. For tonight, she was going to be a girlie girl, with makeup, jewelry, horribly impractical shoes and a Texas man who insisted on buying her dinner.

"This way," she told him with determined cheer.

They headed for the lighted, bark-mulch path that led from the side of the parking lot down to the beach and picnic area. They made their way beneath the glow of overhead lights and the rustle of aspens and sugar maple trees. Her narrow, three-inch heels sank into the loose bark mulch of the pathway. After stumbling a few times, she moved to one side, stopped and slipped off the shoes to stand barefoot on the lush lawn.

Lucky halted to check on her. "You okay there?"

"I'm fine." She picked up the sandals, dangling them from the straps, the grass cool and soft against her soles.

"Is it safe to walk barefoot?"

"The park's well maintained."

He frowned in obvious concern. "I could give you a lift."

"Is that how they do it in Texas? Haul their women around over their shoulders?"

"When necessary."

"It's not necessary. I've been running barefoot through this park since I was two years old."

"You sure?"

"I'm sure." She began walking, passing him. "But thank you," she added belatedly, turning to pace backward so she could watch him.

He had a long, easy stride. His shirt collar was open. She could see the fabric was wrinkled, but his blazer was well cut, delineating broad, and what she guessed were well-muscled, shoulders. She wondered if he also had a six-pack.

"You grew up in Lyndon?" he asked.

"I did."

Technically her family's ranch was two hours west of Lyndon. But she wasn't going to fret over the details. Tonight she was a city girl through and through.

"Brothers and sisters?" he asked.

"Both. You?" She didn't think the question would take them too far down the road to revealing their identities. Mainly, she didn't want him to know she was the mayor's sister, and she didn't want him to know she was really a ranch hand.

He shook his head. "Nope."

"You were an only child?"

"That's right. Watch where you're going."

She turned her head to discover they were only a few feet from the first picnic table. The grass was about to give way to sand.

"Perfect," she pronounced, dropping her sandals to the ground and stepping up on the wooden bench seat, intending to perch on the tabletop facing the lake.

"Hold up there." Lucky swiftly set down the burgers. Stripping off his blazer, he laid it down like a blanket for her to sit on. The simple gesture made her chest tighten.

"Gotta love Texans," she joked, taking in the breadth of his chest beneath the thin, white cotton shirt. The fabric was tight over his biceps, and she was more willing than ever to lay a bet on him having six-pack abs.

"Can't have you ruining your dress," he said.

"So we're going to ruin your jacket instead?" But she sat down on the warm satin lining.

He shrugged, plunking down beside her, placing the burgers and shakes between them.

A couple of fat mallards splashed and waddled their way out of the water, crossing the pebbles and sand to investigate their presence, obviously on the lookout for bread crumbs.

Lucky handed her a foil-wrapped burger. "The jacket will clean."

"So would the dress."

He simply shrugged again.

The wrapper crackled as she peeled it halfway down the thick burger. Then Lucky was handing her a shake with a plastic straw already sticking through the lid.

She transferred the burger to the opposite hand as she accepted the drink, taking a sip of the icy, smooth treat.

"Yum," she acknowledged, then took a bite of the burger. It was juicy and flavorful, with a fresh bun and crisp condiments. Her stomach rumbled quietly in anticipation.

"I'm starving," she muttered around the bite.

"Me, too," he agreed with a nod, digging in to his own burger. "Long day on the road."

"Long day in the office for me."

Then they both ate in silence, while a few more ducks made their way over from a small, reed-filled marsh. Abigail tossed them some bits of bun, and they quacked with excitement, wings flapping, orange beaks pecking the ground.

Satiated, she took a long drink of the milk shake and threw the remains of her bun to the birds.

"Better?" asked Lucky, crumpling his wrapper and tossing it into the empty bag. She tucked hers away, as well, and he set the trash behind them.

"Much better," she acknowledged.

His gaze settled on the black horizon, where the moon was

coming up over the mountains, fading the stars that were scattered across the sky. "So, are you going to tell me?"

"Tell you what?"

"What's going on here?"

She waggled her cardboard cup at him, pretending to misunderstand his question. "I'm finishing my milk shake."

"That's not what I meant."

"Then what did you mean?"

"You must have guys hitting on you all the time."

Abigail coughed out a laugh. "Not really."

She'd spent most of her life in dusty blue jeans, hair in a sensible ponytail, face free of makeup while she worked up a sweat on the land. Things had been slightly different during the campaign. But most of the attention had been on her brother Seth, and most of the people she spoke to in Lyndon remembered her as a little freckle-faced, red-haired girl with pigtails and skinned knees.

Lucky gazed down at her. "First of all, I don't believe you. Second, I'm betting you don't usually accept dinner invitations from strange men."

She took a long, noisy slurp, draining the milk shake. "I do when it's a mountain burger."

He gently removed the cup from her hand, setting it on the table behind them. "Spill, Doll-Face. Who are you hiding from?"

"That's a stupid name." But she couldn't seem to tear her gaze from his.

"Then tell me your real name."

"No." She was enjoying this anonymity. For a brief space of time, she wasn't Seth's campaign manager, or Travis's stalwart sister and ranch hand. She was her own woman, nothing more, nothing less.

"Then Doll-Face is all I've got." Lucky's smooth baritone rolled over her like warm honey.

It really was a silly name, but when he said it, it sounded sweet. He reached up and brushed a strand of hair back from her forehead, and her skin tingled behind the touch.

"Don't do that." She closed her eyes, hiding her emotion as the incredible sensation slowly ebbed.

"Sorry."

She shook her head, regretting the sharpness of her outburst. "Don't worry about it."

"You had to know I was attracted to you."

Had to? No. Suspected? Sure. She wasn't stupid.

After a long moment, he spoke again. "So why'd you come with me?"

She opened her eyes, and it was her turn to drink in the blackened horizon and the sharpening moon. She hesitated to tell him anything remotely close to the truth, but reality had been burning in her brain all evening long, and it seemed desperate to get out. "Because I'm putting off tomorrow," she told him on a sigh. "It's going to be a very bad day."

She expected him to press for details, was already weighing exactly how much she'd say.

But he didn't ask. Instead, he shifted, and the wooden table creaked beneath his weight. "I hear you." He paused. "There's a better-than-even chance that my tomorrow's going to suck, too."

Despite herself, he had her curious. She turned to take in his profile. "Yeah?"

He set aside his own cardboard cup. "Yeah."

"Family?" she probed, promising herself, whatever it was, she'd keep the conversation to generalities.

He shook his head.

"Girlfriend?" she dared, swallowing a sudden lump.

He turned to paste her with a scowl. "While I'm hitting on you? Thanks tons, Doll-Face."

She tried not to feel quite so relieved. "Gambling, drinking, illness?"

"Business," he answered, his tone smoothing out. "There's a problem with my mysterious, yet perfectly legitimate, business interests. But I take it your problem is family?"

"What makes you say that?"

"It was your first guess for me. That makes it top of your mind."

She took in his expression, seeing warmth and compassion and, yes, a little bit of lust. But she was okay with that. It had taken her two hours to dress up for the reception tonight. It was nice to know somebody appreciated her efforts.

Her first instinct was to evade his question. But for some reason, she wanted to be honest with him. "My family needs me to do one thing," she told him. "But I want to do something else entirely."

He canted his head, and he suddenly seemed closer, his chest looked broader, his voice going lower. "Age-old dilemma," he rumbled.

She picked up his woodsy musk scent, getting lost in his warm, brown eyes, and momentarily lost brain function. She braced her hand on the tabletop, gripping with her fingertips. "I guess."

"So what are you going to do?"

She blinked. It wasn't like there was a choice. "Support my family."

The pad of his thumb passed over her knuckles, sending a kick of reaction up her spine. He gave a small smile. "I'd have guessed that about you, Doll-Face. You seem like the loyal type."

"What about you?" she managed to say around a drying throat and laboring breaths. Every single thing about this man oozed sex appeal. "What would you do?"

His hand covered hers completely, warm, broad and strong. "I'd make my own choice. I'd do whatever I wanted."

She was surprised, but also intrigued. "Even if it hurt your family?"

"My family doesn't need me."

"Mine needs me."

"Are you sure about that?"

"Positive."

He lifted an index finger to touch the bottom of her chin.

This time, she didn't wave him off. She drank in the sensation of his touch, anticipating the kiss that was sure to come.

What would it hurt?

What could it hurt?

Tomorrow she'd be back in her blue jeans, and men like Lucky wouldn't give her the time of day. Surely she deserved one single kiss.

Two

Zach figured there was a pretty good chance he was about to get his face slapped. He also figured it was going to be worth it.

He leaned in, anticipating her taste, the softness of her full lips. But a boat horn suddenly blasted from the lake, and Doll-Face abruptly turned away. Then another horn sounded, and another.

Disappointment clenched Zach's gut, even as light and color flashed in the periphery of his vision. He looked toward the lake in time to see starbursts of color cascading in the skies above.

A cheer went up from the crowd that had gathered far down the shore and out onto the wharf. A few people had also arrived in the park, taking up spots on nearby picnic tables. Zach hadn't even noticed them.

Doll-Face settled back to watch the show, bracing her hands and locking her elbows, bringing her dress taut against her breasts, highlighting an intriguing dip of cleavage.

Her skin was honey-toned with a tan. Her neck was long and graceful, her face classically beautiful, with big, golden eyes, dark lashes and a wide, sexy smile.

"Wow," she whispered. "That's spectacular."

"It sure is," he agreed, gaze fully on her, still desperate to lean down and kiss her mouth. Her auburn hair was slightly mussed. Wisps had worked their way free from the updo, along her neck and forehead. He had a sudden vision of her lying back on a white pillowcase, naked, thoroughly kissed, a sheen of sweat glistening on her brow.

He gave himself a shake.

"Oooh," she sang, smiling. Then she glanced up at him. "You're missing it."

He wasn't missing a thing. But he turned to look at the fireworks anyway. "Part of the election celebration?"

"It is," she said. "I should be standing out there on the dock with a glass of champagne in my hand, toasting my—"

He waited, but she didn't add anything to the end of the sentence. "You want to go drink some champagne?" he felt compelled to ask. The last thing he wanted to do was join the crowd down the beach.

"No. I was just wondering if anyone noticed I was missing."

"Did you have a date at the party?" That could easily have been the end of her sentence. Toasting with her boyfriend? Was that what she'd meant to say?

He glanced reflexively at her left hand. No ring. At least she hadn't been talking about toasting with her fiancé.

"No date," she assured him.

He scanned his way from her knees to her breasts, along her neck, returning to her face. Bursts of light danced off her skin, reflecting in her gorgeous eyes. His voice went husky. "Do you have a boyfriend?"

She met his gaze for a long moment, while he tensed, waiting. Then she shook her head. "Not since Russell Livingston, senior year."

"How old are you?"

"How old do I look?"

"Young enough that I should ask."

She grinned. "I'm twenty-six."

He did the math. "So you haven't had a boyfriend in four years?" He found that absolutely impossible to believe. What on earth was wrong with the men of Colorado?

"Not a steady one." She gave a little lift of her chin. "How about you?"

"I've never had a boyfriend."

She threw an elbow to his rib cage. "You know what I mean, Lucky."

He steadied her arm with his hand as she rocked back. "Nobody serious."

She resettled her bare feet on the picnic-table bench. "Since when?"

He reluctantly removed his hand from her arm, shrugging as he took in the glinting copper polish on her toenails. Sexy. How had he missed that up to now? "Since forever."

"You've never been in love?"

"I've never been in love," he confirmed. He'd never had the time. Not that he'd be likely to recognize it if it happened. He'd had no role models, no examples of romantic love in his formative years. He supposed he loved Alex like a brother. But that was a completely different thing.

"Me neither," said Doll-Face. She contemplated the fireworks display for a minute. "But both of my sisters are in love."

"You have two sisters?"

"And two brothers."

"Are your parents still together?"

Her expression faltered for a second, but then she nodded, voice a little quieter. "Yes, they are. And they're still very much in love."

"Sounds like a perfect family." Reflexive resentment flickered inside Zach. But he quickly tamped it down. He wouldn't wish his tough childhood on anyone, least of all this delightful, beautiful creature in front of him.

She laughed. "We're a long, long way from perfect. But there's a wedding coming up. A double wedding."

"Both sisters?" he guessed.

"I'll be the maid of honor." Then she sniffed and wrinkled her nose. "And me, the oldest."

"Oh, that's not good." Zach shook his head in mock concern. "Tragic, really. Pitiful."

"Isn't it?"

"An old maid at twenty-six." He clicked his cheek. "What will the neighbors say?"

Her laughter tinkled. "They'll probably introduce me to every eligible bachelor they can lay their hands on."

Zach knew she was probably right. And he didn't like that image. He had a sudden urge to curl an arm around her, pull her close, tell her to stay away from all those no-good bachelors.

"Funny," she continued, her gaze back on the fireworks. "Marriage has never been a goal of mine."

"Mine, neither," Zach agreed, ridiculously relieved. It was silly, stupid even. He didn't know the woman's name, yet he didn't want to think about her with other men.

"What *is* your goal?" he prompted. The gasps of the crowd and the pops of the rockets once again penetrated his conscious, reminding him of where they were.

She shrugged her slim, bare shoulders. "A career, maybe."

"What kind of career?" This line of conversation definitely beat talking about her future boyfriends.

"Lately I've been thinking about event management, or maybe business."

"What's your degree in?"

"History. Don't you dare laugh."

Did she mean at the impracticality of studying history? "I'm not laughing. I don't even have a college degree."

She waited for him to continue. There was no judgment in her expression.

"Where I come from," he found himself explaining, "high school graduation is about as far as kids go."

"Did you graduate high school?"

"I did." He paused. "But would you care if I hadn't?" He was honestly curious.

"I don't think it's your education that matters. It's what you do with it."

He couldn't agree more.

With the exception of their accountant, DFB Incorporated didn't have a single employee with a college degree. Mostly because they were all foster kids. They'd grown up in group homes, like him, or in a series of short-term, single-family placements. They'd learned to avoid emotional attachment to their caregivers and had spent their childhoods in survival mode. None of them had family ties. None would have had a single penny of support, even if they had wanted to go to college.

"If you want to use your history degree to go into business," he told her, "I'm all for it."

She smiled, and his chest tightened. "Thank you."

He drew a couple of hard breaths. He'd never wanted to kiss a woman quite this badly. But people could see them, and she was trying to keep a low profile. "What kind of business?" he forced himself to ask again.

"I haven't the slightest idea."

"Well, if you start your own, expand slowly. Make sure you don't overleverage."

"Is that what you did?" There was an astute intelligence in those golden eyes. It was as if she'd suddenly shifted modes, staring frankly, seeking information.

Okay, that really shouldn't strike him as sexy.

"We grew fast," he told her, shifting his attention to the lake in order to keep from grabbing her right here in front of everyone. "When you hit a certain size, all of a sudden there are a whole lot of moving parts. We ended up with a weak link. And I'm here to fix it." It seemed silly to stay so oblique. "You want me to tell you what the—"

"No!" It was her hand on his arm more than her words that shut him up.

He glanced down at her slim fingers, the lavender polish, felt the heat through the thin cotton of his shirt, and thought about all the other places he'd like her to touch him.

"It's better this way," she assured him.

It would be better with her in his arms.

The sky suddenly lit up with the fireworks finale. The crowd oohed then aahed then cheered madly as the sky went dark.

"Whatever you want," Zach told her, meaning it in all possible ways.

* * *

Abigail knew the evening had to come to an end. It was after three in the morning. They'd been talking for hours, and she was nearly asleep on her feet as they approached the front entrance of the Caspian Hotel.

Except for the doorman, the place was deserted. He tipped his hat, gave them a welcoming smile and opened the glass-fronted, brass-trimmed door so they could enter.

Lucky slowed his steps and motioned with an outstretched arm for Abigail to go in first. Her heels clicked on the marble floor, echoing through the empty lobby. A front-desk clerk glanced up from her computer screen. Seeing they had no luggage, so obviously weren't checking in, she nodded a greeting and went back to typing on the keyboard.

They crossed the vast lobby toward the bank of elevators, while Abigail struggled for something clever or memorable to say. But everything she came up with sounded either trite or ridiculous.

Lucky pressed the call button, and an elevator door immediately slid open. She wanted to tell him she'd had a great time. No, not a great time, an amazing time. A time that she wished she could repeat again someday. But she knew that was impossible. He was leaving town. And she was going back to her real life. And she didn't even know his name.

He pressed eight, then lifted his brows in her direction.

"Same," she confirmed, her voice raspy over her dry throat.

Their gazes locked, and the air in the elevator seemed to thicken with anticipation.

The door slid shut.

"Imagine that," Lucky observed.

Abigail's skin tingled. She felt heat rush up from her toes to her scalp. She'd never, ever, not even once, had a one-night stand. But she was tempted tonight.

The elevator pinged to a stop.

The door slid open.

She exited first, turning left down the hallway, wondering

what she could say, if she could say it, if she could possibly, actually bring herself to do it.

He fell into step, the heat from his body seeming to swirl out to touch her.

"Eight-nineteen," he told her, extracting his key card, slowing to a stop.

"Eight-twenty," she responded, stopping beside him.

He glanced down.

She looked up.

Her heart pounded hard against the inside of her chest. A roaring sound filled her ears. And her lungs labored as she moistened her dry lips.

He cocked his head ever so slightly toward his hotel-room door. "I'm thinking there'll be a bottle of wine in my minibar."

Abigail tried to make her head shake no, but somehow the message got scrambled. "Red or white?" she rasped instead.

"Either. Both. Whatever you want."

She knew she should say good-night and leave. This was her last chance. If she walked into that hotel room, she would throw herself into Lucky's arms, damn the consequences.

She couldn't tell him no. But she couldn't bring herself to say yes either.

He slipped the key into the lock, and the indicator light turned green. He pushed down on the handle, released the latch and yawned the door wide open.

Abigail took one step then another into his room, her shoes whispering against the thick carpet. The door whooshed shut behind them, clicking with finality.

From behind, Lucky gently touched her shoulder. He turned her, backed her slowly against the closed door, one hand tunneling into her hair, the other coming around her waist, pressing their bodies together while his lips came down on hers. They were firm, hot, moist and tender.

She gave in to the sensation, immediately kissing him back, grasping his arms, steadying herself against the steel of his biceps. She opened wide, welcoming his tongue, marveling at his sweet taste, his masculine scent and the feel of his thighs hard against her own.

He broke the kiss, speaking huskily against her lips. "I've been dying to do that all night long."

"Are we crazy?" she felt compelled to ask, lips hot and swollen, desire permeating every cell of her body.

He captured her gaze once more. "I don't particularly care."

She couldn't help smiling at that. "Am I going to sound preposterous if I say I've never done anything like this before?"

"You haven't done anything yet."

"I'm about to."

"Yeah?"

"Yeah."

"Glad to hear it." He kissed her again, longer and deeper, his fingertips finding their way up her spine.

She wrapped her arms around his neck, tipping back, abandoning herself to the passion building inside her body. She was an adult woman. She wasn't reckless, and she wasn't foolish. She'd thought this through, and she wanted to be with Lucky tonight.

"You're gorgeous," he whispered, smoothing his hand along her shoulder. He pushed her shoulder strap out of the way. Then he tenderly kissed her shoulder and eased the other strap down. "Amazing," he mumbled, kissing his way along her neck. The back of his knuckles brushed the tip of her breast, and she sucked in a breath in response. "I am the luckiest guy on the planet."

"Is that why they call you Lucky?"

He stilled, lips brushing against the tender hollow of her neck. "You're making a joke?"

"I am," she offered without a trace of apology.

He kissed her again, more firmly this time, drawing her tongue into his scorching mouth. "Well, I'm not going to keep calling you Doll-Face."

"Oh, yes, you are."

"What's your real name?"

"Uh-uh." She shook her head.

"You sure about that?"

"I'm sure."

His hands slid their way down to her wrists, and he backed her tighter against the door. "Okay. Then that's pretty hot."

She tipped her chin. "You're pretty hot."

"I'm about to get hotter." His eyes turned to molten chocolate, and a split second later he was kissing her mouth, harder, deeper. One hand slipped up her back, finding her zipper, pulling it down. The tight bodice gave way.

In return, she reached for his shirt buttons, plunking the disks through the open holes, revealing his chest, running her fingers over his bare skin.

He gave a tug on her dress, and it slid to the floor, freeing her bare breasts and pooling in a heap around her feet.

He drew back, his breath whistling out. "Where have you been hiding all my life?"

"Colorado." She pulled his shirttails out of his pants, and stripped the shirt off his shoulders.

He was absolutely magnificent, and they both stilled, staring at each other in silence.

He lifted his broad hand, cupping her face with his palm, leaning in ever so slowly. Her eyes fluttered closed. She inhaled deeper. Her lips parted, and she eased toward him, twining her arms around his neck, feeling his heated skin press tight against her breasts, as his lips came down in a tender kiss that drew itself out for long minutes.

His free hand slipped over the curve of her hip. There, his fingers paused, slipping beneath the strand of her panties. His other hand slid up to cup her breast. Her nipples instantly beaded, and his palm closed around her. His kisses grew more insistent, longer, until they were both gasping for breath.

He kissed her neck, dipping to a breast, drawing the taut nipple into his mouth. Her hands fisted hard, and she moaned at a sensation she'd never experienced. What was he doing? How was he doing it?

Cool air replaced the heat of his mouth, and she loved the

contrast. He switched to the other breast, causing cascades of desire to roll through her.

She needed to do something.

She was just standing here.

She ran her palms up his chest, feeling the burn of his skin, testing the muscles she knew would be steel hard. Then she worked her way down, over the six-pack of his abs, to the waistband of his pants, popping the button and lowering his zipper.

He grabbed her wrist. "I want this to go slow."

"Sure," she agreed, even though her mind screamed for speed. She brushed her knuckles against him.

"You want it slow?" he growled.

"No."

He stilled for a second. Then he hoisted her into his arms. "Good."

He turned in the foyer, cutting across the oversize room, past the sofa, the armchair and television. He set her on her feet next to a king-size bed.

His hands went to his waistband, stripping off his pants and everything else.

She kicked off her sandals and dispensed with the panties.

She straightened, and they both stilled.

"You're beautiful," he whispered, and she felt the edge of her mouth draw into a smile.

"You're not so bad yourself." She dared to reach out, tracing her index finger along his smooth, warm chest. He looked even better out of his clothes than he had in them, and that was saying something.

He took a half step forward. "Is this a dream?"

"I sure hope not."

"Things like this. Things like you don't happen in real life."

"I'm real."

"You're amazing."

Impatient, she took his hand, backing her way to the bed, where she sank down.

His gaze stayed molten on her naked body as he extracted a packet from his wallet and dropped the wallet to the floor.

"I can make this slow," he offered again.

She shook her head. "You're my torrid one-night stand."

"Oh, sweetheart," he whispered.

She smiled saucily in return. This was the only time she was ever going to do this, and she was going to get it right. "Show me what you've got."

He cupped his hands beneath her arms, lifting her, pushing her farther onto the bed, laying her back. His voice was a deep baritone, rumbling through her. "Seriously. Where in the hell have you been all my life?"

She didn't have time to answer because his mouth came down on hers. His body covered her own, pressing her against the soft mattress.

He toured her body with rapid but thorough kisses, while she explored the contours and angles of his. Within minutes, they were face-to-face, him on top, staring into each other's eyes in the dimly lit room.

He flexed, and she moaned, welcoming him inside, arching her back, wrapping her legs, as he set an insistent rhythm that made her head tip back and her eyes close tight. Desire overwhelmed her, and she gripped the comforter, straining for his kisses, her toes curling as he inflamed the passion at her core.

Time lost all meaning. Her body felt somehow weightless. Reality contracted to the feel, the scent and the sound of this man. His ragged breath murmured in her ear. His damp body scorched her skin. And she dragged his essence into her lungs, holding it tight, imprinting it on her subconscious so she could relive it over and over again.

She held on as long as she could, not wanting it to end. But it was a losing battle. A pulse began deep inside her, building to a tidal wave of ecstasy. She clung tightly to him, her cries mingling with his groans, as she crested for an eternity, the intense rush leaving her limp and gasping.

Her chest rose and fell against Lucky's comfortable weight. He braced himself on his elbows, rising slightly above her, sweat glistening his brow, breath fanning from between his parted lips.

They stared at each other in silence.

"That was…" His breathless voice trailed away.

She was similarly struggling for words. "It was," she agreed.

His smile widened. "Somehow we both seem to know just the right thing to say."

A small chuckle formed in her chest. "What do you usually say?"

He smoothed her hair behind one ear. "I have no comparables. You have no comparables. You are one of a kind, Doll-Face."

"That was an awfully good line," she acknowledged.

"It wasn't a line."

They both fell silent, their breathing synchronizing.

His tone when low and intimate. "Should I ask if it was good for you?"

It was the best sex she'd ever had. Hands down.

Without waiting for an answer, he shifted, taking more of his own weight. "You want that wine now, or are you ready for breakfast?"

Abigail glanced to the digital clock glowing on the nightstand. It was four-thirty in the morning. She blinked against grainy exhaustion. "It's pretty much a toss-up between night and morning, isn't it?"

He eased onto his side, propping himself on his elbow, one thigh staying angled across her legs. He brushed a wisp of hair from her cheek. "I'd like it to still be night."

She drank in the sensation of that intimate touch. "I'd like it to still be dinner."

He eased closer. "So we can start our evening all over again?"

She pretended he might have it wrong. "Yeah. Sure. Well, that and the mountain burger."

Closer still, he brought his teeth gently down on her earlobe. "Liar."

"Egomaniac."

"Am I wrong?"

She played dumb. "About what?"

He glanced at the clock. "About us wanting to stop time."

She sobered. Then she shook her head. He wasn't wrong. But

that didn't change anything. "It's a stolen night," she reminded him. They both had places to go and things to do.

"When do you have to leave?"

"Early." She was meeting her brother at the campaign office to close things up before she drove back to the ranch.

Lucky cradled her cheek, placing a long, tender kiss on her swollen lips. When it ended, his arm eased around the small of her back. "But not yet?"

"Not yet," she agreed, desire rising inside her.

He kissed her again, and again, longer and sweeter each time.

"Tell me your name," he demanded.

She shook her head.

"I need to know." He drew back, obviously determined to withhold more kisses until she answered.

Instead, she reached up, slipping her arms around his neck.

He tensed against her pull, resisting, but then he gave in, allowing her to bring him in for a kiss. She twined her naked body around his.

"Oh, Doll-Face," he groaned, capitulating to their passion. He wrapped his strong arms fully around her, holding her close and igniting a new burn deep inside.

"There you are, Abby." Abigail's oldest brother, Seth, mayor-elect of Lyndon City, zeroed in on her as she entered the campaign office on Main Street.

Cardboard boxes covered every available surface, stuffed with leftover posters, flyers, buttons and campaign literature. Half a dozen campaign volunteers were carting boxes and other materials out the back door to waiting pickup trucks, while the staffers who would form the core of Seth's mayoral staff clicked away on their laptop computers or talked on telephones.

Seth tucked a pen into his shirt pocket as he moved across the storefront shop toward her. "I didn't see you at the fireworks last night."

"Weren't they great?" she asked, avoiding any further explanation of where she'd been.

"The good folks of Lyndon know how to do it up right," he agreed.

She gave him a quick hug. "The good folks of Lyndon are excited about their new mayor."

Seth pulled back with a grin. "The display was planned weeks before the votes were cast."

She winked at him. "But I'm sure they'd have canceled if you hadn't won."

He scoffed out a laugh. "Since we both know you're not naive, I'm going to assume that's blind loyalty talking."

"That's supreme confidence talking." She patted him on the shoulder as she glanced around the messy office. "You need any help here?" She was more than a little anxious to get herself out of town. Last night Lucky had said he was just passing through Lyndon. He might very well have left town already. But she didn't want to risk running into him.

She'd sneaked out of his hotel room and back to hers as soon as he fell asleep last night. Though the soft bed, the thick quilt and Lucky's warm, strong body had been powerful draws, she hadn't wanted to risk facing him in the morning. Better to leave things on a high note. A very high note. Wow, had that ever been a high note.

"Abby?" Seth prompted, waving his palm in front of her face.

"The financial records?"

"What about them?"

"What's the matter with you?"

"Nothing."

Seth peered at her curiously. "I just asked if you could do a double check on the donation receipts. And Lisa needs a hand with the database."

At the sound of her name, Lisa Thompson glanced up from a crowded desk in one corner of the room. "I want to make sure we have a clean backup copy before I delete all the information from the laptop. I'm planning to use it in the mayor's office, so I have to get rid of all the campaign records."

"Happy to help out," Abigail agreed, telling herself the odds of seeing Lucky were low, particularly if she was hidden away in the back of the campaign office. She made her way across the room, weaving around the mess of chairs, desks, boxes and trash bins.

Seth's cell phone rang, and he moved to a quiet corner near the back exit to answer the call.

Lisa, blonde, petite, freckled and perky, tracked Abigail's progress from her office chair.

She waited until Abigail sat down and spun the chair, then she wheeled herself to face her. "So, what happened?" she demanded in a conspiratorial undertone.

"What are you talking about?"

"It's blatantly obvious you got laid last night."

"What?" Abigail blurted, glancing swiftly around, making sure nobody could overhear them.

"Don't play dumb with me." Lisa smacked her palm down on the padded arm of Abigail's chair.

"I did not—"

"And don't you dare lie to me either." Lisa rocked back and crossed her arms over her gray Colorado Lions T-shirt, green eyes narrowing. Her voice stayed low. "Your cheeks are flushed. Your eyes are glowing gold. And there's a spring in your step that wasn't there at the party. Plus, you disappeared before ten last night, and I never saw you again. Neither did anyone else. Now, give."

Abigail hesitated. She wanted to lie, but she knew she was trapped. Lisa had her dead to rights.

Obviously taking Abigail's silence as an admission, Lisa grinned and leaned closer still. "Details, please."

Abigail sent a worried glance toward Seth. "Don't you dare tell—"

"I'm not going to tell anybody. I'm not a gossip."

Abigail knew it was true. Lisa would be Seth's executive assistant in the mayor's office, in part because of her brilliance and hard work, but also because they'd learned she was the soul of discretion. She and Abigail had become quite close over the course of the campaign.

"So, what happened?" Lisa hissed. "Who was he?"

"Nobody you know."

"How can you say that? I know lots of people. I've met half the town in the last three months."

"He's not from here."

"Ooh." Lisa's eyes sparkled. "Where's he from? What's he do? What's his name? Is he hot?"

"I don't know."

Lisa drew back. "You don't know if he's hot?"

"I don't know his name," Abigail admitted sheepishly. "I don't know what he does. And I don't know where he's from."

Lisa's mouth opened, then her expression turned positively gleeful. "You had a one-night stand with a stranger?"

Abigail lowered her own voice even further. "Yes."

Lisa's hand tightened on Abigail's arm, as if to hold her in place. "Was he hot?"

"Yes." Hot didn't begin to describe Lucky. In fact, even now, Abigail's body responded with an embarrassing level of arousal at the mere memory of Lucky naked, laconic, gazing at her with that lazy half smile.

"You go, Abby!"

"Shh."

"Yes. Of course. Wow. No wonder you don't want to tell Seth."

"I don't want to tell *anyone*."

Lisa gave a series of rapid nods. "Got it. But if you don't know his name, how are you going to see him again?"

"I'm not." Abigail wouldn't. She couldn't. No matter how much she wished she could.

"But if he's hot and, well, if the look in your eyes is anything to go by, maybe you want to—"

"Lisa, look up the definition of one-night stand."

"One-night stands can turn into something else, you know."

Abigail coughed on a laugh, seizing on the chance to turn the tables. "Actually, I wouldn't know. Would you?"

Lisa wrinkled her nose in the air. "No. Not that there's anything wrong in it. Not with the right person. You know, in the right circumstance."

"Last night was the right circumstance." Abigail wasn't going to regret last night. She refused to regret last night.

She'd never met a man remotely like Lucky. The memory of his voice made her tingle, and the thought of his kisses brought a flood of desire. Her real world was closing in fast, dragging her back into its clutches, while the exhilarating escape with Lucky secretly pulsed just below her skin. She'd lock it away where no one could see, but where she could pull it out to relive that treasured night over and over again.

Fall was on its way to Lyndon Valley. Work on the ranch would begin in earnest now, starting with the roundup. But when the wind howled down from the Rockies, or when she was bone tired out on the range, she'd remember the feel of Lucky's strong arms around her, the heat of his body against her, his whispered words, his endearing sense of humor and the way he'd made her feel like the only woman in the world.

Three

The Craig Mountain Brewery was tucked in the mountains above the picturesque shores of Lake Patricia, an hour north of Lyndon City. Built of stone and mortar, around 1850, in the style of British castles, Craig Mountain had started life as a manor house for a British lord, a remittance man, a reprobate whose family had paid him handsomely to leave England and never return.

The brewery manager, Lucas Payton, shared the story of Lord Ashton with Zach while the two men made their way along the covered pathway that connected the original castle, which was now mostly offices, to the newer industrial complex housing the warehouse and brewery, with its tanks, filtration systems and bottling line.

"They say Ashton bribed a railroad official for information on the planned railway line," Lucas continued, tone animated. "Whether the official didn't know the real route, or he simply lied for reasons of his own, nobody ever found out. But he took the money and left the state, while Ashton built his house a hundred miles in the wrong direction."

"You a history buff?" asked Zach.

Lucas had worked for DFB for three years now. The two men

had met on several occasions when Lucas traveled to Houston for company meetings. But they'd always talked shop, and it had always been amongst a larger group of people.

"You know how it is," Lucas answered, stuffing his hands into his back pockets. "I'm an orphan. So I've adopted some-body's else's ancestors."

"Never thought to do that," said Zach. Interesting, though, choosing a family history based on interest and convenience instead of strict genealogy.

Like all DFB employees, Lucas had come through the foster care system. When Zach and Alex founded the company, they'd promised each other it would be for the benefit of orphans like themselves, people who had no families and few chances in life.

"You should prowl through the top floors of the castle some-time," said Lucas, pulling open a door to the cinder-block ware-house. "There's some absolutely fascinating stuff up there."

"I'm not going to have time for that." Zach stepped inside the cool, dim building, and the familiar tang of hops and malt hit his nostrils. Supplies were stacked twenty feet high on steel shelv-ing, on either side of a wide aisle that bisected the big building. A forklift rumbled unseen in the distance, its backup alarm sounding intermittently with the whir of the tires and hydrau-lics.

"Going right back to the big city?" asked Lucas. "I suppose there's not much to keep you here."

"Not much," Zach agreed, even as his mind slipped back to last night and the incredible encounter with Doll-Face.

When he woke up this morning, the sexy and mysterious woman had already slipped out, leaving him there alone. He'd told himself to let it go. She didn't want to know him, and she sure hadn't wanted him to know anything about her.

It was disappointing, and for a few seconds he'd been tempted to hang around town looking for her. But orphans learned one lesson very early in life. Anything good could be snatched away in a millisecond. It was probably better that it had happened fast this time. Something told him, given half a chance, he could have fallen dangerously hard for the beautiful, intelligent, engaging woman.

He came back to the present as Lucas started through the center of the warehouse.

"It's not the renovation costs that'll get you," said Lucas, turning the conversation back to the reason for Zach's visit. "And there's plenty of room to expand out back toward the hillside."

He pressed a red button on the wall, and a big overhead door clattered its way open. He pointed outside to the vast gravel parking lot, past two semitrailer trucks that were positioned for unloading. "We can build a new warehouse over there, free up some space for more production. The bottling plant and the brewery will have to stay put, but we'd have some options around the coolers and the fermenters."

"If it's not the renovation costs, what is it that'll get me?" asked Zach, used to cutting directly to the chase.

"The water," said Lucas.

"Something wrong with the water?"

"We've maxed out the water license. I asked around after your call on Friday, and it's going to be tough, if not impossible, to get permission to increase our usage."

This was very bad news. Zach frowned. "Why?"

"Moratorium on water-use licenses all across the region."

The unique underground springwater of Craig Mountain was a key ingredient in the beer. The springwater was also the cornerstone of the marketing campaign for C Mountain Ale, the most popular brand in DFB's iconic Red, White and Brew six-pack.

Red, White and Brew contained one beer from each of DFB's six breweries, and it was taking their international markets by storm. Production was already on pace for the new orders at the other five breweries in Montana, California, Michigan, South Carolina and Texas, but Craig Mountain had to catch up.

"The water-rights battle has been going on for months. It's the ranchers versus everyone else, and the ranchers are a very powerful lobby group."

"We're miles and miles from the nearest ranch." Zach gestured through the big doorway. "How can our water use possibly impact them?"

"It doesn't matter," said Lucas, shaking his head. "People have grazing rights nearby. There'll be no new water licenses. No variances to existing water licenses. No temporary permits. Nothing until the new regulations are drafted and they go through the state legislature."

Zach swore.

"You got that right."

Zach smacked the heel of his hand against the doorjamb. He gritted his teeth. Then he straightened and squared his shoulders. "All right. Who do I talk to?"

"Beats the hell out of me. I do beer, not politics."

"Well, who does politics?"

"You could try a lawyer. Someone local, maybe."

Zach nodded. He supposed that was a logical place to start. "Who do you use locally?"

Lucas gave a shrug. "We've never had any legal problems."

"Are there law firms in Lyndon?"

Or maybe he should fly back to Denver. If this moratorium thing was broader than the immediate Lyndon area, he might as well go to a big firm with plenty of capacity.

And his clock was ticking. If the Craig Mountain Brewery construction didn't get started in the next couple of weeks, they'd end up with a shortage of C Mountain Ale, and they wouldn't be able to fill their spring orders for Red, White and Brew. That would most certainly mean the downfall of DFB.

"There are definitely law firms in Lyndon." Lucas answered the question. "Sole proprietorships mostly. And I don't know if they've been involved in the issue. Honestly, if I was going for the greatest concentration of knowledge on this, I'd be going to the Ranchers Association."

"Didn't you just say they were on the other side?"

"I did."

"So, then, that would be a foolish move."

"Well." Lucas scratched the back of his neck. "If you don't

want to go to the Ranchers Association, you can try Abigail Jacobs."

"Who's she?"

"The daughter of one of the ranching families. I was told she has an encyclopedia for a brain and a passion for the water-rights issue."

"She's still the enemy."

"Maybe. Technically."

"So she's not going to help us."

"You can always get creative. You don't have to tell her exactly what you're looking for. Just meet her and, I don't know." Lucas looked Zach up and down. "Tell her she's pretty or something, take her out for dinner and a movie, then ask a lot of questions."

"You want me to romance the information out of some unsuspecting woman?"

"If she's a research geek, maybe she hasn't had a date for a while."

"Did we not give you an ethics quiz before we hired you?"

"I had a dysfunctional upbringing."

"So did I, but I still have standards. I'm going with the lawyer." The clock might be ticking, but Zach had absolutely no intention of lying to this Abigail Jacobs for his own ends.

The Jacobs ranch covered thousands of acres in the Lyndon Valley of western Colorado. As it had become more prosperous, Abigail's grandfather, and then her father, had purchased more and more land. The main house was two stories high, with six bedrooms, overlooking the Lyndon River to the east. To the west the Rockies rose, their peaks jutting to the blue sky behind the three main barns, several horse corrals and a massive equipment garage.

Staff cottages and two low bunkhouses snaked along the riverbank, forming a semicircle around the big cookshack that welcomed cowboys and farmhands with wholesome food and pots of brewed coffee any time of the day or night. Born and raised here, Abigail knew there were many things to love about the

Jacobs ranch, and she now spent her days reminding herself she could be happy here. She climbed the front stairs, the summer day's sweat soaking through her T-shirt, dampening her hairline and wicking into the band of her Stetson. As she started across the porch, she heard male voices through the open living-room windows. The sun was slipping low in the hot August sky. The breeze had dropped to nothing. And a dozen horseflies buzzed a lazy patrol pattern beneath the shade of the peaked porch roof. She slapped her hat against her leg, brushed the excess dust from the front of her jeans, then checked her boot heels for mud.

The voices grew louder, more distinct. One was her brother Travis. The other was vaguely familiar, but she couldn't quite place it.

"And you expect *us* to help?" Travis demanded.

"I could have lied," the other voice returned reasonably. "But in the interest of—"

"Is that supposed to impress me? That you stopped short of lying?"

"I'm not looking to impress you."

Wondering who her brother was arguing with, Abigail moved toward the door. In the week since she'd returned to the ranch, there'd been a steady stream of friends and neighbors stopping by, expressing their congratulations on Seth's victory and inquiring about Abigail's father, who was expected home from the Houston rehab center in the next few weeks.

"Lucky for you that you're not," scoffed Travis.

"I just want some information, and then I'll be on my—"

"You'll be on your way right now."

"Not before I talk to Abigail."

Abigail stopped short. Who *was* that?

"Abigail's not here."

"Then I'll wait."

"I don't think so."

Well, whoever it was, he wasn't going to have to wait long, and it was going to be a pretty short conversation. Abigail had a hot shower in her sights, followed by dinner and maybe a nice glass of Shiraz. Then she was falling directly into bed.

She wasn't exactly out of shape, but it had been several months since she'd done full-time ranch work, and her long shift on the oat field today had been exhausting.

"Nobody gets to Abby unless they go through me," Travis stated.

From the entry hall, Abigail could picture her brother's square shoulders, his wide stance, the hard line of his chin. He was endearingly, if unnecessarily, protective. She pushed down the door latch with her thumb and silently opened the door.

The unknown man's voice came from around the corner, inside the big living room. "Craig Mountain's new usage will be negligible in the scheme of things."

"And what better way to set precedent?" Travis responded. "You're the thin edge of the wedge."

"I'm brewing beer, not setting precedent. It's one little underground spring."

"It's still part of the aquifer."

Abigail dropped her hat on a peg by the door and raked back her damp, dusty hair. Her ponytail was definitely the worse for wear. Then again, so were her dirty hands and her sweaty clothes. But she was back on the ranch now. And she wasn't looking to impress anyone. So who cared?

During the local-water-rights hearings a few months ago, she'd listened to every argument in the book. It wouldn't take her long to send this guy packing.

She rounded the corner. "Hey, Travis."

Her brother scowled.

The broad-shouldered man in the expensive business suit pivoted to face her.

As he did, she went stock-still. Her stomach plummeted to her toes, while waves of sound roared in her ears. *Lucky?*

His dark eyes widened.

"Lucky what?" asked Travis, glancing from one to the other.

Abigail's brain stumbled, and an exaggerated second slipped by. "Lucky I got here when I did," she managed to say on a hollow laugh.

Where on earth had he come from? What was he doing standing here arguing with her brother?

Before she could formulate any kind of question, Lucky stepped forward, holding out his hand. "Zach Rainer. You must be Abigail. It's nice to meet you."

"Mr. Rainer was just leaving," Travis put in with finality.

"I own the Craig Mountain Brewery," Zach continued, his voice betraying none of the recognition evident in his expression.

"I…uh…" Her throat closed over. "I'm Abigail," she managed to rasp, giving his hand a perfunctory shake. The sizzle of his brief touch ricocheted up her arm.

"Then you're the woman I'm here to see. I understand you have some expertise on the regional-water-rights issue."

Travis stepped forward. "Oh, no, you don't."

"I'd like to talk to Abigail."

"But Abigail wouldn't like to talk to you."

"I think Abigail can speak for herself." Lucky raised his brow.

She struggled to shake off the shock. So far, he was keeping their night a secret. Although she had to find out what he was up to, and quickly.

"It's okay, Travis," she said with a quick glance to her brother.

"No, it's not okay. He doesn't get to waltz in here and—"

"I'm not out to harm you." Though Lucky was responding to Travis, he kept his gaze fixed on Abigail.

"You're a liar," said Travis.

Abigail agreed with her brother. Lucky's being here couldn't possibly be a coincidence. Had he set her up from the very beginning? A wave of disappointment and humiliation washed over her.

"I'm not lying," said Lucky.

The odds were overwhelming that he was lying through his teeth, but one thing was sure, she needed to talk to him alone. Bad enough that she'd slept with him, but in the wee hours of the morning she'd also confessed embarrassing secrets. She'd told him how badly she wanted a career in business, that she didn't want to work with her brother on the ranch. She'd said some things that, in retrospect, were downright disloyal.

"It'll be fine," she assured Travis in the calmest voice she could muster.

"You don't need to be polite," Travis pointed out. "This guy's the enemy."

Lucky heaved a frustrated sigh.

"I'm a grown woman." Abigail was firm. "I think I can decide who to talk to."

"Don't start with me," said Travis.

"Can we step outside?" asked Lucky, taking a step toward the door.

Travis barged between the two, facing Lucky, his back to Abigail. "Leave," he commanded.

"Travis," she said from between clenched teeth. "You have to back off."

"No."

"We're only going to talk."

He rounded on her. "I don't understand. Why would you give this jerk the time of day?"

"I'm giving him five minutes."

Travis spread his arms in obvious frustration. "I've already given him ten."

Fine, Abigail was frustrated, too. When Travis got like this, there was no point in arguing with him. But she didn't dare give in, not until she knew what Lucky was up to. She held her palms up in surrender and took a backward step, then another, and another.

When she was clear, she turned for the door, stomping her way outside, assuming Lucky—no, *Zach*—would have sense enough to follow. Her brother was a tough, intimidating man. But Zach seemed as if he could hold his own. And she was hoping against hope they were too civilized to engaged in a fistfight in the living room.

She banged her way through the front doorway, stomped across the porch, down onto the gravel driveway, taking a few steps out onto the turnaround. She pushed back her hair, acutely aware of her disheveled appearance.

She shouldn't care. But she couldn't seem to help herself. Zach had seen her at her best last week, dressed up for the party. Okay, so he'd also seen her naked. But she didn't think she looked that bad naked.

Right now her shirt was wrinkled and covered in grit. She was pretty sure there were dust streaks marring her face. Her hair looked like something out of a horror flick. And she smelled like the rear end of a heifer.

"Abigail?" came Zach's voice, followed by his swift footsteps crunching on the gravel.

She squared her shoulders and turned to face him.

"What are you doing here?" she asked shortly.

"I need your help." He came to a halt a few feet away.

"No. I mean, *what are you doing here?*"

"I don't get the distinction."

"How did you find me? Did you know who I was all along?" She feared she already knew the answer, but she wanted him to admit it out loud.

"I didn't find you. I didn't even know who you were."

"Right," she scoffed. He had to have targeted her from minute one. She could only imagine he'd been laughing at her all night long.

"I didn't know your name," he insisted with remarkable sincerity. "I met Doll-Face. I *liked* Doll-Face." He paused, and an emotion flicked through his eyes. "Why wouldn't you tell me your name?"

"Apparently I didn't need to."

"I didn't know your name," he repeated. "It was only *later* I heard that Abigail Jacobs was the best person to help me with the water license. I put those two things together exactly two minutes ago."

"You expect me to believe that?" Had she come across as completely stupid and gullible? What a depressing thought.

"Yes, I expect you to believe me."

"I believed you were leaving town," she challenged. "That was a week ago, Zach. You haven't left town."

"I told you I was passing through."

"What kind of play on semantics is that?"

"I *am* passing through."

"You set me up from the start." There was no other explanation.

He spread his legs, firming his stance. "I did not know who you were that night."

"Bull."

"I didn't. If I had..." He paused. "Hell, I don't know what I would have done if I had. That night was pretty great."

"You don't get to talk about that night." Not now, not ever.

"It doesn't matter if I talk about it or not." His gaze smoldered for a silent second, transmitting the unspoken message that he remembered it as well as she did.

"It's nothing more than a blur to me," she bluffed.

He eased closer. "You can't lie worth a damn."

"Yes, I can." The protest was reflexive. She didn't want to be a good liar, and his opinion meant nothing to her.

"I need your help, Doll-Face."

She leaned in, pointing an index finger at his chest. "You can't have my help."

"Oh, I'm pretty sure I can." His tone was mild, but his eyes had gone hard as flint.

A cloud moved over the setting sun, cooling the air and darkening the world, while a sick feeling settled in the pit of her stomach.

"I saw your look of panic inside the house," he finished.

"That wasn't panic," she lied again.

"You don't want your brother to know about us," Zach stated.

As if on cue, Travis appeared in the doorway, leaning on the jamb, arms folded over his chest and a scowl on his face.

Abigail didn't dare let Zach know he had the upper hand. "Believe me when I tell you, *you* don't want my brothers to know about us."

"I'll take my chances with your brothers."

Did she dare call his bluff? Was it a bluff? Was he willing to risk her brothers' wrath over a water license? Her skin prickled and her heart rate doubled.

Okay, this might be the beginning of panic.

"I am certain," he continued, voice lower, leaning ever so slightly toward her, "that you want to keep every damn thing we said and did that night a secret."

She refused to answer.

"And that gives me a whole lot of bargaining power."

"Are you blackmailing me?" she demanded.

"Yeah," he admitted. Again, something flickered across his face. It could have been regret, but that seemed unlikely. "Sorry about that. But I'm in a hurry, and I need your brain."

"Was that supposed to be a joke?" she demanded, arms reflexively crossing over her breasts.

"What joke?"

"That you've already had my body?"

"I never said that."

"You thought it."

"You're paranoid."

She swallowed convulsively, attempting to moisten her throat. "How can you do this to me?"

"I wish I had a choice."

"You have a choice," she rasped. "You can walk away right now and forget any of this ever happened."

He crossed his arms over his broad chest. "Forget about today or forget about that night?"

"Go to hell."

Zach didn't flinch.

Travis stalked out onto the porch, and she knew he was about to intervene. He couldn't break this up. Not yet. Not until she convinced Zach to go away and never come back.

"Follow me," she told Zach, turning for the path that led to the river.

With a glance at Travis, Zach fell into step. "Is he going to let us leave?"

"Fifty-fifty," she allowed, wondering the same thing herself.

They cut off the edge of the driveway, moving onto the narrower path, where willows would partially screen them from Travis's view. She took a surreptitious glance over her shoulder, making sure her brother wasn't following.

"It's not like I'm asking you to knock over a bank," said Zach.

"You're asking me to betray my community."

"Don't be melodramatic. Nobody even has to know you're helping me. It'll be a secret."

"So you can blackmail me with it later?" she challenged.

He gave an exaggerated eye roll. "Don't be ridiculous."

"How is that ridiculous? You're blackmailing me now." Her voice came out more shrilly than she'd intended.

"There's only one thing I want from you, Abby."

"Don't call me Abby." That nickname was reserved for her family.

"I like it."

"You don't get to like it."

His gaze stayed on her, while he obviously regrouped. "How can we make this work?"

"You can go away and never come back."

"I'm definitely not going away. I need a variance on my water license. Nothing more, nothing less. Hundreds of jobs depend on it. And from everything I've learned in the last week, you're the only person who can help."

"I'll email you my research," she offered out of desperation.

"I need more than your research. I need to know who to ask, what to ask them, how to write the application and how to fight my way through the bureaucracy."

"My brain is not for sale."

"Yeah? Well, when it comes to my employees, my morals and values are open to the highest bidder." Passion and determination moved into his tone. "Don't push me, Abby. I'll do anything, *anything* to keep them from losing their jobs."

"If I help you set a precedent for varying a nonranching water license, my family's cause gets set back by miles."

"You'll have to gain the ground back later."

"You couldn't care less about me, could you?"

He didn't answer.

Then again, maybe he did. His silence said it all.

She clamped her jaw against her anger, realizing there was nothing left to say, no argument she could make that would change his mind. Zach had given her an impossible choice. She could be secretly disloyal, or blatantly disloyal.

If she was blatantly disloyal, there was no going back. If she secretly helped Zach, maybe, just maybe, the fallout would be manageable. At least she'd know the ins and outs of his strategy for getting around the water license. Maybe she could use that later, in some kind of political counterattack. Maybe.

"Well?" he prompted, and she knew her time was up.

"Fine," she ground out, accepting that she was trapped. "I'll do this for you. But if you ever dare tell my family anything—" she lifted her index finger, jabbing it against his chest "—and I mean anything about *anything,* I swear I will hunt you down and shoot you dead."

"Not a word," he vowed.

She paused, shaking off the sick feeling of disloyalty. "We can't talk here." And meeting in town was also a risk, with Seth and his staff all there.

"Come out to the brewery," Zach suggested.

It wasn't her first choice. But at least it was out of the way.

"It'll take me a couple of days to pull things together," she told him. "And I'll need to come up with an excuse to leave the ranch." She'd only just returned home to help Travis. It was going to take some fast talking to get away again. And she'd be leaving all the work to him. "I hate this."

"I'm not crazy about it either." Zach's eyes unexpectedly softened. His lips parted. A breeze washed over them, rustling the leaves.

He reached out, grazing the top of her hand with his. "You know, I really wish we could—"

"Don't," she warned him, darting away, even as her pulse leaped at his light touch. "Don't you dare try anything. I am *not* going to sleep with the man who's blackmailing me."

He dropped his hand. Then he blinked his expression back to neutral. He gave a sharp nod of acceptance. "Of course you're not. The brewery, then. Thursday morning. Be there."

Four

As she turned onto the Craig Mountain Brewery road, a Sawyer Brown tune came through the stereo speakers, and Abigail cranked up the volume, letting the beat pound its way through her brain. After she'd lied to her brother Travis this morning about where she was going, she'd promised herself she'd give Zach one day. She'd work fast. She'd work hard. And he'd have everything he needed to apply for his license.

Then she'd spend the night in Lyndon, head back to the ranch and forget she'd ever met the man.

Her plan to fantasize about him had come to an abrupt end when she'd learned that he had no scruples. Okay, maybe the end wasn't quite so abrupt. In fact, she was still working on it. It turned out that fantasizing about Zach was a hard habit to break. Which only made her hate him more.

How dare he mess up her life like this? It was a mere one-night stand. Was she not entitled to cut loose and have fun every once in a while? Thousands of women across the country had one-night stands. She was willing to bet things like this didn't happen to them.

Then again, she supposed they hadn't slept with Zach.

It would have been easier if she could just plain hate him. But he'd been such a perfect lover, she couldn't help wishing for the fantasy. If she could have Lucky back, she'd be looking forward to today.

They'd talk and joke and flirt, maybe kiss a little, maybe even cancel her reservation at Rose Cottages....

Whoa. She abruptly pulled back on that thought. She wrestled her imagination into submission as she navigated a series of potholes. Then she rounded a corner, and the massive stone castle of Craig Mountain rose in front of her. She rocked to a halt in the parking lot, fingers going white as she gripped the steering wheel.

The band had changed songs, belting out one about the winner losing it all. Abigail didn't particularly feel like a winner, but the rest fit. Her pride had been battered and bruised, and if she dared let her anger slip out of place, her emotions felt a whole lot like heartache.

Zach greeted Abigail in the brewery's reception area, which was once a foyer to the massive, stone castle. She was glaring at him, displeasure palpable in her flashing golden eyes. She wore torn, faded blue jeans, a powder-blue cotton shirt with the sleeves rolled halfway up her forearms, the top button missing, and a pair of battered cowboy boots, with a gray backpack slung over one shoulder. Her face was scrubbed free of makeup, and her glossy auburn hair was pulled back in a plain ponytail. She couldn't have telegraphed "don't touch me" any louder if she'd shouted it from the highest tower.

He knew she thought he'd set her up. He hadn't. But there was no way to make her believe it. Too bad. Because whatever it was that had attracted him that night wasn't going away anytime soon. She could dress down all she liked. She was still off-the-charts sexy in his eyes.

"Good morning," he offered.

"Morning," she returned, stony faced.

"Thanks for coming."

She scoffed and shrugged her shoulders. "Like I had a choice. Tell me what you need, and let's get this over with."

Zach couldn't help a surreptitious glance at the receptionist stationed at the counter across the room, trying to gauge if she was within earshot. It seemed unlikely, but there was no point in taking chances.

"You want the tour first?" he asked Abigail, using an out-stretched arm to direct her toward the main door.

Craig Mountain Brewery offered tours of the castle, the facilities and the grounds. According to Lucas, there were quite a few tourists willing to make the hour-long, scenic drive to visit a historic castle and sample Craig Mountain beer. At the last managers' meeting in Houston, Zach and Alex had turned down Lucas's proposal to put in a small restaurant. But Zach was now rethinking that decision.

"Why would I want a tour?" Abigail asked without moving.

"Because it's interesting."

She crossed her arms mulishly over her chest. "I'm not here to see the sights."

In his peripheral vision, he saw the receptionist move to the far side of the cavernous room. Nice to know the staff were courteous.

"I need you to understand how we operate here. How else are you going to argue our case?"

"I'm not arguing your case. I'm giving you some information. What you do with it is entirely up to you."

"That wasn't our deal."

"We don't have a deal. We have a blackmail scheme."

True enough. "You're being melodramatic again."

She jabbed a thumb over her shoulder. "Then I can walk back out that door and not worry about any negative repercussions?"

"No, you can't," he admitted.

"I rest my case."

"See, you're good at this."

She frowned. "You expect me to laugh?"

"I expect you to let me show you around Craig Mountain Brewery." He gestured toward the door again.

She gave a hard, exaggerated sigh and hiked up the backpack. "If that's what'll get this over and done with."

"That's what'll get this over and done with," he confirmed.

She lifted her nose in the air, pivoted on those scuffed boots and marched for the door.

He couldn't help watching her rear end as she walked away. The woman had the sexiest body he'd ever seen. He supposed that's what happened when you combined natural beauty, fresh air and healthy living. The hot got hotter.

Abigail was scorching.

He followed her outside to where semicircular, stone steps led to a gravel parking lot. They were bordered by the castle lawns on the lake side and by forests of maples, aspens and evergreen trees stretching up the hill on the other. As August wound to a close, the barest hint of changing leaves had appeared. Beyond the tree line, the mountains turned to scrub and then craggy rock.

The expanse of green lawn stretched toward a rocky cliff that dropped to Lake Patricia. At the cliff's edge was a massive statue of Lord Ashton, chest puffed out, sword drawn, perched on a magnificent charger that seemed to gallop toward the water.

Zach had to admit, if it wasn't for the worry about DFB's future and the discord with Abigail, he would have enjoyed his stay here. He'd taken a small but very comfortable suite on the third floor of the castle. He'd even poked his head up to the small, dusty, rotund turrets. Lucas was right, the castle was a treasure trove of memorabilia.

"That's the statue of Lord Ashton," Zach offered as an opening.

"Is he currently brewing beer?" Abigail tartly inquired.

"He is not."

"Then I don't need to know about him." She rounded on Zach. "Can we move it along? Let's stick to the things I need to know."

Zach couldn't really blame her for being testy. And blackmailing her wasn't exactly his most admirable undertaking. But life was tough. You took your advantages where you could. And in a few days, she'd be finished with him, and she'd be back in the bosom of her family, doing the ranch job she hated, none the worse for wear.

Come to think of it. She should be grateful to him for giving her a reprieve from roping and riding and branding. He wondered if he'd be able to make her see it that way, or at least get her to admit that he wasn't dragging her to the gallows. Helping Craig Mountain get a few thousand more gallons of water each day wasn't going to fundamentally change anything, except the lives of Zach's employees. And that would be for the good.

"The brewery's down this path," he offered, nodding the way.

She reluctantly fell into step beside him. "And I need to see it why?"

"We brew C Mountain Ale up here," Zach began. "It's Craig Mountain's signature product, and its unique taste comes, in part, from the local, underground springwater." They rounded a corner of the path, and the gray, industrial complex came into view. "Nationwide and worldwide, hundreds of microbreweries are going under in today's economy. We're in danger of joining them, except that we have one product that's taking our national and international markets by storm. Our Red, White and Brew six-pack."

"Red, White and Brew?"

"Very patriotic packaging. Consumers love it. It contains one beer from each of our breweries. They're in six different states. All the other facilities can keep up with the increased demand. But we need to triple production of C Mountain Ale."

"Why not replace C Mountain Ale with another beer?" she reasoned.

"Because it's one of the most popular in the pack. When you find the X factor in the beer business, in any business, you don't mess with it."

"Find another water source. It's water, Lucky. Water."

"From where?" He stopped and gestured around them. "From the lake? The river? Surface water is vastly different in chemical composition. It would need a different treatment. The taste would change. And—and this is the most important point—I'd have to get the bloody water license to do that anyway."

She didn't seem to have an answer for that.

"Do you have any idea how hard it is to hit on the exact formula for a popular beer?" he continued.

"Do you know how hard it is to lie to your family?"

"No," he stated flatly. "I don't."

They stared at each other in charged silence.

"Then why are you making me do it?"

Zach's heart contracted, and he was forced to push down an unfamiliar feeling of guilt. "I'm not. You can tell your family anything you want."

"If I'd told them the truth, I wouldn't be here."

"And your secret's safe with me."

"My conscience isn't."

"Your conscience will get over it." People had to do what they had to do in this life. It was a tiny bit of white lie, one of omission really. Zach had done far worse, and his conscience was perfectly clear.

"I'm going to hate you, Zach," she warned.

"I guess I'm going to have to find a way to live with that."

"You couldn't care less, could you?"

"No. I could care a whole lot less than I do." Truth was, he cared far more than he should. But his duty was to Alex and to his employees. He had to stay tough. He couldn't let his personal feelings for Abigail get in the way.

Abigail tried very hard not to show an interest in the inner workings of the brewery. But the manager made the tour quite fascinating, and she found herself impressed by the scope of the operation.

"The bottling plant—" wearing a hat and safety glasses, Lucas projected his voice over the rumble of the motors, the whir of the conveyors and the clatter of the bottles running past them toward the filling station "—is the one place we won't need any kind of upgrade. It's currently only operating at eighteen percent capacity, so there's plenty of room for growth. Good call on that when you bought it." He tipped his head to Zach.

Zach nodded an acknowledgment of the compliment but

didn't offer a response over the din. They bypassed the labeling conveyor to go through a swinging doorway, shutting out much of the noise. Then they headed down a short hallway that seemed to be leading them back to the warehouse.

Halfway down the hall, Lucas opened a door to a large, dimly lit room. It was lined with banks of computers, monitors and electrical panels that featured a host of blinking lights. "This is the nerve center of the operation."

Just then, Zach's cell phone rang. He peeled off the hat and safety glasses they'd been issued for the brewery leg of the tour, excusing himself to move farther down the hall.

Abigail removed her own hat and glasses, handing them to Lucas as they moved farther into the control room. Two staff members were walking from station to station, noting numbers and turning dials.

"We can monitor temperature, humidity, production, supplies and shipping," said Lucas. "You name it."

"Are all of the DFB breweries this big?" Abigail found herself asking.

"Craig Mountain is the smallest," Lucas replied. "But we've had some of the most recent upgrades, so we like to think we can hold our own."

"I'm sure you can. I have to say, I'm very impressed." The place seemed high-tech and very well run.

Lucas rested his butt against the edge of one of the long, black-topped counters. "And I have to say it's nice of you to help us out with this."

She retied her ponytail, compressing her lips. She had no intention of discussing the sordid details, but she wasn't willing to tell an outright lie. "Helping Craig Mountain wasn't my choice," she admitted.

He cocked his head. "I have to admit, I was surprised to hear that you'd said yes."

She tried to guess how much he knew about the blackmail. He seemed to be seeking information.

"Was it out of pity?" he probed.

"I'd call it insanity," she responded. "If Seth or Travis find out I'm doing this—"

Lucas came upright. "Wait a minute. Your brothers don't know you're here?"

Abigail stilled, a sinking feeling creeping into her stomach. "Zach didn't tell you to keep this a secret?"

"You helping us is a secret?"

"Yes."

"Are you kidding me?"

Abigail shook her head. Then she swallowed. Oh, no.

Lucas slipped an arm through hers. With a surreptitious glance at the two employees over his shoulder, he propelled her out the door and into the hallway. There, they all but ran into Zach.

"Please tell me there's more to this plan," Lucas opened, staring accusingly at his boss.

Zach moved his confused gaze from Lucas to Abigail and back again. "What plan?"

"She's *known*, Zach. She's recognizable."

Zach didn't respond, taking a moment to tuck his phone back into his pocket.

Lucas wasn't finished. "How in the hell is she going to explain being here?"

Zach's jaw went tight in obvious annoyance at Lucas's manner. "The details are none of your business."

"This brewery is my business," Lucas returned.

"Let's discuss this in private," Zach ground out.

But Lucas shook his head. "Fire me if you want to, but this isn't Houston or Denver. She's the mayor's sister. She has no anonymity. We need to get her out of here before people start asking questions."

Abigail knew with a sickening certainty that Lucas was right. When she agreed to meet Zach up here, she hadn't realized so many people worked at Craig Mountain. Most of them probably lived in Lyndon. She could only hope her hat and glasses had kept her from being recognized on the tour. But she was playing with fire, and she needed to get out of here.

"Everything we need to work with is in the offices," Zach pointed out. "She has to do it here."

"Well, it can't be during business hours. Bring her back later, preferably in the middle of the night. And put her in a disguise of some kind."

"I'm standing right here," Abigail couldn't help interjecting.

Both men glanced at her.

"You're talking about me as if I'm not," she pointed out, feeling miffed.

"Sorry," said Lucas.

"You don't think a disguise is overkill?" Zach asked Lucas.

Lucas raised a brow to Abigail. "What do you think?"

"I think I was stupid to come here." She glanced from one to the other. "And so, having enjoyed a nice brewery tour, I'll take my leave."

"You still have work to do," Zach insisted.

"She needs to leave." Lucas backed her up.

"Then be here tonight," said Zach. "The second shift ends at ten. After that, nobody'll be here but security."

"Maybe wear a blond wig," Lucas put in.

"I'll phone you later," she told Zach, anxious to make herself scarce. She should have realized the danger. She definitely wasn't cut out for covert operations.

"You'll *come back* later," he insisted.

"It's too dangerous."

"Nobody will see you."

"You can't guarantee that."

"I'll make sure nobody sees you."

"Zach—"

"Abigail."

They gazed at each other for a long minute. Abigail knew a stubborn man when she saw one, and Zach was surely one of them.

"Tonight," he repeated. "The sooner we get our water license, the sooner you're off the hook."

She hated to admit he was right. But he was. The faster she learned about his business and showed him how to do his research and fill out the application form, the sooner he'd leave her alone. There wasn't a single chance they'd succeed, but he'd be forced to admit she tried.

Annoyed by the delay, but knowing she had no choice, Abigail headed into Lyndon for the afternoon. There, she took pity on herself and decided to go for a manicure at the Crystal Pool spa. Discovering they were having a three-treatments-for-the-price-of-two sale, she also had a facial and a wax job. Then she stopped by her favorite clothing store and picked up a pair of black jeans and a sleeveless, shimmering, royal-blue blouse with lace insets and a mandarin collar. The jeans were too long to go with her cowboy boots, and she found a kicky pair of rhinestone-decorated, high-heeled sandals to complete the look.

Afterward, she felt better, confident, more like herself. She checked into the picturesque Rose Cottages down by the river. She'd made the reservation thinking she'd be finished with Zach tonight. Instead, she'd asked for a late checkout, planning to get some sleep there tomorrow before she drove back to the ranch. There was no way she was spending even half the night at the Caspian Hotel, not with the memories of Lucky flitting at the edges of her brain.

Then finally, since she couldn't tell Travis she was spending a couple of days in Lyndon without making a point of visiting her brother Seth, she drove to the mayor's residence on Bainbridge Avenue, pulling the truck up to the historic, white, pillar-fronted three-story house. She truly missed the sleek, shiny Audi she'd leased over the course of the campaign.

Hopping out, she settled her sandals on the concrete driveway, smoothed her blouse, fluffed her hair and strode up the wide steps to the over-height double doors. It was nearly eight o'clock, so she knew she wouldn't disturb dinner.

It was Lisa Thompson who answered.

"Hey, Abigail," she greeted with a beaming smile. "Nice blouse. You look great!"

"Thanks." A warm feeling settled in Abigail's stomach. She liked being pretty. She really did.

"So, how're things at the ranch?" Lisa stepped to one side so that Abigail could enter the formal, octagonal foyer. The house had been built in 1902 and kept lovingly restored by the Lyndon Historical Society. The huge, overhead chandelier sparkled with light, while the marble floor gleamed, and notable, historical Lyndon City figures peered stoically down from gilt-framed oil paintings.

Male voices rose and fell from the depths of the house, something to do with land zoning and property tax. It didn't surprise Abigail in the least that her brother was conducting business into the evening.

"It's all good at the ranch," she answered Lisa's question.

"I didn't know you were coming to town." Lisa closed the door behind them, her black ballet flats whispering as she moved.

"Just picking up a few things," Abigail made the excuse.

"Spurs and saddle soap?" Lisa teased.

Apart from Zach, Abigail hadn't confessed to Lisa or anyone else her trepidation about going back to the ranch. She pasted on a smile. "A new pocketknife and some baling wire."

Lisa laughed. "Around you, I feel so useless."

"*You* are anything but useless. I don't know how my brother got by without you."

"I think he had a whole lot more fun before I showed up. Hey, Seth," Lisa called. "Your sister's here."

Conversation stopped in the back room. It had once been the original kitchen and dining area, but years ago it was converted into a large gathering room where many of the mayor's formal parties took place. A new kitchen had been added to the house sometime in the fifties and updated every decade since.

"Which one?" Seth called.

"It's me," Abigail called. "But you don't need to—"

Seth headed through the curved archway that led into the living room adjacent to the foyer. "Hey, Abby." He strode across the big room and pulled her into his usual hug. "What are you doing in town?"

"A little shopping," she told him cheerfully. "What's up with the zoning?"

He pulled back and waved a dismissive hand. "The usual. The chamber of commerce wants the town boundaries extended past the river bend, and the ranching community is up in arms over the grazing leases. You staying over?"

"I already checked into Rose Cottages."

He frowned. "Why would you do that? You know we've got plenty of room here."

"I plan on sleeping in tomorrow," Abigail lied.

"So what?"

"So, you're here. And you'll be up early. Not everybody wants to keep your manic schedule," she added.

"You've never minded my schedule. In fact, I think you liked it."

"Well, I'm not working for you anymore. And I feel like being self-indulgent."

"And so you should," Lisa stoically defended, linking an arm through Abigail's in blatant solidarity. "Give the girl a break. She'll be up slopping the hogs at the crack of dawn soon enough."

"We don't have hogs," said Seth. He turned, calling out, "Benjamin?"

"Yes?" a young man's voice answered from the gathering room.

"Do you mind running over to Rose Cottages and grabbing Abigail's suitcase?"

"Seth!" Abigail protested, reflexively moving to block the door. She was not going to let herself get shanghaied.

"I'm not letting my sister stay in a hotel."

"And I'm not letting my brother order me around."

Benjamin, a local teenager who was doing a part-time internship with Seth, appeared in the doorway. A bedraggled, black-and-white puppy limped in at his heels, sniffing its way around the legs of a colonial side table.

"Which cottage are you in?" Seth asked Abigail.

She jerked her attention back to her brother. "*None* of your business."

"Don't start, Abby," Seth warned.

"Back off," she responded. She was usually quite amiable when it came to her family's desires, but she couldn't give in this time.

"I just opened a bottle of ninety-six St. Germain," he cajoled.

"I'm not thirsty."

"Come on."

"Boss," Lisa put in, in a warning tone. "Didn't we talk about this?"

Abigail was a little surprised that Lisa was willing to come to her defense. Lisa was brash and bossy at the best of times, but she was usually quite deferential to Seth.

"This is an entirely different circumstance," he intoned.

"It's exactly the same circumstance."

"What?" Abigail couldn't help asking.

"Problem solved," said Lisa, propelling Abigail from the room. "She'll stay at Rose Cottages, but join us for a drink now. Bring some glasses, Seth." Then she lowered her voice, leaning toward Abigail's ear. "So, what's going on?"

"Nothing," Abigail whispered in reply.

"Like hell," Lisa harrumphed as they made their way toward the gathering room. "You've got something going on tonight, or you wouldn't be fighting with Seth over where you slept." Then she raised her voice as they switched rooms. "Luis, Harlan, you remember Seth's sister Abigail."

Both men came to their feet from a sofa grouping where they were going over some kind of report.

"Nice to see you again." Luis nodded.

"Hi, Abigail," Harlan echoed.

She barely had a chance to say hello because Lisa kept her moving toward an alcove with a bay window. Tucked into the corner of the L-shaped room, it was furnished with a low, round table, several broad-leaf plants and a half-round, floral-print bench seat.

"Are you okay?" Lisa asked with obvious concern as they plunked down on the soft cushions.

"I'm fine," Abigail assured her, putting on a smile.

Lisa's eyes narrowed. "Something's off."

"No, it's not," Abigail lied.

The quick denial seemed to pique Lisa's curiosity. "It's just us girls…"

"There's nothing going on."

"Really?"

"Yes."

Lisa tsk-tsked. "It's a good thing you don't have to lie for a living."

"I'm not lying. Why would I be lying?" Abigail glanced to where her brother had followed them into the room. She wondered if he'd take Lisa to task or pick up his argument with Abigail. But, instead, he paused to joke with Luis and Harlan while he poured the wine.

"Because you're embarrassed, or you're up to no good. Or, hey, here's one, you're going to see that guy again. Making it a two-night stand."

Abigail felt her face heat up. She couldn't think of a single thing to say.

The men's voices rumbled and glasses clinked. The puppy scampered its awkward way over the patterned carpet toward them.

Lisa's eyes went wide, and her mouth formed an O. "No way."

"Exactly," Abigail told her firmly. "No way."

"You *are* planning a two-night stand."

"I'm not. No. Definitely not."

"You do realize you're protesting way too much."

"I'm protesting exactly the right amount because you're dead wrong." Dead wrong. The very last thing in the world Abigail was about to do was sleep with Zach again.

"Ladies," Seth's voice preceded him. He strode forward, offering each of them a crystal goblet of merlot.

"Thanks," Abigail managed to say, scanning his expression to gauge if he'd overhead anything.

"You're a very good mayor," Lisa told him approvingly as she accepted the other glass of wine.

"You might want to remember that," Seth retorted.

"How could I forget? It's in every other speech. Now go away." She shooed him with the back of her hand. "We're having girl talk."

"Yes, ma'am." He backed off with good humor.

Lisa returned her attention to Abigail. "You've got me worried here. You're acting weird."

Abigail heaved a sigh. If she was acting weird, she couldn't help herself. She wasn't any good at this cloak-and-dagger stuff.

"Fine." She took a bracing drink of her wine. "I am meeting someone tonight. But it's not what you think."

Lisa leaned in. "A man someone?"

"Yes, a man. But it's not like that. I'm helping him—" She stopped herself, searching for the right words. "It's a research project."

"A *research project?* At night? What is this, freshman year?"

"It really is a research project."

"Uh-huh." Lisa slipped off her flats and curled one leg beneath her simple, sky-blue dress. She gave an exaggerated sigh. "I'm envious of your private life."

"You really ought to focus on your own," Abigail advised.

"It's not the same. There's nothing going on in mine."

"I don't believe you," Abigail challenged, seizing on the opportunity to change the topic from herself to Lisa.

But Lisa wasn't so easily swayed. "You're the one with the hot guys on speed dial."

"Nobody's on speed dial."

"Then how're you contacting him?"

"He's not a hot guy."

"You're blushing again."

"Okay, he is a hot guy." Abigail regretted admitting there was a guy involved. "But it's not about sex."

Lisa chuckled. "It's always about sex."

"Do tell." Abigail raised her brows meaningfully, trying again to switch the focus to Lisa.

"I wish," Lisa scoffed.

"There must be somebody. You've been in Lyndon for three months now."

"I've been busy. Working hard. As you well know."

"What about the guys on the campaign?" Abigail glanced at Luis and Harlan. She caught Seth looking at Lisa, a funny expression on his face.

Lisa's earlier challenging and teasing of Seth came rushing back.

"What about Seth?" she blurted out.

Lisa's jaw dropped, and her cheeks flamed.

"Ah-ha!" said Abigail. "I knew there was something—"

"Not Seth." Lisa adamantly shook her head.

"Hey, I know he's your boss, but—"

"Not *Seth*," Lisa repeated, the flush turning to pallor as her gaze flicked across the room.

Abigail reached out. "What is it?"

"Nothing."

"What's going on?"

Lisa mutely shook her head.

Abigail couldn't help another glance to her brother. His brow furrowed as he watched their exchange. She pasted a smile on her face and rose to her feet, reaching for Lisa's arm. "Let's step outside."

Obviously upset, Lisa complied, and the two moved through an open set of French doors to a wide veranda that overlooked the mansion's extensive gardens. The scent of roses permeated the air, and crickets chirped over the backdrop of the light traffic on the distant interstate.

They stopped beside the far railing.

"Dish," Abigail ordered.

Lisa pushed back her blond hair and squeezed her eyes shut.

"I won't give you up," Abigail promised in a quieter tone, knowing Lisa had to have fallen for Seth. "You're not the only one who can keep a secret."

Lisa blinked open her blue eyes. "You sure?"

"Positive."

Lisa downed her remaining wine. "Oh, man. I can't—" She closed her eyes for another long second. "Okay. Fine. It's better than you thinking I've got the hots for Seth."

"Okay..." Abigail waited, not exactly sure what would be so terrible about being attracted to Seth.

Lisa looked directly into Abigail's eyes. "You know about Nicole, right?"

"Who's Nicole?"

"Nicole Aldrich. Your mother's younger sister."

Abigail drew back in surprise. She hadn't heard that name in years. "I know she died young," Abigail allowed. "I never met her, of course. And nobody really talks about her."

"She died at eighteen, right after I was born."

Abigail stilled. Then a tingle rushed over her skin. Her heart expanded in her chest. Could Lisa be saying...? "And...?" Abigail prompted impatiently.

"And I'm definitely not attracted to Seth," Lisa stated with a toss of her head. "As it happens, I'm his cousin."

Abigail gave a muted squeal, every muscle in her body contracting in delight. "And *my* cousin. *Our* cousin." She wrapped Lisa in a tight hug. "Why on earth wouldn't you tell us?"

"I didn't know how you'd feel."

Abigail drew back. "I feel great. How could you not know we'd be thrilled?"

Lisa gave a self-conscious laugh. "Because I didn't know you. That first day, I was just going to check you out. And you all assumed I was a campaign volunteer, and it seemed easier to go along with that. And then I found out about your dad, and that your mom was away. And then Seth hired me, and I loved the job, and I started to get scared that if he knew..."

"You thought Seth might fire you for being our cousin?"

"I thought he might fire me for secretly spying on him."

Seth's dry voice interrupted. "He might fire you for lying to him."

Lisa jerked back, her attention shifting to where Seth had silently appeared on the deck. "I never lied."

"You never told the truth."

"I was working up to it."

Seth crossed his arms over his chest. "And you pumped me for information."

"I did," Lisa admitted. "Your mother wasn't around, and you were the only one old enough to remember Nicole."

"I was six when she ran away."

Abigail glanced from one to the other. "I don't understand. When she died, why didn't they bring you to us?"

"About a week before the car accident, she left me with the Sisters of Charity—anonymously."

"You were abandoned? Raised by nuns?" Abigail couldn't help asking, her brain scrambling about a hundred miles an hour as she cataloged the revelations.

Lisa shook her head. "I was adopted by a wonderful family. It was only two years ago when I started looking for you. Records were sketchy, so it took a while—"

"And you're positive it's us?" Seth challenged.

Abigail socked her brother in the arm. "This is *good* news, Seth."

"I'm not after your money," Lisa protested.

"But you were after a job."

"Go away, Seth," Abigail ordered tartly, grasping Lisa's hand. "If you can't play nice with our new cousin, you can go do something else."

"I'm not going away."

"I'm sorry," Lisa offered to Seth. "I was scared."

Seth's expression seemed to soften. But there was a moment of meaningful silence before he spoke. "I do get it." Then he sighed and his arms dropped back to his sides, while the corners of his mouth turned up. "I knew there was something I liked about you."

A tremulous smile grew on Lisa's face, and she blinked rapidly. "Yeah?"

"It must be the stellar genes."

"It must be."

Seth's hand went to his chin. "I'm not sure how I feel about Travis and me being outnumbered four to two."

Abigail laughed in relief. "I can't wait to tell my sisters Mandy and Katrina."

Just then, the puppy scampered out the open door, skidding on the deck as it clumsily rounded the corner.

"So, you're heading back to the ranch tomorrow?" Seth asked Abigail.

"Yes." Abigail's own complex life came back to her in a rush. She hoped it was true. She hoped she could map something out for Zach in one night, catch a nap at Rose Cottages then head home. If not, well, she'd have to make up a new excuse for to-morrow night.

"Good," said Seth, reaching down to scoop the gawky puppy up in one hand. "Take this guy with you, will you?" He rubbed his chin on the top of the puppy's head. "He's the last of the litter, and they were going to put him down. He has a gimpy leg, blind in one eye, and he's got one ear up and one ear down. Nobody wanted him."

"Uh…" Abigail didn't know how to refuse. What the heck was she going to do with the puppy between now and when she went back to the ranch?

But Seth dropped the puppy into her arms. "Butch and Zulu will make a man out of him."

"He is a bit skittish," Lisa put in as she reached out to pet the pup.

Abigail tried to protest. "I'm not sure I can—"

"We named him Ozzy," said Seth.

"Now, that's just mean." Abigail felt a sudden rush of pro-tectiveness for the pathetic puppy.

"No, I like it," Lisa interjected. "It's not like we could name him Spike or Killer."

"I guess not," Abigail slowly agreed. She had to admit, Ozzy would probably be happy at the ranch. As long as he learned to stay away from the horses and the cattle, it was pretty much doggie heaven. And Butch and Zulu were good with smaller animals. They didn't even bother the cats.

But she wasn't going back there for at least twenty-four hours. "Can I pick him up tomorrow?"

Lisa gave her a curious look, and she could see the wheels turning inside her newly discovered cousin's head. The last thing Abigail wanted to do was reprise their conversation about her plans.

"Never mind," Abigail quickly said. "He can sleep in my cottage tonight."

She hoped Zach liked dogs. And she hoped Ozzy liked road trips. They had a ways to drive before she could settle him in his new home.

Five

The pathetic little puppy scampered across the hardwood floor of Zach's compact suite on the third floor of the castle. He sideswiped the sofa, canted out of control and bumped his head against the ottoman, giving a little yelp.

Abigail glanced up from where she was typing on Zach's laptop. He'd set her up at the small dining table in one corner of the living area and logged her onto the company network.

"He's blind in one eye," she explained.

"He's also a little lopsided," Zach noted, observing Ozzy's odd gait. One front leg was shorter than all the others. The puppy sniffed his way along the fireplace hearth.

"That's why nobody wanted him." Abigail paused in her typing and turned in her chair.

Zach let his gaze rest on her pretty face. She'd changed into a feminine blouse and a pair of snug-fitting black jeans that showed off her curves. Her shoes were sexy now, too. She'd told him she'd stopped by her brother the mayor's mansion in Lyndon. He supposed the mansion had a stricter dress code than Craig Mountain. Or maybe it was because she liked her brother enough to dress up for him—unlike the way she felt about Zach.

"Do you always take pity on strays?" he asked.

The puppy plunked himself down at Zach's feet, gazing hopefully up at him with big brown eyes. Since Zach's heart wasn't made of stone, he lifted Ozzy into his lap.

"One more out at the ranch won't make a difference."

"You could have said no."

She shrugged. "Why would I?"

Zach felt a sudden curiosity about this welcoming family utopia that was apparently the Jacobs ranch. He speculated how much of her description translated into real life.

She turned back to the laptop. "How many new jobs will the Craig Mountain expansion create?"

"I don't know yet."

"Got a guess?"

"Why?"

Ozzy settled into Zach's lap.

"There are three mandatory exemptions to the water-license moratorium. One, if a state of emergency is declared in the region. Two, if a strategic regional industry is threatened. Or, three, if the issuing of the license or variance has a fundamental impact on employment creation in the region."

"Maybe a dozen new jobs," he reasoned. "Give or take."

She frowned. "That doesn't sound like much of an impact."

"Can we argue that beer is strategic?"

"This *is* cowboy country." She allowed what seemed like a reluctant smile along with her answer.

"And who has to declare the state of emergency?"

"The governor."

"So, not me."

She ended up smiling at that one, too. "Not you."

"So much for a mandatory exemption."

She hit a few keys. "Our other option is to make representation to the committee."

Ozzy shifted his little body, whimpering in his sleep, and Zach smoothed his palm down the puppy's soft coat. "How do we do that?"

"We fill out form 731-800(e) and submit appendix Q along with supporting documentation and letters of intent."

"I should be paying you to do this."

She typed out a sentence on the screen. "You think money's going to make me feel any better about the situation?"

Ozzy shifted again and twitched, his eyes blinking open.

"It would make *me* feel better."

"You should feel great. You're getting exactly what you want. Free of charge."

Ozzy whined and twisted, sniffing at the arm of the chair.

"Any chance this little guy needs a walk?" asked Zach.

Abigail paused to look at them. She grimaced. "Probably, he does."

"Okay, champ," Zach rose, lifting Ozzy to the floor and brushing traces of black-and-white fur from his lap.

"Care to check out the grounds?" he asked Abigail. The walk would be a whole lot more fun if she came along.

"Sure," she agreed. She quickly rose and headed directly for the suite door, obviously considering time of the essence.

The three of them made their way down the narrow hall, along a back staircase to the second floor, where they picked up the grand staircase that led to the foyer.

The ancient hinges creaked as Zach pushed open one side of the heavy, oak doors. He couldn't help admiring Abigail as she passed by. There was a sinuous grace in her movements, and unconscious sensuality in the sway of her hips, the tilt of her chin and the silky flow of her hair.

"The mayor's office has a dress code?" he asked, falling in behind her as they crossed the lighted porch toward the illuminated front grounds. Stars were scattered in the black sky, while the moon rose above the northern horizon.

"I did a little shopping in town." There was a hint of censure in her tone. "Had some time to kill this afternoon."

"Sorry about that."

She shrugged as they started down the wide, stone steps. "Oh, well, I needed a manicure anyway."

He glanced down at her fingers, noting what must have been her favorite lavender color. "I guess ranch work can be hard on the hands."

Ozzy chugged enthusiastically ahead, beelining for a clump of shrubbery.

"A little," she allowed, following in the general direction of the puppy.

As she stepped onto the thick lawn, she stumbled in her high shoes. Zach quickly reached out to grab her, steadying her with a hand at her hip, another on her shoulder. His body's reaction was instantaneous. His muscles zipped tight, and his senses went on high alert. Her soft scent surrounded him, and he remembered her taste, craved the feel of her in his arms.

"I'm fine," she insisted, pulling to get away.

But his brain was slow to react. He didn't let go.

"I'm *fine,*" she repeated, jerking back.

He forced himself to release her.

He cleared his throat. "So, how are things going back home?"

"Fine." She made a show of straightening her blouse.

"You're really not much of a conversationalist, are you?" But he knew it wasn't true. He'd talked to her for hours on end that first night, one topic flowing into the other, discovering a shared sense of humor and shared opinions on books, films and many current news events.

"You know perfectly well how I feel about the ranch," she pointed out.

"I do," he allowed.

"So, why do you think I'd want to talk about it?"

"Exactly how unhappy are you?" Not that he could fix it for her. But he realized he would if he could.

She tossed her auburn hair and lifted her pert nose. "I'm not unhappy at all."

"I didn't take you for a liar."

"And I didn't take you for a blackmailer."

They faced each other, and the night air seemed to smolder between them. Every nuance of their lovemaking rushed back to him. He searched deeply into her eyes, subconsciously easing closer. His hands twitched with the need to reach out to her. But it wouldn't be right, and it wouldn't be fair. She'd made her position clear, and he'd already made the hard choice between his company and his feelings for her. There was nothing left but for him to be a gentleman.

"I really do like you, Abby," he allowed himself.

"Funny, I don't like you at all."

"Liar," he whispered.

"Not about that." But her golden eyes had gone liquid, cheeks flushed, and her lips softened in the glowing light. Her chest rose and fell with deep, indrawn breaths.

Zach threw propriety to the wind. "Tell me you don't want me to kiss you."

"I don't want you to kiss me."

He shook his head. "I guess that was predictable."

She pivoted sharply away from him, taking a couple of steps across the lawn. "Ozzy?" she called. "Where are you, puppy?"

Zach glanced around the expanse of lawn, searching for the pup's movement. The lawn was night black, interspersed with pools of lamplight. He squinted to find the flashes of white in Ozzy's mottled fur.

"Ozzy?" Abigail called again, voice louder this time.

They heard a yelp, then a whimper. It was from the direction of the cliffs.

Abigail glanced back. "Zach?"

"He probably banged into a boulder." But Zach quickened his steps, striding toward the rocky ledges that overlooked the lake.

Ozzy whimpered again, and the sound of the waves grew louder.

Abigail took a few running steps, catching up to Zach. He saw that she'd stripped off her shoes.

"Wait here," he instructed as they came to the edge of the lawn. "The rocks are sharp."

"Ozzy?" she called.

The puppy let out a long whine.

Zach zeroed in on the sound. "I'll get him," he assured Abigail.

Walking carefully from rock to rock, skirting the biggest boulders, he made his way toward the cliff edge. He'd been out here this afternoon, so he knew it was dangerous terrain. He also had a pretty good idea of how close he could safely get to the edge.

Ozzy barked, and Zach stopped, looking right.

In the traces of moonlight, he could just make out the shape of the puppy. He'd either jumped or fallen into a rocky depression that boxed him in. It couldn't have been more than two feet deep, but he seemed perplexed by the task of climbing back out.

Zach chuckled low, squatting on his haunches to reach down.

"You poor, poor thing," he muttered, scooping his palm under the pup's belly.

Ozzy went limp with compliance, content to have Zach lift him out. Zach secured him against his chest.

"Got him," he called out to Abigail, rising to make his way back across the uneven ground.

She looked relieved as they approached.

"He's a bit of a candy-ass," said Zach. "I hope ranch life won't be too tough for him."

She reached out and scratched the pup's head, her knuckles grazing Zach's chest, causing him to suck in a breath.

"Kind of reminds me of my sister Katrina."

"Katrina?"

"Yes, she's a gorgeous, graceful ballerina in New York. But ranch work was too much for her."

"So, she gets to live her dream instead?"

"She does." There was pride in Abigail's eyes as she glanced up. "She's a principal dancer with the Liberty Ballet in New York City."

"But you don't get to live yours?" he asked.

"She started boarding school when she was ten years old. She only comes back for visits, not to work the ranch."

"So?"

"So, it's a completely different thing."

"I don't see how."

"That's because you're not trying." She dropped her hand and headed for the castle.

He began walking next to her. "I'm simply pointing out a double standard."

"What've you got against my family, anyway?"

"I've never even met most of them."

"But you're judging them."

"I'm judging you. And your apparent unwillingness to stand up to them."

"I don't hate ranching, Lucky."

She didn't appear to notice her use of his nickname, and he wasn't inclined to correct her. He liked hearing that name on her lips.

"Life isn't about doing things you 'don't hate.' It's about doing things you love."

"Easy for you to say. I'm sure your family has absolutely no problem whatsoever with you being a rich, successful brewery owner."

"I don't have a family."

"I mean your parents. You already told me you don't have brothers and sisters."

"I don't have parents either."

She stopped to look at him. "Did they die?"

"They did. When I was two."

Her eyes widened. "Seriously."

Zach was long past the place where having been orphaned was a problem for him. It simply was. He nodded in answer to her question.

"Wow," her breath whooshed out.

"Happens to a lot of people," he told her.

"I know." She nodded. "So, were you adopted?"

"I grew up in foster homes. Well, foster homes when I was really little, then a group home."

"A group home?"

"Like an orphanage. But smaller and less, you know, Oliver Twist."

"Oh, Zach." She blinked a couple of times.

"It's fine." He gave her an encouraging grin. "This conversation isn't about me."

"It is now."

"No, it's not. I'm all grown up. Everything's good."

"But you have no family."

"I have Alex. And I have my company."

"But—"

"It's okay, Doll-Face. Now stop looking at me like that."

"I'm sad for you."

He rolled his eyes. "You should be sad about mucking out stalls, not about my misbegotten childhood."

"We have hands who muck out the stalls."

"That's good to hear." Zach turned to start back to the castle again, thinking Abigail's feet must be getting cold, and Ozzy was probably getting hungry.

They walked a few yards in silence, Ozzy snuggled contentedly against Zach's chest, watching the nighttime world go by.

"My cousin was adopted," said Abigail.

"That's nice."

"I only just met her tonight. I mean, well, I'd met her lots of times before. She was involved in Seth's campaign. But I only just found out tonight that she is my cousin."

"While you were down in Lyndon?"

"Uh-uh. We got to talking." Abigail paused. "We were talking about her and about Seth, and she blurted it out. She came here looking for us a couple of months back. We never even knew about her. Did you ever look for your family, Zach?"

"Nobody to look for."

"Did you ever think about trying?"

"The state of Texas had no wish to pay for my education and upbringing. Believe me, if there'd been long-lost relatives to foist me upon, they'd have found them."

Abigail fell silent at that. And they made their way to the castle and mounted the stairs, heading back inside. Though there'd been a few moments in Zach's childhood when he'd fantasized about finding some long-lost relatives, he was a realist. Even if there was somebody out there with a tenuous genetic connection to him, what would be the point in finding them? His life was what it was, and he fully intended to live it.

* * *

Abigail blinked open her eyes to bright sunlight. It took a couple of seconds to realize she was on Zach's couch. The laptop was on the coffee table in front of her, and she was covered in a soft quilt, a throw pillow tucked under her head.

She'd reviewed the annual reports from Zach's six breweries until her eyes blurred and her head began to pound. As near as she could remember, she must have dozed off around five. She wasn't sure how long she'd slept, but it wasn't nearly long enough. Her eyes were scratchy, and a painful pulse throbbed at the base of her neck.

The suite was completely quiet.

She pulled into a sitting position, checking her watch and discovering it was nearly 10:00 a.m. She threw back the quilt then staggered her way to the bathroom, washing her face and scrubbing toothpaste across her teeth with her finger. She combed her hair and did the best she could to straighten her clothes. The small window provided a view of the front grounds and the parking lot. Several dozen vehicles were parked, and a number of people wandered the area. They looked more like tourists than employees, but she knew there'd be employees working both in the castle and the brewery by now. There would definitely be people down there who might recognize her. She suddenly felt like a princess imprisoned in a tower.

Ozzy's little nails clattered on the living-area floor, and she opened the bathroom door.

"Morning," Zach intoned, setting a tray down on the small corner table.

"You let me sleep," she accused, slipping out of the bathroom.

"You were exhausted. I slept, too."

"I should have gone back to Lyndon."

Delicious aromas rose as Zach removed the silver covers from the tray. "You were way too tired to drive."

"But it's daytime and I'm not supposed to be here."

"Nobody'll see you up here."

"So, I'm your prisoner?"

He lifted a silver pot and began to pour coffee. "You do have a flare for the dramatic."

She was drawn to the coffee, and moved across the room. "Can I leave?"

"Not in the daylight."

"There you go. I'm not being dramatic, I'm simply stating the facts at hand."

He grinned in response to her indignation. "You need anything?"

"Coffee." She lifted one of the cups and took a grateful sip. "I don't do well on five hours' sleep."

"Cream or sugar?"

"Straight up is fine with me."

"Like a cowboy?" he joked.

"I can do it over a campfire if necessary."

"Not necessary this morning." He gestured to the fine china and silver. It was quite beautiful.

"Where'd you get this stuff?"

"I think it might be antique." He pulled out a chair and gestured for her to sit down. It seemed pointless to argue, so she sat.

"Lucas is lobbying to open a small restaurant here at the brewery," Zach continued, taking the chair across from her. "He says people like touring the castle as much as they like touring the brewery, and this would help make Craig Mountain a destination."

"Seems like a good idea to me." Abigail helped herself to a small pot of strawberry jam and spread it on a slice of toast.

"I'd only consider it if it helped to market the beer."

"You don't want to diversify?"

"We're not a bed-and-breakfast."

"Could've fooled me." She bit down on the toast.

Zach chuckled. "These are extraordinary circumstances."

Abigail contemplated while she chewed and swallowed. "Zach, how many people do you think you could reasonably employ in a new restaurant?"

He raised his brows. "Are you thinking about the employment exemption?"

"We're definitely not going to get anyone to declare a state of emergency. And we'll never sell you as a strategic industry."

"I can ask Lucas. But I'm guessing, maybe twenty."

She knew it wouldn't be enough. "Even combined with the additional brewery staff, I don't think that'll work. You'd need to be adding a couple hundred new jobs at least."

"That's definitely not going to happen," said Zach, cutting into the omelet on his plate.

"Then we're back to the committee presentation."

"What about job losses if we close?"

"Those don't count."

"Why not?"

She shrugged. "I guess because every business in the valley that wanted a change to their license would threaten to close."

"How long do you think the committee process will take?"

"Weeks, at least. The application will take a while to write, and there's no guessing how long the committee will take to review it." The process was going to be longer than she'd hoped, that was for sure.

Zach set down his fork. "The bulldozers show up tomorrow."

"What bulldozers?"

"First thing we need to do here is dig the foundation for the expansion."

She sat up straight. "You're starting already?"

"I've got no choice. If we're not up and running by November, and into increased production by January, we won't make our spring orders."

"But—"

"There's no point in me sitting on my hands while you fill out the paperwork."

"But what if you don't get the license?"

He lifted his coffee cup in a mock salute. "I'm counting on you, Abigail."

Her stomach instantly hollowed out. He'd already told her DFB was in financial trouble. He was about to spend hundreds of thousands, if not millions, of dollars on what might be useless renovations.

"*Don't* count on me," she begged. Then she reflexively reached for his hand. "Seriously, Zach. This a long shot." She could fill out the paperwork for him, but many had tried this route. So far nobody had been successful.

His steel gaze moved from her hand to her face. "I don't have a choice."

She squeezed. "Of course you have a choice. You can wait to spend your money until we know for sure whether you're getting the variance."

"The clock's ticking."

"This is a mistake."

"It's a risk, not a mistake."

She swallowed, letting go of his hand and pushing back from her breakfast. Then she closed her eyes for a long second, knowing she had to be honest with him. "You're not going to get it, Zach. They're not going to grant you license variation."

"They will if you help me."

She shook her head. "I'm not magic. I'm trying because you're forcing me to try, but it's not going to work."

"We don't know that yet."

She rose to her feet, pacing to the window. "Lucky, you're living in denial. Don't do it. Call off the bulldozers. It's too big a risk."

He rose more slowly. "Everything I've ever done in life has been a risk."

"Not like this."

"Exactly like this. If I wait any longer, there'll be no point in even getting the license, because we'll lose the spring orders and the company will go under."

She advanced on him. "The Craig Mountain expansion will tie a brick to the entire company and drag it straight down to the bottom."

His dark eyes seemed to pin her in place. "You can do this, Abby."

She slowly shook her head.

He placed a reassuring hand on her shoulder. "I know you can."

"Don't put this on me. It's too much. I can't be responsible—"

"I'm only asking you to do your best."

For some reason, her eyes stung. "My best won't be good enough."

He stepped forward, gathering her in his arms and holding her in a comforting embrace. He spoke against the top of her head. "It'll be good enough."

Her voice was muffled against his chest. The thought of having that much riding on her work was overwhelming. "Let me quit. Let me go home."

"I can't do that."

He continued to hold her, and the warmth of his body seeped into hers. She breathed in his scent and fisted her hands against the overwhelming rush of desire that swarmed her. She wanted to hug him back, to hold him close, to kiss him hard and deep and bury her emotions in the passion she knew they'd find all over again.

He drew back, gazing down at her, palms rubbing circles against her shoulders.

She told herself to step away. She had about five seconds to make the right choice. His eyes darkened, and his lips parted. She knew that expression, could feel the pulse of his thoughts. She held her breath as he bent forward.

She forced herself to jerk back. "No."

The word stopped him cold. His jaw clenched, and his hands convulsed, squeezing her shoulders for a second longer.

"We can't," she managed to say.

He dropped his hands and stepped back, voice clipped. "Sorry."

She turned her head, afraid to look at him while she gave a short nod. "I'll get back to work."

"Yeah."

She heard him turn. Heard the clatter of Ozzy's footsteps. Heard the door open then close, and their sounds disappeared.

* * *

Zach slouched in a dusty, French-provincial chair in the topmost reaches of a castle tower, Ozzy curled sleeping in his lap, and his cell phone squeezed in one hand as the bulldozers rumbled into the rear, gravel parking lot. Alex was speed-dial one, but Zach couldn't bring himself to press the button just yet.

Abigail had agreed to stay another day. She'd made it crystal clear that she had her doubts about their success with the license. Truth was, he had his doubts, too. But he couldn't dwell on that. There was only one route forward.

He'd signed off on the construction contract this morning, and it was the right thing to do. It was the only thing to do. In his experience, any action was better than no action. He knew that if he sat here and did nothing, the company would trickle down to an inevitable death.

He pressed his thumb on the one key and lifted the phone to his ear.

Alex picked up on the first ring. "Hey, Zach."

The clatter of background noise quickly faded as Alex obviously moved to a different location.

"How's it going?" Zach asked his business partner.

"I just found out that Shetland Trucking went bankrupt," Alex rattled off in a matter-of-fact voice. "There's a mechanical breakdown at the bottling plant in Charlotte. And Stephanie walked out on me last night. So, pretty much business as usual."

"Again?" Zach asked.

"Which part?"

"Stephanie."

"It was inevitable," said Alex.

"She serious this time?"

"If she's not, I am. I don't know what other guys do, but I'm not into working sixteen-hour days then coming home to talk about my feelings."

"So, how're you feeling about that?" Zach couldn't help joking.

"Shut up."

"We can talk about it if you like."

"Then can we braid each other's hair?"

"You get a new trucking company?" Zach went back to business.

"As of this morning. What about you?"

"I'm looking at the bulldozers now."

"Fantastic. So, you got the license?"

"Not yet."

Alex paused. "What do you mean, not yet?"

"Abigail's still working on it."

Another pause. "But you started anyway?"

"We're out of time."

It took a minute for Alex to speak. "You're putting it all on one roll of the dice?"

"I am."

"And if we don't get the license?"

"Is that a rhetorical question?"

"It's a veiled criticism."

"You'd have done the same thing."

"Maybe. Probably." Alex heaved a sigh. "Hell, what've we got to lose?"

"Beer."

Alex coughed out a laugh. "At least we're both still employable as bartenders," he said, referring to the first jobs they'd had after they left the group home.

"I could start all over." Zach wasn't worried about himself. He'd give up the Houston penthouse, the sports car and his platinum credit card in the blink of an eye. Some of the happiest times of his life were when he and Alex had shared a tiny basement suite while they saved up the down payment for their first brewery.

But he'd hate to be forced to lay off even one employee. Many of them had kids and mortgages, and for the first time were settling into normal lives.

"Need a roommate while you start over?" asked Alex. "The apartment lease is in Stephanie's name."

"You're homeless?"

"I am."

"You've got my spare key."

"I guess it's either your place or the Four Seasons."

"Hey, we're on a budget now." Zach glanced at the third bull-dozer rumbling and clanking its way off the trailer. If this all went bad, their days at the Four Seasons were definitely over.

"The Family Inn on Hawthorn Street?" Alex suggested.

"Get your ass to my place."

"Yeah, I probably will. How long do you think you'll be in Colorado?"

"A couple more days, anyway. Hopefully, Lucas can take it from there."

The aging door to the tower room creaked. Both Zach and Ozzy looked toward the sound. Abigail peeked around the end of the thick, oak panels.

"Gotta go," said Zach, meeting her eyes.

"Keep me posted."

"Will do."

"You'd better bring this one home," Alex warned.

It was probably the hundredth time Alex had said that to Zach over the years. They'd been in many tight spots before, taken plenty of risks, but this was truly a make-or-break moment.

"I know." Zach clicked off the phone and tucked it into the breast pocket of his shirt. "Hey."

"Hi." She moved around the end of the door and into the room, glancing at the curved walls, dusty furniture, boxes and crates, and the collection of knickknacks and outright junk that covered every horizontal surface.

"Wow," she breathed.

"Quite the collection," he acknowledged, dislodging Ozzy as he came to his feet.

"Don't get up."

"I'm already up."

She gave him a rueful grimace. "I just came to tell you that something's come up."

He didn't like the sound of that. "To do with the license?"

"To do with me. I have to go to Houston."

"Why?" Was it an excuse to get away from him?

"It's a long story. My parents are down there. And, well, I told you about Lisa, the newly discovered cousin? We need to tell my mom about her before other people find out. I just talked to Seth and then to Travis. They want me to do it. In person. Of all the sisters, I know Lisa best. And Katrina and Mandy are—"

"Living their own lives?"

"That's none of your business."

"I suppose not," he allowed. Though it still galled him that she seemed to be the one in the family bearing the most burden.

"I know you're in a hurry." Despite everything, there was an apology in her voice.

"We can keep working while you're in Houston," he pointed out. "In fact, it'll be easier. DFB headquarters is there."

"Whoa." She held up her palms. "I'm not going to have spare time in Houston."

"You won't be busy twenty-four seven."

"Zach—"

"Abby—"

"Abigail."

"Yeah, 'cause that's our biggest problem." It might not be fair to her, but he was frustrated by the situation. And he was getting genuinely worried about losing his entire company.

Her tone was tart. "I have to focus on my family right now. I'm sorry if it slows down your personal agenda for me, but I have obligations."

He pointed out the window. "See that? Do you have any idea how much it costs per hour to dig that hole?"

She tightened her jaw. "You don't own me, Zach."

"Maybe not, but we have a deal."

"I'm altering the terms."

"That's not your choice to make."

"Are you drawing a line in the sand?"

He was. But maybe that wasn't the smart choice. Maybe he'd pushed her as far as he could. It was time to change tactics. "You can have time with your family in Houston."

"Thank you so *very* much."

"But you'll also need to find time for me. Five other breweries are waiting to press the go button on spring orders. If I can't confirm Craig Mountain, I'm going to have a way bigger problem than a useless hole in the ground."

She hesitated, and her teeth came down on her bottom lip.

"I'll spring for your plane ticket." He sweetened the pot. "Hell, for your hotel, your meals, anything you need." He didn't give a damn about the cost.

"My sister Mandy's fiancé has a jet."

"He coming with us?"

"There is no us."

"I need you, Abby."

He realized the words were true on far too many levels.

"We can bring Ozzy," he offered. "He can stay in my penthouse."

She cracked a smile at that. "You're bribing me with a dog?"

"I am."

"You're going to spoil him," she accused. "And then he's going to hate me when I make him live at the ranch."

Zach bent and picked up the pup, scratching under his chin. "He really doesn't strike me as the ranch-dog type."

There was total sympathy in her eyes when she gazed at Ozzy.

"Fine." She capitulated. "You take the dog, and I'll see you in Houston. But I'm not promising anything. I'm going to be busy."

"Thank you," Zach offered sincerely.

"Are you ever going to be out of my life?"

He hesitated over his answer. What an intriguing question. He didn't really want to be out of her life. And he sure didn't want her out of his. Not yet, anyway, and it had nothing whatsoever to do with any water license.

Six

Abigail was happy to see her father looking so well. He'd been in rehab in Houston for several months following a stroke in the early summer. Luckily, her sister Mandy's fiancé had been in the valley with his jet plane that night, and they were able to whisk everyone to Lyndon and then Denver for his treatment. Ultimately, they moved him to a state-of-the-art facility in Houston. After months of therapy, he was nearly ready to come home to walk Mandy and Katrina down the aisle at their double wedding, coming up in a few weeks.

Now Abigail and her mother, Maureen, moved to a shady table in the lush garden of a restaurant a few miles from the facility. The scents of roses, asters and sage mingled beneath the oak trees in the September afternoon. They ordered iced tea and spinach, raspberry salads, settling comfortably into padded rattan chairs.

"And how's Travis doing with the ranch?" asked Maureen, stirring some sugar into her glass.

"He seems good," Abigail answered. "Though I've actually seen more of Seth lately than Travis."

"But you are back on the ranch."

"I was for a few days. But I'm back in Lyndon." Abigail drew a breath. "Speaking of which, your sister Nicole's name came up the other day."

A look of obvious shock contorted her mother's face. "Nicole?"

"You never talk much about her."

Her mother's fingers trembled ever so slightly as she rested them on the table. "Even after all these years, it's hard for me to think about her. She was so young and beautiful and full of life. It hurt a lot to lose her."

"Seth said she ran away from home?"

"Sadly, she did. All she could talk about back then was the bright lights and the big city. I tried to convince her to pick out a college." Maureen squared her slim shoulders. "But I couldn't. She thought she was going to become a model or an actress or some such craziness. Seven months later, she was in that accident."

"Seven months?" Abigail's stomach flip-flopped.

Maureen's eyes shimmered. "I can only guess what happened. I adored her. But she always partied too much, was constantly finding excuses to stay in town on weekends. She smoked and drank with her friends. There was no holding her back."

While her mother spoke, Abigail's brain did the math. The nuns had told Lisa she was two weeks old when her mother dropped her anonymously into their care. Nicole had died a week later. That made her ten or twelve weeks pregnant when she left town.

Lisa's father was from Lyndon. But that would have to wait until later.

"We were told the pair of them were leaving a bar," Maureen continued, a faraway look on her face. "We later found out his family didn't know Nicole, had never met her. They were estranged from their son, too." Maureen absently restirred the iced tea.

"Mom." Abigail reached forward and took her mother's hand.

"Yes, dear?"

"I have something to tell you. It's surprising, maybe even shocking."

Maureen frowned. "Are you ill, honey? Is something wrong?"

Abigail quickly shook her head. "No, no. Nothing like that. It's good news. At least I think it's good news."

Her mother waited.

"It's Nicole, Mom. She had a daughter."

Maureen blinked, her expression frozen in the dappled sunlight.

"A daughter," Abigail repeated. "She was adopted out to a very nice family. She started looking for us a couple of years ago. And now she's found us."

Maureen's voice was paper dry. "Nicole had a baby?"

Abigail smiled, squeezing her mother's hand. "My cousin. Your niece."

Maureen's eyes welled up with tears, and her hand went to her chest.

"Her name's Lisa," said Abigail, speaking more quickly. "I've met her. In fact, I know her. She helped with Seth's campaign."

"I can't believe it," said Maureen, but a smile was forming on her face. "Okay. I do believe it." The smile turned into a shaky laugh. "Nicole was never a careful or cautious person."

"So, you're okay? You'll like her. She's a wonderful woman."

"You said she helped on Seth's campaign? Is she in Lyndon?"

"She came to town a few months ago. But right now…" Abigail paused. "Right now, she's in Houston."

"She's here?"

"She wants to meet you. And she wants to meet Mandy and Katrina and everyone. But we wanted to start with you."

"Oh, well in that case." Maureen promptly stood up, dropping her napkin onto the table. "Let's go."

Abigail laughed. "Hold on."

Her mother paused, waiting.

"We don't have to go anywhere." Abigail nodded across the garden to a far table. "She's over there."

As Maureen turned to stare, Lisa caught the gist of the body language and came gracefully to her feet. She was wearing a white, sleeveless tank dress, her blond hair loose and framing her face. She looked nervous but brave as she walked forward on delicate, white, strapless sandals.

Abigail rose and moved to stand next to her mother as Maureen approached them.

"Nicole," Maureen whispered, groping blindly to grasp Abigail's hand. "She looks just like Nicole."

Abigail found her own eyes filling with tears.

Maureen let go of her hand, rushing forward to pull Lisa into her arms.

Lisa's eyes fluttered closed as Maureen rocked her back and forth and stroked her hair.

"Oh, my darling." Maureen spoke in a choked voice. "I'm so glad you've come home."

It didn't take Abigail long to realize Zach's employees were like a family. Thirty people worked in the executive offices, with another hundred and fifty or so between the sales, marketing, accounting and human resources offices on various floors in the office tower in downtown Houston. All of them greeted Zach by his first name. They all seemed to know he'd been in Colorado, and they were all anxious to hear how things were going with Craig Mountain.

She'd been in Houston for three days, and between visiting her father and watching her mother and Lisa get to know each other, she'd managed to power through the application for Zach. Now she sat in a corner boardroom on the thirty-second floor, gazing out the bank of windows at the lights of the surrounding buildings and the clear, night sky. The water-license variance application form 731-800(e) was on the table in front of her, neatly printed out, supported by charts and graphs, and a letter of intent, complete with the company background, prospectus and all the technical data she'd been able to pull together from her previous water-table research. It was a great report, probably the best she'd ever done.

Half the double doors opened, and Zach entered with his partner, Alex Cable. She'd met Alex earlier and really liked him.

He seemed smart and motivated, with a wry sense of humor. She knew he'd just broken up with his girlfriend. She also knew he was staying with Zach. Though Alex was fairer than Zach, with blue eyes, light brown hair and a lankier build, the two had a lot of gestures, expressions and speech patterns in common. If she hadn't known better, she would have taken them for brothers.

Zach glanced at the cover page of the report, then looked to Abigail. "That it?"

"That's it," she confirmed. She was done, officially free from his blackmail, ready to go back to her old life.

"It's really nice of you to help us out," Alex put in.

Abigail shrugged. "It was no problem." Then she caught Zach's ironic brow lift, and she amended the statement. "Uh, not much of a problem. I am glad to be finished, though."

Zach lifted the report and thumbed through it.

"We should celebrate," said Alex.

"You don't have a variance yet," Abigail pointed out, taking her clutch purse from the table and tucking it under her arm. She should be rushing from the room, but, for some reason, she found herself hesitating.

Her mother was resting at her rented condo right now, tired from her emotional few days with Lisa. She'd taken a shine to Ozzy, and the puppy was keeping her company. It was nearly eight o'clock, and Lisa had asked Abigail to meet for a late dinner or maybe hit a club before they flew back to Colorado in the morning.

It was a strange feeling of déjà vu. Abigail was having a final night on the town before heading back to the ranch. She was trying hard not to rehash the Lucky and Doll-Face evening in her mind, but it was proving impossible. She was also trying hard not to think about leaving Zach forever, but that was causing her trouble, as well. Despite everything that had happened, she couldn't seem to stop herself from liking him.

"How long will the committee deliberations take?" Zach asked.

"Weeks, probably," she answered, avoiding looking into his

eyes. She had to be strong for another five minutes or so, get out of here and forget about looking back.

"We don't have weeks."

"You don't have a choice."

"Anything we can do to speed it up?" asked Alex.

"You want to try bribing a legislative committee of the state of Colorado?"

Alex coughed out a laugh. "Not a good idea?"

"Not if you enjoy life outside the Colorado penal system," she responded. Then she shot a stern look at Zach. "And there's not a thing in the world you can blackmail me with on that one."

"Blackmail?" Alex glanced from one to the other, clearly in the dark about the details of her and Zach's working relationship. No matter. It was over now, and Zach could explain himself however he wanted.

"Ask your partner," she told Alex, starting for the door. "By rights, he should already be in jail."

"Who'd you blackmail?" asked Alex.

"She's exaggerating," Zach drawled.

"Abigail." Alex's voice stopped her.

She turned, prepared to answer his question, acknowledging that she'd been the one to drop this bomb into the conversation.

"He actually blackmailed you into helping us?"

It was all a moot point now, and she didn't really care enough to keep the secret from Alex. Mostly, she just felt tired. "He did."

"Go, Zach." Alex whistled in obvious admiration. "What'd he use?"

"He slept with me then threatened to tell my brothers."

"Abby." Zach dropped the report back onto the table.

"What?" She stared at him. "You embarrassed about sleeping with me, or embarrassed about committing a felony?"

"It wasn't like that," he protested.

"It was exactly like that. And now you've got what you want."

"I threatened to tell them you hated the ranch."

"I don't hate the ranch." Though she once again felt as if a set of walls was closing in on her. By this time tomorrow, she'd be in blue jeans and boots.

He moved toward her. "I was never going to kiss and tell."

She was vaguely aware of Alex discreetly backing his way out of the room.

"Then you lied to me," she told Zach as he came to a halt directly in front of her.

"I guess I did." His eyes reflected the desire she couldn't deny.

"Yet another sin on your head." But her pulse sped up at his proximity, and her skin flushed with heat.

"Yet another sin," he agreed. "You want to go get something to eat?"

She sputtered a laugh. "A date? On my last night in town?"

"Something like that."

"You looking for another one-night stand?"

He gently took her hand in his, rubbing the pad of his thumb over her knuckles. "Absolutely."

Her mounting desire peaked and crested. She struggled not to stammer. "You have got to be kidding."

He leaned in, voice lowering to a husky drawl. "I'll understand if you say no."

Her breath hitched. "How very magnanimous of you."

"But I'm still going to ask."

"I'm saying no," she managed to say.

"Yeah. I figured." But his hand moved up to her cheek. His fingers brushed her sensitized skin, and he dipped his head toward her. "At least let me kiss you goodbye."

She ordered herself to move, to back away, get out of the danger zone. But her feet weren't cooperating, and her head was tilting to accommodate him. Her lips were parting, and her eyes were fluttering closed.

When his lips touched hers, desire exploded within her. A small sound escaped from her throat. Her knees went weak, and her chest became a tight band of emotion. Before she could form a coherent thought, her arms wound their own way around his neck.

His free arm pulled her close, pressing their bodies together, while his tongue found its way into the hot recesses of her mouth. The kiss continued for long minutes before he broke it off.

"I've missed you," he moaned, cradling the back of her head, pressing her cheek against his strong chest.

Her voice was muffled. "You've barely let me out of your sight."

"You know what I mean."

She did. She'd missed him, too. But that didn't make sleeping with him again a good idea. Okay, it would be great. It would be fantastic. But it would also be foolish.

She shook her head and tried to pull back.

"I can't let you go."

"You have to." She swallowed, forcing herself to stay strong. "You're out of ammunition, and I'm going home."

She braced her hands on his shoulders and broke free of his arms, stumbling a couple of steps in her high heels.

He reached for her, but she'd already put enough space between them.

"Goodbye, Zach."

He stilled. But then he dropped his shoulders and gave a sad smile. "Goodbye, Doll-Face."

Her eyes started to burn, and she quickly turned away, walking out the door.

Watching her two sisters dancing under the sparkling lights of the central ballroom at the Ten Peaks Country Club in downtown Denver, Abigail couldn't stop smiling. Mandy's gown was clean and classic, strapless with simple lines that flowed gracefully as she danced in Caleb's arms. Katrina's dress had a sweetheart neckline and glittered with shimmering embroidery, beadwork and sequins. Where Mandy had gone with a silver-link necklace and hoop earrings, Katrina wore cascades of white sapphires, interlaced to a point just above her cleavage. Her dangling earrings and elegant bracelet made up the set. She looked delicate and beautiful in Reed's arms.

Abigail had served as maid of honor, while Lisa was a bridesmaid. Seth and Travis stood up for the grooms. Their father was sitting now, at the head table near the multitiered cake that was flanked by two bridal bouquets. But he'd done an impressive job of escorting his daughters down the aisle. After the wedding, he and Abigail's mother were definitely considering an extended stay here.

The lights were dim around the dance floor as everyone watched the two bridal couples in their first waltz. Abigail's feet were sore, but in a good way. It had been weeks since she'd worn high heels, and she felt feminine and beautiful in her knee-length, plum-colored bridesmaid dress. Made of airy chiffon, it had a soft, strapless bodice, a two-layer skirt and a sleek waist-line.

"Abby?" A deep voice resonated close to her ear, sending a shiver down her spine.

She twisted to come face-to-face with Zach. She blinked, unable to make sense of his appearance.

"Hi," he offered.

"What are you *doing* here?"

He was dressed in a well-cut three-piece steel-gray business suit, his silver tie in a sharp knot, his crisp, white shirt allowing him to blend with the other guests.

"I need to talk to you," he whispered.

"I'm a little busy."

The crowd broke into applause as the final strains of the waltz came to a close. The string quartet immediately launched into another song.

Mandy picked Seth from the crowd, while Katrina laughingly asked Travis to dance. Reed Terrell snagged Abigail's hand and smoothly pulled her onto the hardwood floor. He swung her gracefully into his arms. For a large man, he'd always been a great dancer. He'd been a year ahead of her in high school, and they'd danced together many times before.

"Who's that?" he asked, leaning to be heard above the music.

Abigail glanced back at Zach. Her heart tripped at his hand-some, sexy looks.

"Zach Rainer," she told Reed. "He owns Craig Mountain Brewery."

"He was invited to the wedding?" Reed's tone was incredulous.

"He's here looking for me."

Reed stopped.

"Don't," Abigail warned. She knew her neighbor well enough to realize he would step in to solve whatever problem was at hand. Dressed in a wedding tux or not, he was completely capable of tossing Zach out on his ear. "I'll handle it."

Reed hesitated a second longer, but to her relief began dancing again. "Why's he crashing my wedding?" he asked.

"I don't know yet. I haven't had a chance to talk to him."

"He a friend?"

"Sort of."

Reed stared down at her, eyes narrowed. "There something you're not telling me?"

She gave a light laugh. "There are many, many things I'm not telling you, Reed. But don't worry about it. It's all good."

"Are you in some kind of trouble?"

"Not at all." Unless you counted her overwhelming desire to haul Zach off to the nearest hotel room and ravage him. That was a whole lot of trouble.

"He looks ticked off."

"He's impatient."

"Well, he can bloody well wait until my wedding's over."

"Stop," Abigail ordered. "Katrina's going to kill me if I get you all riled up."

"I'm not riled."

"Yes, you are."

"You don't know riled, Abby."

Abigail grinned. "Welcome to the family." She stretched up and gave him a kiss on the cheek.

"You've got a great family," said Reed.

"It just got greater." She glanced at Caleb who was laughing with Lisa. "Two new brothers, and a new cousin."

"Seth just thanked me and Caleb for evening things up between the genders again."

"We women did have the upper hand there for a few weeks."

The song wound down.

"You better get back to Katrina."

Reed scowled in Zach's direction one more time. "You let me know if he gives you any trouble."

"Absolutely," Abigail lied.

As Reed walked away, she felt someone come up behind her.

"Care to dance?" asked Zach.

She turned. "You're not supposed to be here."

"Like I told you, I need to talk to you."

"Can it not wait?"

Without waiting for permission, he drew her into his arms.

It seemed simpler to dance than to make a scene by arguing about it. Plus, that would bring Reed to her side in a heartbeat, so she went along with Zach.

He settled her close. "You want to meet up later instead?"

"I do not."

"It was worth a try."

"You crash my sisters' wedding, and now you're hitting on me?"

"I can't seem to help myself."

"Try, Zach. Try."

His tone stayed intimate, and his hand moved up and down her back, tracing the bare skin between her shoulder blades. "You take my breath away, Doll-Face."

She steeled herself against the softer feelings creeping into her psyche. "You see that guy over there? The groom? The one I was just dancing with?"

"I do."

"See how big he is? Well, he likes me. And he's already ticked off at you."

"I like you, too."

"You like me naked." The second the words were out of her mouth, Abigail realized they were a colossal mistake.

She mentally braced for his retort, but Zach didn't reply. Instead, he gathered her closer, seeming to mold his body to hers. She fought the arousal that gripped her body, but it was useless. Images of their night together were back in force.

"I need to talk to you," he repeated, voice barely a rasp. "And I can't wait. Can we go outside?"

His tone brought a thousand questions into her mind. Why was he here, after all these weeks? Had he missed her? Had he come back for her, to pursue their relationship?

She tried to control the hope that surged inside her. She realized in a split second that she wanted him to pursue her. She wanted to be with him again, free from all the complications that had tangled them in knots.

She gave him a mute nod, and he took her hand in his, leading the way from the dance floor to patio doors that led to a lighted garden. Conflicting thoughts continued to spin around in her mind. Sure, he lived in Houston, while she lived in Lyndon. But there were airplanes. There were hotels. Maybe they could spend weekends together someplace in the middle.

Anticipation tightened her chest as she realized she was going to say yes. If he wanted to try something long-distance, she'd agree to it. And then maybe they could find that nearest hotel right now and spend the night in each other's arms. Her breath caught and her heartbeat thudded deep.

He came to a halt at the far edge of the concrete patio, turning to face her, taking his hand from hers. The music and voices wafted out from the reception, while pot lights glowed softly from the hedges and garden beds, reflecting off the planes and angles of his face. He was an incredibly attractive man.

"Abby," he started.

"Yes?" She waited, not moving, not breathing.

"The application was rejected."

She blinked. It took a second for her brain to switch gears.

"The committee turned us down," he elaborated.

"The water license?" she all but stammered.

"Yes."

She took a shaky step back, mind refusing to accept reality. "You dragged me away from my sisters' wedding to tell me you didn't get your precious water license?"

He looked confused. "What else?"

Excellent question. She pressed her fingertips against one

temple. "Oh, I don't know. Nothing, I guess. What *is* your problem?"

"I just told you my problem."

"And this couldn't have waited until tomorrow?"

"You're leaving tomorrow."

"Yes, I am. Goodbye, Zach." She took a step toward the reception.

He snagged her upper arm. "Hear me out, Abby."

"No." She was not going to let him do this. She'd done her best. She'd caved to every single thing he'd asked of her. And to add insult to injury, she'd apparently become infatuated with him along the way.

"I need you."

She glared at him. "You need a bankruptcy attorney."

"You're giving up? Just like that."

"Just like that? There is no 'just like that.' I did everything I could, everything I could think of. Every fact, figure, argument and rationale I could dream up went into that paper, Zach. There is nothing, nothing more I have to offer."

"I don't believe you."

"Too bad."

He dropped his hand from her arm, raking it through his short hair. "There *has* to be something."

"There's nothing. You and a hundred companies like you want variances. The State has decided you can't have them right now. They've made a rule, and they're following it, Zach. You're just ticked because they won't break it for you."

"I'm not asking anyone to break the rules. I'm only asking for a little logic and reason."

"You're asking a government for logic and reason."

His lips flattened in obvious anger.

"You see the flaw in that, right?" she pressed.

"I see you giving up."

"This is not my problem."

"You're right. It's my problem. But while you stand there secure in that knowledge, Abby, ask yourself one thing." He stepped forward, crowding her. "Ask yourself what you would do if this was your family."

His gaze held hers, and she felt her resolve falter.

"If it was your ranch on the line. If it was Seth's and Mandy's and Katrina's and Travis's jobs. Would you throw up your hands in defeat? Or if you thought I could help, would you not track me down, back me into a corner and force me to agree?"

"By blackmailing you?" She'd like to think she wouldn't, but maybe she would.

"By any means possible."

Her throat became dry, and her voice became strained. "I tried to help you, Zach. I truly, truly tried."

He took the last step that brought him directly in front of her. "One more time?" he asked. "Tonight. When you're done here, before you go back to Lyndon. Let's think it through one more time. You and me."

There was no point. "I read every single word of the moratorium. I've looked up precedents and past cases. I followed their template to the letter. I dotted every *i*, I crossed every single *t*."

"We're talking hundreds of jobs. Hundreds of people without anything but the livelihood and the family they get from working at DFB. A couple of hours, Abby. Can you give me that?"

Her mind screamed no. But there was something in the raw honesty of his plea that got to her.

"If it was your family?" he asked more softly this time, "what would you do?"

She tipped her chin and tossed her head, telling herself she was capitulating for a good cause. "Fine. We'll try one more time."

He was silent for a moment, almost as if he couldn't believe she'd finally said yes. "Thank you," he breathed, in obvious relief and gratitude.

She was hit with an unexpected rush of pleasure. Which was silly. She might feel good about helping him, but that didn't change the cold hard facts. "I wish I could be magic, Zach. I truly do."

He gently took her hands. "You are."

Despite everything, she wanted to throw herself into his arms, squeeze him tight and forget the rest of the world existed. "Go away," she murmured. "Leave me alone for the next few hours."

He nodded, and with a final, reflexive squeeze of his fingers, he let go and walked away.

She stared into the dark reaches of the garden, struggling to bring her emotions under control.

Lisa's voice came from behind her, skirt rustling, heels clicking rhythmically on the concrete as she approached. "Now, who the heck was that?"

Abigail shook her head and gave a helpless laugh. "Nobody."

"Come on. Anybody who looks at you that way is not a nobody."

Abigail was tired of keeping all this locked tight inside her chest. She gave in to temptation. "Cone of silence?"

"Cone of silence."

"That was my one-night stand."

Lisa whistled low, turning to look at the doorway where Zach had disappeared. "Oh, mama."

"You got that right." Abigail gave a wry grimace. "He was also my midnight research project. And tonight I'm meeting him after the reception."

"Really?"

"Yes."

"You okay?"

"No."

"You want to tell me what's going on?"

"Yes," Abigail admitted. "But I can't."

Lisa moved closer. "Oh, but you can."

"I really can't." Abigail hadn't gone to all this trouble to blurt the truth out to Lisa.

"I'm family now," said Lisa. "Plus, I'm discreet. And I'm not above feeding you champagne until you reveal every single secret locked away in your little heart." She nodded to a waiter standing just inside the doors. "You might as well do it without the hangover."

It was tempting.

Lisa rapidly rubbed Abigail's arm. *"Tell me."*

Abigail gave in. "I lied to and betrayed my entire family."

"You did not."

"Yes." Abigail nodded, looking square into Lisa's eyes. "I did."

"Then wait right here."

Lisa swiftly crossed the patio, helped herself to two glasses of champagne and returned, handing one of them to Abigail.

Abigail took a swallow. "I slept with Zach. He's that guy you just saw. Only, I didn't know he was Zach then."

"You're an adult."

"I know."

"Was it good?"

Abigail shot her an incredulous look. "That's irrelevant."

"Yeah, but was it good?"

"Yes."

"So far I'm not hearing anything particularly problematic."

"Yeah, well, it gets better. He blackmailed me. Threatened to tell Travis and Seth—"

"Tell them what you like in bed?" It was Lisa's turn to be incredulous.

"No. No. It was something that I *told* him in bed."

"Oh, good. Though I have to admit, you had me curious." Lisa waggled her brow. "Little Bo Peep outfit, handcuffs, whipped cream."

"Give me a break."

"It's not as if you can tell by looking at a person."

"I'm not into handcuffs."

Lisa shrugged. "So what'd you tell him?"

Abigail was having second thoughts about the conversation. She glossed over the facts. "The important point is that he blackmailed me into helping him get a variance to his water license."

"He *got* a variance?" Working in the mayor's office, Lisa was well aware of the contentious water issues.

Abigail shook her head. "The committee turned him down. And now he wants me to try again."

"Wow, Abby. Unless we're talking black leather and whips, and even then, just tell him no."

"This isn't about kinky sex."

"Then just tell him no."

"There are hundreds of jobs at stake." Abigail found herself defending Zach. "Hundreds of orphans' jobs at stake. Because that's what Zach does. He grew up in foster care, and he's built this whole brewery conglomerate to give jobs to other foster kids. You should see the place, Lisa. The headquarters are in Houston, and the people who work there, well, they all but worship Zach and his partner, Alex. He's given them all a real shot in life, given them a place to belong. And I'm the only person who might be able to help him save it."

"What does this have to do with water?"

"They need to up production at their Craig Mountain brewery. To do that, they need water. If they don't, it all falls apart like a row of dominoes."

"It's still not your problem," Lisa told her gently.

"They're his family."

"And you want to help them."

"I do," Abigail admitted. "I know it'll set a precedent that will hurt the ranchers. But I want to do it anyway."

Lisa smiled. "He must be damn good in bed."

"He is." Abigail felt her cheeks grow warm. "That's irrelevant. But he is."

Lisa's grin widened. "Then you'd better help him."

"And betray my family." That was the conundrum. She might sympathize with Zach, but the facts remained the same.

Lisa linked arms with her. "It's not the worst betrayal in the world. Besides, if they kick you out of the house, I'll take your room."

Abigail tried to smile at the joke, but she couldn't quite pull it off.

"Chill, Abby," said Lisa. "The water battle will go on for a long, long time to come. And in the end, Zach's variance will be a mere blip on the radar."

"*If* I pull it off," Abigail reminded her as they started for the door. Having met some of Zach's employees, she truly wanted to save their jobs. "I honestly don't know what I can do to change the committee's mind."

"Seth told me about all the research you did on this," Lisa reminded her. "The paper you wrote, your presentation in Denver. You didn't let those bureaucrats intimidate you. The Ranchers Association thinks the world of you. He also told me he credits you with getting him elected. You wrote every speech, developed every policy. You've been a straight A student since first grade. You're brilliant, Abby. If anyone can do it, it's you."

Seven

It was after midnight. Having finished a phone call to Alex, Zach moved from the bedroom of his hotel suite to the living room where Abigail was curled up on the sofa, reading her way through one of the papers from the thick rejection file. She still wore the filmy, plum, strapless bridesmaid dress. It draped enticingly across her thighs, highlighting her toned, tanned, sexy legs. Her feet were bare. Her hair had come loose from the updo and now framed her face with those same auburn wisps he'd fallen for the first night he'd met her. Her makeup was slightly smudged, and a hint of cleavage peeked out from her bodice. It was all he could do not to stride across the room and pull her into his arms and kiss her until they couldn't see straight.

He knew she didn't want that. But he also knew she was still attracted to him. And, right now, he wanted it enough for the both of them.

She lifted her gaze to look at him, those golden eyes all but glowing in the soft light from the table lamp.

He knew she'd caught him staring. And he imagined there was no mistaking his thoughts, since he was all but salivating at the thought of her.

But she didn't seem to notice, or else she didn't care. She smiled serenely. "I've got it."

He had to forcibly pull back from the sensual path he'd been on. "Got what?"

"The solution." Smile broadening, she asked, "You got any champagne around here?"

"I can order anything you want."

"You might want to order some champagne."

"Why?" he prompted.

She chuckled softly, coming to her feet. "It's so simple. It was there all along."

He knew she couldn't be talking about sex, but, man, did he wish she was. "What was there all along?"

"You move your company headquarters to Lyndon."

Her words didn't compute into anything logical in his brain, so he didn't respond.

"That's the answer, Zach."

"Is that a joke?" If it was, she was keeping a pretty straight face.

"It's not a joke."

"It's ridiculous." DFB had only recently agreed to a new five-year lease for the office space in Houston. His two-hundred-strong at headquarters had houses there, families there. They were all Texans.

"You do that," she singsonged, obviously ignoring his reaction. "That's over two hundred new jobs in the Lyndon area. Your variance application then has a fundamental impact on employment creation in the region, and you've just earned yourself mandatory exemption."

Against all odds, the woman truly was serious.

"Do you have any idea what it would take to make that kind of move?" he asked. "There are legal and incorporation impacts, taxation impacts, export-licensing impacts, not to mention up-rooting two-hundred people and their families."

She sauntered toward him. "I think what you mean to say is, 'You're brilliant, Abigail. Thank you so much for giving me a real solution to an impossible problem'."

He knew she was brilliant, but he couldn't quite wrap his head around the magnitude of her suggestion. His words were confrontational, but his tone was soft. "I believe I mean to say, 'You're insane, Abigail. This will never work in real life'."

She came to a halt in front of him, all soft and sexy and proud. "You coerced me. You blackmailed me. You stalked me."

"How did I stalk you?"

"To the wedding."

He considered that. "Okay. Fair enough."

"And now, after all that, after I practically made my brain bleed thinking this through, you're refusing to take my advice?"

"Your advice is frightening."

"It's brilliant."

"I don't see how it can work."

"It can work." Her eyes took on that glow of intelligence as her brain obviously clicked through a catalog of facts. "Or maybe it can't work. But it's all I've got."

He recognized that it was an extraordinary plan. The only flaw was that it wouldn't work, at least not for him, not for DFB. But that didn't change the fact that she'd been clever to come up with it.

"They tell me you're a genius," he found himself saying.

His words clearly took her by surprise. "Who are they?"

"People I talk to. People in Lyndon. Are you a genius, Abigail?"

"I'm smart enough that you should be listening to me."

"And I'm stupid enough to think there's another way."

"You're not stupid. Exactly."

"Ouch."

"I'd say you were self-confident to a fault."

"It's taken me a long way in life." He felt compelled to defend himself.

"That doesn't mean it shouldn't be mitigated."

"You're really quite fearless, aren't you?"

"Where did that come from?"

"Nobody challenges me like this. Nobody pushes me, nobody

makes me second-guess myself. I've missed you," he confessed, easing closer to her.

"In a good way?"

Was it his imagination or was she leaning slightly toward him?

"My life seems flat when you're not around."

"Mine seems a whole lot simpler when you're not around."

"You want simpler?"

She hesitated, brain obviously cataloging again. Finally she shook her head.

"Neither do I," he muttered. He gave in to impulse and lifted his hand, cupping her cheek, easing his spread fingers into her hair. "I want you."

Her eyes closed, and she turned her face into his palm. "When you touch me," she breathed, "nothing else seems to matter."

"Everything matters," he countered. "But you matter the most."

"Zach…" She sighed. "What now?"

He moved in. "Now I hope I kiss you."

"We shouldn't."

"Agreed. Not the way things have been between us. But you're free from me now. From here on in. No matter what, I'll never bother you again."

"So I can leave? And you won't try to stop me?"

He held his breath, afraid she'd do exactly that. "You can do anything you want."

But she didn't move. In fact, her lips softened and parted, and her pupils dilated ever so slightly.

"Kiss me, Zach."

His arms went around her instantly. He tried to be gentle, but passion pushed him on. He kissed her deeply, holding her tight, reveling in the feel of her body pressed against his own. He'd missed her so much. Every minute of every day they'd been apart, he'd missed her.

She was soft to his hard, supple to his taut steel. She smelled like wildflowers, and she tasted of champagne.

She kissed him back, her delicate hands gripping his shoulders, her tongue tangling with his, opening to him, molding against him. Desire crested in his bloodstream, and he knew he was careening toward losing control. He forced himself to pull back.

"I'm sorry," he rasped. "I didn't mean this to get out of hand."

"It's out of hand?" She was equally breathless, and her hands went to the buttons on his shirt.

"Abby," he warned.

"What?" she asked, glancing up, tone falsely innocent, eyes blinking up at him.

"You're a very smart woman."

"I am," she agreed, still unbuttoning.

"You're unbuttoning my shirt."

"Also true." She separated the fabric and placed a hot kiss on his chest.

"You know what this means."

"In fact, I do."

"Just so we're clear."

"We're clear."

"I can't keep my hands off you."

She smiled impishly up at him. "You're doing a pretty good job so far."

He scooped her into his arms and strode for the bedroom. "Let's fix that."

Her luscious lips went to his neck. "Please do."

He was in the bedroom in seconds, setting her down on the bed, stretching out beside her, kissing her lips, her neck, her shoulders, inhaling deeply as he ran his fingers through her soft hair.

"This is the sexiest dress ever," he told her.

"Katrina picked it."

"Remind me to thank her." He released the zipper and pushed the fabric down over her breasts.

Abby groaned. "I'm trying to picture that conversation."

He kissed one nipple, bringing the tip to a bead.

Her fingertips dug into his shoulders.

"Picturing it now?" he teased.

"Huh?"

"Nothing."

With a free hand he drew her dress up along her bare thighs, reveling in the soft, tender skin, his thumbs drawing circles as he moved higher.

She finished with his buttons, pushing his jacket and shirt off his shoulders. He let them fall to the floor, taking her lips in a deep kiss.

He touched the hot silk of her panties, and she gasped against his mouth. Her panties were filmy, barely there, and he easily pulled them off, down her gorgeous legs, tossing them to the side. In answer, her hands went to his pants, fumbling with the button and his zipper.

He retrieved his wallet, working with one hand for a condom as she pulled down his zipper, grazing him with her knuckles, her hand surrounding him through his boxers.

He followed the contours of her body, reveling in her soft skin, kissing her from her hairline to her toes and back again. Then he finally rose above her, watching her expression, the moue of her pink mouth, the glow of her golden eyes, the sheen of sweat on her forehead, and he gently pushed inside.

He groaned out loud. "How can anything be so good?"

A haze was taking over his brain. A roar had started in his ears. And all nonessential systems were shutting down.

Abigail was the center of his world. The blackmail was done. From this moment on, she had the power.

"Oh, Lucky." She kissed his mouth, wrapped her arms around his neck, tightened her legs around his waist, her entire body cradling his.

He'd never felt anything like it. Explosions started at the base of his brain, growing in intensity, fanning out.

He heard her cry, felt her body ripple around him, and he let himself cascade over the edge.

Their breathing was ragged, and long minutes passed while he held her to him, passion slowly throbbing its way from his body.

Neither spoke. Her body was limp, and her head was tucked into the crook of his neck.

"I thought about what you said," she whispered.

"What did I say?" Whatever it was, he'd say it again.

"About your employees being your family. It made me want to help you. To throw my heart and soul into it."

"Thank you," he said simply.

"You really do need to move your headquarters."

"Can we talk about this later?" Though he accepted that she was right. He and Alex had to sit down and seriously talk about how that might work.

"There is no later," she told him, tone regretful. "I've got a 9:00 a.m. flight."

Stay, his mind screamed. "Back to the ranch?" he asked instead.

She nodded.

Her words made him feel helpless. She didn't want to go back there. She shouldn't have to go back there.

"Have you told them?" he asked, already knowing the answer.

"I'm never going to tell them, Zach. And you can't either."

"You can't live your life for your family."

"You're living yours for your employees."

"That's different." He loved his job. He loved working with Alex, and he took immense satisfaction in the success of Red, White and Brew.

She gave him an ironic smile and cocked her head.

"Hot tub or bed?" he asked, deciding to assume she was staying the night. Before she could refuse, he touched the bottom of her chin with his index finger, placing a gentle kiss on her swollen mouth.

"Bed," he decided for her on a whisper. "Don't make me let go of you just yet."

Wrapped in Zach's discarded dress shirt, sleeves rolled up a few turns, Abigail gazed through the window of the darkened hotel bedroom, watching the distant spot of light that was an early flight taking off from the Denver airport. It trailed across the sky, disappearing into a blend of stars on the horizon. It wouldn't be long before she was on a plane just like that, winging her way north, while Zach made his way south.

She heard him moving behind her, and then his arms were around her, drawing her back against him.

"Hey." His voice was husky above her ear.

"I didn't mean to wake you," she apologized.

"I wasn't asleep."

She drew a breath and allowed herself to absorb his warmth. He seemed so strong, so sure, as if nothing in the world could slow him down. She tried to imagine how he'd become such a successful man, how he'd overcome what must have been innumerable challenges in his childhood.

"What was it like?" she found herself asking.

"What was what like?" he asked.

"Growing up. Alone. In the group home."

"You don't want to hear about that."

She turned in his arms. "Yes, I do."

He gazed at her for a minute, eyes dark, expression serious. "Unremarkable," he finally answered.

That didn't come anywhere near to satisfying her. "Were you happy, sad, lonely?"

"We were all lonely."

She looped her arms loosely around his waist, studying his expression. "I'm trying to imagine what it must have been like when you were little."

"It was like having a hundred brothers."

"But no parents."

"Parents, no. Workers, yes. Around the clock. Some of them stayed for years. Some of them seemed to like me a lot. Well—" he gave a wry smile "—when I was little, anyway. But then I met Alex, and we were typical, active boys, and we mostly made the workers all crazy."

Abigail smiled back, but her heart couldn't help aching for him.

"What about you?" he asked. "What was it like when you were little."

"Seth and Travis were horrible to us girls."

"I can imagine."

"They teased us unmercifully. I was the oldest. Mandy was pretty tough. While Katrina was always really small and delicate. They weren't too bad with her. I guess even as kids, they realized it would be cruel to go after her."

"What did they do to you and Mandy?"

"Everything from putting spiders in our beds to throwing us into the freezing-cold lake in the spring. Travis sneaked into my bedroom once in the middle of the night and glued my hair to my pillow. The next morning, Mom had to cut it off."

Zach smoothed back her hair. "Travis get a whipping?"

"My parents didn't believe in spanking. But he spent the next two weeks shoveling manure in the hot sun."

"Learned his lesson?"

"He never did anything like that again. But I don't think manual labor ever bothered him much."

"At St. Stephen's they had a big old leather strap."

"They beat you?"

"They didn't call it beating back then. They called it discipline."

She cringed just thinking about it. "Did you…"

"Oh, yes."

"Oh, Zach." She put a sympathetic hand to his cheek.

He covered it with his. "It wasn't that bad. Schoolyard fights were worse. But it toughened Alex and me up. By the time we left, there wasn't much the world could throw at us that we couldn't take."

She didn't buy his dismissal. She knew how cruel kids could be, and she'd always had her parents as champions. And she also had her brothers and sisters by her side. Though Seth and Travis would tease them at home, they'd staunchly defended them to any outsiders.

It had been interesting when she started dating.

"Did you go to a local school?" she asked Zach.

"Classes were at St. Stephen's."

"So, boys only."

"Boys only."

"How did you date?"

"We didn't. From about fifteen on, we had supervised outings. We sometimes came across girls, at local fairs or movie nights. But it was always in groups, always supervised, never a chance to steal a kiss or cop a feel."

"How'd you learn about sex?" she asked. Somewhere along the way, he'd become awfully good at it.

He grinned. "Hearsay and rumor, and the occasional contraband girlie magazine."

She smiled along with him. "And how old were you when you left St. Stephen's."

"Eighteen."

"So, how long did it take you to get lucky, Lucky?"

His gaze warmed on her. "A long time. I got very lucky a few weeks ago, in Lyndon, Colorado. With a woman who was ten times more beautiful than anyone I'd ever seen in a magazine."

"Oh, *good answer,*" she approved with a nod.

"I mean it."

"You've learned a lot about women along the way, Zach Rainer."

"I'd like to learn more about you."

She sobered. "You've got about two hours."

He drew her closer. "Two hours. And that's it?"

"That's it." She'd been absent from the ranch far too much since the election. It wasn't fair to Travis. And for the next week, they were also helping to take care of the Terrell place next to theirs while Caleb and Reed were on their honeymoons with Mandy and Katrina. She couldn't afford even one more day in Denver.

Back in Houston, two hours after his plane had landed, Zach sat across the boardroom table from Alex.

"You're serious," Alex stated unnecessarily.

"You don't think I've come at this from every possible angle?"

Alex drummed his fingers rhythmically on the tabletop. "And you trust her?"

"What's not to trust? There's nothing in this for her."

"It gets you to Lyndon."

"I don't think she wants me in Lyndon." Zach could get big-headed about this and decide that Abigail had some interest in him beyond their brief fling. But he was realistic. Her goodbye this morning had been final.

Not that he blamed her. He'd forced her to go against her family. And if he knew anything about Abby, it was that she was loyal to the core. Though their lovemaking was explosive, it was temporary and in some ways selfish. She wasn't going to let herself do that again.

Alex leaned back in his chair, twirling a silver pen between his fingers. "Then I guess we get the legal department assembled this afternoon."

"And Accounting," said Zach. "Relocating is going to be expensive. We'll have to break our lease. I can't imagine what it'll do to our taxes. And we should offer employees some kind of moving allowance."

"Are there even enough houses for everybody in Lyndon, Colorado?"

Zach realized it was a good question. "I wonder if we could stage it out, maybe plan the bulk of the move for next summer. That way, people with kids wouldn't be so inconvenienced."

"You think people will quit?"

"Some might," Zach reasoned. "But at least they'll have the option."

Alex's frown deepened. "You are absolutely sure there's no other way?"

"I am absolutely sure." He'd had three of their lawyers look over the moratorium and Abigail's suggestion. They proclaimed her a genius and told Zach they'd hire her as a researcher in a heartbeat.

"There is a bright side," said Alex.

"Yeah?"

"I'm starting to think Stephanie might have been bluffing."

"Will you take her back?" Zach was often baffled by his friend's relationship with his girlfriend Stephanie. It seemed to cause him a whole lot more angst than happiness.

When she wasn't angry, she was pouting. She demanded nearly all his attention. If he was half an hour late leaving the office, she was on the phone. And when he traveled on business, she was always convinced he was going to spend time with other women.

"I don't want her back," said Alex. "But she does have her ways. I figure it's safer if I leave the state. I'll go be the advance man in Colorado. Keep me away from temptation."

"I don't understand how you can possibly be tempted."

"That's because you've never been in love."

Zach might not have ever been in love, but he couldn't imagine love was anything like Alex and Stephanie's relationship. If a guy was going to go to all the trouble to be with one woman, she should at least make him happy. A vision of Abigail flashed through his mind. Okay, he wouldn't exactly call every moment with her happy. Exhilarating, yes. Exciting, absolutely. And the highs were very, very high. But the lows sure sucked.

Then again, the lows were mostly when she left him.

"It's not all laughs and sunshine," Alex put in.

"Apparently not."

"The good is very good."

"And the bad is very bad." Zach shifted his mind back to Alex and Stephanie. "Seems to me it should at least be a fifty-fifty proposition to make it worth a guy's while."

"It'll happen to you one day."

"Not like Stephanie."

"Yeah, well." Alex brought his hands down on the arms of his chair. "Stephanie ain't going to happen for me either. To make sure of that, I'm going to Colorado."

"No forwarding address?"

"Probably for the best." Alex stretched. "Damn, this is going to be expensive."

"That it is," Zach agreed. "Only thing it's got going for it is that's it's better than the alternative."

"True enough."

Zach started to rise, but Alex spoke again.

"So, you going to call her?"

"Abigail?"

Alex set his pen down on the table. "Yes, Abigail. The woman you slept with last night."

"I never said I slept with her."

"Are you going to call her?"

"No." Zach would like to call her. He'd love to call her. But he'd bothered her enough for one lifetime. It was time to back off.

"You mind if I call her?" asked Alex.

"What for?"

"To ask her out."

Zach's fingers curled tightly around the arms of his chair. "On a *date*?"

"There's got to be some kind of nightlife in Lyndon."

"Over my dead body."

"So she's off limits?"

Zach leaned forward. "Look me in the eye, Alex. What do you see?"

"My body chopped up into tiny little pieces if I so much as look sideways at Abigail Jacobs."

"Close enough."

"But you're not going to call her."

Zach wished he could. "She doesn't want to hear from me."

"Got a minute?" Lisa's head popped up above the roofline of the shed where Abigail was perched while she replaced some broken shingles. Seth was perpetually busy on civic matters in Lyndon. Mandy and Caleb were honeymooning in Hawaii. Katrina and Reed had opted for Australia. Abigail's parents were staying in Denver for a while, to be close to the medical facilities while her father completed his recovery. As expected, Travis and Abigail were left holding the fort.

Ozzy gave a belated, warning bark from his post at the bottom of the ladder.

"I didn't know you were coming today." Abigail pulled a couple of roofing nails out of her mouth and dropped them back in the pouch on her leather tool belt.

"Drove in with Seth." Lisa stepped up two more rungs and maneuvered herself around the top of the ladder.

"Careful," Abigail cautioned. She was wearing heavy, leather work boots with thick-tread soles, while Lisa sported a pair of expensive pumps.

Lisa's gauzy, pastel-patterned blouse billowed in the breeze above her skinny jeans. "Wow. Quite the view up here."

Abigail glanced around. She'd been focused on work for the past few hours, but now she noted the fall colors against the evergreens and newly snowcapped peaks in the nearby foothills. October was well under way, and they could expect the first snowfall in a few weeks.

Lisa sat down next to her on the sun-warmed, black shingles. "How's it going?"

Abigail shrugged. "Busy." Fall was a frantic time on the ranch. Along with roundup, they had to make sure everything was winterized and battened down. Colorado was a beautiful state, but it had its fair share of rain and snow. "How about you?"

"Busy in Lyndon, too. We're knee-deep in next year's budget. The environmentalists have turned the Canada goose into a poster child, and the flocks are wreaking havoc at the airport. You know, the usual."

Abigail scooted backward on her canvas work pants, setting another shingle strip in place.

"Saw an interesting application at city hall today," said Lisa, swiping her hair back from her face as the wind raced up the pitch of the roof.

Abigail hammered in the first nail.

"For a business license," Lisa continued. "Corporate headquarters of DFB Incorporated."

Abigail hit her finger with the hammer. "Ouch!"

"It's the parent company for Craig Mountain Brewery."

"I know who they are." Abigail shook the pain out of her hand, her mind reeling. Zach was going to do it. It had been three weeks since she'd presented her idea, and she hadn't heard a word about his decision.

"Did Zach tell you he was doing this?"

"He didn't."

"But it was your idea," Lisa guessed.

"It was," Abigail admitted, taking a breath and setting the next nail.

"It was absolutely brilliant."

It had been a brilliant idea. But it was also a very radical idea.

"I didn't think he'd actually go through with it. He's uprooting more than two hundred people."

"The water license exemption was attached to the business application."

Abigail looked up. "So it's signed, sealed and delivered?"

She wanted to ask if Lisa had seen Zach, if he was in town. But she forced herself to stay silent. He knew full well where she was, and how to get hold of her. The fact that he hadn't bothered contacting her told her everything she needed to know.

"They want to take over the Buskell Building on Fourth. That means a variance to zoning, and they'll need to make provisions for parking. But all that's minor stuff compared to the water license."

"So he's really doing it."

"Looks like."

Abigail let the hammer rest on the roof, gazing across the river, trying hard not to remember her last night with Zach.

"What did he have on you?" Lisa asked softly.

"It's not important."

"You look sad."

Abigail mustered a smile. "I'm not sad. Dad's doing better. Mandy and Katrina are having fantastic honeymoons. The price of beef is up."

"You can't fool me." Lisa scooted closer. "I know you too well."

"You've only known me for five months." Ironic, really, considering Abigail's own family hadn't picked up on anything being wrong.

"It's the genetic link. You have my eyes. And they're sad."

"Your eyes are green and round. Mine are hazel and almond shaped."

"What did he have on you, Abby?"

"You're like a broken record." But deep down inside, Abigail wanted to share with someone.

Lisa leaned back on the heels of her hands. "I'll just wait."

"Okay." Abigail set up for another strip of shingles, then another and another, moving farther away from Lisa, while her mind went to war with itself.

Finally, she dropped the hammer and rested her hands on her upraised knees. "Fine," she called out.

"Yeah?" Lisa called back.

"Yeah."

Lisa stood up, made her way across the roof then plopped back down again.

"Cone of silence?" Abigail asked.

"Always."

"I told him I didn't like working on the ranch." There. She'd said it out loud.

Lisa drew back in obvious surprise. "You don't?"

The rest of the words seemed to leap out. "I loved the campaign. I like the city. I like office work. I like power lunches and research and analysis."

"So, why are you here? You could get a hundred jobs in Lyndon or anywhere else."

"Because they need me. The family needs me."

"No, they—"

"They need me," Abigail repeated with certainty.

Lisa was silent for a long moment. "Yeah, I guess they do."

"If I was going to say something—" Abigail plucked at a seam on the leather belt "—I should have done it sooner. But now Seth's gone, and Mom and Dad bought that condo in Palm Springs, and Mandy's up at the Terrells, and Katrina was never here in the first place." She drew a breath. "And I can't abandon Travis."

"So, you're going to stay here forever?"

"Not forever. But until something changes, yes. Maybe Travis will find a wife. Maybe she'll love ranching. Maybe they'll have sons or daughters who want to take over."

Lisa shook her hair so that it was blowing back from her face. "That sounds like a pretty long-term proposition."

"It does," Abigail agreed. But hoping something would come along to change the circumstances was all she had right now. She couldn't change the circumstances herself. It all depended on external forces.

"Wish I could help," Lisa offered. "But I don't know a heifer from a milk cow."

Abigail chuckled. "You're helping Seth."

"Seth's doing a great job."

"I know he is." Abigail hesitated, desperate to ask about Zach, but not wanting to give Lisa the wrong idea. Or maybe asking would give Lisa exactly the right idea, since Abigail had pretty much been obsessing about him since Denver.

"The business license," she ventured. "Was it…submitted locally?"

"Are you asking whether Zach's in town?"

"Yes." There didn't seem to be any point in denying it, especially to Lisa, who seemed to have an uncanny knack for figuring things out.

"I take it you have feelings for him?"

Abigail shook her head in denial, more for her own benefit than Lisa's. "I slept with him, so…you know…it's weird. If I'm going to run into him, I'd like to brace myself."

"The application was signed by someone named Alex Cable."

"That's Zach's business partner." So, no Zach. Just as well. The last thing in the world she needed was to see him again.

Eight

Zach almost didn't see the guy as he wheeled his Jaguar around the corner on the dark Colorado highway, setting the car up for the turnoff to Craig Mountain. But there he was, hood to his pickup truck propped open, leaning inside in the drizzling rain, feet planted carelessly on the side of the road where somebody could easily clip his legs.

Zach hit the brakes, bringing his car to a halt behind the pickup. He put it in neutral, set the park brake, and left his lights on so nobody else would miss seeing the vehicles. Then he exited his Jag, hiking his suit collar up against the rainy weather.

"Need some help?" he called, extracting his cell phone from his jacket pocket. Hopefully, the cowboy was registered with the auto club.

"I think I've— Ouch! Crap." It was a female voice. "Got it."

He came around the end of the hood. "Abigail?"

She twisted her head to stare incredulously up at him in the gloom.

"What happened?" he asked, keeping his voice even, trying not to react to the shock of seeing her again. She had a grease smudge on her cheek. Her clothes were worn and muddy. And the battered hat on her head was dripping with rainwater.

She'd never looked more gorgeous.

He had to force himself to gaze down into the engine.

"I replaced the fan belt," she informed him, voice unsteady.

But then his eyes focused on a spreading dark patch on her bare forearm. "You're bleeding!" He reflexively reached for her, but then abruptly stopped himself, not wanting to hurt her any further.

She lifted her injured arm and dispassionately inspected the wound. "It'll stop."

"What do you mean, it'll stop?" A stream of blood was trickling off her elbow onto the engine.

"Do you mind cranking the key?"

"Abigail."

"You don't want to help?"

"You've been injured."

"Fine." She extracted herself from under the hood, setting a wrench on the fender and turning for the driver's door. "I'll do it myself."

"Get into my car," he commanded, checking his cell phone, finding no signal.

She kept walking. "The truck will start now."

He followed. "You need medical attention."

"Don't be melodramatic." She opened the door and twisted her arm to get a better look in the glow of the dome light. "A few butterfly bandages will do the trick."

The wound was even worse than he thought. "I am not letting you drive like this."

She swung into the driver's seat. "It's not your decision."

He quickly snagged the key from the ignition.

"Hey," she protested.

Ozzy popped to his feet in the passenger seat and barked once, then wagged his tail at Zach and clambered onto Abigail's lap to get closer.

"Give me back the keys, Zach."

Zach scratched the dog's head. "What's he doing here?"

"He likes road trips. Now give me the keys."

"Not a chance." There was no way in the world he was sending her out injured on a dark, rainy highway.

She gripped the wheel with her good hand, glaring at him in anger. But her mouth was also tense with pain, white at the edges, and sweat had beaded on her forehead. "You can't do this to me."

"What the hell are you trying to prove?" he demanded.

"Nothing."

"That you're tough? Fine. I believe you're tough."

"I'm not trying to prove a thing to you. I couldn't care less what you think of me. I'm trying to get these supplies to the ranch."

He scooped Ozzy from her lap and tucked the pup against his chest. "Not tonight you're not."

She leaned back. "Zach, stop it."

He put his free hand on her shoulder, and tried to keep his voice gentle. "This truck is a stick shift."

"So what?"

"So you need both hands to drive it."

"I have both hands."

"We're thirty minutes from the hospital in Lyndon, or thirty minutes from the paramedic at the Craig Mountain construction site. Which is it going to be?"

"I'm going back to the ranch."

"We're two hours from the ranch."

"There is no we."

"There is right now." Giving up completely on logic and reason, he pocketed her keys, paced back around the front of the truck and slammed the hood with finality. He swore the woman had lost her mind.

He returned to find her eyes closed, teeth gritted, arm limp by her side. Her cheeks had gone a shade paler.

"I'm taking you to the hospital," he announced, trying to figure out how to force her into his car without hurting her.

"Craig Mountain," she retorted, opening her eyes, glaring in defiance.

Fine with him. The job-site paramedic was highly qualified.

"I'm sure they'll have some morphine for the pain and a local anesthetic for the stitches."

She coughed a cold laugh. "I'm a cowboy. All I need is an aspirin and some alcohol."

"For rubbing or ingesting?"

"A little of both."

Impressed by her attempt at humor, he braced his hand firmly beneath her arm. "Come on, partner."

"I'll bleed all over your Jaguar."

"That's why they invented detailing shops."

She eased her way out of the cab. "I don't need stitches."

"How about we let the medical professionals decide that."

"You are so stubborn." But the fight was gone from her voice.

"Yeah," he drawled. "I'm the stubborn one."

They made their way to his running vehicle, and he settled her into the passenger seat, placing Ozzy on the small backseat behind her. Glancing at her arm made him grimace. She had to be in a whole lot of pain.

"This is completely unnecessary," she complained.

"Humor me." He stripped off his suit jacket, tossed it back next to Ozzy. Then he began unbuttoning his cotton shirt.

"What are you— Oh, seriously, Zach. It can wait till we get to the castle."

"I don't think so." He doffed the shirt, bent on one knee and loosely wrapped it over her arm.

"Ever think of becoming a nurse?" she asked.

"Not until now."

"You're very gentle."

"You're very brave."

"It's just a scratch." But she was beginning to shiver.

"Cold?" he asked, worried that it might be a sign of shock.

"Little bit."

He set her arm in her lap then retrieved his jacket, draping it around her shoulders. He turned the heater dial to full, softly latching the door before rounding the hood to get into the driver's side.

"So, how've you been?" he asked as he eased out the clutch and pulled onto the dark highway. "I mean, up until now."

"Fine," she answered, sounding a lot more frustrated than faint. Maybe she wasn't going into shock. "And you?"

"Busy. I guess you must have heard?"

"That you wised up and took my advice? Yes, I had heard that."

"When you're right, you're right," he allowed.

He took the first few turns of the mountain road.

"So you're moving to Lyndon?"

He couldn't identify the emotion in her voice. And, under the circumstances, maybe he was foolish to try. But he would love to know if his moving made her happy? Sad? Ticked off? If she was ticked off, she had no one to blame but herself. It was her idea.

"I am," he told her.

"When did you get to town?"

"Today. Alex has been here for a while. He's taking care of setting up the new head office in Lyndon. I've got some work to do at Craig Mountain."

The pavement abruptly ended, and he hit a pothole on the gravel stretch.

Abigail hissed in a pained breath.

"Sorry."

"No big deal. I also heard it was official. You got the water-license exemption."

Zach was sure the jolt had caused her considerable pain, but there seemed little point in arguing. Maybe discussing his business would take her mind off the injury. "Your plan worked like a charm," he told her. "Thanks for the help."

"No problem."

He couldn't help chuckling at that. "That's not what you said a few weeks ago."

"I'm over it."

"I'm glad to hear that."

She shrugged. "In the end, you made it easy. It was nothing

I said or did. An exemption is an exemption. Anybody could have gotten one by bringing in two hundred jobs."

"I wouldn't have known about the exemption, if not for you."

She cast a sidelong glance his way. "But we're still keeping that our secret, right?"

"Right."

"Along with everything else? There's no expiration date on a blackmail payoff," she confirmed.

"I said yes."

"Just so we're clear."

"We're clear." He paused. "But I didn't think there were official rules for blackmail."

"Honor among thieves."

"We're not thieves."

"We'd've been good at it, though."

He chuckled.

"Trickery, subterfuge, deception and clandestine meetings."

"We'd also have to steal something," he pointed out.

She leaned her head back. "I don't need anything."

"Except medical attention."

"Do we need to steal it?"

"We do not." He nodded out through the windshield. "See those lights up ahead?"

She squinted. "Way up in the trees?"

"They're farther up the mountain. That's the new building for Craig Mountain. The walls are up. The roof is on. And it'll be clad to weather by the end of the week."

"Congratulations."

"There's a long way to go. But so far we're on schedule."

"Did you decide whether or not to do a restaurant?"

He pretty much had, but he hadn't made if official yet. "I'm not sure," he hedged, to keep the conversation going. "What do you think I should do?"

She got a faraway look in her eyes, and her tone softened. "I think people would love to have dinner at the castle."

"Yeah?" he prompted. "Why?"

"It's beautiful, for one thing. And the place has enormous

potential. If I was you, I'd take a bunch of that stuff out of the towers, polish it up and use it to decorate the restaurant."

"Anything in particular?"

"Whatever you want. The paintings, for one thing. The furniture. There were some awesome silver pieces up there, and the dishes. Did you see the dishes?"

Her growing enthusiasm surprised him. He hadn't paid much attention to the stuff in the towers. "Will you show me what you mean?"

"Sure. Seriously, Zach. It could be as much a museum as a restaurant. Imagine the experience you could conjure up for guests. Costumed staff, vintage dishes." She gave an impish grin. "Flagons of mead and ale served by lusty wenches."

He grinned. "I like the way you're thinking."

"You just like the lusty wenches."

"No. I have a thing for your brain."

"Once word got around, the restaurant would practically market itself."

"I'm sold," he told her.

She waved him off. "You don't have to humor me. I'm only suggesting you think about it."

"I have thought about it." He gave in to impulse. "Help me plan it. Help me design it."

She scoffed out a laugh. "Yeah, right."

"Why not?"

"I don't have time."

"What? You need to herd more cows? Shovel more manure? Repair more engines?"

His anger bubbled up as he was reminded of her injured arm. What kind of family sent her out on the highway all alone at night? What was she doing repairing a pickup truck by the side of the road? What the hell else was she up to on the ranch? Bronc riding? Bullfighting?

"Don't go there," she warned.

He gripped the steering wheel, but held his tongue, concentrating on choosing the smoothest path through a series of potholes.

The silence stretched.

"When you're right, you're right," he finally allowed.

Now, if only she'd be smart enough to figure out what was right for her. She was obviously still working as a ranch hand. And she was obviously exhausted by it. There were fatigue lines around her eyes, and she looked thinner than he remembered.

She hadn't deserved to get hurt today. And she shouldn't have been hauling freight on a dark highway in a pickup truck. She had so much more potential than that. And if she wasn't in so much pain, he'd tell her so.

"I apologize. Please show me what you liked in the towers. I won't pressure you. I'll simply take any and all advice you care to give."

She eyed him with suspicion. "Are you being nice because I'm hurt?"

"No."

She pursed her lips in obvious disbelief.

"I'm being nice because I'm nice."

"You are not."

"Am too," he retorted in a childish voice.

"You're a meanie," she mocked.

"You're a tomboy."

She sobered, glancing dubiously down at her dirty jeans. "Okay, well, you're right about that."

He was hit with a sudden jolt of guilt. Why was he picking on her? "You're also very beautiful," he corrected himself.

"Oh, don't kid-glove me, Zach. I'm not hurt all that bad."

"Well, you really are all that beautiful."

"I'm covered in grease."

"Doesn't matter. It's not something you can hide with grease."

She shifted in her seat, grimacing and cradling her arm. "Can we stop arguing?"

"Absolutely."

"I mean it."

"I'm *agreeing* with you."

"Okay." But her tone was cautious.

"Take a look up there." He nodded through the windshield

again, to where the lights were growing stronger through the trees. "Wait till you see how much work they've done on the brewery."

Abigail had tried to convince Zach to take her on a quick tour of the impressive new building. But he was adamant that they go directly to the medical trailer and let somebody look at her arm.

Despite herself, by the time the paramedic finished cleaning her up, she was feeling woozy. She'd said yes to the stitches, but no to the painkillers. After the medic finished, her forearm was covered in a thick layer of gauze and also a thin plastic bag to keep it dry. Zach escorted her to his suite in the castle and insisted she take a hot shower. When she looked in the mirror, she realized why.

Her hair was full of dirt and specks of rust from the inside of the truck's hood. Her hands and face were smeared with grease, while her clothes were damp and dusty.

"Wow," she whispered to her reflection. "Way to impress the guy, Abby."

Then she shook her head at the hopelessness of the situation. What did she care what she looked like in front of him? He knew she was a cowboy, and all they ever did was fight. And it wasn't as though he'd even bothered to tell her he was coming to town. No. They were living different lives again. She was focused on her family, and he was focused on his. Difference was, she understood his commitment. He absolutely refused to see the worth of hers.

Good to know where she stood.

Then again, for now, it would also be good to get clean. Wallowing in self-pity wasn't going to get her anywhere.

She twisted on the ancient taps and stripped off her clothes. She was careful of the water, washing her hair and scrubbing her face with one hand, while holding the other up, out of the stream. The hot water helped ease some of the tension from her body. And she was thinking about what to tell Travis as she dried awkwardly off and wrapped herself in Zach's voluminous, cream-colored robe.

She combed through her wet hair and stepped out of the bathroom, directly into the small living area.

"She wouldn't let me take her to the hospital," Zach was saying into his phone. He sat in an armchair, Ozzy on his lap.

Abigail moved to the small Queen Anne sofa next to him, frowning as she sat down. Who was he talking to about her?

"Not tonight, for sure," he said.

"Who is that?" she mouthed.

"Travis," Zach mouthed silently in return.

Her eyes went wide. "What?" she hissed. Why had he called Travis? *How* had he called Travis?

"You want to talk to her?" Zach asked into the phone. Then he paused. "Sure." He rose and held out the phone, her phone, she realized. That explained how he got the number.

"What did you do?" she muttered as she reached for it.

"Let him know you weren't dead," Zach whispered back.

She glared at Zach while she moved the phone to her ear.

"Travis," she chirped in a cheerful voice.

"You okay?" asked her brother from the other end of the line.

"Perfect."

"How's the arm?"

"Couple of stitches. No big deal."

Zach frowned, and she waggled her finger at him to warn him off.

"Good to hear," said Travis. "I guess you're not coming home tonight."

Abigail glanced at the clock on the mantel. It was nearly ten. "Tomorrow," she told her brother.

"I can send someone for the truck."

"Not necessary. I can drive it home in the morning."

"You sure?"

"I'm sure." With the topical anesthetic wearing off, her arm was beginning to throb, but it would take more than that for her to go into damsel-in-distress mode. "Sorry if Zach exaggerated," she told Travis.

"It was good to get the information."

"I would have called you myself," she said, more for Zach's benefit than hers.

"He was just being neighborly."

"Right." If Travis had any idea just how neighborly Zach had been with her in the past, this would be an entirely different conversation.

"You sure you're okay?" Travis asked.

"Perfect. I'll talk to you in the morning."

"Bye, Abby."

She pressed the end button with her thumb. "Why did you do that?" she asked Zach.

"I thought it would be one less thing for you to worry about." His gaze was steady, sincere.

"You weren't worried he was still ticked off at you?"

Zach shook his head. "You said it yourself. It was an exemption. That rule applies to everyone. And your brother doesn't know you helped me." Zach paused, his expression inscrutable. "Travis thinks he won our last fight, and I went away."

She thought about taking Zach to task again for making her lie to her family, but she honestly didn't have the energy. The throbbing in her arm was growing worse. She wished she'd said yes to the painkillers the medic offered. "Travis thought you were being neighborly."

"I am. How's your arm?"

"It's fine." She set the phone down on an end table, resisting the urge to cradle her injury. She hoped it didn't keep her awake tonight.

"I won't think any less of you because you feel pain, you know."

"I know that."

"Good. Then let's try that again. Abby, how's your arm?"

"It's sore," she admitted, tossing back her damp hair and raising her chin. "Can we move on now?"

He gave what looked like a reluctant smile. "Yeah. We can move on. Shot of whiskey, cowboy?"

"Sure. Why not."

He rose smoothly to his feet. "I've got a thirty-year-old Glenlivet." He opened a cupboard in the small kitchen alcove. "That ought to be in keeping with the theme of our surroundings."

It sounded good to Abigail. She hoped he made it a double.

"On the rocks?" he asked, setting two short, crystal glasses on the countertop.

"Please."

The ice cubes clinked, and the cork made a hollow popping sound as he pulled it out of the bottle. She watched as he poured the amber liquid over the small ice cubes. It looked like at least a double. Good. That would help her sleep.

He lifted both glasses and turned. "Do you think it would compromise beer sales if we were to offer scotch whiskey at the restaurant?"

"I think most customers would like to have the choice," she answered.

"Me, too." He handed her one of the glasses then sat back down in the armchair. "I liked your idea about flagons of ale. I think we could do a lot with a historic theme." He swirled his glass and inhaled appreciatively. Then he took a first sip.

Abigail followed suit. The liquid burned her throat, but in a good way, and she appreciated the warmth that radiated out into her bloodstream. She took a second sip. This was going to feel very good on her arm.

"Alex has always been a bit of a scotch aficionado," Zach continued. "He got me into it, too. There's no reason why we couldn't make that a specialty, maybe do a bit of recon through Scotland, check out some of the lesser-known distilleries, the rarer brands."

Abigail found herself nodding. What a fantastic job that would be. And what a fun addition to the restaurant. She took another sip. It had taken her a while to develop a taste for scotch, but now that she had, she found it a very satisfying and civilized beverage.

"If you feel up to it tomorrow, will you help me hunt through the upper floors?"

"I have to get back to the ranch." Though, at the moment, driving the stick shift didn't sound very appealing.

"A hundred different people can drive the truck to the ranch," said Zach. "You're the only one who has a vision for my restaurant."

Though she knew he was only being kind, her heart warmed at the compliment. She did have a vision for his restaurant. At least, she had a vision that she liked. There was no way to know if anyone else would like it. Staying definitely sounded more appealing than going.

Then again, staying anywhere lately sounded more appealing to her than going home to the ranch. She didn't know whether she'd become spoiled or lazy. But she needed to get past that.

"I really have to go home," she told him, knowing there was a trace of apology in her tone.

"Let's play it by ear." He swirled his drink.

Good enough.

She knew she wasn't going to change her mind, but she could always tell him that in the morning.

She lifted her glass to her lips and realized she'd emptied it.

"Went down good?" he asked.

"Too good," she acknowledged.

"Refill?"

She shook her head. She was already pleasantly woozy, and more than a little tired.

"You want to lie down?"

"I should try to sleep," she admitted, coming to her feet. "Down the hall?" she asked, remembering there were a couple of smaller bedrooms between the suite and the back staircase.

He rose with her. "Take my bed."

"Oh, no, no, no." She shook her head.

"Give me a break. I mean you should sleep in it alone. You've got the bathroom here, and it's comfortable—"

"I'll be fine anywhere. I've slept beside campfires and in line shacks half my life."

He moved toward her. "Good for you. But not when you're hurt. And not on my watch."

"I'm not made of spun glass, Zach."

"Really? Could have fooled me, cowboy." His arm encircled her shoulder. "What with all your pouting, impatience and temper tantrums."

"Stop mocking me."

He urged her away from the couch, while Ozzy settled himself in the warm spot she'd left behind. "Humor me. Please. I'll feel like a cad if I send you to a cold bedroom down the hall while I snuggle in here."

She couldn't help chuckling. "Snuggle?"

Once he had her walking, he steered her to the bed. "Yes. I want you to snuggle." He pulled back the covers.

"Fine," she reluctantly agreed. She was here. She was tired. She was sore. If he was going to insist, she'd bloody well sleep in his bed.

She sat down on the crisp sheet, and the robe slipped off her knee. After a moment, she was aware of Zach's still silence. She glanced up at him.

"What happened?" he demanded.

She followed the direction of his gaze, coming to a purple, half-healed bruise on the middle of her thigh.

"Oh, that." She covered it up with the robe. "I was painting the other day. I tripped halfway down the ladder and smacked into one of the rails."

"You were painting a house?"

"A shed."

"And you fell down a ladder?"

"It wasn't a big deal." Embarrassed that he was going to think she was a hopeless klutz, she pulled her legs up onto the bed, curling them under the covers.

"And this?" he asked.

Too late, she realized the robe had fallen off her shoulder. Zach's thumb traced a barely visible bruise on the tip.

"Pulling a horseshoe."

"Oh, Doll-Face." He sighed.

Before she knew what was happening, he'd leaned in and kissed the fading bruise.

"Zach," she warned.

"Scoot over."

They couldn't do this. *She* couldn't do this. No matter how much she might think she wanted to do this.

"I can't," she managed to say.

"That's not what I meant. You're hurt. You're tired. You're a little drunk."

"I'm not drunk."

"I gave you a lot of scotch."

"It helped."

"That was the point."

"But I'm not drunk."

"I just want to hold you." He eased her to the middle of the bed. "Just for a few minutes."

"Why?" she asked with suspicion, holding herself stiff.

He stretched out beside her. "I don't know." He circled an arm around her, but stopped before he touched her. "Any other sore spots I should know about?"

"My ribs," she answered before she thought it through. She probably should have kept that to herself.

His expression darkened. "What happened to your ribs?"

"I came off a horse. It happens a lot."

He closed his eyes for a long second, but then his arm curled ever so gently around her stomach. "It never happens to me."

She couldn't help smiling at that. The warmth of his arm felt very good against her stomach. As her body relaxed, he put his own head down on the pillow.

"You need to find a safer job," he muttered.

"I need to find someone who won't fight with me all the time."

"Can't argue with that."

"Well, *there's* a first."

Abigail awoke in Zach's arms. There was no way to tell how long he'd stayed with her last night. The whiskey had put her into a sound sleep, and this morning he was showered and changed, lying on top of the quilt, while she was tucked underneath it.

"Morning," he intoned in a deep, lazy voice, smoothing her hair back from her forehead.

"What time is it?" She stifled a yawn.

"Nearly nine."

"Nine?" She started to sit up, but a jolt of pain shot through her arm. She gritted her teeth, just barely controlling an outburst. "I have to call Travis."

"I already did."

"Excuse me?" She must have misunderstood.

"I called Travis. He's sending someone out to the highway to pick up the truck."

Abigail struggled to a sitting position, using her good arm to hold the covers across her chest where the robe had come open while she slept. "You had no right to do that."

"You're definitely in no shape to drive home."

She groaned out a frustrated exclamation.

"Hungry?" he asked.

"I don't even know what to say to that."

"Yes?"

"Since when did you become Travis's best friend?"

"I told him about the stitches."

"He already knew I had stitches."

"You downplayed it. And we agreed it would be better for you to wait a day or two before going back to work."

"What is *wrong* with you?"

"He offered to come and pick you up, but I told him I'd make sure you got home."

"Seriously, Zach. You can't just up and plan another person's life."

"I consulted your family," he defended with a straight face.

"That's not the point."

"You've always made it clear their opinion was important."

"Oh no you don't." She shook her head vigorously. She wasn't about to let him use her family against her. She might love and respect them, but that didn't mean Zach got to do an end run around her own wishes.

He moved to a sitting position, swinging his legs so that his feet rested on the floor. Then he twisted back to look at her. "Do you really want to go home right away?"

Part of her did, and part of her didn't. There was always plenty of bookwork for her to do at the ranch. So she could rest up for a couple of days and still be useful. Then again, Zach had her enthusiastic about the restaurant, and it would be fun to prowl through the castle for a few hours.

"This afternoon would be fine, I guess."

He smiled at that. "I washed your clothes."

Okay, that embarrassed her. "Really?"

"They're on the counter in the bathroom." He stood. "I'll go get us some breakfast. You need anything else? A couple of painkillers?"

"Some aspirin would be nice."

"I can get you something stronger."

"What are you, my dealer?"

He chuckled at that. "I'm just trying to make you comfortable."

She realized that he was. She was the one being surly and antagonistic. All the poor man had done was rescue her from the side of the road, get her medical attention, inform her family and take care of her truckload of ranch supplies, while she was doing nothing but give him grief.

"Aspirin will be fine," she told him, determining to do her best to help him gather some ideas for the restaurant. It was the least she could do to pay him back.

"See you in a couple of minutes."

He left the room with Ozzy at his heels, and by the time she'd freshened up and gotten dressed, the pair of them were back, Zach carrying a tray of coffee and two stacks of delicious-smelling pancakes.

"Where did you get all this?" she asked, taking a seat at the small table. There were two aspirin tablets sitting next to a glass of orange juice, and she popped them into her mouth and washed them down.

"There's a kitchen in the staff area. Staff members do some cooking for lunches and things, since we're so far from any services up here. But, in this case, I got the food from the catering truck set up for the construction site." He sat down across from her, pouring syrup onto his plate of pancakes. "You need any help?"

She bit back the sarcastic retort that formed on her tongue. What was the matter with her? "I'm fine," she answered pleasantly.

He waited a moment before responding. "Good."

"Would you still like some help picking out furniture and things to decorate the restaurant?"

"Absolutely. But only if we don't wear you out."

"You won't wear me out." She cut into her pancakes with the side of her fork, spearing a bite. She'd skipped dinner last night, planning to eat once she got back to the ranch. But after the breakdown, there hadn't been an opportunity. So, this morning, she was famished.

They ate companionably, talking about housing, schools and services available in Lyndon. Abigail had a hard time wrapping her head around the fact that DFB headquarters was moving to Lyndon. And hearing Zach talk, she realized just how complex an undertaking it would be. They had lawyers, accountants and real estate agents working overtime. It was a major disruption to the lives of all his employees.

Listening, she found herself feeling guilty for having pushed the move on him. Then again, there really wasn't another solution to expand Craig Mountain Brewery. And if the expansion was as important as Zach made it out to be, then she'd provided the only solution possible.

They finished breakfast and headed for the north tower. She'd already been up in the center tower. It was easily accessed by a half flight of stairs from the fourth floor. The north tower was a little tougher to access. They made their way to the rear service area, where they came to a narrow, curving, stone staircase that spiraled up in a dim passage. Ozzy gazed up the stairs as if considering his options, then, evidently having decided to skip the climb, settled on a worn, padded bench seat in the stream of sunshine from a recessed window. He wasn't the most athletic dog in the world.

"You're not planning to imprison me up here, are you?" Abigail couldn't help joking as she and Zach made their way up.

"It'd be perfect for that, wouldn't it?" he said over his shoulder.

"If you ever had a fantasy about being an evil count, this would definitely be the place to act it out."

"Scream as loud as you like, sweet darling," he intoned in a dramatic, dire voice. "No one will ever hear you."

"I wonder why they built it this way." She couldn't see any particular use for a room this inaccessible.

"According to Lucas, Lord Ashton modeled the entire castle after one his family owned back in Britain."

"Either that, or he had a crazy wife he needed to imprison."

"That would be my second guess." Zach stopped at the top of the steep staircase, bracing his shoulder against a thick, rough-hewn, oak door.

"I hope she's not still in there," Abigail joked as the hinges squeaked.

"I don't think anyone's been up here in fifty years," said Zach.

"Seriously?" Now she was really curious.

"I'm joking. Apparently they clean up here periodically."

She socked him in the back. "Not funny."

"I wasn't really spooking you, was I?"

"No." Well, not exactly. Coming across the skeletal remains of someone's long-dead, imprisoned, insane wife—now, *that* would have truly spooked her.

The door opened to reveal a surprisingly brightly lit room. It was wide and round, with an abnormally high ceiling and at least a dozen lead-paned windows recessed into the stone walls. The air was still, warm and musty, and most of the contents of the room were boxed in cardboard or aging wooden trunks. It didn't seem to have antique furniture like the center tower and some of the other upstairs rooms. She supposed nobody would want to carry a dresser or cabinet up that staircase.

"I can't even imagine what's inside all these." She glanced around, feeling like a kid on Christmas morning.

Zach pushed his shoulder gently against hers. "Have at 'er. All this is the property of DFB Incorporated." Then he took the easiest pathway through the boxes to one of the windows, pushing it open and letting in a welcome breeze.

She zeroed in on the trunk that looked the oldest. There, she crouched down on her knees, popped open the center latch, flipped the two end catches and eased up the lid.

Zach squatted beside her. "What did you find?"

"Candleholders." She pushed wads of yellowed newspaper to one side, lifting the first of a matched set of ornate, thickly tarnished silver candleholders. It was heavy in her hand, and Zach took it from her, lifting it and the other, and setting the pair on the floor between them.

"And serving trays," she announced, leaning over the edge of the trunk and digging deeper. To her delight, she also found a tea service and a velvet-lined, mahogany chest of silverware.

"This is great stuff," she enthused, reaching into the depths of the chest.

"Be careful feeling around in there," Zach advised. He reached to the very back of the trunk and pulled out a long, silver object. Rising, he revealed a sheathed sword. He took a step back and withdrew the blade.

Abigail turned, taking the burden off her knees by sitting down. She leaned against the side of the trunk as she gazed up at the sharp, jeweled-hilt sword. It was pretty impressive. Then again, it might be the man brandishing it who was impressive. "That would go great on the restaurant wall."

He stepped back, swishing the blade through the air. "Lord Ashton…" He whistled. "What did you get up to?"

Abigail chuckled. "I hope we find a diary, or some letters or something. I'd love to know more about these people. Hey." She had a sudden idea. "What if we used an old-English-script motif for the menus? We could go with parchment and leather bindings."

"Sure," he agreed, carefully replacing the sword in its sheath. "We'll do them however you want."

She couldn't help feeling pleased by his approval.

He set the sword aside and again peered into the crate. "Here we go."

"What is it?"

"The other sword. It's a matched set. I guess when you challenge someone to a duel, you're obligated to offer evenly matched weapons."

"Or it could be a spare," she reasoned. "Do you think Lord Ashton had a shield to go with them?"

"Not in this trunk." It was obvious they'd come to the paper-lined bottom. "But let's open another."

Nine

Zach watched Abigail's slow smile as, one by one, she unveiled the watercolors they'd discovered behind a canvas sheet against one wall of the north tower. He was content to stand back and observe her reaction to the paintings. Time had slipped away while they worked. Midafternoon, and they were now surrounded by treasures both valuable and absurd. He had no desire and no intention of reminding her that it was getting late.

She favored her left hand as she awkwardly lifted one of the larger paintings. He quickly stepped up and took it away, positioning it so that she could get a better look. It was the view from the cliff beyond Lord Ashton's statue, a man standing in the foreground on a sunny summer day, with Lake Patricia and its two small islands as the backdrop.

"Whoever painted these did a really good job," Abigail observed.

Zach squinted down in front of himself, trying to make out the scrawled signature in the bottom corner. "E. Ashton." At least that's what it looked like to him.

Abigail stepped around the clutter on the floor, dusting off her jeans with one hand as she moved. "E. Ashton," she confirmed.

"Lord Ashton's wife was named Elise."

"I guess she must be the artist. Elise's paintings are *definitely* going on the walls of the restaurant."

"Whatever you say." Zach couldn't keep his gaze from Abigail.

There was a smudge of dust on her smooth cheek. Her eyes were deep gold in the streaming sunshine. Her lips were full and dark, and her mussed hair framed her face like a halo.

"You're beautiful," he breathed.

"Sarcasm?" she returned without missing a beat.

"I'm dead serious." Despite her family's obvious attempts to turn her into some latter-day Cinderella laborer, he'd never met any woman who could hold a candle to her.

"I'm dirty and sweaty, and I haven't worn makeup in two weeks." She held up her blunt, unadorned fingernails. "Look at these."

Setting aside the painting, he reached forward and took her hand, giving in to impulse and gently kissing at her knuckles.

"Doesn't matter," he told her. "They can't erase your beauty."

She fluttered her long lashes. "You're starting to sound like a courtly Lord Ashton."

"I'm beginning to like Lord Ashton."

"I bet he danced a mean quadrille."

Zach lifted her hand and spun Abigail in a pirouette, earning a grin. "He strikes me as more of the pheasant-hunting type. Or maybe wild boar."

"Wild boar?"

"Isn't that what they do in England?"

"I think they go fox hunting. In those tight little red suits. Quite the dandies back then."

"I suppose," he allowed. "I mean, when he wasn't busy loading a cannon or fighting a duel."

"Over the honor of a lady?"

"What other reason would there be to fight a duel?"

"Would you fight for my honor?"

"In a heartbeat." He sobered, his voice going husky, using their joined hands to draw her close.

She didn't pull away, but fear clouded her expression.

"Don't look so scared."

"I'm not scared."

"Good." He couldn't resist brushing a smudge of dust from her cheek.

"Zach?"

"Relax."

"That seems unlikely."

"Let's stop time again."

She went still. "I don't think—"

"I don't mean jump back into bed," he quickly assured her.

"Yes, you do," she countered.

She was right about that, but he wasn't going to press her. "I mean you should stay here. For a couple of days. Help me put together some ideas for the restaurant."

"I told Travis I'd come home today."

"Call him back and tell him you've changed your mind."

"They need me—"

"I know they need you. And I know you love them. And they can have you back. But not yet. Stay here with me and heal." He searched his brain for something else to say, some other argument that might sway her.

He realized that he couldn't bear to let her go back to the ranch while she was still injured. He wanted her here, with him. And, yes, he wanted to sleep with her. He wanted to pull her into his arms and never let her go. But he'd take her with or without lovemaking. He'd take her however he could get her.

She drew a breath. "I don't need to hide to take a few days off. There's some office work at the ranch that I can—"

"Stay, Doll-Face." He gazed deeply into her eyes, all out of reasonable arguments. "Just... Stay."

She was silent for what seemed like an eternity. "Okay," the word whispered out. "For a couple of days."

The tension rushed from his body, and his hand tightened around hers.

He tried to fight the impulse, but he couldn't resist brushing a tender kiss across her soft lips.

The tenderness didn't last. Passion leaped to life inside him, shattering his control. He deepened the kiss, parting her lips, releasing her hand to snake his arm around the small of her back. He reveled in the satisfying feeling of her curves pressed against his taut body. He'd missed her so much, he could barely stand it.

And he wanted more.

He wanted her naked.

He wanted to make love to her so badly that he was nearly shaking with need.

But that wasn't fair. He forced himself to pull back. He let her go, refusing to take advantage of the situation and risk hurting her.

"The west hall," he managed to say.

She blinked at him in obvious confusion, her pupils dilated, lips parted, dark and moist. "Huh?"

He mustered his strength and focused. "We should go look at the west hall. See if it's big enough for the restaurant. I like the high ceilings, and the archways. If it's too small, we could include the mezzanine level. It wraps around the main hall, one story above." Zach knew he was babbling, but it was either that or haul her back into his arms and make love to her on the stone floor, or maybe up against the curved wall, or on one of its long trunks.

Damn it. He had to stop letting his mind wander like that.

"The west hall?" he repeated with a steely will. "We can go down there and take a look." He waited for her response, inordinately proud of his self-control.

She tipped her head to one side, her soft brows going up. "Or," she proposed in a perfectly reasonable tone, "we can stay up here and have sex."

His jaw dropped.

She eased in closer, coming up against him, a sultry smile growing on her face. "Come on, Zach. We both know that's why I'm staying."

"There's more to it than that." There was much more to it than that. Abigail wasn't just about sex to him.

She leaned a cheek against the front of his shirt. "I suppose there's the restaurant. That'll be fun, too."

"Abby," he protested. "I'm not asking you to—"

"I'm just sayin'." She walked her fingertips up his chest. "We can have a quickie now and then concentrate on the restaurant for the rest of the afternoon. Or we can pretend to work, while doing nothing but lusting after each other for the next few hours."

Zach was honestly speechless. The woman was one in a million. No, one in a billion. How many people out there were so forthright and pragmatic? He'd swear she didn't have a manipulative bone in her body.

He put his arms around her and tugged her flush against him. "My room?"

"What's wrong with here?"

"Nothing."

"Good. It'll be more efficient."

"Efficient? That's your priority?"

"A girl gets more done that way."

Chuckling, he popped the snap on her jeans, released the zipper and whisked the denim and her panties down her legs. Then he lifted her and set her on top of a waist-high trunk in one smooth motion.

"Happy to help this girl get things done," he drawled.

She kicked off her boots and got out of her jeans, while he shucked his own pants.

As soon as he was done, she put her hands on his hips and pulled him between her legs. She met his lips in an open-mouthed, carnal kiss that went on and on.

Then she wriggled forward, and their bodies met in intimacy.

"Condom," she prompted.

"Wait a minute, don't you want—"

"What?"

Didn't she want foreplay, soft words, hugs and sexy whispers?

In answer, she braced herself on her elbows, and her legs slipped up to his waist, solidifying the angle between them.

Okay. Apparently not.

"You always this slow on the uptake, Lucky?"

He tore open the condom. "You always this impatient?"

"Never."

"So, it's just me?"

"It's just you."

"Should I be flattered?"

"Absolutely. I'm usually a very deliberate, methodical person."

Taking her at her word, he pressed fully inside.

Her eyes fluttered closed. Her head tipped back, revealing her slender neck. She moaned.

"Good," he agreed, his own voice guttural, mouth going to her neck to taste the delicate skin.

"So good." She arched toward him.

Zach wasted no time. He cupped her bottom with his other hand, pulled her against him, moving immediately into a solid rhythm. Then he stripped off her T-shirt, popped the clasp of her bra and tore off his own shirt, scattering the buttons in his impatience. He needed to feel her hot skin against his, all the length of their bodies.

He inhaled her scent, tasted her sweet lips, cupped her breasts, bringing first one nipple then the other to a beaded point. Her nails dug into his back, her thighs tightened around him. Arousal was like a freight train inside his brain, moving at full speed. There was no stopping it, and there was definitely no turning back.

Abby obviously felt it, too.

He sped up, and she met him thrust for thrust. Her head sank back, and he kissed her neck again, her shoulders, her breasts. His subconscious took over, body arching and withdrawing in a primal rhythm. Her gasps grew higher and shriller, until the contractions of her body sent him completely over the edge.

He locked his knees, stabilizing them both, until the waves of pleasure dissipated. When the strength came back into his muscles, he lifted her, turning her onto his lap, perching himself on the trunk to give his legs a reprieve.

"That wasn't exactly fast," she gasped.

"Complaining?"

"No. But it's a fact, once we get going, we don't seem to want to stop."

He touched his forehead to hers. "I don't ever want to stop."

Her grin was blurry so close to his eyes.

"Maybe long enough to plan a restaurant," she said.

"Maybe long enough for a shower and dinner." Forget the restaurant. They could plan it any old time. Right now, he wanted her in his bed as soon as humanly possible.

"Don't be a slacker, Zach."

A laugh rumbled through him, bringing him partway back to reality. "Nobody's ever accused me of that before."

"It's barely four o'clock. We've got half the day left."

"How late do you usually work?"

"Eight, sometimes nine. It depends."

"You need to join a union or something."

"I'm one of the ranch owners."

"Well, the other ranch owners are taking advantage of you."

"They're working just as hard."

"Most of them left, Abigail."

"You mad at me?"

He drew back in surprise. "No."

"You haven't called me Abigail in a while."

He gazed into her eyes. "I'm not mad at you, Doll-Face. I—" He stopped himself. What the hell had almost popped out of his mouth? "Like you a lot," he finished.

It was true. He liked her. A whole lot. She was so fresh and fun and unpredictable.

"I like you, too, Lucky. But we have a restaurant to plan."

"You'll sleep with me tonight?" he confirmed.

She molded more closely against him. "I'll sleep with you tonight."

His body shuddered in intense relief. He might have missed sleeping with her even more than making love with her. Tonight, she'd lay naked in his arms for hours and hours. Her warm, supple body would wrap around his. He'd sleep deeply, and wake up to her scent, her touch and her voice, knowing she was safe, knowing she was cared for, knowing nothing could harm her as long as he was there.

Abigail knew she was being utterly self-indulgent. She'd been at Craig Mountain for three days now, sleeping with Zach at night, and undertaking what felt like a dream job of planning his restaurant during the day. He was busy with DFB work, either out in the brewery, with the construction contractor, on the phone with Houston or, today, working with Alex who had arrived in person last night.

She'd quickly figured out that Zach was content to leave the restaurant planning entirely in her hands. She dived into the research, contacting other theme restaurants across the country, even recruiting a manager, who'd suggested a head chef. From the west hall today, she was calling graphic design firms and interior decorators, looking for some expertise in putting together themes and branding.

"There you are" came Seth's unexpected voice.

She jolted back in surprise, seeing her brother strolling into the cavernous hall.

"What on earth are you doing here?" she called out.

"I could ask you the same question." His footfalls echoed on the stone floor of the mostly empty room.

She came to her feet, pushing back the big chair. She'd set herself up with a laptop, printer and telephone on what was likely once the master's dining table. It was ornately carved mahogany, with pedestal legs and at least two dozen matching chairs. Right now, it was covered with everything from architectural drawings to fabric swatches and knickknacks from the tower rooms.

"I'm getting better," she answered as Seth made it to her, pulling her into a hug.

"Glad to hear it." He let her go, glancing meaningfully at the cluttered table. "You convalescing or running a business?"

She waved a dismissive hand over the work supplies, swallowing her guilt over focusing on Zach's project instead of her family. "I'm just offering my opinion on a few things."

"Hmm." Seth looked skeptical.

"What's up with you?" she said, changing the topic. "How are things in the mayor's office?" And what was he doing at Craig Mountain?

"Same old, same old," Seth answered, strolling around the table, glancing more closely at her work. "Travis said he'd talked to you yesterday."

"I'll probably head home tomorrow," Abigail found herself saying. "Or maybe the next day."

Seth took in the bandage on her arm. "How's the wound doing?"

"Getting better and better." She moved back to her chair, motioning for Seth to sit in another of the velvet-upholstered dining armchairs.

He took his seat slowly, bracing his hands on the carved, mahogany arms. "So, little sister, what's with this Zach guy?"

She tried to gauge his expression, but he was too good at keeping a poker face. "What do you mean?"

"You want me to be blunt?"

"Please, be blunt." She braced herself.

"Who is he to you? Why are you here instead of at home?"

Abigail gave a studied shrug. "He found me at the side of the highway."

"Travis told me."

"My arm was too sore to drive a stick shift."

"That was three days ago."

"Zach's going to drive me back to the ranch soon." Truth was, it was Abigail herself who was putting off going home. She loved it here. Zach was fun and exhilarating and amazing in bed. She found the restaurant project fulfilling, and she was trying to drag it out just as long as she could.

"I can drive you back today."

"That won't be necess—"

"I'm going out to the ranch anyway."

Abigail couldn't think of a single comeback. There was absolutely no logical reason for her to stay at Craig Mountain instead of going back to the ranch with Seth. She could hardly tell her brother she was having a really great fling. And she sure couldn't tell him she wanted to finish planning the restaurant. It could take weeks, even months. But if she left today with Seth, she wouldn't have a chance to give Zach a proper goodbye, to maybe figure out what happened next.

She hoped something happened next. They'd done their best to stop time once again, to steal a little fantasy with each other amongst their divergent lives. And that might be all that was happening here, a longer, but equally temporary, fling. But she truly hoped it wasn't. She liked Zach. She more than liked Zach. She didn't know what it felt to fall head over heels for somebody, but it had to be close to this.

"Abigail?" Seth prompted.

She blinked at her brother, struggling for the words that would buy her a little more time.

Then Lisa's voice interrupted. She came through the same entry Seth had used. "This place is amazing!" She gaped at the high ceiling. "Did you see the grounds?" she asked Seth. "Hey, Abby. How are you doing? The mayor and I are officially checking out the newest business development in the Lyndon area."

Abigail felt a surge of relief at seeing Lisa. Maybe Lisa could help her finesse the situation. Or at least she could help Abigail stall for a bit.

"You should definitely take a tour of the grounds," Abigail told her brother. "While you're here, check out the new brewery construction. It's moving along at record speed."

"I don't need a tour of the grounds," he responded.

"Well, at least look outside. If you take that staircase—" she pointed to the far end of the rectangular room "—you'll get to the mezzanine above. The bay window down at the other end gives you a view of the lake. But if you look north, you can also see most of the construction."

"Go take a look," Lisa prompted, grasping the back of Seth's chair. "You should at least see the lake and the statue of Lord Ashton."

Seth kept his gaze fixed on Abigail. "Travis doesn't know what to think of this guy."

Abigail met his eyes. "That's because Travis doesn't know him."

"Neither do you."

"I know enough."

"What are you saying?"

"Seth?" Lisa intoned from behind him. "Quit giving your sister the third degree."

"She's needed at the ranch." Seth still spoke directly to Abigail.

"And I'm coming back," she assured him.

"Good." Seth brought his hands down on his thighs.

"Go look out the window," Lisa prompted.

"Fine." Seth came to his feet, tone turning sarcastic. "I don't know why I employ such a bossy woman."

"Because I'm a smart bossy woman." Lisa immediately slipped into the chair Seth had vacated.

He looked down at her. "You're not coming with me?"

"I just saw the statue and the lake."

With a roll of his eyes and a shake of his head, Seth paced for the staircase.

"What the heck is going on?" Lisa asked Abigail, leaning forward on the table. "You're still with one-night-stand guy?"

"I guess it's a five-night stand."

Lisa gave a half laugh, half gasp.

"And what's with Seth?" Abigail returned. "He's acting so..."

"So like *Seth?*"

Abigail supposed that was true. "Does he know anything about Zach?"

"Travis told him Zach tried to get your help with the water license."

"But he thinks I said no, right?"

"He thinks you said no."

"And he doesn't know Zach blackmailed me into it?"

"No, no. Not the blackmail. And not that the two of you had a one-night stand." Lisa grinned. "Well, five-night stand. But he does know about Zach's initial fight with Travis. And he's pretty ticked off about that."

"You can't tell him the rest," Abigail reminded Lisa.

"I'm never going to tell him the rest."

Seth's footfalls sounded directly above them, and they both glanced reflexively up. Abigail leaned closer in and lowered her voice. "Can you help me out here? I'm not ready to go home yet."

Lisa's eyes lit up. "You falling for this guy?"

"Maybe," Abigail admitted, her face growing warm. "Kind of. Just a little bit."

Lisa's grin grew. "He's living in Lyndon now. So you never know what might happen."

Nothing was going to happen, at least nothing that really counted. Not as long as Abigail supported her family, and not as long as Zach wanted her to let them down. "It's all brand-new. And Travis isn't crazy about him. Now Seth doesn't like him."

Lisa waved a dismissive hand. "You can't please your entire family every minute of the day."

"I'm not pleasing anyone at all right now." Every day she stayed here, she was letting Travis down.

"You're pleasing yourself."

"That's not exactly an admirable character trait."

Lisa gave another shrug. "You're human. Live with it."

"I've seen the lake" came Seth's tense voice as he made his way back down the stairs. "And the statue. Are we ready to head home now?"

Abigail's body went stiff. Surely he didn't mean right this second. She was in the middle of working. And Zach didn't even know she was thinking about leaving today.

"Abby needs to say goodbye," Lisa interjected. "Gather her things, thank Zach for his hospitality."

"So this was a social visit?" Seth's jaw was set, his gray eyes hard as steel.

"Come on." Lisa grabbed Abigail's hand, clearly intending to remove her from Seth's line of fire. "Let's go get your stuff."

Abigail allowed herself to be pulled to standing. She glanced longingly from the sketches to the phone messages to the fabric samples. She wasn't ready to leave. She was waiting on return calls. She was waiting on emails, and more samples, and there was still the south tower to explore. But Travis needed her, and Seth was tapping his foot, looking implacable. And she couldn't come up with a single plausible reason to prolong her stay.

Zach entered the west hall, expecting to find Abigail in her usual spot, expertly juggling the hundreds of details around the restaurant project. Instead, he found a grim-looking man in an expensive suit, glaring daggers at him as he approached.

"Can I help you?" Zach asked, searching his brain for context. Was he a building inspector? A tax collector?

"Seth Jacobs," the man announced without offering his hand. "I want you to explain why the hell you've been blackmailing my sister."

Zach stopped short, eyes narrowing. "You're the mayor?"

"I'm the mayor. Now, start talking."

Zach glanced to the corners of the room. "Where's Abigail?"

"None of your business."

"What did she tell you?" Why would Abigail bring Seth in on the secret? What could possibly have happened while Zach was down at the brewery?

"Also none of your business," Seth snapped. "You don't need to worry about how I know. You just need to worry that I do."

"That's all over and done with." Zach's mind was working quickly, trying to assemble pieces of information.

Did Seth know they'd slept together? Did he know Abigail hated working on the ranch? Was everything out in the open? And what did she expect him to do here?

One thing was certain, until he talked to Abby, he wasn't giving her brother any more information.

"*Nothing's* over and done with in my book." Seth took a menacing step forward. "You come after my sister, you deal with me."

Anger flashed deep in the man's eyes. His jaw was set. His fists were clenched. Despite the business suit, he looked a whole lot like his brother, Travis. They might love their sister, but they sure didn't understand her.

Zach responded in the most reasonable tone he could muster. "What's between Abigail and me is none of your business."

"You blackmailed a member of my family. That is my business."

Zach realized Seth was bluffing. The accusation was too vague. "You don't know what happened, do you?"

"If it was sex, you're a dead man. And we mean that literally in Colorado."

"I'm from Texas," Zach responded with equal determination. "If I blackmailed a woman into having sex with me, I'd stand here while you killed me."

Seth drew back in obvious surprise.

Zach used what he hoped was a conciliatory tone. "It might have started off rocky, but things are fine between Abigail and me."

"Well, they're pretty far from fine between me and you."

"She's not doing a single thing she doesn't want to do."

"So says you."

"It's the truth."

"Forgive me if I don't take the word of a blackmailer."

"Former blackmailer."

"You think you're *funny?* Okay, then laugh about this." Seth pointed his index finger to the center of his chest. "I'm the guy who approves your business license. I'm the guy who approves your zoning. And I'm the guy who approves your parking variance."

A block of lead settled itself in Zach's stomach. The idea that Seth could block DFB's move to Lyndon was sickening.

"Not so funny anymore, is it?" Seth taunted.

"You're blackmailing me?"

"Ironic, isn't it?"

"What do you want?"

"I want you to stay away from Abigail. Forever."

"No." The word burst out of Zach. That was the one thing he couldn't do.

"No?" Seth asked with obvious incredulity. "You *want* me to destroy your business?"

"I want you to let your sister make up her own mind." It was all Zach could do to keep silent about Abigail hating the ranch. "Let her make up her mind about me, and about everything else."

"You didn't let her make up her mind about you. You took that choice away from her, didn't you?"

Zach didn't have an answer for that accusation. Seth had him. Zach had behaved shamefully, and there was no arguing the contrary.

"I'm walking out this door. I'm taking Abigail with me. And if you dare touch my sister, talk to my sister, even look at my sister ever again, I will take you and DFB down so fast and so far, you'll never get out of the hole."

"That's abuse of power," Zach pointed out. Seth could lose his office, possibly go to jail.

"That's protecting my family," Seth countered. "And I know a hundred ways to do it and not get caught. Don't test me, Rainer. I'm holding all the cards."

"I'd never hurt her," Zach told him plainly and levelly.

"You already have."

Once again Zach didn't have an answer. Seth was right. He'd already hurt Abigail. He'd betrayed her trust. He'd coerced her. And everything that had happened since was tainted. Seth was right, and Zach was wrong.

Ironic didn't begin to describe the situation.

He gave Seth a curt nod of acquiescence and left the castle. There was no chance Seth would let him say goodbye. Abigail was gone, out of his life, back to her family. He'd never deserved her in the first place.

After two days of silence from Zach, Abigail's guilt turned to frustration. After four days, her frustration turned to anger.

She'd sent him a text. She'd left him a voice mail. So he knew she'd gone home with Seth. But instead of calling to talk about it, he'd cut her off.

She finally realized this was Zach's way of making her choose. And it had worked. She'd take loyalty over betrayal, her family over a one-night stand, any day of the week.

She hoisted a saddle onto Diamond's back, settling it on the hunter-green blanket. She was home, and this was where she was staying.

"Need any help?" her sister Mandy offered from the opposite side of the hitching post as she slipped the bit into Happy-Joe's mouth.

"My arm's fine," Abigail assured her. The gash was nearly healed. She'd have a scar, but hopefully, it would fade over time.

"You always were a trouper."

"That's nothing unique in the Jacobs family."

Mandy grinned in return. She was dressed in blue jeans and a quilted plaid shirt, her favorite Stetson planted firmly on her head. Abigail had slipped into a pair of old blue jeans this morning, topping them with a faded gray T-shirt and a sturdy denim shirt against the cooling autumn air. Her boots were familiar and comfortable, as were the sights, sounds and smells of the ranch.

She inhaled deeply. It was good to be home.

"The Jacksons put their place up for sale," said Mandy.

"I didn't know that." Abigail waited until Diamond exhaled, then swiftly tightened the cinch.

"Prices are down because of the water licenses but Edward's health has been going downhill, and with no kids to take over, they have no choice." Mandy tucked in the end of the cinch strap and adjusted the stirrups.

Abigail felt a twinge of guilt at the mention of the water licenses. Not that she'd done anything that anyone else couldn't have done. Still, she had helped Zach.

She determinedly placed her booted foot in the stirrup and mounted the horse, pushing the man from her mind. Then she gazed around their vast ranchland, the oat fields rippling, the leaves turning. She tugged on her leather gloves and settled the reins across her palm. "I can't imagine selling."

"I'm not worried about the Jacobs clan." Mandy swung up

into her own saddle. "Between the five of us, I'm liking our chances of coming up with a new generation of ranchers. Even Katrina. With Reed's genes mixed in there, we might get a rancher out of her yet."

Abigail laughed at the joke, but her shoulders felt heavy. Between now and the next generation, everybody would be counting on her.

Her cell phone pulsed three short buzzes in her pocket, signaling a text message. Her mind went immediately to Zach, and she stripped off a glove, digging into the front pocket of her jeans while Diamond started into a walk, falling in beside Happy-Joe.

It was Travis, not Zach. Abigail hated the jolt of disappointment. She was going to get past this stupid infatuation. Her family was her future, not Zach. Even if she didn't produce any babies herself, a new generation of Jacobses running around the ranch would be a wonderful thing.

She read the text. "Travis wants us to check on Testa Springs." As the summer ended, watering holes started to run dry, and the cattle needed to be shifted from place to place.

"Makes sense," said Mandy. "We can take the Buttercup Trail."

Abigail replaced her phone and pulled the glove back on, shifting her seat and focusing on the day. "Diesel went up two cents last week."

Though the Jacobs ranch was prosperous, and her father and grandfather's investments provided a cushion against the ups and downs of ranching, Abigail worried about the others in the valley, particularly those with smaller holdings that had higher overhead and big mortgage payments.

"Are you going to tell me about Craig Mountain?" Mandy switched topics.

The question didn't exactly take Abigail by surprise, but that didn't make her any happier about it. Thinking some more about Zach was the last thing she wanted. But she knew being coy with her sister was only going to prolong the conversation.

And there was no reason to hide it from Mandy. Well, most of it anyway.

"Not much to tell," she said breezily, reminded of the times she'd encourage Mandy to go to Caleb's hotel room to be with him. They'd always been honest with each other about men. "I met a guy. Hurt my arm. We had a fling. And I'm now home again."

Mandy turned to look at her, obviously fighting a grin. "I hate it when you go into so much detail."

"That's all there was to it."

"It's going to be a long ride."

"I know how long the ride is."

"I'm just saying you might want to help the time pass by filling in a few more details."

"They're building a restaurant up at the brewery," Abigail offered.

"I'm more interested in what Zach—it's Zach, right?—in what Zach looks like naked."

"Does your husband know you're wondering about that?"

Mandy laughed. "Was he great? I mean, he must have been great. You stayed up there five days."

And she would have stayed longer if not for Seth. And she'd go back, if not for Zach's stubborn insistence she walk away from her family.

"It was great," she admitted to Mandy. "He's a smart, fun, sexy guy, and he was letting me help him design his restaurant. I liked that," she admitted.

"Why'd you leave?"

"Irreconcilable differences."

"What, over the tablecloths and menu choices?"

"Something like that."

"Abby."

"Can we drop it?" Abigail's tone was sharper than she'd intended.

Mandy went silent. Abigail focused on the sound of the horses breathing and their hooves rustling the grass as they made their way up a slight rise.

Mandy's tone went sympathetic. "Did he break your heart, Abby?"

Abigail's chest tightened, and her throat tingled in reaction. She wanted to be strong, keep the secret to herself. But she needed her sister's shoulder to lean on. "Only a little bit."

They came to the top of the rise, and a vast valley spread out in front of them. Abigail stopped Diamond to take a long look.

"His fault or yours?" Mandy asked softly.

"His. Mostly. Well, mine, too." She had left abruptly with Seth. Maybe she should have told her brother to mind his own business. Maybe she should have stood up to him in that moment and bought herself a few more days with Zach.

"So what are you going to do about it?" Mandy asked.

Abigail shook her head in answer, both to her sister and to herself. "There's nothing I can do."

"You can talk to him. These things never run smoothly. Heaven knows Caleb and I had our share of rocky moments."

"Zach's not Caleb."

"You can still talk to him."

Abigail gripped the saddle horn. There was a catch she couldn't quite keep out of her voice. "I've left messages. He didn't call back."

Without giving Mandy a chance to respond, she kicked Diamond into a trot.

Abigail couldn't seem to get Mandy's words out of her head. Was it better to try to talk to Zach or would a smart woman simply walk away? She couldn't decide. And she was afraid her judgment was clouded by her intense desire to see him again, no matter what the circumstance.

Then again, she reasoned, if her own judgment was clouded, maybe she should go with Mandy's. Mandy was a smart woman. Her advice had been specific and concrete. Abigail should take it. After five miserable days she didn't see how things could get worse.

She knew she could use Ozzy as an excuse to return to Craig Mountain. When she'd left with Seth and Lisa, she hadn't been able to find the puppy. Not surprising, since Ozzy had taken such a shine to Zach. They'd probably been together.

Mind finally made up, she headed for the brewery, easily finding Zach alone in an office.

She breezed in, playing it cool, pretending there hadn't been a seismic shift in their relationship. Half of her hoped he'd pull her into his arms. The other half knew that was a hopeless fantasy.

"I tried to call you," she began, hoping against hope for a simple, logical explanation that would switch everything back to normal.

But instead of answering, he stepped behind the wide desk, obviously putting some distance between them. His expression was guarded. "You shouldn't have come here, Abigail."

Her faint hope fled. "You should have returned my call."

"I didn't want to disturb you. I knew you'd be busy. You've told me what it's like on the ranch." His tone was cool. His eyes were cold.

She wanted to run from the chill, but she forced herself to step closer, coming up against the desk. She gathered her courage. "Is this you pouting?"

"No."

"I didn't pick my family over you."

"I didn't say you did."

"Then why won't you talk to me?"

"We're talking now."

"This isn't talking."

He drew a tight breath. "Trust me, Doll-Face. This is *talking*. And you need to listen." His words dropped like icicles. "It was always going to be temporary between us."

Her lungs went tight, and she couldn't catch her breath.

"And it's over," he finished, and her heart sank like a stone.

She shouldn't have come. She'd completely misjudged the situation. How she wished she'd stayed away. He'd wanted her to leave.

She swallowed hard, a sick feeling bubbling up from the pit

of her stomach. Oh, no. Had he been *waiting* for her to leave? Maybe he'd asked her to stay only out of politeness.

She took a shaky step backward, a chill coming over her body, while humiliation washed through her. The fling had run its course, and she'd embarrassed them both by showing up like this.

She struggled to speak, her voice going small. "I came back to get Ozzy."

Something flashed through Zach's eyes. "Ozzy's fine."

She gathered her pride. "I'm sure you took good care of him, and I thank you for that."

"He can stay."

A fresh flash of pain seared Abigail's chest.

"I don't think he likes the ranch," said Zach.

"He'll get used to the ranch." The puppy was hers, not Zach's.

"Why should he have to do that?"

"Because it's his home. He's my dog, not yours." If she couldn't have Zach, she could at least have Ozzy. She knew her emotions were off kilter, but giving up the puppy suddenly seemed like a final defeat.

"Leave him here, Abby."

Her voice rose. "I want my dog."

"He's more my dog than yours."

"That's not true."

Zach braced his hand on the desktop. "He's happy here. Let him be happy. Why don't you want him to be happy?"

"I do want him to be happy. I want him to be happy with me."

"You Jacobses are all alike," Zach snapped.

"What is that supposed to mean?" He'd barely met any other Jacobses.

"It means…" Zach paused, and for a split second she saw raw pain in his dark eyes. He backed away from her. "It means…"

"Zach?"

His back came flush against the office wall. "You need to leave. Right now."

Her anger immediately vanished, replaced by a hollow loneliness that shattered the last vestiges of her pride. "What did I miss? What happened?"

"Life happened. Your life. My life." He crossed his arms over his chest, and his stare went cold again. "Time started up again, Abby."

Her heart ached, and her stomach clenched. "So you're ending it between us."

"Yes."

"It was a fling, and you're ending it."

"How many ways do I have to say it?"

She tried to laugh, but it didn't quite come off. "I'm sorry. I guess I'm a bit slow on the uptake. I've never done anything like this before."

She'd never had a one-night stand, never had a fling, never fallen in love and had her heart broken.

"I'm sorry," she said again, voice breaking.

"It's all right," Zach returned, without a trace of emotion.

"You can keep Ozzy." Everything Zach had said was true. Ozzy was happier at Craig Mountain. He and Zach should stay together.

"You can take him," Zach unexpectedly offered.

But Abigail shook her head, backing toward the door. She might as well make a clean break of it. She didn't know what she'd expected by coming out here. But she hadn't come after Ozzy. She'd come after Zach.

Zach didn't want her. It had only ever been about sex for him. Well, sex and the water license. And maybe it had only been about the water license. The sex was a bonus. He really was lucky. He got everything he wanted and then some.

She groped for the doorknob, twisting it with a slick palm, letting herself out and rushing back down the hallway, desperate to end this sorry episode of her life.

Ten

Zach was going through his days on autopilot. Though he was far from being an expert, he strongly suspected he'd fallen in love with Abigail. Worse than missing her was the knowledge that he'd hurt her, and he was now powerless to do anything about it. He had to fight with himself every single day to keep from calling to see how she was feeling.

One day he spotted her on Main Street. He nearly called out, but then he saw Travis coming out of the hardware store behind her. He was under no illusion that Travis felt any differently than his brother, Seth. Zach gripped the door handle of his Jaguar, watching her move alongside the ranch pickup truck, wondering if she'd recognize him from this distance, honestly not sure what he would do if she saw him. He didn't think he could bring himself to ignore her.

She was carrying a cardboard box. It was impossible to tell if it was heavy, but the urge to stride down the block and lift it from her arms was overpowering. And then he saw she was limping. He swore from between clenched teeth.

What had happened this time? Had a cow stepped on her foot? Or maybe she'd tripped and twisted an ankle, or come off a horse again, or maybe she'd fallen off a roof. Angry at her, angry at her family, and furious with himself at having abandoned her, he yanked open the driver's door. He slammed his way into the car and peeled out of town.

He brooded in the depths of the castle until Alex caught up with him in his suite that night.

"Missed you at the meeting this afternoon," Alex said easily, but his expression was watchful as he crossed the room, taking a spot on the sofa.

"Got busy," Zach responded vaguely, not wanting to talk about his abrupt departure from Lyndon. He rose and made his way to the makeshift bar to pour them each a scotch.

"No big deal," said Alex, letting it go. "Accounting wants a new software package. Ariel-something. They say it'll pay for itself in staff savings within the next couple of years."

Zach collected the drinks and turned back. "Did you okay it?"

"Wanted to run it by you first."

Zach walked over to Alex and handed him his drink. "Whatever you think."

"I think yes."

"Good enough." Zach sat himself down.

Ozzy immediately waddled over, dropped onto his rear end and whimpered at Zach's feet. Zach automatically scooped the puppy up into his lap.

"Laziest dog in the world," Alex mused.

"He's not lazy."

"He can't even be bothered to jump into your lap."

"He's not lazy. Give the little guy a break."

Alex chuckled.

Annoyed, Zach stared levelly at his friend. "They were going to put him down. Because he's imperfect, and nobody wanted him. You know what that's like."

Alex took a sip of his scotch. "I do know what that's like. But I don't think he should use it as a crutch for the rest of his life."

"One of his legs is shorter than the other," Zach felt compelled to explain. "And he's blind in one eye. It's hard for him to jump."

"He'll never learn if you don't make him try."

"He is trying," said Zach, anger percolating inside him. "I can tell he's trying. But he's not cut out for jumping. He's not cut out to be some robust ranch hand, running after cattle and horses."

"Ranch hand?"

"He'll get hurt." The day's frustrations clouded Zach's brain, coalescing into outright anger. "He might even get killed. And the people who claim to love her should stop putting her in danger."

Alex peered over the rim of his glass. "Her?"

"Huh?"

"You said her."

Zach gave himself a shake. "I meant him."

"You said her."

Zach downed his drink in one swallow. "He's just a little puppy. I'm going to take care of him. So sue me."

Alex rocked back. "Okay, Zach. What the hell's going on?"

"Nothing."

"You're all bottled up."

"I've been working hard, and I'm tired. We're all tired."

"Bull," said Alex. "You love this stuff. When things get frantic and risky, you love it even more."

"I hate it." Zach hated everything today. He hated uprooting their headquarters. He hated moving halfway across the country. And he especially hated depending on Seth Jacobs. If he didn't need to set DFB up in Lyndon, nobody, *nobody* would stop him from going to Abigail.

Alex was silent for a long minute. He polished off his own drink. "It's her, isn't it?"

Zach tried to take another drink, but his glass was empty, nothing but a sip of melted ice on the bottom. "I don't know what you're talking about."

"You've been on edge since Abigail left."

Zach gave a grunt of disagreement.

"Why don't you call her?"

Zach would like nothing better than to call her. "Not gonna happen."

"I know what you're going through. I've been there with Stephanie. You're going to feel like this until you call her."

"I can't call her."

"I know you *think* you can't call her. But, believe me, you can. You'll get used to the indignity that comes with having a girlfriend."

"You think this is about my dignity?" Zach scoffed. If it had been that simple, he'd have kept her here when she came back for Ozzy. No, that wasn't true. If it had been as simple as his dignity, he'd have never let her leave in the first place.

"What else would it be about?" Alex asked.

Zach wasn't a heart-to-heart kind of guy, but he was too tired to fight it tonight, too tired to do anything but admit the truth.

"It's about you," he admitted to Alex. "You and DFB and everybody else. If it was just about me, I'd do whatever it took. In a heartbeat. Anything."

"You're in love with her," Alex stated.

"Absolutely." There wasn't a doubt in Zach's mind.

Alex rose, crossed the floor and retrieved the scotch bottle. He poured a measure into each glass. "Then it's not about me."

Zach contemplated the new drink, a sense of eerie calm coming over him as his mind went places he never could have imagined. "How would you feel about starting over?" he asked softly.

Alex sat back down. "Starting over how?"

"You and me, in a cheap basement suite, working as bartenders again while we save up a down payment for another business."

"Not great," said Alex. "But I'd do it. Why?"

Zach hesitated a moment longer. "Because her brother threatened me."

Alex was clearly confused. "Threatened you with what?"

Zach set the glass down. "The mayor told me that if I ever so much as spoke to his sister again, he'd turn down our business license and make it impossible for DFB to operate in Lyndon."

"Why?"

"He thinks he's protecting Abigail. He knows I blackmailed her. I imagine he thinks I coerced her into sleeping with me."

Alex stared reflexively into space, and the minutes ticked by.

Zach knew he'd put his friend in an impossible position. He was sorry about that. But he didn't think he could bring himself to abandon Abigail.

When Alex finally spoke, there was a thread of laughter in his voice. "He actually forced you to choose between her and me?"

"He did."

"And you chose me? I'm flattered, Zach. But…you're an idiot."

"Choosing her would have destroyed the company."

"You're still an idiot."

"Are you saying I should have turned him down?" Zach challenged.

"I'm saying, for starters, you should have told me we were being blackmailed."

"Yeah," Zach was forced to agree. "I should have told you that."

How many other mistakes had he made in all this? He found himself picturing Abigail in his robe, the night he'd rescued her from the highway, her bandaged arm, the fading bruises, her sore rib cage. His stomach churned.

"I can't leave her there, Alex. It's not right. She's not happy. The work's dangerous. I'm afraid it might kill her."

"So go get her."

"I do, and I risk everything we've ever worked for."

"We'll build something else." Alex made it sound ridiculously simple.

"And what about our employees?"

"If worse comes to worst, we'll sell the assets and give them all a fat severance package."

Zach snapped his fingers. "Just like that?"

"You don't get to give up Abigail for me, Zach. Because if

I find the right woman, and I have to choose—" Alex grinned and shrugged "—you're toast, buddy."

"Good to know where I stand."

"Isn't it?"

It was.

And it was great to know that Alex had his back, just as he always had. No brother in the world could be more loyal than Alex. Because of him, Zach didn't need to stand around and watch Abigail suffer. He could do something about it, damn the consequences.

When Abigail heard Zach's voice in the foyer of the ranch house, she shot to her feet from the sofa, gaping in astonishment as he elbowed his way past Travis, wheeling into the living room.

Her brother Seth jumped up from an armchair, squaring his shoulders and widening his stance. "What the hell are you doing here?"

Lisa appeared from the kitchen, obviously drawn by the raised voices. She stopped in the archway and took in the three men.

"Zach?" Abigail managed to say, the breath leaving her body. What had happened? Why did he look so angry?

Instead of responding to her, he spoke to Seth. "You," he growled, "can take your business license and shove it."

Travis stopped short behind Zach.

"Zach?" Abigail repeated, taking a step forward, half hopeful, half confused.

"Get out of this house," Seth ordered.

"I will close my business," Zach vowed, his voice low and menacing.

"What the hell?" Travis interjected.

"Leave," Seth repeated.

Zach didn't take his gaze off Seth. "I'll chuck it all and start from scratch before I sacrifice Abby."

Sacrifice her?

"Have you lost your mind?" Travis demanded of Zach.

Good question.

"I'll do whatever she wants. I'll hire her," said Zach, still fixating on Seth. "I'll marry her. I'll protect her. The one thing I won't do is let the family who supposedly loves her work her into the ground."

"That's enough," Seth shouted.

"What's he talking about?" Travis had also turned his attention to his brother.

"Nothing," said Seth.

Zach gave a cold laugh. He turned to Travis. "Your brother didn't tell you he was blackmailing me?"

Abigail gaped at Seth.

His nostrils were flared, and his face had turned ruddy.

"Seth?" Travis insisted.

"He's the one who was blackmailing her."

Abigail's stomach dropped like a stone. Her gaze shot to Lisa, but Lisa shook her head in incomprehension.

"He seduced her," Seth continued. "Then he threatened to run to us with the tale."

Zach coughed out a sharp laugh. "You think *that* was my threat? That I'd kiss and tell?"

"Stop it!" Abigail demanded, afraid she knew where Zach was going.

"I threatened—"

"Shut up, Zach."

Zach stared coolly into her eyes but kept right on speaking. "To tell you that she hates working at the ranch."

The room went completely silent.

Abigail mouthed the word no, slowly shaking her head in denial.

"They need to know, Abby."

No, they didn't. They never needed to know. She couldn't believe Zach had betrayed her. "You promised," she whispered.

"I guess I lied."

"How could you?"

Travis stepped up, clamping a hand on Zach's shoulder. "Time for you to leave."

"We need to talk," Zach said to Abigail.

"Why did you come back?"

His tone went soft, and so did his brown eyes. "Because I couldn't stay away."

"Out," said Travis.

But Lisa spoke up, advancing on Seth. "What did you do?"

Seth puffed out his chest. "I protected my sister."

Abigail stood in mute misery, knowing she'd been the cause of all this.

Zach's voice was deliberate. "Mayor Jacobs advised me that if I ever spoke to his sister again, he'd deny the DFB business license and bankrupt my company."

"*He* was blackmailing *her*," Seth protested.

"How did you know that?" asked Lisa.

"Stop it!" Abigail cried. "Everyone, please, just stop." She couldn't stand that Seth had compromised his principles. And she hated that Zach had outed her.

Lisa's arm closed on her shoulders.

Abigail found herself searching Zach's face, as if his expression might give her a hint of why he was doing this.

"You hate the ranch?" Travis asked.

"She's had enough," said Lisa.

Zach shook off Travis's hand, turning on him. "You might want to think about letting her leave this place before you kill her."

Travis sneered. "Don't be absurd."

"Ask her for an inventory of her bruises someday."

Seth had gone quiet. Now he turned a concerned look on Abigail.

"Get out," Travis ordered.

"Right," Zach capitulated. "I'm leaving." Then his icy stare took in both brothers. "But that doesn't mean I'm gone."

His last look was for Abigail. His eyes turned to mocha, and his mouth flexed in a half smile. His deep tone brought back a thousand memories. "Take your time, Doll-Face. Decide what you want to do and let me know."

* * *

An hour later, Abigail blinked against the shaft of light from the hallway as her sister Mandy pushed open the door and stepped into the dim bedroom, quietly pulling it shut behind her.

Abigail shifted into a sitting position on the bed, drawing up her knees. "It didn't take them long to send for reinforcements."

Mandy smiled as she padded across the room, wrapping her hand around the newel post on the footboard. "Sounds like I missed all the fun."

"You call that fun?"

"I call it exciting." Mandy sat down at the foot of the big bed and leaned back.

"It was that," Abigail allowed.

"Your life's not usually that exciting."

"Not so you'd notice." Though, lately, it had had its moments.

"So, what's the real story with this guy?"

"It's a bit complicated."

Her sister shrugged. "I'm not going anywhere." Then she grinned. "Seriously, Abby. I'm not going anywhere anytime soon. So you might as well start talking."

"I met him in Lyndon." Abigail settled back against the headboard, preparing to give her sister the whole story. Though she felt battered and bruised, and confused by Zach's behavior, she felt strangely calm. It was all out in the open now. For better or worse, they could all stop sneaking around.

"When?" Mandy prompted into the silence.

"Election night. He was a stranger then, probably the only guy in town who didn't know who I was. He thought I was elegant and sophisticated."

"You are elegant and sophisticated."

Abigail's glance went to her tattered fingernails. "Not usually."

"You were that night. It was one great dress."

"It was," Abigail agreed. She thought back to her and Zach's nighttime picnic. "I was pretty hot that night. It was all very sexy. I wouldn't let him tell me his name, and I refused to tell him mine. But we slept together."

"No way."

"Way. It was great. And then I sneaked away the next morning."

"And he tracked you down to blackmail you?"

"No. He didn't know who I was." Abigail believed that now. "He needed a variance on his water license. Somebody gave him my name. And when I refused to help him, that's when he blackmailed me."

"And you're still sleeping with him."

"Yes. Well, I was until Seth threatened him, and he broke it off." At least Abigail now understood Zach's sudden withdrawal. She was going to have a long talk with both her brothers.

"He's a great guy," Abigail continued. "In a ridiculous situation." She thought back to the DFB employees she'd met in Houston, and his determination to do right by them. And when you added to that Seth's blackmail, and Zach's stunning reaction tonight... A reaction that was only now coming clear inside her head.

She sat up straighter. "I'm pretty sure he said something about marrying me down there."

"I heard. Lisa told me."

"What do you think he meant by that?" Could it have been metaphorical? Even if she took into account Zach's rather single-minded determination to get her away from the ranch, offering to marry her seemed a bit extreme.

"Let's see..." Mandy tapped her temple with her index finger. "What could a man possibly mean when he offers to marry a woman?" She gave an elongated pause. "I know. Maybe he wants to *marry* you."

"Why?"

"To love, honor and keep you all the days of his life?"

"That's silly. Zach doesn't love me."

"You sure about that?"

Abigail wasn't sure about anything right now. And her head was starting to ache.

She changed the subject. "What on earth was Seth thinking?"

"That he was protecting you."

"Ha, he botched that. I'm a grown woman. He needs to stop interfering in my life. So does Travis."

Mandy leaned forward as if to share a secret. "Maybe if you hadn't lied to him, lied to all of us."

"I never lied."

"You didn't tell us you hated the ranch."

"I don't hate the ranch."

"You hate working on the ranch."

Abigail pushed back her messy hair. A sheen of sweat had formed at the hairline. "Yeah," she admitted. "I hate working on the ranch."

"You should have said something."

"And then what? Leave Travis stuck here all alone?"

"He can hire more help."

Abigail's voice rose. "It's not the same. You know it's not the same."

Mandy scooted to the middle of the bed, placing a hand on Abigail's upraised knee. "That doesn't mean you get to be the sacrificial lamb. Travis doesn't want you to do that. None of us want you to do that. Would you want Katrina to do that?"

"It's different with Katrina."

"It's not different at all." Mandy squared her shoulders. "You're not staying, Abby. We're not going to let you stay."

Abigail gave a sad smile. She had mixed emotions about that. She didn't want to abandon Travis, but she desperately wanted her freedom.

Mandy wasn't finished. "And while you're thinking about where to go, did you happen to give a listen to what Zach said down there? Did you watch him stand up to Seth and Travis? Did you see that he was willing to give up everything for you? His company. His fortune. Alex, and everything they've ever worked for. And he didn't know how our brothers would react. There were two of them and only one of him, and he barged onto their land to get you."

Abigail had seen all that. She'd been shell-shocked at the time. But Mandy was right—it was pretty amazing.

"Love doesn't get much better than that," said Mandy.

Abigail's chest squeezed tight. Could it be true? They pushed and pulled and prodded each other. He was frustrating and opinionated, and she was stubborn. But they also made amazing love. And they laid for hours in each other's arms afterward. And they shared joys and fears and secrets. And if she'd had her way, she might never have left Craig Mountain.

She loved Zach. She loved him so very much.

Mandy tossed back her hair. "So, what are you going to do now?"

"I don't know."

"Yes, you do."

Abigail groaned at the bedroom ceiling. "I should never have let him walk out of here."

"You love him."

"Yes."

"Then you should have thrown yourself in his arms, told him that and walked away from the ranch with him by your side."

"I'd be halfway to Craig Mountain by now." Abigail paused, hope glowing to life inside her. "Is it possible that he really wants to marry me?"

"He asked you."

"In a roundabout way."

"In a very public and possibly hazardous way. He didn't know how Seth and Travis would react."

Abigail's heart thudded, and the hope grew stronger.

"Go ask him," Mandy whispered. "Better yet, answer him. Tell him you love him. Say yes to the marriage proposal."

"Drive on up to Craig Mountain." Abigail couldn't help remembering what had happened last time she'd tried that.

"Yes."

"Tell him I love him."

"Yes."

"Step off an emotional cliff with no safety net."

"He already did that for you."

Abigail felt herself smile.

He had. He'd waltzed right in here and gambled everything. Mandy was right—the very least Abigail could do was meet him halfway.

She put her hand on top of Mandy's and squeezed. "I'm going to Craig Mountain."

"You want me to drive?"

"I think I need to do this alone."

"It's late. And it's a long way. Caleb will—"

"I'm a big girl, Mandy. I can drive myself."

Mandy sucked a breath through her teeth. "Yes, you can. Call me when you get there."

Abigail came to her feet, feeling an overwhelming urge to run to the nearest vehicle and speed to the highway. "I might be busy." She started for the door.

"Then phone me after," Mandy called out. "And drive carefully."

On the stone front patio of the castle, Zach lounged in a deep, wood-slat chair, Alex in the one next to him, Ozzy curled at his feet, a bottle of cold C Mountain Ale condensing against his left palm.

"So, you proposed," Alex was saying. "But you left without getting an answer."

"She was pretty upset by the whole thing," Zach responded. "I don't think she's had time to think it through."

Ugly as it was, he didn't regret his actions tonight. He'd meant every word he said to Seth and Travis, and to Abigail. Whatever she wanted, whatever she needed, he was here, and he wasn't going anywhere.

"You probably should have waited for an answer," said Alex.

"Maybe," Zach admitted. He'd gone over it a thousand times on the drive back. But he truly didn't know if he should have stayed. "Maybe I should have kidnapped her when I had the chance."

Alex chuckled. "I can't see her brothers letting you haul her out of the family house."

"I suppose."

They both took a swig of beer, while the crisp wind whistled across the lake, crackling the bright fall leaves and sending them fluttering down to the grass around the castle.

"So we might be bankrupt, and we might not," Alex mused.

"I don't think Seth will hold it against us."

By the end there, it was obvious Seth was rethinking the situation. Out of everyone in that room, Zach was willing to bet Seth got that Zach would defend Abigail against anyone, including her family.

Alex contemplated his beer bottle. "Which means, the company is saved, and we'll still be able to drink free of charge?"

"Damn fine beer," Zach intoned, chuckling at the memory of their silly, teenage name for the company. Their original plan had been to buy a small brewery, create jobs for themselves and be able to drink for free. That's as far as their dreams had gone in the early days.

"DFB," Alex echoed. "It's been one amazing trip, buddy."

A pair of headlights appeared in the distance, flashing through the trees as the vehicle bounced on the rough road. It was coming in at quite a clip.

"You don't suppose..." Alex ventured.

"A guy can hope." Zach's chest tightened. He took a reflexive swig from the bottle, draining it and setting it on the patio beside his chair.

Restless, he came to his feet, gazing into the night, waiting for the moment when the vehicle came around the bend and he'd know if it was her or not.

"Jacobs Cattle Company." Alex spoke in the same moment Zach read the logo on the door of the blue truck.

"I hope it's not Travis with a shotgun." Zach squinted at the windshield, but the parking-lot lights were reflecting off the glass, and he couldn't see inside.

"I thought you said he wouldn't hold it against you."

"That was Seth."

Travis was definitely a wild card with an attitude.

The truck rocked to a halt.

It was her.

Zach's chest tightened further as she slammed her way out of the driver's seat. She rounded the hood, wearing scruffy jeans, a gray T-shirt and tan cowboy boots. Her hair was mussed, her makeup nonexistent, and her mouth was pursed in a moue of determination.

God, she was beautiful.

"Yes," she shouted shortly as she mounted the stairs.

"Yes, what?" he called back.

She trotted toward him. "You told me to decide what I wanted."

"I did."

She stopped in front of him. "And to let you know."

She didn't look angry, and he dared to really hope.

"Uh-huh," he prompted, gazing into those gorgeous golden eyes.

He was vaguely aware of Alex coming to his feet behind him.

"Hi, Alex," said Abigail, her glance flicking past Zach's shoulder.

Zach touched an index finger to the bottom of her chin, turning her attention back to him. "Yes, what?"

A beat went by. "Yes, I'll marry you."

Pure, unadulterated joy shot through him, but he kept it together. "You will?"

A trace of uncertainty crossed her face. It was adorable. "Were you serious? Or were you just trying to protect me?"

He had to struggle to keep a straight face. He also had to struggle to keep from hauling her into his arms and kissing the life out of her.

"I was trying to protect you," he admitted. He tried to pause, but he was impatient. "I was also trying to love you."

"Gettin' anywhere with that?" she asked, her spunk clearly back.

"Yeah." He gave in and wrapped his arms around her waist. "I've succeeded. Completely."

"Then say it."

"I love you."

"Good."

"Your turn."

"I love you, too, Lucky. A whole lot." She came up on her toes, snaking her arms around his neck.

He met her halfway in a searing kiss.

"Uh, Zach?" came Alex's voice.

Zach broke the kiss and turned. "Are you still here?"

Abigail giggled against his chest.

"I thought you might want this." Alex tossed a small wooden box that Zach caught in midair. "I found it in the north tower."

Puzzled, Zach flipped the brass catch with his thumb and opened the top. There sat a gorgeous little emerald-and-diamond ring, the brilliant stones nestled in polished gold.

"I don't know its history," said Alex. "But then, we orphans never really know for sure, do we?"

"We never do," Zach agreed. An heirloom ring from Craig Mountain Castle. Somehow, it seemed fitting.

"And now I'm leaving." Alex's footsteps sounded on the porch until the door closed behind him.

Zach turned to show Abigail the ring.

"Will you marry me?" he whispered. "I love you so much."

"Yes," she breathed, her eyes sparkling brighter than the ring. Then she looked down. "It's absolutely gorgeous. Lord Ashton's?"

"I'm really starting to like that guy."

The first day of spring was opening night at Lord Ashton's Alehouse. Over the months Abigail had worked on the project, the restaurant had expanded until it was a whole lot larger than Zach had first envisioned. There'd been a buzz about the place around the whole state since New Year's, and the restaurant was booked up past the end of the month.

A bright wood fire roared in the massive fireplace, vintage black tools hanging from hooks against the worn stones. Lord Ashton's swords and shields decorated the walls, and Abigail had even found a couple of suits of armor to place in the corners of the room.

The dinning tables were made of worn, rough-hewn beams. An elaborate candelabrum sat in the center of each one. The chairs were upholstered in soft leather, designed to look worn, with the wooden arms and backs crafted to look antique. Lady Elise Ashton's paintings graced the entrance, and the multitude of sunken windows were decorated with heavy, emerald velvet curtains.

"Is it really wild boar?" Mandy asked, pointing at the leather-bound menu from her place at the table next to Abigail.

"They assure me it is," Abigail answered, smiling around the big table at Seth and Travis, Mandy and her husband, Caleb. Alex was at the foot of the table kitty-corner to Lisa. And even Reed and Katrina had flown in from New York City for the weekend. Her parents were still in Denver, settling in nicely to the social life in a retirement complex.

"I'm going for it," said Mandy. "And I'm definitely trying the Yorkshire pudding."

"I don't know how you people can eat so much," Katrina put in from across the table.

"Try the garden salad," Abigail advised her youngest sister. The downside to being a famous ballerina was keeping your figure so trim.

"I'll be eating even more pretty soon," said Mandy.

"Going on a trail ride?" asked Seth, helping himself to one of the fresh rolls placed in baskets in the middle of the table.

"Eating for two," Mandy announced matter-of-factly.

The wide, proud grin that stretched across Caleb's face confirmed the news.

Abigail squealed. "You're pregnant!"

Mandy nodded, while Abigail pulled her into a tight hug.

The men offered congratulations to Caleb, and Katrina rushed around the table to join her sisters.

"I'm going to be an auntie," Abigail breathed.

"I can't wait to take her to plays and shops and museums," said Katrina.

"Might be a boy." Mandy laughed.

Katrina pooh-poohed with a wave of her hand. "If it is, you can always try again."

Abigail laughed, glancing down at her sister's flat stomach. "Do Mom and Dad know?"

"I called them this morning."

While her brothers came around to hug Mandy, Abigail felt Zach's hand wrap around hers. He urged her to him, out of the fray, then drew her down onto his lap in the roomy armchair at the head of the table.

"What about you?" he whispered in her ear.

"What about me?" she whispered back.

"You interested in having kids?"

"I am." She rested her cheek against his, inhaling his familiar scent and letting her body mold against his strength, while her family's voices seemed to fade. "You?"

"I'm the only one of my line," he said, voice gruff. "So, yeah. I'd like to carry it on."

Abigail's heart squeezed hard.

"We can have lots of children," she told him around a suddenly clogged throat. "You, Zach Rainer, are going to be the start of something big."

"Can we start now?"

She couldn't help smiling at that. "We haven't even had the appetizer yet."

"I don't need food. I need you."

"After dessert," she whispered with a surreptitious glance over her shoulder to the commotion around Mandy. "We'll go get pregnant."

He stared deeply, lovingly into her eyes. "Do you think we should get married first?"

"Sure."

He hesitated. "So, we'll wait?"

"I'm thinking, if we take the Jaguar, we can be over the Nevada border in six hours."

He drew back. "Elope?"

She nodded.

"Won't that upset your family?"

She smoothed a hand across his cheeks, burrowing her fingers in his hair and moving in close. "I've stopped living for my family, Lucky." She kissed him gently on the lips. "I'm living for you now. And we should do whatever we want."

"Oh, Doll-Face," he groaned, hugging her tight. "Marry me. Do it now."

* * * * *

LET'S TALK
Romance

For exclusive extracts, competitions
and special offers, find us online:

 facebook.com/millsandboon

 @MillsandBoon

 @MillsandBoonUK

Get in touch on 01413 063232

For all the latest titles coming soon, visit
millsandboon.co.uk/nextmonth

MILLS & BOON

THE HEART OF ROMANCE

A ROMANCE FOR EVERY KIND OF READER

MODERN

Prepare to be swept off your feet by sophisticated, sexy and seductive heroes, in some of the world's most glamourous and romantic locations, where power and passion collide.
8 stories per month.

HISTORICAL

Escape with historical heroes from time gone by. Whether your passion is for wicked Regency Rakes, muscled Vikings or rugged Highlanders, awaken the romance of the past.
6 stories per month.

MEDICAL

Set your pulse racing with dedicated, delectable doctors in the high-pressure world of medicine, where emotions run high and passion, comfort and love are the best medicine.
6 stories per month.

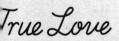

Celebrate true love with tender stories of heartfelt romance, from the rush of falling in love to the joy a new baby can bring, and a focus on the emotional heart of a relationship.
8 stories per month.

Indulge in secrets and scandal, intense drama and plenty of sizzling hot action with powerful and passionate heroes who have it all: wealth, status, good looks…everything but the right woman.
6 stories per month.

HEROES

Experience all the excitement of a gripping thriller, with an intense romance at its heart. Resourceful, true-to-life women and strong, fearless men face danger and desire - a killer combination!
8 stories per month.

DARE

Sensual love stories featuring smart, sassy heroines you'd want as a best friend, and compelling intense heroes who are worthy of them.
4 stories per month.

To see which titles are coming soon, please visit

millsandboon.co.uk/nextmonth

JOIN US ON SOCIAL MEDIA!

Stay up to date with our latest releases, author news and gossip, special offers and discounts, and all the behind-the-scenes action from Mills & Boon...

 millsandboon

 millsandboonuk

 millsandboon

It might just be true love...

MILLS & BOON
True Love
Romance from the Heart

Celebrate true love with tender stories of
heartfelt romance, from the rush of falling
in love to the joy a new baby can bring,
and a focus on the emotional
heart of a relationship.